D0099455

# The Savage Instinct

M. M. DeLuca

This novel is a work of fiction based, in part, on real-life events and individuals, but including imagined elements and characters. See the author's note on page 369 for further details.

Copyright © 2021 M. M. DeLuca
All rights reserved.

No part of this book may be reproduced, stored in a retrieval system, or transmitted in any form or by any means, electronic, mechanical, photocopying, recording, or otherwise, without express written permission of the publisher.

Published by Inkshares, Inc., Oakland, California
www.inkshares.com

Edited by Adam Gomolin, Avalon Radys, and Kaitlin Severini
Cover design by Lauren Harms
Interior design by Kevin G. Summers

ISBN: 9781947848672
e-ISBN: 9781947848689
LCCN: 2018963778

First edition

Printed in the United States of America

*To Ethel Jane and Charlie*
*and all the good people of Low Moorsley*

*Experience declares that man is the only animal*
*which devours his own kind.*
—Thomas Jefferson, 1787

*Mary Ann Cotton, she's dead and forgotten*
*She lies in a grave with all her bones rotten*
*Sing, sing, oh what shall I sing*
*Mary Ann Cotton is tied up with string*
*Where, where? Up in the air*
*Sellin' black puddens a penny a pair*

# Durham

## Spring 1873

I BECAME ACQUAINTED with madness at the age of twenty-six.

During that same year, I met the accused murderer Mary Ann Cotton and learned that the evil ones amongst us are not confined to the filthy alleyways of the poor. They mingle freely in the polished parlours of the middle classes and the gilded ballrooms of the wealthy.

I'd always viewed the world with an artist's eyes. Drawn to edges, angles, curves, and texture. The way light plays with shade and casts surfaces into bold relief, revealing the beauty of their imperfections. But now I know this does not apply to people, whose flaws can be so loathsome, so vile, so entrenched, that nothing—no earthly or heavenly light—can redeem them.

And I fear the shadows now, for they conceal a familiar figure with a chequered shawl, blank eyes, and a pitiless soul. She stands at the foot of my bed, holding a cup in her outstretched hand.

"Drink, drink," she says, "for two penn'orth of arsenic dissolves nicely in a hot cup of tea."

She poisoned my life with a secret.

One that must be guarded with lies.

But I read once in a poetry book that a lie is but the truth in masquerade, so I am not afraid, for this past year I have survived by subterfuge and pretence.

The train glides into Durham station. Shiny as a new toy, its bottle-green engine bears the gleaming gold lettering of its name, *The Flying Scotchman*. I step forwards to greet it, conscious I present a sombre figure, shrouded in dark veils and beaded black travelling clothes.

Widow's weeds.

I face a long journey to London, King's Cross, then on to the Folkestone ferry. But now, as the train brakes and clouds of steam billow into the air, I am reminded of another journey that brought me here to Durham only a few short months ago.

# 1

# Autumn 1872

THAT JOURNEY TO Durham was long, a struggle between body and mind to maintain a quiet demeanour. To pull my fingertips away from the window frame before their frenzied drumming drew the attention of my fellow passengers. To remember Mrs Parsons's words in my final days at the Hoxton Private Asylum, that I should cultivate the gentle, timid manner befitting a professor's wife.

"Be on your guard against wildness and self-abandonment, Clara," she called as I climbed aboard the train, shut the door, and leaned out of its open window. A flock of starlings burst into the sky and my mind thrilled with the rush of freedom.

"Have no fear, Mrs Parsons. Your treatments have saved me from ruin."

I slammed the window shut. I had no desire to heed any more of her blather, and the hissing train engines had wrapped her in clouds of steam, wiping her from my life.

My blood raced with anticipation, but I found my compartment before my nerves got the better of me. An elderly couple clad in worn grey travelling clothes lay slumped across the seat sleeping, hands entwined. I took my place opposite and closed my eyes, trying to block out the frantic activity outside the window. After so many months of confinement, I was like a child stealing through the nursery door, facing the world alone, marvelling at all its wonders, yet cowed by the relentless ebb and flow of life: the clank of train wheels, the conductor's shrill whistle, the rush of a last-minute passenger leaping through an open door.

"Gentle, timid, modest," I mumbled, then reached into my reticule and found my *Guide to the Ancient Cathedral City of Durham.* Mercifully, my breathing steadied as I studied the description of my future home.

*Durham is an ancient city situated on seven hills, in a beautiful winding of the River Wear, along the banks of which are pleasant walks, covered with woods and edged with lofty crags. The cathedral is a fine building and the castle is a curious relic of antiquity.*

Perhaps Henry was right, that a new beginning in a quiet northern city, far away from the grime and smoke of London, would help me forget what had happened almost a year ago.

The calamity that had transformed me into a wild and vicious creature.

The events that had led to my confinement.

*For my own protection and the protection of others.*

Henry had visited me at Hoxton before leaving for Durham to take up his new position as professor of mathematics at the university. He sat opposite me in the morning room, his shoulders tense under his greatcoat, peering at me as if I were an insect pinned beneath a specimen glass. I gazed beyond him at the view outside the window, which seemed to me like a painting by Constable. Woolly masses of clouds floated across a sea-blue sky, and sunlight dappled the treetops.

Henry's head was bowed—his shoulders twitched and shook. It was the first time I'd seen him cry, and though the sight stirred my heart, my hands were bound together with leather straps, so I could not comfort him. Then he snorted and cleared his throat as if he were about to commence a mathematics lecture. He gazed at me with reddened eyes.

"My darling Clara, you know I admire your passion for poetry and art. Indeed, the first time I laid eyes on you, you were standing by the piano in your blue dress, reciting 'The Lady of Shalott.' I remember thinking you were such a rare beauty. Fragile, yet perfect. But I fear our modern industrial world is so cruel, it will crush your romantic temperament. For sadly, you inherited a nervous disposition from your mother and must battle the same hysterical impulses that drove her to an untimely death."

Then he took my shaking hands in his and told me not to fear, that he would always be there to guide and protect me.

"I have made a thorough study of the works of many eminent mind doctors and they all agree that in cases like yours, any exertion of your intellect or imagination could lead to complete nervous collapse."

"But when can I go home?"

"Only when you are fully recovered. Grave circumstances brought you to this place."

"Circumstances, Henry?"

"Do not speak of it. Put all thoughts of those dark times behind you and stay here until you are entirely well. If your release is too speedy, you may have another relapse, and we cannot risk that."

Just then Mrs Parsons wheeled in a groaning tea trolley filled with toasted tea cakes, strawberry preserves, a wedge of cheese, and a silver bowl of butter. A lavish show of plenty in contrast to our usual daily rations of thin porridge, mealy bread, and gristly mutton stew.

Mrs Parsons was a woman entirely bleached of colour. Starched white apron and cuffs, a halo of flimsy silver hair, linen-white skin, and milky eyes magnified behind gold-rimmed spectacles. But my eyes were drawn to her hands—masculine hands with broad, flat fingers that struggled to grasp the teapot's delicate handle.

"I must compliment you, Mrs Parsons," said Henry, helping himself to a tea cake, a spoonful of jam, and a thick slice of Stilton. "This establishment is far superior to the Bethlem Hospital, where Clara was first housed. That place seemed more akin to an army barracks, with attendants shouting orders and marshalling squadrons of lunatics about the grounds."

"Highly unsuitable for the more refined class of patient," whispered Mrs Parsons as she leaned intimately towards Henry and handed him the cream jug. "Dirty floors and the patients packed in like sardines. The poor wretches there, so vile and filthy. Why, they're only a shade removed from beasts of the field."

I recalled the anguished souls.

Their wild shrieks.

Their howling and yelping like a pack of wild dogs.

"No—the dirt was tolerable," I whispered. "It was the cursed noise."

Henry coughed and turned his head away, and Mrs Parsons continued pouring the tea, her mouth a tight line in her angular face.

"I witnessed old hags in every stage of decay sharing the dining table with my wife, wiping their soiled lips on the tablecloth, and that I could not tolerate," he said, slurping a mouthful of tea.

"Well, thankfully, you are an enlightened man, Mr Blackstone. And a sensible one," she said, offering him the sugar bowl. "You saved your wife from that hellish den and brought her here to us."

Henry grimaced, then shovelled three more sugar lumps into his tea. "Precisely, Mrs Parsons. As a mathematician, I pride myself on being a man of science and reason, not a man steeped in superstition and grim morality. Why, such a man might have written off his wife as a hopeless lunatic and forced her to stay there indefinitely," he said, glaring at me until I dropped my eyes to my lap.

"Well, you must clear your mind of worries, Mr Blackstone. Here at Hoxton, we pride ourselves on quality care along with good food and plain common-sense cures."

*Cures.*

Dr Barnsley, a robust man with hooded eyes, heavy whiskers, and a stained yellow waistcoat, had ordered me to lie immobile for hours of bed rest. "Frequent feeding and rough massage," he ordered the attending nurse. "Keep her mind from morbid thoughts until she passes into a state of placid contentment and brainwork has ceased."

I thought of leaves, drifting on water.

Each morning, a swarthy girl in a starched apron took me from the bed and led me in silence to a chilly bathroom so white and stark, it reminded me of a butcher's shop. There I endured long, frigid showers. Afterwards they strapped me to a table and applied the cold douche. I screeched until my throat gave out. But they applied it again and again, until my insides were numb and my teeth chattered so violently, the sound echoed in my head.

I could not conjure leaves then.

"You must tell them to stop the cold-water treatments," I begged, tugging at Henry's sleeve. His brows knit as he frowned, and he pulled his arm away from my grasp. "I cannot endure them."

"Pay no heed, Mr Blackstone. They are all marvellous whiners. And ungrateful," Mrs Parsons said, slathering butter over a hot tea cake. "Now, we must fatten up this starved slip of a girl. More flesh will bolster her blood supply."

"Though not so much to encourage corpulence," added Henry with a wink, so that Mrs Parsons covered her mouth with a large hand and giggled like a young girl.

"Oh, you're a saucy one, Mr Blackstone. Of course we'll keep a close eye on her waistline."

"Then eat your fill, Clara. We want to see that bloom on your cheeks again."

And though the smell of it nauseated me, I allowed Henry to cram pieces of dripping tea cake into my mouth. Perched on the edge of their chairs, the two of them stared at me like beady-eyed hawks.

I chewed and swallowed until every crumb was gone, my stomach turning as the warm butter dribbled down my chin and soaked into the front of my dress.

After eight long months, Dr Shepton arrived at Hoxton.

He called me to his office just before the first morning shower. Unlike Dr Barnsley, who barricaded himself behind piles of documents stacked on a vast mahogany table, Dr Shepton, a young pink-cheeked man with precisely groomed hair and whiskers, sat to the side of a tidy desk, his legs crossed. I fixed my eyes on a large silver inkpot that held three pens, all leaning outwards at precarious angles. I imagined them tipping out and spraying rivers of ink across the neatly stacked papers.

"Please look at me, Mrs Blackstone. Do not be afraid."

My gaze drifted upwards, past the well-shone shoes, the neat pin-striped trousers, and the gold fob and chain that gleamed against his crimson silk waistcoat. His eyes were clear and brown, his expression sincere and unwavering, unlike Dr Barnsley, whose restless gaze never seemed to settle on anything for more than a second. Dr Shepton reached into a glass jar and took out a pear drop.

"You are shaking," he said, holding the sweet out to me.

I slipped it into my mouth.

"Mrs Blackstone, I am afraid to admit that our medical system has treated you rather brutally. We know now that many women suffer extreme changes in temperament after reproductive complications like yours, when infection and blood loss can temporarily disrupt normal behaviour. Your reaction was a natural one to the shock and trauma you endured. Rest, good nutrition, and gentle care are usually the best remedies, not confinement amongst chronic lunatics and maniacs. Indeed a spell in a quiet country village or at the seaside would work wonders."

My head reeled. "No more water cures?" I whispered.

"All treatments will cease as of this moment. You must go home to your family as soon as I contact the Lunacy Commission and arrangements can be made to complete the release papers."

I could have leapt across the space between us and embraced him, but he had already plucked one of the pens from the inkpot and was scribbling out a letter. Instead I backed out of the room, muttering my thanks and praying that I was not dreaming.

Despite Henry's letter of protest to Dr Shepton that my release was highly premature, he grudgingly signed the papers. I packed my belongings three weeks later, the train ticket to Durham safely stowed in my bag.

I gazed out of the window at sun-stippled fields and forested hillsides blazing in their autumn glory. Further along the line we slowed down by a stream so clear, I could glimpse the shape and colour of the stones that dotted its bed. Beyond a little bridge, a gate with rusted hinges opened into a wide farmyard where a mound of dried leaves smouldered. A man in a brown smock poked at the pile with a pitchfork, sending a thin plume of smoke into the air as two children skipped round the bonfire. Their mouths moved and I imagined them singing a nursery rhyme. I put my cheek to the window until a cloud of steam blotted out the scene and we picked up speed again. The colours rushed by in a haze of gold, crimson, and ochre, flooding my starved senses until I thought my head would burst. So much life and beauty in every corner, and I had missed it all for far too long.

*Durham is an ancient city situated on seven hills . . .*

I took out Henry's most recent letter, folded into the back cover of the Durham City guidebook. I'd read it so many times, the words seemed to blur and shift on the page:

*Dearest Clara,*

*I cannot tell you how refreshing it has been to get away from London's crowded streets. I am absolutely sure coming to Durham was the right decision for many reasons; most important, you will find it far easier to put the past behind you, meet suitable new friends, and thus recapture the essence of ideal womanhood that made you so dear to me in the early years of our marriage.*

*Your husband,*

*H. B.*

I tried to put my dark thoughts away. Thoughts of the icy marble floor, my legs paralyzed from the cold, my innards aching. Thoughts of unspeakable months before in Bethlem. Of the room that stunk of human waste. Of the hopeless souls whose bodies rocked in constant motion. Of sitting for hours on rigid, straight-backed benches until I could not feel my legs. Of getting off the train at York and simply disappearing.

*Durham is an ancient city situated on seven hills, in a beautiful winding of the River Wear . . .*

Then the ache of loss and grief rose like bitter gall in my throat, and I could have thrown open the window to scream out my agony for all the world to hear.

*. . . along the banks of which are pleasant walks, covered with woods and edged with lofty crags.*

But I had learned from Mrs Parsons not to give vent to such wild, unbridled feelings. To do so would jeopardise my freedom. If I was to survive outside the asylum, I must be placid, calm, and docile to avoid unnecessary attention.

*The cathedral is a fine building and the castle is a curious relic of antiquity.*

Even after leaving York, my two travelling companions remained sound asleep, clutching each other's wizened hands like a pair of old friends. I reached into my reticule for the provisions Mrs Parsons had packed for me, but the cheese was clammy, the bread dry, and the cloth reeked with the sour stink of the asylum. I rose and edged my way to the door, anxious to leave the stuffy compartment and rid myself of the last vestiges of Hoxton.

Outside in the passageway, the train wheels thundered underfoot and I had the terrifying sense of rushing onwards towards an uncertain future. I heaved the cloth and its evil contents through the open window and watched them scatter across the gravel. *Food for rats,* I thought as we picked up speed and passed a farm where a lone horse kicked and pranced its way across a meadow. Beautiful and free, it seemed somehow oblivious to the smoke and racket of the passing train.

I leaned my head out of the window to feel the wind in my hair and the sun on my face.

I remembered my first days at Bethlem.

How long had I cowered in the corner of a damp cell, watching a pale square of sky through a tiny barred window far above my head?

But in an instant, the fields and forests suddenly slipped away, tumbling downwards into a deep gorge. I shrank back from the window as we crossed onto a narrow viaduct. My heart drummed in my ears as Durham City suddenly blazed out of nowhere, a brilliant canvas unfurled across the horizon. The lofty grey towers and filigreed spires of the great Norman cathedral presided over the entire city, resting on steep, thickly treed riverbanks. Beside it, the stone turrets of a medieval castle emerged from lush groves of crimson and gold. A profusion of red-roofed houses clung to the hills that surrounded the meandering river, all leading uphill towards the mighty cathedral.

I had not lifted a paintbrush or touched a pencil for over a year, and here were sights so breathtaking, I could have spent every waking hour trying to capture them on canvas. And yet the thought of it was such a burden, weighing me down with the worry that anything I attempted would be worse than a child's primitive scribbling. Dr Barnsley's prescription of *a lifestyle with strict limits on brainwork* had dulled my mind and banished my imagination to some hidden recess I couldn't reach.

I remembered the lines from a poem I'd read in the guidebook:

*Grey towers of Durham*
*Yet well I love thy mixed and massive piles*

I whispered them to myself as the gorgeous scene slipped away and we approached the dull, grey station buildings.

In haste I returned to the compartment to make final preparations for my arrival. The shock of the door sliding open and the sudden rush of air launched the whiskery old man into paroxysms of coughing. His wife fished in her reticule and produced a flask of brandy, which he sipped like a suckling babe until his fit subsided.

I glanced in the mirror above my seat. My skin was deathly pale. Dark shadows smudged the hollows under my eyes. A year of scant eating had shrunk the flesh away from my face, making my cheekbones appear sharper and more angular than before, and my eyes so large and feverish, they seemed to consume my face.

*Would Henry be repulsed by my transformation?*

In a sudden panic, I pinched my cheeks until the colour returned and applied a dab of rouge to my lips. The old lady's eyebrows rose to alarming heights. Finally I fluffed the little curls peeping out from the front of my bonnet and arranged the thick coils of hair at the back so they would fall in waves to my shoulders, just the way Henry liked. My heart beat faster as the train slowed down.

The brakes hissed.

The conductor's whistle blew.

The doors flew open, and a flurry of porters entered the carriages.

"Ken I tek yer bags, mum?" said a short red-haired young man with the most musical accent I had ever heard.

I followed him down the train steps into the bustling station. A glass and metal canopy spanned each platform, supported by a long row of black-and-white striped arches. The porter disappeared into the milling crowds of travellers and busy workers pushing carts loaded with trunks and bags and parcels.

Families clasped their relatives in tearful embraces.

Overwhelmed by their joy and unsure which direction to take, I stopped for a moment and closed my weary eyes. The air felt fresh and soft, far from the clammy heat of London, with its teeming streets and pestilent fog.

"Lost in thought as always."

The sure voice cut above the din of the platform.

I whirled around and Henry stepped out from behind a pillar, stiff in his starched white shirt and black frock coat.

A flicker of displeasure furrowed his brow, fleetingly, like a cloud passing over the sun, and my skin prickled from the sudden chill.

# 2

FOR AN INSTANT I had the sense I was facing a stranger, until his frown slipped away and his lips curled upwards in a tight smile. But his eyes remained steely as he stepped forwards to greet me, clasping my shoulders with gloved hands as he drew me to his chest.

"You will get used to me again in no time, Clara," he whispered, his warm breath ruffling my hair. "The peculiar feeling will pass."

When I nestled against his jacket, the lemon scent of his shaving soap and the wiry coarseness of his beard awoke dim memories of another time and place, now shrouded in a fog of grief. I pulled away and studied his closed, inscrutable expression, searching my mind for something to say.

"You are changed. Your cheeks seem ruddy."

"There's no London smog here. Just good, fresh air."

I continued staring at him, unable to shake the sensation that I had somehow stepped out of my body. Even miles away from that frigid marble bathroom, I could not move my legs. He scanned the crowded platform, then leaned in close to whisper, “Clara, it’s natural that you should feel at odds with everything, but I’ll be patient as long as you try to get well again. You understand?”

“I’ll do my best,” I said, trying to quell the fluttering in my stomach by smoothing out the wrinkles in my gloves.

“I have a carriage to take us to our lodgings,” he said, offering his arm. I slipped my hand under his elbow and let him guide me along the busy platform to where the porter waited patiently, leaning against my luggage. “On the way, you must tell me all about your journey.”

We crossed from the station into the commotion of the neighbouring street, where cabs and carriages jostled for space, their horses stamping, snorting, and tossing their fine heads.

As the cab trundled down the bank, I gazed at Henry’s profile, trying to reacquaint myself with the man who had been my husband for five years. The small bump on the bridge of his narrow nose, the heavy eyelids that drooped at the corners, the pale lashes, the curled reddish beard, and the wheat-coloured hair. I knew that face so well, but when he glanced down at me with a solicitous smile, I felt a tightness, as if the air were being pressed from my lungs. Then my hands began to shake until I thought the tremor would spread like a current through my entire body.

“You must tell me what you’ve learned about the city,” I said in a childish voice that seemed to come from somewhere outside of me.

“Just sit up and look, Clara. Open your eyes to the charms of Durham.”

Henry kept up a steady commentary as we rode along North Road, past the long row of shops and businesses, until the cathedral loomed out again, high and majestic above the river. Beneath it, the river’s swirling grey waters flowed under the great arches of the bridge, upon which throngs of people strolled back and forth.

"Durham on the Wear," Henry announced proudly. "This sight of the cathedral nestled amongst the trees and set in the oxbow bend of the river has been named as superior to Pisa on the Arno."

I couldn't tear my eyes from those three mighty towers silhouetted against a twilight sky peppered with faint stars. A pale husk of moon hung above the tallest turret and my hands itched to hold a paintbrush again, to capture the mystery of that ancient monument.

Seconds later I felt a sharp tap on my shoulder.

"Clara, are you listening?" said Henry. "I was just telling you how humble and forthright people are here—not tainted by insufferable London smugness. They truly respect my talents. In London I was just another anonymous face amongst the crowds. Here I'm certain to rise up in the academic ranks."

I smiled, forcing myself to pay attention as the carriage emerged from a narrow lane into a wide-open marketplace. In its centre stood a large domed pavilion topped by a figure of Neptune astride a gaping fish, his muscular arms brandishing a forked trident.

I, too, had coiled into myself like a dying fish and slithered across a marble floor, my body numb with cold, whilst a nurse towered above me.

"That, my dear, is called the pant, and it has been a source of water since medieval times, though I believe there was some concern about its purity. Oh, and there you can see the statue of Charles William Vane Stewart, Third Marquess of Londonderry and founder of Seaham Harbour."

Henry's words faded to a low-pitched drone when I spied a massive copper statue of a swaggering Hussar astride a rearing horse, its muscular forelegs threshing the air.

It reminded me of the day Henry moved me from Bethlem to Hoxton. Two glossy chestnut horses had pulled our carriage, and after so many months locked away in the fetid gloom of the asylum, I revelled in the fresh gusts of wind rushing at my face. Henry sat opposite, ashen-faced, covering his mouth and nose with a handkerchief. The stale reek of Bethlem still soiled my body and clothes, causing him to recoil from me as if I were a creature that had crawled from a swamp.

My mind snapped back to the present and I moved to touch Henry's hand for reassurance, but he flinched, removed his hand from mine, and made a great show of adjusting his collar. It was exactly as I thought. Even though I was free and far away from those nightmarish places, I'd never rid myself of the taint of madness, and Henry would never forget it.

"Clara?" Henry's voice echoed in the distance.

I saw that we had already moved out of the marketplace into a narrow road lined with shops. Mrs Parsons had warned me that simple conversation might prove difficult. That my mind would tend to drift away into itself. That I must force myself to meet the eyes of those who addressed me, and maintain a neutral though placid expression, making sure to incline my head at the appropriate times.

*Like a dumb, nodding doll.*

"I'm sorry, Henry. I was merely admiring the statue and wondering about its history."

"As it happens, there is an intriguing story behind that monument," he said, lurching forwards suddenly as the coach slammed to a screeching halt. My reticule flew to the floor, and in the confusion of trying to rescue it, I heard yelling and jeering and the clatter of many footsteps on the street. Henry shoved the window open.

"What the devil is going on?" he shouted to the driver.

A mass of people swarmed from behind us, swallowing up the coach as they closed ranks in front to meet another crowd advancing from the other direction. The two groups seemed to hover and circle like a cloud of insects, then merge into one swarming mob in pursuit of a long black wagon, drawn by two jet-black horses and driven by two uniformed guards.

The coachman yelled above the noise of the crowd. "It's the Black Maria, taking some poor soul up to the prison."

"But what scoundrel would attract so much attention?" asked Henry, craning his neck in the direction of the wagon, which slowly wove its way through the crowd.

The coachman tapped a skinny youth on the shoulder with his crop. The boy cupped his hands around his mouth and shouted something before the crowd jostled him along, surging forwards, pushing and shoving one other aside to get close to the wagon with its row of tiny barred windows. Old men hobbled along, grasping gnarled walking sticks, and ragged beggar children wove their way around serving women in aprons and men wearing flat caps and work-worn suits. A man staggered drunkenly forwards, balancing a smut-faced child on his shoulders. Others brandished brimming bottles of beer. All were shouting and jeering as they clawed their way to the front of the mob.

The coachman leaned towards us, his face gleaming with sweat. "It's Mrs Cotton, the Auckland poisoner. They're fetching her from the assizes at Bishop Auckland. An evil witch she is, what with all the husbands she's seen off. They say she's bound for the hangman."

When I tried to lean out of the window to see better, Henry tore my wrap away from my shoulders when he jerked me back inside the cab, his face wild with panic as he wound the shawl tightly around me again and beseeched me not to look outside. But I had already smelled the stench of sweat and musty clothing from the crowd as they rocked the black prison wagon from side to side.

When riots happened in Bethlem, I would hide under a table. The blood coursed through my veins as I'd once watched two women wrestle and claw and rip at each other's hair, snarling like lionesses. Bloody skeins of brown hair landed by my feet.

Henry reached across me to secure my window catch just as a handful of rocks flew by, striking our horse on the flanks, causing him to whinny and toss his head. The driver yanked hard on the reins to settle the poor creature down, then cracked his whip until the horse was still.

"I'll force my way through this riffraff if I have to," roared the coachman, finally spurring the horse onwards. "I'll crush the scoundrels."

I shrank back into the plush upholstery as a young woman's white face pressed against the window, the toothless mouth forming a damp circle on the glass. She squinted to see inside. Her left eye was swollen and black.

At Bethlem, the walls shook as the brown-haired woman's head smacked against the floor with a damp thud. The nurses dragged her shrieking attacker away, her hands reddened with blood.

Now fear clutched at my throat as the coachman flicked his whip again, sweeping the young woman away so she collided with a fierce heavyset man who grabbed her by the shoulders and hauled her out of his way. She writhed like a wildcat, causing a stout red-faced woman to launch herself onto the man's back and slap at his ears.

His friend hooted with laughter and tried to drag her off his back, ripping her clothing in the process to reveal a pendulous breast. A nearby constable charged at the man, truncheon raised, cracking him across the head so hard that blood splattered across the faces of the horrified onlookers. He crumpled to the ground and his legs folded under him like a marionette's. That was enough to incense the crowd, which surged from behind us like a flood tide, jostling the coach towards the Black Maria.

My heart almost leapt from my chest as we drew level with the barred window of the black prison wagon. I looked over at Henry, who was glued to the other window, watching constables drag the bleeding man away. I tugged at his jacket. "What has she done to enrage such a mob?" I begged.

Before he could answer, the coach lurched sideways, throwing us against the wall of the cab. Now we were stuck fast amongst the bodies. A line of constables marched towards us, their brass buttons glinting in the lamplight.

Heart racing, I turned and dared to look at the prisoner. But instead of a wild ruffian in chains, I glimpsed a small black-haired woman sitting straight as a ramrod, shoulders back and chin held high as if to defy her captors. She seemed to stare straight at me, her dark eyes glittering like granite. Then she raised her arms and lunged forwards, grinning, and I saw her hands were bound with straps like those I'd worn at Hoxton.

I heard the coachman's voice as if through a fog. "Why, there's the evil vixen, the one who killed all her babies."

My stomach turned and I fell back against the seat, pressing my gloves against my mouth to stop myself from crying out.

My baby was limp. I'd strained to pull myself up from the fog of ether to hear its cry above the doctor's mumbling.

*Silence.*

Then Henry's face had loomed like a pale moon in the shadows, his eyes wide with fear. They told me it was a stillbirth, but I barely heard them beneath the sound of my own screams. And when I struggled to see the little body, strong, blood-streaked arms held me back.

"She's on her way out now. You'll catch a look at her," the coachman cried.

Henry stood up to look, one knee wedged on the opposite seat as two guards held the prisoner under the arms and carried her down the steps of the wagon. Her feet were manacled with heavy steel chains. Bareheaded, she was clad in a black dress with a broad chequered shawl pinned around her shoulders. Two burly policemen supported her as she shuffled through the jeering crowd, eyes trained ahead at the yawning black door of the prison.

The line of policemen linked arms and stood fast, holding the crowd back from the small procession. Though my stomach churned at the thought of her crimes, I studied her closely: the small white triangle of a face distinguished only by a thin sullen mouth and dark distinct eyebrows. Eyes hard and cold as slate, defying the screaming crowd.

It was then that I heard a chant coming up from the people—like a child's nursery rhyme.

*Mary Ann Cotton, Mary Ann Cotton*
*The rope will break yer neck*
*And yer'll be dead and buried and rotten*

At the sound of the words, she stumbled, and a woman from the front of the crowd rushed forwards, kicked at her, and spat in her face, shouting, "Baby killer!" The prisoner, Mrs Cotton, bent her head and raised the manacled hands to wipe the spit from her cheek.

Just then the mob surged forwards like a great wave, slamming into the back of our coach and pitching me headlong into the opposite wall.

I heard a dull thud as my head hit the corner of the seat. I felt my teeth snap together and the darkness engulfed me.

# 3

I WOKE TO the sound of splashing water and my stomach rolled.

I squeezed my eyes shut again.

Was it the hiss of the showers at Hoxton, or water from Eva's bucket slopping across the bathroom floor? I waited for the familiar sound of her rheumy coughing and the sour stink of vinegar and carbolic, but all I could smell was the fresh, earthy scent of rain.

I opened my eyes. A candle flickered beside me. This was not the narrow box of a room I had spent the last year in, with its blank white walls, and the plain wooden crucifix hanging above the bed.

*Only follow the Lord and he will deliver you from the devil's clutches.*

Dr Barnsley was a great believer in purging the soul as well as every nook and crevice of our wretched bodies.

I shuddered as raindrops spattered against the half-open window, and I remembered I was in Durham.

A cool breeze sent the lace curtains billowing inwards. Tree branches scratched at the glass and the moon threw shadowy patterns onto the walls.

Then I remembered I was a free woman. This was my new home. *Our new home.* Henry, my husband, was here somewhere with me. My throat tightened. Where was he? I could summon no recollection of getting here—to this house, to this room. Had he carried me?

I lay back against the pillows and touched a small, hard swelling on my forehead. I remembered the coach, the mob, the brass buttons glinting on the policemen's jackets, and the murderer. The baby killer. She'd stood so proud, so defiant, her eyes glinting like obsidian.

The coach driver had said she'd murdered her children, but surely the authorities were mistaken. I had endured a wave of grief that ripped my body apart when I lost my baby, felt the tearing anguish that turned me into a wild and hopeless creature, so how could that small, unassuming woman deliberately kill not one, but many of her own children?

My mind began to race and my head felt so light, I thought it would spin clear away from my body. I clutched at the mattress and told myself, *Be still, put those thoughts away inside your head. That is the only way to behave.*

I'd learned the rules of survival from Annie, a weary seamstress committed to the asylum by her devious husband to clear the way for a younger, more comely wife. Now I heard her voice in my head.

*Keep your mouth shut and your eyes open. These medical men want nothing less than your soul. Make a show of giving it to them, but curse the bastards to high heaven inside your head. Only, make sure your eyes are blank as a doll's and your head bent in submission when you do it.*

And so I'd survived the endless hours lying in a bed like a corpse, counting the dust motes suspended in a ray of sunlight whilst an inferno raged inside my head.

I threw the sheets aside and swung my feet to the floor, eager to breathe in fresh air and put away the memory of that stifling place. Pushing the window up, I thrust my head outside. Moisture beaded the leaves of a huge elm tree, its trunk wrapped in creeping ivy. A streetlamp cast a glow on the road, and two figures, a man and a woman, stepped into the pool of yellow light, their heels tapping across the cobblestones. I pulled back into the shadows for fear they would see me, then peeped out again as they crossed the street and made their way towards our front door.

I tiptoed across the room and pushed the bedroom door open onto a long landing. The moon shone through the far window, silvering the walls with spectral light, and for a moment I thought I was sleepwalking. But when someone rapped at the front door with two good, sharp cracks, I knew I was awake. I had just stepped over the threshold when the door opposite my room swung open and Henry loomed out of the darkness.

"Why did you not call for me?" he snapped, his face swimming out of the shadows. "You could have fainted and struck your head again."

Two more loud raps boomed into the silence.

"Will you not answer that?" I asked. Henry's eyes flitted to me, then towards the front door.

"Go back into your room," he whispered, moving towards the stairs, but turning to keep me in his sight. "And stay there until I come back. I cannot risk another accident."

I backed into the doorway, a cold sweat misting my forehead, and stood still as a statue, listening. The front door creaked open, letting in a swish of cold air that set the hallway curtains fluttering. I heard low, muffled voices but couldn't make out the words, so I stole across the room to the open window and peered around the lace curtains to see our visitors.

A man and a woman stood at the front doorstep. An unusually tall, broad-shouldered man, wearing a bowler hat that obscured most of his face, though reddish wisps of hair and whiskers sprouted from underneath it. All I could see of the woman was smooth silver hair under a wide black bonnet. Raindrops glistened on the shoulders of her coat. She thrust a large saucepan into Henry's hands, then the two of them disappeared into the darkness, though I fancied I heard a carriage door close somewhere beyond the streetlamp.

Henry's footsteps echoed across the hallway tiles, growing gradually fainter until I heard the clink of pots from the back of the house.

I stood at my door, paralyzed by indecision.

*Should I go downstairs?* I asked myself. He'd told me to wait in my room.

*Just be an obedient wife and he will soon trust you again,* the voice said, so I stayed in the doorway.

But I'd forgotten how to be a wife, and the thought of intimacy filled me with such dread. I bit my knuckles to stifle the sudden surge of panic. Passion was a distant memory, driven far away by the horrors of that cold white bathroom.

I peered around the doorpost to see if Henry was about, and my heart lurched when he appeared again at the head of the stairs, carrying a tray.

"The visitors left?" I asked, for the want of anything better to say.

"I told them you were indisposed. They brought soup. You must eat some to get your strength back."

"But I should have liked to thank them."

"Another time," he said, appraising me coolly and placing the soup on the bedside table. "That was the college chaplain, Reverend Buckley, and his wife. You were not in a proper state to meet them today. They'll come back when you're settled."

I touched my hair. The combs had come loose and tangled strands hung down to my shoulders. My dress was creased and spotted with blood.

"I'm such a sight—I'll clean myself up."

He shook his head and beckoned me towards the bedside table. "It's late, Clara. Almost bedtime. Eat first and then rest again. It's been a trying day."

He motioned towards the room behind him. "We'll keep separate sleeping quarters for now. Dr Barnsley said you must get plenty of sleep and avoid any excess of emotion; otherwise, you could suffer an immediate relapse."

An image flashed across my mind. Lying like a gutted fish on a cold marble slab, my naked legs blue with cold, my teeth grinding together as white-aproned figures poured icy water into long rubber tubes and I tried to separate my mind from my body to disguise my absolute terror.

I still couldn't endure the idea of being touched now.

He pushed past me and placed the tray on my bedside table. "You do want to get better, Clara, don't you?" he asked, moving closer so I could see that his lips were dry and scaly. I shuddered as he dampened them with his tongue. I wanted to back away, but my feet were stuck fast to the floor.

"Yes . . . yes, I do, Henry," I whispered. "But what happened . . . to the murderer . . . the wounded man . . . all the blood?"

When I tried to say more, Henry placed a finger on my lips. "Don't fret, Clara. You survived a terrifying experience, and you mustn't speak of such unpleasantness. Just concentrate on happier thoughts. That's the only way to get well." He bustled about the room, pulling the curtains shut and shovelling more coal onto the fire. "Now eat your soup and I'll be up to check on you later."

He left, pulling the door slowly shut.

I realised then, I hadn't eaten all day.

I sat down in the fireside chair and consumed the entire bowl of soup, barely stopping to take a breath.

I looked around at the room to distract myself. Faded green floral wallpaper spread like a leafy web across the walls. All my familiar treasures were arranged on the carved mahogany dressing table. Izzie's silver vanity set, the jade and walnut jewellery box Father had brought Mother from India, and a crystal perfume atomiser.

I ran my fingers across the cool surfaces. So familiar yet still strange. I had not seen these objects for so long. All my earrings and necklaces were carefully placed inside the jewellery box, including the silver locket Henry had given me when he proposed. I could scarcely imagine those distant times now, but I supposed they'd been happier. I laid the necklace on the dressing table and went to explore the wardrobe, where my dresses and coats hung limply, a row of headless corpses waiting to greet me after a long time away. I shivered and shut the door, remembering the sour, grey strong dress from the asylum. I would reacquaint myself with all my clothes later.

Restless, I pulled open the curtains, then pushed up the window and leaned out into the night. But the sound of Henry's footsteps creaking along the hallway outside drove me away from the open window.

"You'll catch your death keeping that open at such a late hour," said Henry, making straight for the window and tugging it down. Dressed in a loose open-collared shirt, he appeared softer, more vulnerable. "We're in the northern climes now and there's a creeping dampness in the air here."

"Thank you for arranging my things on the dressing table," I said. "They remind me of home."

He drew himself up and seemed to hover over me. His eyes strayed to the open collar of my nightdress, then darted away as if he were afraid to look me in the eye. "This is *our* home now, Clara. I hoped they'd make you feel more comfortable here." He glanced at the locket lying on the dressing table. "But you must put this on now that you're home."

I turned and let him drape the chain around my neck, trembling as the cold silver touched my skin. He grasped my shoulders from behind. "Now we are truly man and wife again," he whispered into my ear.

He rummaged through his trouser pocket and produced a small vial and a spoon. "Mrs Parsons advised that you continue with the sleeping draught. You need to get plenty of rest."

I backed away, shaking my head. "But it makes my mind so foggy."

He sat me down on the bed.

"No more protests, Clara. It's just a little medicine." He took my chin firmly in his hand and pushed the spoon into my mouth until its edge scraped against my teeth. "You do trust me entirely?"

He tugged at my chin until I opened my mouth wide, allowing the medicine to slip down my throat. "Well, don't you?" he whispered, his eyes so close to mine, I could see bloodred flecks in the amber irises.

"I do," I croaked, my throat almost too dry to utter the words.

"Good, then we'll have no more silly dramatics," he said, releasing me with a little shove and pocketing the bottle. "Sleep well, my dearest."

And then he was gone and all I could hear was the dull thud of my heart against the silence of the room.

Despite the medicine, I tossed and turned, thoughts of the murderer, Mrs Cotton, swirling through my mind.

I dreamt it was night, and I came upon the black prison wagon. It stood alone in the deserted marketplace, shining like polished ebony. Three black horses snorted and pawed at the ground, their breath clouding the air. Then the wagon door swung open and Mrs Cotton descended the steps through the sheet of mist. *See how I am free,* she said, shaking off her manacles and floating towards me like a pale strip of moonlight, her features shifting and changing so I could see only the impression of a face. And then a great black fog swept through the air, causing her to stumble and fall to her knees. And there were eyes in that fog that watched her creep like a broken-winged bat across the cobbles.

I backed away and put my hands to my ears to drown out the sound of her shrieking, then I woke, sobbing.

I'd cried out in my sleep.

I stuffed the corner of the sheet into my mouth to stifle my cries and held my breath at the sound of footsteps in the hallway outside.

But it was too late. Henry had heard me.

My blood froze as a ribbon of light spread across the narrow gap below the door. He was outside, waiting and listening. I heard the rush and catch of his breath when he placed his ear to the keyhole.

I pressed myself flat against the mattress, my mind racing, trying to remember a time when he had held me to his chest and murmured words of comfort. I cast my mind back to some dim, distant time in the early years of our marriage when I had first miscarried and wept until my eyes were dry. Now I willed him to go away and leave me in peace with my misery.

*I needed no consolation now.*

After a few moments more, the footsteps retreated.

I flew across the room and tried the doorknob. The door creaked open onto the dark, empty corridor.

Relieved, I edged the door shut, placed my cheek and hands flat against the wood panelling, slid to the floor, then crushed my knuckles into my mouth for fear of crying out again as I remembered Annie's wise words.

*Live inside your head.*

# 4

I AWOKE TO a tray of tea and toast set on the fireside table.

So Henry had already been to my room. I wondered if he was downstairs dining alone or had left for the university. I reminded myself to become familiar with his movements so I could fit seamlessly into his daily routine.

I took a slice of toast and wandered over to the window. The sun was out and a light wind shook the leaves of the great elm tree. A passing milk cart told me the world was at work, and suddenly all the strangeness of the previous day slipped away.

Henry had left fresh water in the bowl, so I sponged my face, changed my clothes, and brushed my hair. I cleaned the spots of soup from my travelling dress, unpacked the small bag with the few effects I'd had at the asylum, and opened every drawer to inspect its contents. Many were filled with clothes—petticoats, chemises, and scarves I remembered from my life in London. Henry had spent a good deal of time organising all my things. Even my old letters from Izzie had been tied with string and stowed away neatly in a pretty walnut writing desk.

My dear grandmother Izzie had raised me from the age of ten. Now she was in India, where the climate was kinder to her failing lungs. And yet, I had written letters to her from Hoxton and never received any reply. I began to sort through the letters, checking the date on each postmark, when I heard footsteps outside the door. I thrust the letters back into their pigeonhole and slammed down the roll top.

Henry stood in the open doorway, smart in his frock coat and tie. He glanced beyond me at the writing desk, then fixed his eyes back on my face, his lips curving into a smile. "You look more rested, Clara. I trust you slept well."

"Very well."

"I must go to work now. My lectures begin in an hour," he said, checking his watch. "Will you be all right on your own?"

"I'll spend some time acquainting myself with the house," I said, trying to nudge some enthusiasm into my voice.

He stepped back. "Of course, Clara. You haven't even been downstairs. You must explore our new home and make yourself comfortable here."

My insides fluttered as I tiptoed past him and fled down the stairs. Glancing back, I saw him watching me, his arms folded, his expression unreadable.

When he disappeared into his bedroom, I could breathe again.

I looked around me. An open doorway at the foot of the stairs revealed Henry's study and a desk strewn with papers and piles of books. On the far side of the hall, another door led into a parlour, its faded wallpaper scattered with exotic birds and tropical flowers, scrubbed by a vigorous hand until the shapes were blurred. A grand fireplace took up one wall. On its mantel, a brass carriage clock ticked away the hours, flanked by two stout brass candlesticks, like sentries overseeing the slow passage of time.

I caught sight of my face in the gilded mirror above the mantel. When had my eyes become so dull? My complexion so pallid? *Where was the young, energetic woman who painted and read and loved life?* Then I reminded myself I was here to recover. To regain my strength.

I ran a finger across a polished side table. Dust furred every surface and I vowed to make a start on cleaning the house as soon as I had settled in.

The other door led to a dining room and beyond that, a narrow but airy kitchen with rose-sprigged wallpaper, a scrubbed wooden table and bench, and a heavy wooden mantel above a leaded coal range. Two blackened kettles were set against the sooty brick of the chimney flue wall and a hearty fire burned behind an iron grate. Two chairs were arranged at either side of the range, each with its own footstool. Perhaps Henry expected me to be up and ready with a blazing fire in the hearth and breakfast on the table. But it had been so long since I'd run my own household, I felt nervous at the many hinges and flaps on the range. And when I wandered into the tiny whitewashed scullery, the row of hanging copper pots and baskets of kitchen implements resembled an armoury.

I heard a rustle behind me and whirled around. Henry appeared in the kitchen doorway, shrugging on his greatcoat.

"I slept so late," I muttered. "Did you eat breakfast?"

He began to do up the buttons. "I've learned to look after myself this past year. Men can be very resilient when faced with adversity." He pressed his lips together and glared at me with such acrimony, I stopped dead in my tracks.

"It must have been difficult for you."

"You have no idea, Clara," he said, turning away and taking up his gloves from the table.

My heart pounded in my head.

If only he knew how I'd suffered.

I bit my lower lip. "I'm sorry," I whispered, lowering my head and following him out into the front hallway.

I glanced at the floor, afraid to meet his eyes for fear my rancour would show itself. Sunlight splashed red shapes onto the tiles through the stained-glass windows on the front door. As if the floor were daubed with blood, like the ragged blotches on the doctor's apron.

Henry put down the gloves and took me gently by the shoulders. "Poor Clara. So melancholic and lost in your thoughts. I fear for you. Just remember how your mother was. Surely you don't want to go the same way as she did?"

I shook my head, turning my face away from the odour of stale tea on his breath. He never missed an opportunity to remind me of my poor tragic mother.

"Good. Then you know I'm here to make sure that doesn't happen. Do you understand?" he said, shaking me until I looked at him.

"Yes, Henry. I do." The blood rushed in my ears.

"Then we'll keep our heads up and look forwards to the future. Forget the morbid events of the past."

He released me and I stood in the beam of sunlight, my body limp and deflated.

Finally he pulled on his gloves, put on his hat, and took up his briefcase. He opened the door and turned to look at me. "You look so well rested, I'll tell the Buckleys to call in this afternoon. I think it's time to let my colleagues know I'm a happily married man, not a reclusive bachelor. And you'll meet Reverend Buckley's wife, Emma. She's a fine woman."

"A new companion would be a great comfort to me," I said, massaging my palm with my thumb.

Henry scowled at me. "Stop fidgeting, Clara. You must learn to conduct yourself with more composure now that you're home."

I dropped my hands to my sides, unsure how to occupy them.

He shook his head. "You should spend today preparing the tea service and making sure the parlour is spotless. I will fetch some cakes from the baker's on my way home."

I nodded obediently as he strode out smiling into the fresh air, the door slamming shut behind him.

I wandered into the kitchen. All those long hours spent at Hoxton, *resting* and blankly staring into space, had numbed me, made me cautious and unsure of how to act.

As I poured a cup of cold tea, I searched my memory for details of my life before the asylum. I tried to picture myself performing the small morning routines of boiling water, cutting bread, measuring tea leaves into the pot, and sitting at breakfast opposite my husband, a sweet smile fixed on my face whilst I offered him the sugar bowl. But I could never see myself in that cosy tableau. Instead I appeared as a shadowy figure, a blurred, half-formed creature drifting on the periphery.

I drank the rest of the tea and put the dishes into the scullery sink. A small storage room nearby revealed an assortment of dusters, brushes, and buckets. I would clean the parlour and dining room to pass the time.

As I dusted and swept, I chided myself for being so ungrateful. How could I complain when I'd left behind so many hopeless souls who'd never leave Hoxton? I remembered Ivy, a skinny slip of a girl, diagnosed with chronic hysteria, abandoned there three years before my arrival when she'd refused to marry an elderly judge. She'd run away from home at least four times to escape that fate. Her stepfather claimed he couldn't tolerate another blow to his reputation; neither had he sufficient funds to support two women. He'd dropped Ivy off at the asylum for some *moral management*, then taken her mother off to live in South Africa.

Ivy's lovely thick hair had been cut short when she refused to eat. The day before I left, she rushed to my room and clung to my arm. Her hair stuck out in ragged points like the head of a scrubbing brush and her scaly lips were flecked with spit.

"You must take me with you, Clara," she begged. "I cannot stay here a moment longer or I will lose the brains I had. I'll become a wild animal if I stay here."

Nobody would ever come for her.

And neither could I go back.

An obedient, submissive manner was my only hope of being free.

I passed the time polishing the furniture, arranging the dishes, and sorting out the best cups and saucers. Then I moved on to the parlour. Potted ferns flanked a small piano that stood along the adjacent wall. A carved mahogany desk with its ladder-backed chair sat in a corner by the garden window. I could have sat there and read or written in a journal, but Henry had declared such "brainwork" as an excessive mental drain on my fragile mind.

"The stress will result in total emotional depletion, Clara," he'd said the previous evening. "Concern yourself with gentle, repetitive tasks instead."

I sat in that ladder-backed chair and gazed out the window. The sun had disappeared behind banks of grey clouds and the wind was whipping the last of the autumn leaves from the branches. I longed for diversion—something to stimulate my deadened brain. Yesterday's newspaper lay on the desk. I rustled through it until I caught the word *poisoner* in one of the titles. Straightening out the page, I read:

## THE AUCKLAND POISONER: POSSIBLY TWENTY DEATHS AT HER HANDS

*The prisoner, MARY ANN COTTON, is presently remanded in Durham Prison on the charge of murder by poisoning of her stepson Charles Edward Cotton. She herself states that whilst she was in the south of England, she had four children to her first husband, William Mowbray, all of whom died. The other deaths occurred as follows:*

*Margaret Jane Mowbray (4), June 22, 1860*
*John Robert William Mowbray (1), September 20, 1864*
*William Mowbray, husband (47), January 15, 1865*
*Margaret Jane Mowbray (4), April 30, 1865*
*George Ward, husband (33), October 20, 1866*
*John Robinson (10 months), December 21, 1866*
*Mrs Stott, mother (54), March 15, 1867*
*James Robinson (6), April 20, 1867*
*Elizabeth Robinson (8), April 25, 1867*
*Isabella Jane Mowbray (9), April 30, 1867*
*Margaret Isabella Robinson (3 months), February 28, 1868*
*Frederick Cotton, husband (40), September 2, 1871*
*Fred Cotton (10), March 10, 1872*
*Robert Robson Cotton (14 months), March 28, 1872*
*Joseph Nattrass, lodger (35), April 1, 1872*
*Charles Edward Cotton (7), July 12, 1872*

Twenty deaths in only twelve years. Babies less than two years old and so many little children. My mind strained to grasp the possibility that one small woman could be capable of such hideous crimes. To have poisoned all those innocent people—her own flesh and blood. How was a human being capable of such savagery? Was she inhuman—a monster?

A sudden crack of thunder robbed the breath from me. I imagined those small stiff corpses lying in a row, like a fleeting impression from a forgotten nightmare. Thrusting the newspaper down, I hurried to the window. A storm was blowing in. Outside, the elm trees creaked and groaned in the gusty wind. Rain lashed against the windowpanes, turning the street outside into a watery blur.

A wave of dizziness washed over me. I wanted nothing more than to lie down and sleep. To push those terrible thoughts away. I dragged myself up the stairs and set off along the hallway, past Henry's locked bedroom door on the way, but when I noticed the spare room door was ajar, I stopped outside. It had been locked when I arrived and was the only other room I hadn't explored.

I stood at the threshold and hesitated before stepping inside.

# York

## Spring 1873

THE SLOW HISS of brakes signals our arrival in York, the first stop in my long journey to India, Izzie, and freedom. A conductor in a navy coat and brass buttons slides the door open to tell me they will stop for refreshments. I say I will stay in the carriage. He nods in silent understanding, his eyes drifting over the heavy black veil that obscures my eyes. Then he gives a shallow bow and retreats into the narrow passageway, now filled with passengers stopping off at York.

Alice, our maidservant, prepared a feast of sandwiches and cold chicken for the journey before she left for her new position at St. John's rectory. She was such a comfort to me in those final weeks at the house. I hugged her close, told her to be good to her family, and urged her to forget the terrible crime she had witnessed.

She cried and said she would never, ever speak of that night, for that was the only way she could move on. Now I hope she finds happiness with the vicar and his wife, since joy was scarce around Henry and me.

Steam clears from the train window, revealing the towering spires of York Minster. I pull aside my veil to see the great cathedral, silhouetted against a brilliant blue sky. Ochre-stoned and palatial, it lacks the haunting austerity of Durham Cathedral. My father was born here and yet I never visited the place. His people moved south to Bristol when he was only ten. It comforts me to think of him now and, as the doors open to let in new passengers, I wish I could step out for a whilst to walk the streets that he'd skipped along as an innocent child. My father was a trusting man who believed all people were good and kind and loving. A gentle man of deep thought and infinite patience.

I sip at the warm flask of tea, remembering him as a tall bear of a man with heavy black brows and a head of dark curls, which I twirled around my fingers when he carried me on his shoulders amongst the apple trees in our orchard. He'd stop to let me reach the higher branches and pick the ripest fruits. He'd click his tongue and make *clip-clopping* sounds as he loped around the garden, making me giddy with laughter and dizzy from the dip and lurch of his shoulders. But he worked for the Foreign Office and was often away for weeks at a time. The house always seemed stale and empty without his colossal presence. Mother and I missed him terribly, but when he returned, my mother ran to him and leapt like a child into his arms whilst I clung kitten-like to his coattails. Then the two of them would disappear together upstairs and I'd sit in the kitchen with Cook and Janet, the parlourmaid, who'd wink at her and say, "Good thing the mattress is getting a right beating. One less job for me."

Mother was a raven-haired artist who painted intricate pictures set in fairy woodlands and glades. When I was a child, she'd lock herself in her studio for hours at a time. Afterwards she swooped out and ushered me inside to scour her latest canvas for tiny creatures hidden in the leafy undergrowth. But at other times, when my father was away, she slipped like a shadow from the darkened studio and took to her bed, with the curtains drawn and strict instructions not to be interrupted. Then I'd wander into her abandoned studio only to find the canvas splattered with black and grey paint and the brushes strewn across the floor. I spent hours tidying up the mess and cleaning the palettes until she crept down the stairs, her face white as the plaster she used for sculpting moulds, her arms crisscrossed with faint bloody lines. She'd crush me to her chest and carry me upstairs, where she'd tell me bedtime stories about a rabbit named Belinda.

Even now I wonder if I inherited my father's generosity of spirit or whether I am more my mother's daughter. Excitable, passionate, impulsive.

Unpredictable.

Unstable.

When I think of that spare room, I feel the sense of precariousness that always unsettled me when I was in the house at Durham.

I pull the dark veil across my eyes again, then sit back and close them.

Some things are too painful to remember in the harsh light of day.

# 5

DARKENED BY THICK velvet curtains, the spare room had a musty smell; the air tinged with the smoky stink of London streets. The familiar scents of my old life.

Furniture from our London house was stacked against the wall—a child's table and bench set against a rocking chair, a washstand, and a baby's swinging cradle. I ran my hands over the rough wicker surface of the cradle. A gift from Izzie.

I hadn't laid eyes on it for so long.

Ribbons hung like ragged streamers from its corners, but the soft cotton mattress was clean and unsullied. My baby should have been lying there sleeping, its lashes resting against its rosy cheeks.

All at once the wind blew up again with more force, setting the door creaking on its hinges. I heard the echo of branches tapping against the chimney pot, the wind whining in the chimney, and it seemed like a mist parted before my eyes as I recalled the events of the day I lost my baby.

I was sitting on a rose upholstered rocking chair by my bedroom window in London, crocheting a baby's sock and listening to the wind whistle down the chimney flues. Right beside my bed, the wicker swinging cot shone like a little sailing ship, covered in snowy-white lace and muslin, and trimmed with pale green ribbons.

The afternoon sun beamed into the room, illuminating the display of white baby garments fanned out on the bed.

I placed the finished sock beside its matching partner, and hoisted my swollen body out of the chair to admire my handiwork. I pictured myself in just a few more weeks, pulling those tiny socks onto my precious baby's feet.

Then Henry called me from the downstairs hallway to tell me our carriage had arrived. He had arranged a ride for us in Kensington Palace Gardens. I crossed the room to answer him, but pains slashed through my body like hot knives stabbing my gut. I hunched forwards, clasping my belly, and flopped back onto the rocking chair, the breath searing my lungs as a slow, wet warmth oozed between my legs.

I screamed and clenched my teeth, squeezing every muscle in my pelvis to keep the baby inside, to stop its life from seeping out of me, but a crimson stain soaked down the sides of the chair. I howled until the sound deafened me.

After that, I remember only a string of ragged images.

I lay on a wooden pallet in a dimly lit room, the sickly sweet smell of ether in the air. My abdomen throbbed as if hot sticks were beating it. My entire body convulsed with searing pains. A blurry, whiskered man's face hovered over me, hands like crimson-coated talons. His shirt, blood-smeared like a butcher's apron. "It's done," he said as I turned to retch into a bucket at the side of the bed. But in that bucket I saw a pink mass of flesh with a transparent blue-veined head, its filmy eye fixed in a stare. Like the eye of a dead fledgling. The doctor grabbed the bloody bucket and shoved it towards a nurse in a starched white cap. I struggled to stop the man who would put my baby in a slop pail—to throw it in the drain with all the stinking sewage. Writhing and spitting, I bit at arms, hands, warm flesh until I tasted the metallic rush of blood. I grasped a scalpel and stabbed at the air. Two nurses appeared. White angels in the gloom. I felt the snap of leather straps, pulled so tight that my limbs were caught, as if in a vice. Henry loomed in the background, a grey shape swimming in the shadows, his terrified eyes like bruises on his pale face. Then someone thrust a rubber plug into my mouth and forced my tongue downwards until I began to choke.

The dull thud of something dashing itself against the windowpane roused me from the grip of my nightmare. I hoisted myself up and rushed to the window. On the gravel below, a large crow lay stunned, its wings trembling, a blue film creeping over its eye. Then I felt the tears come, hard and fast, bending me in two and forcing me to my knees. I braced myself, palms flat on the floor, as the sobs tore through my body.

Afterwards, when my eyes were dry and the tears spent, I lay facedown on the floor, too weak to move. My mind drifted back to the day before I left Hoxton. I was sitting by Dr Shepton's desk, gazing at the vase of yellow chrysanthemums next to his inkpot. I marvelled at the bright petals.

"You will soon enjoy many such sights, Mrs Blackstone," he said, looking up from his writing, "but you can learn something from these flowers. Remember, it is natural to grieve and give vent to your pain." He touched a full golden bloom. "Here is an open heart, ready to receive all that life has to give, and here," he said, touching a dried-up bud, "is one that clutches its fears and sadness into itself until it withers and dies."

A sudden weariness came over me. I lay there, grief bearing down on my shoulders like a heavy yoke, but the pain was preferable to the numbness I had felt for so long. As I drifted into a deep sleep, the wind tore at the shutters and I thought of Mrs Cotton and her life, so steeped in death. I dreamt she was standing on the riverbank, the rain cutting across her face and soaking her hair so that it hung to her shoulders in slick, wet tendrils. Then the wind whipped up the river into choppy waves that boiled and swelled, lapping up against her feet until the water rose into a monstrous wall of blackness that rushed towards her, sweeping her into a maelstrom of churning water, river mud, broken branches, and sodden, bloated corpses.

I awoke to the sound of the grandfather clock striking four, and I sat up in a rush. The Buckleys were arriving at half past four. Hurrying to the door, I listened for voices, but the house was silent except for the snap and flutter of the curtains at the landing window. My thoughts raced. I should tidy myself, light a fire, boil water, set out the cups.

The storm had abated, but the sky was still clouded over and the evening was drawing in quickly. I ran back into the bedroom. Only an inch of water remained in the bowl. I wiped my face as best I could in the dim light, then arranged my hair and pinched my cheeks to get some colour into them.

It was almost half past four when I hurried downstairs, praying the fire was still burning in the kitchen grate. But the kitchen was dark and chilly, the ashes almost cold. Desperate, I grabbed a newspaper from the table, threw some scraps onto the ashes, and fanned the faintly glowing embers with the rest, sending a shower of dust and ash into the air. Finally the paper began to burn, so I shovelled on more coal and flapped the newspaper hard over the growing flames. Soon the fire began to crackle and spit. All I had to do was put the kettle on the hob and heat the water for tea.

When the key turned in the front door lock, I slammed the kettle onto the hob and hurried into the hall.

Henry was hanging his coat on the stand. A tall, square-shouldered, florid man with bushy eyebrows, a shock of reddish hair, and flourishing whiskers materialised behind him. His lips appeared so unusually plump and pinkish, I felt a wave of nausea.

"Good day, Mrs Blackstone," he said in a deep, plummy voice.

Henry took his arm. "Clara, this is Reverend Donald Buckley, college chaplain and dean of mathematics. He and his wife kindly brought us soup yesterday when you were recovering from your injury."

Vivid memories of the murderer and the mob and the coach lurching forwards flashed into my head, temporarily disorienting me. I struggled for the right words. "I . . . I thank you. The soup was most delicious."

"Think nothing of it, Mrs Blackstone," said Reverend Buckley, moving closer to peer at my forehead. "Though I was sorry to hear you were indisposed. I told Henry I'd be happy to take a look at that bump. One cannot be too careful with blows to the head."

I edged away. "It's nothing."

"Of course, I have some knowledge of matters related to healing. I had the privilege of studying medicine for two years at Edinburgh University under the tutelage of the great surgeon Dr Andrew McPherson."

"And then God called him," said a soft female voice. A plump middle-aged woman appeared beside him, a basket slung across her arm. Smooth-faced, with clear grey eyes and grey-streaked hair tucked into a starched lace cap, she had such a calm manner, my apprehension subsided.

Reverend Buckley propelled the woman towards me, his arm wrapped around her waist. "May I introduce Mrs Emma Buckley, my wife, the moral compass of my life, the guardian of my soul, the angel at my hearth."

Her face appeared rosy in the light. "My dear Clara, I've so looked forward to meeting you," she said, clasping my hand, though I pulled it away when I noticed black smudges on my palm.

Henry's brows knit in a bemused expression.

"I was stoking the fire."

"Is that why your dress is covered in ashes?" he said.

Emma cupped my chin and scrutinised my face. "Don't fuss, Henry. It's high time you showed everyone you aren't a lonely bachelor. And Clara's jasmine-tinted complexion and exquisite Grecian nose is quite perfect. Now, dear, just permit me to wipe that smear from the side of your chin."

When she took out a handkerchief and dabbed at my cheek, Henry's eyebrows rose. "My apologies, Emma. Clara has an overactive mind and tends to be easily distracted."

Reverend Buckley sniffed and patted Henry on the back. "Have no worries, Henry. Emma will soon take her in hand."

As she dusted down the front of my dress, Emma continued to chat. "Of course, Donald and I have so enjoyed looking after Henry these last few months. I'm sure he would have starved if we hadn't fed him dinner every night."

Henry looked sheepish. "I'm afraid I've imposed on your generosity for far too long."

"We're already missing your company at suppertime, but now I must step aside for Clara to take over," Emma said, with such a tinkling laugh that I couldn't help but feel I'd disturbed their comfortable arrangement. "Now, please let me be of assistance. I know how daunting one's first tea party can be in a new setting."

"I won't hear of it," I said, struggling to hang the coats on the rack. "Please join Henry in the parlour, and I'll get the tea."

Henry lunged forwards just as I was about to drop Reverend Buckley's hat. "Clara, I insist you accept Emma's offer. Now, be a good girl and do as I say. I will take the coats."

Angry, I led Emma to the kitchen. Henry had addressed me like a scatterbrained child.

Emma darted around the kitchen like a busy chicken. She opened the tea caddy and sniffed at the tea leaves, checked the inside of the kettle, then clucked her tongue at the messy floor.

"You must get the broom, dear. The floor is covered in ashes."

As I swept, she brought teacups and saucers in from the dining room, then sniffed the milk I'd taken from the pantry. "Curdled, as I expected. One can't trust a man to do the shopping, but never fear, I came prepared."

She placed the basket onto the table. "Now, be a dear and plate these jam tarts whilst I pour this cream into the jug."

Minutes later we entered the parlour carrying the tea things to find Henry and Donald deep in conversation.

"I trust Emma has everything in hand," said Donald, his hands clasped behind his back as he stood in front of the fireplace, rocking to and fro on his heels as if he were the man of the house. "My dear mother always loved to impress upon me that there is no more fruitful source of family discontent than a housewife's badly cooked meals and slovenly ways, so I must say, Emma's fastidious nature has made our home a place of harmony and contentment."

Henry stroked his beard and glowered at me as if I had already failed tonight's test. "I am sure Clara will strive towards such exacting standards once she's settled in."

"Y-yes, of course," I stammered.

"Though you simply must hire some help, Henry," said Emma. "Clara cannot be expected to take care of everything in the house. Especially if she's to join our ladies' circle."

"Naturally," said Henry, studying the movement of my hand as I poured the tea. "Perhaps you could recommend a suitable girl."

"As a matter of fact, I do have someone in mind," said Emma, handing the plate of tarts around. "I'll make further enquiries tonight."

"The ladies have a very active group," said Reverend Buckley, reaching for the sugar and placing four lumps in his tea. "Of course, my wife does not favour gossip or vain pursuits. She has a philanthropic nature and prefers to involve herself in charitable activities."

"Well, I'm sure Clara would be happy to accompany Emma in one of the less taxing roles," said Henry, biting into a tart and looking over at me. I gulped at my tea and focused on the droplets of jam that dribbled down his beard.

"Naturally, we wouldn't overburden her," said Buckley. "The nervous temperament cannot tolerate overstimulation."

My hands began to sweat and I put down my cup before it slipped from my hands. *How much had Henry told them about me? About the past year?*

Buckley put down his cup and inhaled deeply. "Henry, you'd be advised to read the works of the great Dr Maudsley, who claims that intellectual exertion is an excessive mental drain on a young woman's mind. He uses the brilliant metaphor of a bank to illustrate his theory. As he says, 'What nature spends in one direction, she must economise in another.' Hence, intellectual or creative pursuits will drain a woman's body, causing headache, fatigue, and insomnia, and in the more severe cases, epilepsy and complete mental breakdown."

I rose from my chair. "I'll get more hot water," I said, grabbing the teapot and hurrying to the kitchen, where I steadied myself against the scullery sink and listened to the hushed voices in the other room. *So I am to be the invalid, the hysteric, poised forever on the brink of insanity, nerves strung tight as piano wires. An object of cloying sympathy and the subject of medical speculation.*

I poured more hot water into the teapot and fixed a placid smile on my face before venturing back to the parlour. Hearing the name Cotton, I realised the conversation had shifted to talk of the poisoner. Reverend Buckley still held court as Henry and Emma looked on in rapt admiration.

"What is our society coming to when the beauty of motherhood is defiled by such brutal and vicious actions? How can a mother suddenly become deprived of reason? Is she insane? Instead of surrounding her family with a halo of love, she turns into a cunning murderer, an angel of death dispensing suffering in the guise of care. I'll warrant her madness and degeneracy is inherited. Passed down from one generation to another."

I almost dropped the teapot onto the tray. Henry's eyes flashed a warning when he steadied my hand. "I'm sure she'll soon feel the full weight of the law," he said, his lips twisting into a strained smile. "More tea?"

Reverend Buckley reached in his waistcoat pocket and pulled out a gold pocket watch. After checking it and stowing it back into its place, he puffed out his chest and rubbed his palms together before standing up. "I think now we shall take a brisk walk homewards. Good for the constitution, Henry." He clapped a meaty hand on Henry's shoulder. "You might consider joining us one evening. Or perhaps accompanying us on a weekend outing to the coast. Gets the blood flowing from head to toe. Mrs Buckley swears by it. Don't you, my dove?"

"Absolutely. And the air is so fresh in these parts. We'll have you ruddy and glowing in no time, Clara," she said, following her husband out into the hallway.

Henry shook Reverend Buckley's large hand like a thirsty man pumping water and Emma leaned close to my ear. "Look after yourself, my dear. Plenty of rest and good food will help you recover from your recent troubles." She pulled on her gloves. "And I hope to see you both at our home on Saturday. We're hosting a little soiree."

Henry's mouth drooped at the corners when he glanced over at me, whilst Buckley's eyes followed his every move. "My wife's dinner creations are not to be missed, Henry. We'll expect you there at six."

"And I do so want to introduce Clara to the other ladies," added Emma, eyelashes fluttering like an ingénue as Buckley held the front door open for her.

"Till the weekend, Mrs Blackstone," said Buckley, stepping out into the yellow glow of the streetlamp.

"We look forward to it," said Henry, waving and closing the door.

I turned to go to the parlour and clear up the teacups when Henry caught me by the arm.

"Just a moment, Clara," he said, steering me around to face him. "I must be honest with you for your own good. Your social behaviour needs some attention. You seem flat and impassive, with little to offer in the way of conversation, and your hands shook so much, I feared you would drop the teapot."

"I've been here only two days, Henry. You said you'd be patient."

He ran a hand through his hair. "So I did. I suppose everything seems strange to you still."

I nodded. "As you said, Henry, it will take time but I promise to try my best."

Henry reached for me again and sighed. The light from the streetlamp shone through the window, casting his face into darkness. "I'm certain you'll soon be back to your old, sweet self, Clara, and I will be waiting."

"I'm grateful for your patience," I mumbled, despite the dryness of my throat.

He exhaled, his eyes glinting in the shadows, and stroked my hair. "That's better. Now, get to bed and rest. I'll be up shortly with the sleeping draught."

I climbed the stairs, my legs heavy and my eyes searching the gloomy hallway for something friendly and familiar to fix on to. Something to make me believe I could be happy and secure here in my new home. But the silence in the house felt ominous, the curtains dark and shivering, the pictures hung slightly askew, the floor tilted away from me.

That woman I used to be was long gone—wiped away by the busy hands of the eminent mind doctors. Bludgeoned by their theories.

Broken by their cures.

# 6

THE DAY AFTER the Buckleys' visit, I ventured out into the city.

Warm autumn sun shone onto ragged shrubs and faded rosebushes in the small garden by the front gate. A carriage clattered by. A man walked in the other direction, pushing an elderly gent in a wheelchair, followed by two children bowling hoops. Then two servant girls with white aprons and caps chattered as they swung their shopping baskets on their arms.

I turned to look at my house, a low two-storey building of pale brown stone with blue-painted shutters, dwarfed by taller houses on either side, both obscured by trees.

When the gate slammed behind me, I stood, wondering which way to walk, but a farmer's cart passed by, loaded with turnips and potatoes, so I followed it, hoping I was headed in the right direction for the town centre.

The road took me past terraces of grey stone houses into the very marketplace I'd crossed with Henry. Crowds swarmed around the market stalls, where merchants stood behind piles of turnips, carrots, cabbages, and potatoes. My stomach rumbled at the scent of pies and fresh loaves of bread, but my appetite abated at the sudden sight of a butcher's stall, where three skinned hares dangled from their bound feet. I stumbled onwards until a street hawker stepped into my path and thrust a bag of hot chestnuts in my face. Smoke curled from the coals in his cart, reminding me of London's murky air, but I shook my head and pressed on. I'd left that place and all its sad memories behind.

Further on, a knife grinder in a battered top hat and ragged greatcoat held a blade to the stone, throwing out a shower of sparks as he worked a pedal. He puffed at his clay pipe and held up the knife so the metal glinted in the sunlight, its edge sharp as a razor. When he turned towards me, I saw that his left eyelid was fused shut and a ragged scar had gouged the side of his face from eye to chin. For a split second an image burst into my mind of Mother brandishing her palette knife, the soft skin of her inner arms a maze of bloody lines.

"Watch it, miss," he said as I stumbled backwards into a circle of children gathered around a peddler selling spinning tops. They stared at me as if I were mad. I mumbled my apologies and hastened towards a large crowd gathered at the corner of the marketplace. The crowd jostled a harried news seller who stuffed newspapers into outstretched hands as fast as the pennies were thrown at him. On the front page was a cameo-shaped portrait of a woman. Her pale face, with its narrow, brooding eyes and sulky mouth, glared out at me. The same face I'd seen in the Black Maria. A bold headline painted on the display board read:

**THE SUSPECTED WHOLESALE POISONING AT WEST AUCKLAND**

"Did ya want a paper, mum?" asked a ruddy-faced woman in servant's clothes.

I nodded, gave her a penny, and watched her dive into the crowd, jostle a young boy with her meaty elbows, and secure a paper. She held on to it for a moment until I fished out an extra farthing from my purse.

"Many thanks," she muttered, and scuttled away down the street. I sidled up to the edge of the group to listen to the paper seller chat to a small crowd of onlookers.

"They're calling her the Black Widow," said a serving woman in an apron. "No man was safe from her wicked scheming."

"And they say she's pleading the belly," said one man in a white butcher's coat. "Already four months gone."

"Aye, she'd spread her legs that many times for money, it's not surprising she'd do the same to save her own neck," said another.

"And those children—poor bairns—all poisoned by their mother's hand," said the paper seller.

"And yer wonder if there's a god, giving her the gift of an innocent baby again after what she's done to the other poor wretches," said the butcher.

"Must be the devil's spawn," said the serving woman.

I clutched the paper.

*She is pregnant.*

*The murderer is pregnant.*

I turned away and hurried down the street, my heart burning. *How could a woman accused of murdering her own children have been granted the gift of another? Surely her tainted blood is incapable of nurturing another innocent life.* My eyes stung and my vision blurred as I pressed on, determined to get home and read more about this infamous poisoner.

I burst into the kitchen, hung the key back in its place, and piled more coal onto the fire. Sitting by the bright flames, I studied the portrait on the front page: the haughty expression, the bold knitted eyebrows framing cruel, heavy-lidded eyes that dared me to look on her and know her crimes. Her face flickered in the firelight as I turned the page to read.

## STARTLING REVELATIONS IN THE POISONING CASE AT WEST AUCKLAND

*On Wednesday, the woman Mary Ann Cotton was brought up at the Bishop Auckland police court and charged with the wilful murder of Charles Edward Cotton (7), her stepson. The boy died under such suspicious circumstances that it was deemed necessary and advisable to hold an inquest and have a postmortem examination made on the body. The first doctor found no trace of poison; consequently the coroner directed a verdict of death from natural causes. This gave a great dissatisfaction to certain members of the public and a thorough enquiry resulted in Mrs Cotton's arrest. An order was obtained from the Home Office, and the body was exhumed, the stomach and intestines sent for analysis to Dr Scattergood of Leeds, whose report indicates the boy's whole system and every major organ was completely saturated with arsenic. The boy was insured for £4 10s.*

*Since the committal of the prisoner, considerable excitement has prevailed in the district, not so much on account of her ill treatment of the little fellow, but as of the conspicuous manner of other deaths that have occurred in her house in which she had a pecuniary interest. It is said that no fewer than twenty deaths have taken place in her home, including three husbands, and in most of these deaths, if not all, it has been found that the prisoner has benefited financially, either by insurance or otherwise.*

*On 7th July 1870, the prisoner had obtained a situation as housekeeper to Frederick Cotton, a pitman. In October of the same year, he married her at St. Andrew's Church, Newcastle upon Tyne. The pair then lived in Walbottle. The woman was married under the assumed name of Mowbray. There is reason to believe that she has been four times married, that three of her husbands are dead, and that one, the third in order, was alive at the time of the fourth marriage.*

*When residing at Walbottle, a number of fat pigs died, and she was suspected. The place became so uncomfortable that they were obliged to leave and came to reside at West Auckland, where her husband procured employment as a pitman at the West Auckland Colliery. At that time the family consisted of herself; Frederick Cotton, her husband; Frederick Cotton, stepson (9); Charles Edward Cotton, stepson (6); Robert Robson Cotton (14 months), their son.*

*Nine months after their coming to West Auckland, Frederick Cotton, the head of the family, died. His illness was sudden, his suffering apparently great. A medical certificate stated the cause of his death to have been gastric fever. All the children followed soon after.*

*These events have given rise to much speculation: Who and whence is this woman in whose presence death has reaped such a rapid harvest? The prisoner's account of herself was that she came from Rainton to West Auckland, and that she was 35 years of age. In these points the investigation so far brings out a different story. The person who was married to Frederick Cotton is a woman who has lived in various parts of the north of England, chiefly in the neighbourhoods of Sunderland and Newcastle, and in the colliery districts of Durham; and in whose various residences deaths have been numerous; and that the unfortunate persons dying near her were all insured in some benefit club or other, and left behind them "funeral moneys" or other small bequests.*

*Assuming this is established, Mary Ann Cotton is 40, not 35 years of age. She was born in the village of Low Moorsley in the parish of Houghton-le-Spring, halfway between Hetton-le-Hole and Pittington, and spent her girlhood in Murton Colliery village. The story of her subsequent career, up to the terrible denouement now impending, is one of the most ghastly and revolting character.*

I had come across many violent women in Bethlem. Fierce, snarling creatures who put their faces close to mine and hissed through toothless gums that they'd beaten their children's bodies with buckled belts or stuck a knife under their husband's ribs or smothered their bastard baby. They'd pull away, howling and crying or shrieking with laughter. But every one of them seemed powerless to let go of those terrible memories, doomed to dwell forever on the vicious acts that had unhinged their minds.

Not so Mrs Cotton, who held her head high and proud in the face of the mob.

I sat, gazing into the blazing fire, the thoughts turning round in my head until the front door slammed and brought me sharply back to the present.

Henry was home early.

As his footsteps approached the kitchen, I plucked the paper from my lap and threw it into the fire, where it blazed like a raging inferno, wheezing and crackling as the witch murderess burned and the flames consumed her cunning face.

"Stand back, Clara. Your dress will catch fire," bellowed Henry as he swept into the kitchen and shoved me backwards. He lunged towards the fire, jabbing at the blaze and pushing the burning paper scraps down amongst the coals.

"Heavens, you'd have set the place on fire if I hadn't come back early."

Sweat trickled down my neck, and I felt a dull pounding in my head. My mind was fixed on the word saturated. An innocent child's body saturated with poison. I couldn't speak.

Henry peered down at me, his brows knit. "And look at your dress, Clara. Covered in dirt."

"I was cleaning," I said, the lie slipping easily from my lips. "The upstairs is thick with dust."

Henry placed one hand on his waist, his elbow jutting out to the side.

"It's a good thing the domestic help will be here in a day or two."

I backed away towards the door and he cast me a long, hard look, his lips pressed tightly together, eyebrows furrowed.

"Don't cower in the doorway like a frightened rabbit, Clara. We have Reverend Buckley's dinner party to look forward to tomorrow."

I fled from the kitchen, breathless. The murderess's story had pierced the frozen core of my heart and awakened my curiosity.

That night, as the sleeping draught began to dull my consciousness, my mind fixed on the words from the newspaper article.

*Who and whence is this woman in whose presence death reaped such a rapid harvest?*

I dreamt I stood at the door of a ruined barn, its roof split open to the moon. I saw a dark-haired woman standing in a pigsty, and as the pigs swarmed round her ankles, she stroked their bristled snouts and whispered, "Thou shalt rest well soon, my husbands."

Then she saw me and seemed to float through the muck and swill until I felt her behind me, whispering in my ear: *I am in the city now. Come to me.*

I followed her to a vast churchyard, where cracked headstones were lit with a reddish glow from the hunter's moon that hung low in the sky. "It is a blood moon," she said, staring upwards. Then she tiptoed over the rain-soaked moss and stood by a great tree, its branches twisted like the fingers of a convulsing man. "Now, come here and see what I've done," she whispered, looking down into a black, yawning grave.

# 7

REVEREND BUCKLEY'S HOME stood at the corner of a long terrace, set back from the street. It seemed a grand place, with large windows spanning the entire upper storey. Henry helped me down from the carriage and steered me past a row of manicured rowan trees towards the red front door with its heavy brass knocker.

"I will be watching you tonight, Clara," he whispered, his breath tickling my ear. "Pay attention to me. If I raise my eyebrows, smile and try to make conversation."

I felt a sudden rush of apprehension as we climbed the steps. Social chitchat with polite company was unnerving after months spent locked away amongst the mad and hopeless. In Bethlem I'd heard language that would make Henry's hair stand on end.

*How you must miss your smart London friends, Clara,* the Buckleys' guests might say. And how they would quail when I told them of the bald woman with cow eyes who came to me carrying loops of her hair and said, *Won't you give this to my husband so he remembers me when he fucks his whore?* Or the toothless old crone who hitched her dress up to her waist and shrieked, *The king can kiss my silken arse!* And Henry wanted me to engage in polite chitchat with the Buckleys.

The maid showed us into a cosy walnut-panelled parlour where lamps threw a golden glow over bowls of yellow chrysanthemums. Emma swooped over to greet us as the girl took my wrap.

"Donald is immersed in a debate about Newton's *Principia.* Join him, Henry. Clara and I will occupy ourselves with lighter fare."

Henry strode towards the knot of men gathered at the far end of the room. Buckley's voice boomed above the chatter of the other guests and Henry was immediately swallowed up in a frenzy of hand-shaking and shoulder-patting.

Emma's hand on the small of my back steered me away into a cavernous drawing room decorated in green and gold. Potted ferns bordered the tall windows and an abundance of family portraits lined the walls. The largest, a massive portrait of Reverend Buckley, hung above the carved oak mantel, though the artist's overdependence on white tones made the subject's face appear ghoulish. And with the thick swath of red hair waving back from a lofty forehead, and the short neck emerging from a ruffled collar, I was reminded more of a garish circus clown than a man of the cloth.

I averted my eyes to the clusters of guests sitting around the perimeter of the room. Their heads turned to survey us as we entered. Instinctively, I pulled back, aware their keen eyes weighed, measured, and dissected my appearance as they whispered their verdicts behind raised fans. Fortunately, Emma whispered, "Take courage, dear," and propelled me towards a trio of ladies who reminded me of the woodland creatures from my mother's paintings.

First was the rabbit, with pointed ears, a twitching pink nose, and prominent front teeth. Next the badger, a bulging woman in purple brocade with a streak of grey in her dark hair, a long, sleek snout, and heavy eyebrows knit together in one bold line. Last, the long-necked doe with dappled hair and limpid brown eyes who held court from a crimson velvet chair. I forgot their names as soon as Emma introduced them.

"So many new faces and so much to take in," said Emma, shaking me out of my reverie and steering me towards a nearby sofa. I had been gawking so shamelessly at the assembled company, they were already cupping their hands over their mouths and whispering to one another. "But you will soon get to know all our dear friends and feel comfortable here."

"I hope so," I whispered, attempting a smile.

"Can I get you a glass of punch?"

I nodded and she motioned to the maid, who hurried over with a glass. I sipped it, grateful for the distraction, and tried to maintain that polite smile, directing it towards the trio of women.

"Emma, how is your daughter, Amy, faring?" asked the rabbit woman.

Emma reached for her embroidered hanky and mopped at her eyes. "She has spent the summer in Venice. How I miss her."

The woman patted the back of Emma's hand. "Be patient. She will soon return."

"But it seems such an age since she left." Emma sighed.

"My own boys have brought me a lifetime of joy and worry," said the badger, "but now they're all married and quite settled." She turned to me, her eyes flaring wide. "How old are your children, Clara?"

My face burned. "I-I am childless," I stammered like a half-wit. My stomach clenched.

"And you have been away for the better part of a year?" asked the doe, her eyebrows raised as if in anticipation of some juicy morsel of gossip.

"Clara has experienced some recent health troubles," said Emma. "But I am sure our brisk northern air and a nourishing diet of plain, healthy food will restore her strength."

Just then, the dinner gong sounded and the ladies' attention switched away from me.

Still smarting from their curiosity, I followed the company to the dining room. They had already labelled me an object of pity, a half-woman. The childless wife, condemned to the margins of polite society with the aging spinster sister. Henry's mother, Adeline, had visited us after my first miscarriage. I remembered her pursed mouth and her comments—*We countrywomen come from more hardy stock. Our sturdy hips are better suited for childbearing*—which only served to remind me of my complete and utter failure as a woman. Nothing less than successful motherhood would reverse her opinion.

I took my seat, barely noticing the glinting silverware and the arrangements of pink roses.

When we were all assembled round the table, Reverend Buckley tapped on his plate and raised his glass of punch.

"We have already received Henry into our circle of friends and colleagues, and he has proved himself an excellent scholar *and* man of principle, but now let us welcome his charming wife, Clara. We sincerely hope her arrival here will mark an end to her previous misfortunes."

All eyes turned to me, and the bird wings flapped in my ears again. I tried to smile, but my face felt stiff, my head muddled. What secrets had Henry revealed to make them gawk at me like slack-mouthed fools? He sat opposite, his eyes hard as flint. Scrutinising every tremor in my expression, every movement of my eyes. I forced my mind to empty, my body to become still until I could muster another blank smile. Satisfied, the company turned its attention to the arrival of the soup.

I peered from beneath lowered eyelids at the bobbing heads of the ladies; like clucking hens, they dipped their beaks to sip from silver spoons. At Bethlem the women cradled their tin bowls in the crook of their arms, slurping up the thin stew as if it were their last meal on earth and growling at anyone who tried to seize it. Now, mindful that I might appear gluttonous, I slowed down the motion of my spoon and mimicked the rhythm of the other guests, just as Reverend Buckley waved his spoon in the air.

"My dear friends, if we are to believe everything written in our newspapers, it seems that crime, drunkenness, and moral depravity have spread like a contagion amongst the working classes. Look no further than the crimes of the despicable poisoner Mrs Cotton as a testament to their degeneracy. Only the fittest and wiliest survive in this underclass. Kill or be killed is their motto, and I hear she took this advice to heart."

When I heard the poisoner's name, I dropped my spoon with a loud *clink*. Henry mopped his lips and directed a warning glare at me, eyebrows raised. He cleared his throat.

I picked up my spoon and stirred my soup.

"I agree, Reverend Buckley," he said. "Dr Maudsley calls it 'the stigmata of degeneration,' innate traits and inclinations strictly related to breeding and natural selection. I have no doubt Mrs Cotton hails from similar brutal stock."

Reverend Buckley nodded. "Quite right, Henry. A former colleague of mine claims Cotton's maiden name, Robson, places her as a descendant of the notorious reivers, those bloodthirsty border raiders from centuries past."

"I read somewhere she claims to be thirty-five," said the badger woman, wiping the corners of her mouth with a napkin, "but the newspapers have mapped out the events of her life and say she is closer to forty years of age."

"Apparently she drifted for years like a gypsy around Durham County, leaving death and misery in her wake," said the rabbit woman's husband, a ferret-faced man with a wispy beard. "It seems incredible that her crimes have remained undetected until now."

"Then she is an enchantress, casting spells on those poor, unsuspecting husbands who fell under her power," added his wife, one hand clasped to her breast.

"A witch," blurted the badger woman, leaning forwards to scan her neighbours. "Only a witch would dabble in such dark practices."

"They say she laid a curse that caused some pigs to die," said the rabbit woman, her face so flushed, the tips of her ears glowed red. "So she must be an emissary of the devil."

"Then they must check her for the devil's marks," said the badger woman.

"Enough," cried Reverend Buckley, slamming his palm so hard on the table, the salt cellars rattled. "Enough of these fantastical ravings. The answer lies in the science of modern medicine. She is merely an uneducated pauper woman with a delusional mind. Typical of the criminal underclasses."

"Well, it's not surprising," said a red-haired bear of a man, grinning. "Darwin believes the illiterate masses are not so distant cousins to the apes." He nudged his mousy wife, who covered her mouth with a napkin and giggled.

The doe woman had kept her silence, but now she turned her elegant head to direct a disapproving glare at the couple. "Gentlemen, we are all God's creatures, and every one of us is capable of aspiring towards a better life. I have worked for many years educating miners' children and have witnessed the most encouraging results."

"But how can Mrs Cotton be one of God's creatures when she acts against her natural feminine instincts?" said Emma. "Only a monster would kill its own children."

The room seemed to spin so that I struggled to hold my body upright, to fight back the bile that rose, bitter in my throat.

Donald's eyes flashed. "Precisely. She cannot be called a woman. In fact, the newspapers have called her the Black Widow. A ruthless creature with salacious appetites."

Emma persisted. "And all children who came into her care died horrible deaths. Not to mention her husbands. That cannot be coincidence."

All at once I pictured the swell of the murderer's belly under her rough prison dress, imagined the innocent child growing there. I felt a shifting inside me, a sudden swell of loss, grief, and bitterness. My cheeks burned as the words burst from my throat. "And now she is pregnant again. It is inconceivable—a travesty that she should be blessed with another child when the autopsy showed the stomach, liver, and intestines of her last one were saturated with arsenic?"

The company fell silent. Twenty faces turned to gaze on me. Some of the women held napkins to their mouths. Henry's eyes darted round at their stunned expressions, his face ashen.

"You must excuse my wife's emotional state. We ran across a wild mob gathered to watch Mrs Cotton taken into the jail and Clara hit her head when the coach was pushed from behind."

The attention switched immediately to Henry as the guests peppered him with questions about the prisoner. *Was she handsome? Had they shackled her? How was she dressed? How was the mood of the crowd?*

I sat utterly still, the spoon clenched so tightly in my hands, I could have snapped it.

*I had lost control for a few seconds.*

*It must never happen again.*

After supper, the men retired to Buckley's library for port and cigars. Emma guided me to the parlour, where the women had gathered to drink coffee.

"It's clear you need worthwhilst pursuits to occupy your time, Clara. Perhaps you might consider doing charitable work. Many of the ladies here find rich reward in helping the less fortunate members of our community."

"I make regular visits to the colliers' school," said the badger lady, helping herself to a slice of sponge cake. "There are so many children in need of motherly guidance."

"And I volunteer at the hospital," said the doe. "The infirm and elderly do so love someone to read to them."

I shook my head. "I'm not sure if Henry would allow it."

Emma waved her hand in the air. "Nonsense, dear. Henry wants you to be part of our community, so he'll encourage it. Donald was delighted when I became a lady visitor at the prison. It's challenging work, but when you are doing good deeds, the rewards are manifold."

At the mention of the prison, my heart began to race. I pictured Mrs Cotton alone in her cell, her hands folded neatly on her lap, her eyes tracing the fine mesh of cracks that spread across the walls of her cell like narrow roads that led to nowhere. Only back to their beginning. In my dream she had said, *Come to me.* Was it some strange call for solace? Or the need to make a confession?

Could I help her shed the unimaginable burden of her guilt when I still struggled with my own, almost a year after the stillbirth?

"How can you even sit in the same room as those degenerate creatures, Emma?" asked the badger woman, stirring me from my thoughts. "Aren't you afraid for your life?"

Emma shook her head until her ringlets bounced under her lace cap. "On the contrary. They become meek as lambs when they hear God's blessed words."

I saw myself sitting at the open door of a cell, like a prim schoolmistress, holding a Bible and reading a Psalm to the flint-eyed poisoner, whose expression burned with defiance.

"We are there to exert a calming influence on the women. To be kind without being indulgent, patient without being patronising," Emma continued, her lips curving into a virtuous smile.

I remembered a time in Bethlem when a group of lady visitors had come to keep us company. The attendants had selected the quieter patients to meet them. They scrubbed our faces and braided our hair and we sat, silent and submissive on a row of hard-backed chairs, sniffing at the scent of roses that wafted from the visitors' clothes as they walked down the line.

"And what brought you here?" said the oldest one, their leader, a buxom lady in black bombazine trimmed with glinting jet beads. The other women crowded behind her broad back, staring openly at us.

"You mean me, ma'am?" asked Ethel, a washed-out scarecrow of a woman.

The lady nodded.

"Overwork," said Ethel. "I were the only servant in a twenty-room house. In the winter, the lamps had to be lit before dawn and the fires all burning in every room, not to mention the chamber pots emptied, the stove blacked, the silverware polished, the washing done, and the floors swept and scrubbed. I were up at four and crept up to my bed no earlier than ten at night."

"You poor woman. It's no wonder you broke down," said the visitor. "And how are they treating you here?"

Ethel leaned forwards, grinning. "Tell the truth, I never ate so good. They gives us porridge, bread, cheese, broth, *and mutton.*"

"I'm sure you'll have a swift recovery, then."

"I hope not," mumbled Ethel, dropping her chin to her chest.

The woman frowned and moved on. "What about you, dear?" she said to the pale, doll-eyed girl beside me. I'd never spoken to her, but remembered that she sat all day in the same corner, only moving when the attendants called us for supper.

She looked around at all of us, then back at the visitor, who nodded so that her jet earrings swung from her fleshy earlobes.

"Yes, you, my dear," said the woman, smiling benevolently.

"Oh," the girl said, crossing her hands in her lap and moistening her lips. "I threw my baby down a pit shaft because the father left me. I was obliged to throw the little beggar over. It made such an awful row."

The visitor made a terrible clatter when she fainted to the floor. It took four attendants to move her out to safety.

"All professional lady visitors obtain a general order to visit the prison," said Emma, jolting me back to the present. "We guide the women towards a godly life and an honest living."

"But what if they're simply deceiving you and pretending repentance?" said the rabbit woman.

Emma drew back her shoulders. "With experience, one comes to know the false converts. But most of the prisoners are grateful for our interest. Our kindness often reaps results that last long after they leave the prison."

Something stirred in me at the thought of visiting the prison. As if a sharp blade had pierced the toughened shell of my heart. At the asylum, Annie always said, "Turn yourself to stone, Clara. A hardened heart expects no tenderness and feels no grief." But now I saw a chance to redeem myself. To ease my own burden by helping another shed hers.

I felt a tap on my shoulder and turned to see Emma, head tilted to the side, smiling at me. "Why, Clara, you were quite lost in your thoughts. But if you are interested, come to hear Donald's sermon tomorrow at St. Giles' Church. He's drumming up support for charitable works at the prison. I'm sure you will all be moved by his devotion to the less fortunate amongst us."

I was compelled to employ some slyness on the way home from the Buckleys' to convince Henry that we should accompany them to St. Giles' Church the next day.

"At Hoxton I took great comfort in attending the chapel services each week," I said, my eyes averted downwards to the scuffed toes of Henry's boots. "I should like to continue my devotions. Dr Shepton always said a life of piety and quiet contemplation of God's bounty is a life of peace and contentment."

"Wise words," said Henry, though I fancied his brow creased in doubt. "I have been remiss in my churchgoing, but now that you've nudged my conscience, we'll go tomorrow."

That night, after Henry gave me the sleeping draught, I lay in bed and imagined myself again, standing at the doorway of a prison cell, reading the Bible to a dead-eyed woman with hunched shoulders and a sour expression. I drifted off to sleep asking myself, *Where had God been in the asylum? How had God looked out for me and all the other women there?*

Then I dreamt I stood by a towering stone fortress—in front of a black-panelled door. I raised the Bible in my hand and the door swung open, allowing me into a long, dank corridor. A veiled woman stepped into my path, her white hand extended towards me. She took the Bible from my grasp and slipped a weighty iron key into my hand, only turning to point in the direction of a reddish light that danced ahead. I followed that light through the cloying darkness, unlocking every door until I reached the cell of the murderer, Mrs Cotton. She stood with her back to me, facing a blazing fire. "You are here, my sister, she said, without turning. I knew you would come."

I said, "I am not your sister. How can I be sister to a murderer?"

Then she turned to me, cradling a bundle in her arms that she clutched to her bosom, rocking it back and forth. And as I stepped closer, I saw two lifeless lumps of flesh, like newborn rabbits with bluish smudges where their eyes should be.

"I have your babies," she said, holding them out to me. "Are these not the ones you killed? Did they not wither and die inside that barren body of yours?"

She handed them to me, and I pressed my face into their cold flesh and sank to my knees, crying for forgiveness. But a cold wind blew through the space, turning the fire to ash, and the walls faded away. I knelt alone in a gritty wasteland marked only by twisted trees sprouting from rocky ground. In my hands I clutched two empty white shrouds.

And then I beat at my hollowed-out body with my fists until the blessed darkness came and swallowed me up into a dreamless sleep.

# 8

THE FOLLOWING MORNING, on a drab, rain-spattered Sunday, Henry and I travelled to St. Giles' Church, a dowdy, stark building with a steep slate roof and tall, narrow windows that resembled portals in a grim fortress. Two clover-shaped windows were the only decoration to relieve the plainness, besides a tiny bell tower that perched atop the roof like a birdhouse.

The musty stink of wet clothing permeated the air as clusters of faithful parishioners crowded in from the rain, their reddened noses and watery eyes a testament to the great sacrifice of leaving home and hearth on a bitter cold day to do their Sunday duty.

Henry and I joined Emma in the second row of pews, just below the great lectern—a fearsome brass eagle with outstretched wings—and waited for the assembly to settle themselves for the arrival of the choir. At the sound of the organ, they filed in, those pink-cheeked boys in starched white surplices clutching hymnals, their sweet voices soaring in perfect harmony like the ringing of finely tuned bells.

It was so unlike the chapel at Bethlem and the bizarre chorus of female patients—a cacophony of shrieking and caterwauling, of tuneless moaning and wild cackling, with the occasional reedy soprano searching vainly to retrieve the errant melody. We were a sorry sight—bowed heads, eyes cast to the ground except for the occasional rebel who escaped from her pew, cast off her dress, and twirled with abandon in time to some wild inner melody only to be dragged, giggling and bleating, back to her seat.

Reverend Buckley marched imperially behind the local vicar, a stocky man with a bald pate and grizzled grey muttonchop whiskers. Buckley towered above the drab little man, in an embossed purple stole across a spotless white surplice that only served to emphasise his florid cheeks. I followed his progress along the aisle, imagining how I would sketch those swollen lips pursed tightly beneath the drooping whiskers in an expression of stern and righteous self-examination.

"Don't stare so," whispered Henry, nudging my arm. Alarmed, I cast my eyes to the floor and concentrated on how the intricate patterns of black-and-white tiles formed perfect stars.

After the vicar had delivered the opening prayers, Reverend Buckley took to the pulpit, grasping the edges of the lectern as he leaned forwards and scanned the assembly with blazing eyes. Emma shifted her legs and pressed her gloved palms together. Henry cleared his throat and turned his fob watch in his hand whilst I sat perfectly still. Eight hours in a rigid-backed chair with an attendant passing back and forth, watching for the mere twitch of a finger, was perfect training for church. With a deep intake of breath, he began.

"We are indeed a great and wealthy nation. If you will, the greatest and wealthiest nation on earth, but as citizens of this great country, shall we engage in a placid and self-satisfied contemplation of our charities and philanthropic endeavours? Or should we strive to do more? I am here today as visiting chaplain at the prison to address a delicate topic concerning the female prisoners. I come here to plead the state of those who have miserably lost their purity of heart. Who have given in to vile, primitive urges, who have sunk to the very depths of evil and depravity and now sigh for penitence, but have none to guide them to it. These suffering souls long to quit their hell on earth by shedding their monstrous load so they may hear their many sins forgiven."

My heart gave a sudden jolt. It seemed he had read my thoughts from the previous evening. I caught my breath and averted my gaze to Henry to see if he had noticed my reaction, but he sat, stolid and immobile, staring ahead, his eyelids drooping as Buckley's voice continued like a dreadful incantation.

"In my work at the prison, I encounter thieves, murderers, drunkards, and fornicators—weak, desolate souls who are lost and abandoned. Some have been tempted or betrayed—made outcasts of society. Some are victims of men's lowest passions. Preyed on by scurrilous men—vile panderers to human lust, their purity ruined by the contaminating society of the fornicator and adulterer."

A few men with reddened cheeks fidgeted with their stiff collars at the onslaught of righteous indignation. Their wives sat, unflinching, their eyes betraying nothing. I imagined they didn't dare to turn their heads for fear of catching even the slightest trace of guilt on their husband's faces.

"We must set our faces as flint," he continued, "against these gluttonous parasites, these villains whose unhallowed passion has wreaked misery upon thousands. Who, in their desperate pursuit of pleasure, spread vile, disgusting diseases to their unsuspecting wives."

My mind drifted away from the booming voice to Mary, a jaundiced ghost of a woman, racked by constant seizures, who wore a scarf across the lower half of her face to hide her disintegrating nose. The result, Annie told me, of advanced syphilis passed on by her husband, a frequenter of local brothels. I felt a swell of indignation, surprised that Buckley's words had actually spoken some truth to me.

"So, I ask you," he said, leaning closer to his captive audience, "what can you do? Well, the answer is simple. These unfortunates crave the attention and sympathy of educated, pious women. Loving, faithful daughters of the church, not encumbered by any special family duties. Our pious spinster sisters, our widows, our childless wives who sigh for a life of greater usefulness. These aimless women might become ministering angels to their fallen sisters. I can assure you that many of our prisoners are knocking on the doors of forgiveness, seeking to escape the pitiless storm of misery, remorse, and anguish raging within them. And so I say, to their cries of 'Help me or I perish,' you will say, 'I do not condemn thee. I will stretch out my hand to welcome you. Go and sin no more.'"

I could almost hear the exhalation of a thousand breaths as Buckley stepped back from the pulpit, scowling like a headmaster. But I had felt a rush of elation. The path stretched ahead of me, and my way was clear. I must go to the prison and visit the poisoner as soon as I could arrange it. And though the elation was tempered by a small thrill of fear, I sang along with the hymn, the music seeming to lilt with joy.

Later we shared a carriage home with the Buckleys. Though my head ached from the mildewed stink of the church, I welcomed the fresh air on my face.

Reverend Buckley wiped the condensation from the carriage window with his coat sleeve, then turned back to us, resting his head against the seat and revealing a small dribble of egg yolk on the corner of his lips.

He sighed. “My duty today was to bring discomfort to the complacent and to spur them on to extend their charity towards our fallen women at the prison. I hope I did that.”

Henry grunted and nodded in enthusiastic assent.

Emma patted my hand, though her movement brought a salty waft of fried meat into the air between us. I imagined the two of them only hours previous, eyes gleaming, knives and forks poised over a hearty breakfast of fried mutton chops, poached eggs, and blood pudding. Reverend Buckley would pierce his poached egg and swiftly mop up the pooling yolk with a thick heel of bread.

“Do not let us forget, Donald,” said Emma, grasping my hand, “Clara has already expressed her interest in going to the prison—that sanctuary of broken souls and fallen sisters.”

Henry’s eyes seemed glassy and blank, as if he struggled to comprehend the full implications of their words. “But can it be advisable for Clara to be a prison visitor? Surely, in her vulnerable state, there is danger of her being sullied by close contact with women of devious character?”

Reverend Buckley spread his hands across his thighs and directed a tight smile at Henry. “I assure you, Henry. So wise and so well framed are the rules by which the prison is governed that you need not fear for the purity of Clara’s mind.”

“I suppose if she is not tempted to wander off alone, there can be no harm in trying it,” said Henry, narrowing his eyes at me until I was forced to look away.

“Then she shall accompany me there tomorrow,” said Emma gleefully, squeezing my fingers until I winced and was forced to turn away towards the window, though not before a swell of satisfaction forced my lips into a smile.

I had not smiled in a year.

# 9

ALICE KEMP, OUR new maid, arrived the next morning on the back of a weathered wooden flat cart.

The ancient horse snorted to a standstill at our front door and the driver jumped down from his perch, twisting a battered cap in his hands. A map of spidery black lines spread across his cheeks and etched the outline of his eyes. He bowed, then flashed a gap-toothed grin at us.

"Arthur Kemp. Delivering me daughter Alice into your service. Alice," he barked without looking around. A young girl of about fifteen years sprang down from the side of the cart. She wore a threadbare brown dress and a battered black bonnet. Though her face was fresh and rosy, a lazy left eye gave the impression of slyness.

"Has she no other clothes?" I asked, noting the cloth bundle clutched in her hand.

"We have six other young'uns to clothe. We reckoned you'd be wanting new togs for Alice," said Kemp without flinching.

"Fair enough," said Henry. "We'll clothe her and deduct the expenses from her wages."

"As you please, sir, and now I'll be off—but might I trouble you for some fresh water for me and my horse, Gracie?"

I took a step towards the horse, a stoop-necked grey mare, and stroked the rough grey-white hair of her muzzle.

He nodded at the horse, which nuzzled gently at my hand. "She's only been out of the pit a year now and she suffers terrible with her lungs. Would have gone blind if they hadn't freed her."

I smiled at her velvety touch on my palm. Henry cleared his throat. "Clara, take Alice inside and fetch Mr Kemp a cup of water and a slice of pie. I believe there's a bucket in the back shed for the horse."

Alice stood inside the hallway, staring in wonder at the stained glass inset in the front door.

"I've never been in such a grand house," she said, her eyes so wide and shining, I felt a stab of sympathy for her.

I showed her into the kitchen. "Just sit at the table and wait for me."

I busied myself with the water and the pie, then rushed outside to find Mr Kemp talking with Henry.

"Aye," he said, licking his lips at the sight of the food. "Dinna be afraid to bray her with a belt if she's contrary."

"I'm sure we'll try kindness first," said Henry coolly.

Kemp wiped a sleeve across his mouth. "I telt yer, spare the rod and spoil the child is what I say, and I know. I've had eight of the little buggers and strapped them all. Though my youngest lad is dead and gone. God bless his soul."

He took a bite of the pie and closed his eyes in bliss as droplets of grease caught on the ends of his moustache. His tongue darted out to lick them. I gazed at him, wondering how it was that so many children were born into such poverty, yet I was still childless at twenty-six. What justice was there in the world when my child had never drawn a breath?

My gaze drifted to the slight bulge of his trouser fly. I looked up again only to see him grin and wink at me just as Henry bent down to put the bucket in front of the horse. Mortified, I busied myself with the empty plate and hurried into the kitchen, where Alice was rummaging through the cupboards. She slammed a door shut.

"Sorry, mum, didn't mean to pry—just seeing where everything's kept," she said, sliding closer to the hearth and fixing me with a direct stare.

Her boldness caught me off guard. I forgot the plate in my hands and the fork slid to the floor with a loud clang. She lunged forwards to pick it up as I fussed with the plate. "So clumsy," I mumbled, sliding the plate onto the table.

"No matter, ma'am, that's why I'm here," she said, hauling herself upright. Her cheeks were flushed and her brow gleamed with sweat. I wondered what I should say to her. Should I take charge and go over her daily duties? I searched my mind for the right thing to do.

"There is water in the kettle. You might go to your room and clean yourself up."

"Me mam was a demon with the washcloth," she said in a surly tone. "There's no nits in my hair."

"You'll find suitable clothes on your bed in the attic. Mrs Buckley loaned them to us in case you had none of your own."

"I suppose I'll get changed, then," she said, her eyes darting towards the front of the house, where the *clip-clop* of horse hooves signalled her father's departure, but she made no move to say goodbye. When I turned to go, I swore I heard her mutter *good riddance* and I whirled around, but her eyes were cast to the floor.

"I'll be accompanying Mrs Buckley to the jail this morning, so you can go to the market afterwards. I'll leave a list for you."

She stood there, gaping at me.

"Is there something else, Alice?"

"Will you be seeing Mrs Cotton?"

"I doubt it."

"She's an evil monster who murdered her own bairns."

"She has only just been arrested, Alice. A jury will decide if she is guilty."

"All the papers say she even murdered her own mother then sold her few belongings."

"You must be careful not to get carried away by gossip and rumour. Besides, who are we to judge her? That's the duty of the court."

"I suppose so," she said, sniffing and wiping a hand across her nose. I raised my eyebrows and her hand dropped to her side. "Sorry, mum, only she come from near us in West Auckland. Me da knew her last lodger. Says he ran wi' a right crowd of ruffians—one o' them were a rascal come from Pipewellgate, a right filthy slum in Gateshead. Da says that butcher gambled his week's wages away at the pub, then followed the bloke that pocketed his money and slit his guts so bad, his insides fell out."

I could not have Henry hearing such talk and blocking my prison visit, so I lowered my voice to a whisper. "That's enough silly gossip about Mrs Cotton. You understand, Alice. This is not the colliery street."

"I know that, mum," she said a little sulkily. "Is that all?"

"You may go," I said, alarmed at her boldness.

She scuttled upstairs just as Henry strode in, carrying the bucket. "She's settled?"

"I sent her to change."

"Very good," he said, striding past me, swinging the bucket. "She seems a well-mannered, modest girl, don't you think?"

"Make no waves," Annie had said. "Keep bold opinions in check or you may invite unwanted concern and attention."

"Why yes, Henry, a very docile and compliant young woman," I said, my attention diverted by the sound of hooves on the cobbles outside and the dark shape of Emma's carriage slowing to a gradual halt at the front door.

# 10

MY FIRST GLIMPSE of the prison was through a blurred coach window streaked with rain. We crossed a muddy expanse of field and approached a collection of grim grey-brick buildings stacked behind high stone walls whose upper edges were packed with jagged fragments of broken glass and barbed wire. Not a single shrub or blade of grass grew against that towering wall, which was so stained with damp and moss, it seemed to have sprouted from out of the mud that surrounded it. I wondered how many unfortunates had escaped their cell and clambered up the other side only to reach the top and have their legs shredded to ribbons before falling back to the ground, where uniformed guards and snarling dogs awaited them.

The prison buildings stood beyond a gatehouse. Four-storey-high, soot-streaked rectangles with rows of barred windows stamped into each level and topped with smoking chimneys, through which the entire building belched its foul breath into the leaden sky. The whole effect was one of rigid sameness, of unrelenting ugliness. I pulled my shawl more tightly around me and shivered at the sound of a clock chiming the half hour, its loud, tuneless clang reminding the prisoners of the creeping monotony of time.

We climbed down from the carriage and the gate porter let us through onto a narrow pathway between two buildings. As the gate slammed shut, I looked upwards at the pale rectangle of sky above. The buildings seemed to close in on me, as if they would crush me between their sooty walls. I stopped in my tracks as an image burst into my head.

A moment when a strong hand clamped around my wrist and steered me along narrow, winding hallways, damp with mildew like the stone walls of a dungeon. At the end, a door opened into a low-ceilinged room. My hands were tied, my arms bound to the sides of my body. Someone thrust me inside a room where the stale scent of sweat and fear hung like a noxious fog in the air.

Emma strode on ahead of me, swinging a cloth bag, but then stopped and waited until I caught up with her.

"Bibles, prayer books, and poetry," she said, holding out the bag. "You'd be surprised how words of truth and goodness can reach even the most hardened souls."

I hesitated for a moment, breathing deeply to steady myself. I imagined reading the Bible and reciting prayers to Mrs Cotton as she bowed her head and held her palms together in prayer.

"Let's hurry along and I'll introduce you to the governor," she said, stepping up to a large iron door on our left and nodding to the guard at the entrance. "All visitors must report to him."

She ushered me into a vast entrance hall, thick with the oily reek of floor polish. I had a sudden recollection of that smell mingled with the sharp stink of urine and carbolic. I felt a slight constriction of my throat when the doors creaked shut behind me, but Emma marched confidently ahead and I had no choice but to follow.

The governor's office smelled of leather and roast meat. The governor, a short man with bushy brown whiskers and a sour face, rose from behind his desk as we entered. A half-finished plate of beef and gravy lay beside his paper and pens.

His eyes flickered in disapproval. "So you've brought another friend to work with our fallen women, Mrs Buckley."

"This is Mrs Clara Blackstone, wife of my husband's colleague, Professor Henry Blackstone," said Emma.

He bowed briefly and turned to face the window, his hands clasped behind his back. "I must tell you ladies, we have had many ghoulish characters of late who present themselves as philanthropists, when their true motive is to gain an audience with Mrs Cotton, our infamous new inmate." He turned around to face me. "Mrs Blackstone, I trust you are not one of those morbid thrill-seekers."

I shook my head and spoke without blinking. "I only seek to bring solace and comfort to those who have nowhere else to turn. To show an interest in their improvement."

The governor continued: "Good, then. Our purpose here, Mrs Blackstone, is to allow our prisoners time to reflect on their crimes. They have rebelled against the laws of society and must be punished and confined. These women face insurmountable odds, since most of them were raised in poverty and ignorance and not born to the advantages you enjoy; therefore, their natural inclination is towards degeneracy and crime."

"And that is why, as a lady visitor, you must offer them moral guidance—help them find a more godly way to live," said Emma.

The corners of the governor's mouth twitched at Emma's interruption. "Precisely, Mrs Buckley. But Mrs Blackstone must never forget that these women are hardened criminals.

They may seem calm, some even docile and modest. But beneath that surface, a vicious creature lurks, capable of lawless behaviour and deadly violence. It is simply a matter of circumstance whether that other being is unleashed."

A sudden, vivid memory of my teeth fastening on to firm flesh and the taste of blood on my tongue forced me back against the wall. I pressed my palms against the cool plaster and focused on the movement of the governor's lips.

"I warn you, Mrs Blackstone," he continued. "Never turn your back on any of them. They are marvellous actors and liable to pick your pocket or slit your throat on a whim. And now, begging your pardon, I must prepare notes for an important meeting. The deputy matron, Mrs Callahan, will escort you to the cells." He gave us a shallow bow and strode back behind his desk.

I followed Emma outside again. Mercifully the rain had stopped and the sun shone weakly through milky clouds.

We passed a paved yard studded with weeds and surrounded by a high wire fence. Emma pointed towards it. "That is the female prisoners' airing grounds. The women will be most pleased that the weather has turned. I expect they'll be let out for a walk later."

An iron door at the other end of the yard opened to reveal a heavy-browed man in uniform sitting at a desk. He wished us a good day and made us sign the visitors' book.

When I hesitated, he pushed the book closer. "'Case yer gets lost, mum," he said, his dour face splitting into a wide grin. "Then we know who we're lookin' for."

A thin woman in a severe grey dress appeared behind him. Her hair was drawn tightly back into a small knot, and her face seemed the colour of dry putty, as if her skin were starved for sunlight. "Nobody gets lost on my watch, Mr Boxted."

He raised a hand. "The charming Mrs Elsie Callahan, deputy matron."

Emma ventured forwards. "This is Mrs Clara Blackstone, who is keen to become a lady visitor."

Mrs Callahan surveyed me from head to toe, her lips pursed into a tight line. "Happy to meet you, ma'am."

"Perhaps you could just give Mrs Blackstone a tour of the facility today," said Emma, peeling off her gloves. "I must meet my husband at the chapel."

"As you wish," said Mrs Callahan, her eyes searching my face as if she could lay bare the false creature beneath. And when Emma took her leave, I felt a nervous fluttering in the pit of my stomach.

"I must trouble you to empty out the contents of your reticule, Mrs Blackstone. We are obliged to search every person who enters here."

Emma had given me a Bible and a small pamphlet of poems. Mrs Callahan flicked through its pages, squinting at the contents. "Well, I can't see as this could be of any harm. More likely none of them will have any idea what it's about. Just make sure not to leave anything in the cells."

"We cannot lend a book to them?"

She shook her head. "Had a terrible incident only two months ago, ma'am. One of the chronics had—by means unknown to us—secreted a knife in her cell. She lured one of our new assistant matrons into her cell, saying she'd found a beautiful verse in Bible. '*Come and look at it*,' she says, holding the book up. Once the young matron was inside the cell, that prisoner shut the door, leapt onto her back, and stabbed at her face and throat. Poor woman was dead before we could get to her."

I felt the blood drain from my face and yet the story did not shock me. I had seen worse.

"I'll be careful to abide by the rules, Mrs Callahan."

She led me along a narrow corridor that opened into a massive gallery, two storeys high with metal walkways on each level, and all along these were doors, each with its own tiny window.

"These are the chronic offenders," said Mrs Callahan, nodding towards the first few doors.

In one, a white-haired old woman with a sunken face and caved-in mouth glanced up at me.

"I gets bad food here," she hissed through toothless gums. "The gruel's laced with poison and they puts cow piss in my cocoa."

"Curb your tongue, Grice," said Mrs Callahan, rapping the bars with her stick. "You'd have been dead long ago if we were trying to poison you."

In another, a white-faced, angular woman sat upright, her hands tied together with leather straps. Her haughty eyes blazed. "Judgement Day is upon us," she cried. "The flames of Hell are waiting. Devils haunt me at night. They sit around my bed and torment me for my sins."

"And that one is bound for the asylum as soon as we can arrange it," the matron said. "The prison surgeon has already been told."

"Not the madhouse, you old bitch!" the woman screeched. "Can't you see I need the priest to cast the demons out?"

We hurried on, the clanking of keys and slamming metal doors echoing in my head.

Next we passed a row of windows that looked down onto a bare yard surrounded by high brick walls. Suddenly, from out of a small doorway, a line of women in drab prison dresses and bonnets issued forth, each following the other in perfect order like a row of grey ducklings. At their head marched a stout, black-garbed matron in a stiff cloak. The women circled the yard, never breaking their formation. Once they had reached the far corner, a small woman wrapped in a brightly chequered black-and-white shawl, a black dress, and a black ribboned bonnet emerged from the same doorway, flanked by two matrons in grey dresses. In contrast to the other regimented women, she strolled around that rubble-strewn yard as if taking the air on a breezy seafront esplanade. I slowed down to watch. Mrs Callahan nodded towards them.

"That's our famous poisoner, Mary Ann Cotton," she said with a sniff. "Special treatment and no hard labour for that one whilst she waits for her trial."

I held my breath and pressed my palms tight against the window until the dampness seemed to seep into my skin. She walked with a slight limp and the swell of her belly under her dress was unmistakable. *So the child was real.* I strained forwards, eager to catch a glimpse of her face under the black bonnet, but her head was bowed and she seemed deep in conversation with the matrons.

I was so close to the glass, my breath fogged the windowpane. When I went to wipe it in an upwards motion, Mrs Cotton passed below. She stopped in her tracks and her eyes seemed to snap upwards, as if she felt my presence and thought I was waving to her. I drew back but not quickly enough. She stared straight at me with a knowing look in her eyes. Not with surprise or curiosity. But exactly as if she'd been expecting me. As if her thoughts had trickled into my dreams and she'd willed me to come here.

"You look like you've seen a ghost," said Mrs Callahan, taking my arm and steering me round the next corner. "She's only flesh and blood, though the papers would have us believe otherwise."

"It gave me quite a turn to see her."

Mrs Callahan shook her head and tutted. "When you've witnessed all the abominations I have, nothing can shock you, though I have to say hers is a dreadful case."

We came to another long row of cells. Mrs Callahan stopped and cleaned her glasses before commencing. "Now, in this section, the prisoners will not speak unless spoken to because this is their work time. Most of them are sentenced to hard labour, a fitting punishment, for there's nowt like plain, hard work to tame the wildest, most wilful creatures."

"What kind of work do they busy themselves with?" I asked, trying to show interest, though my mind was still fixed on the poisoner.

"Oh—weaving, mat-making, oakum, and ragpicking, and for those who choose to mind their behaviour, they're rewarded and sent to do laundry or kitchen work."

As we walked, she stopped and opened a sliding panel to reveal the occupant, who glanced up momentarily then lowered her eyes to resume her tedious labours.

She supplied short descriptions: "Bella Ross. Her fifteenth stay. Theft of money and bed linen. Six months hard labour. Elsie Kelley. Stealing poultry from her employer. Three months hard labour. Jane Gilbert. Stealing a purse. Drunk and disorderly and a habitual prostitute and pickpocket. Fifteen months hard labour."

Some were so young, I could not disguise my shock. We stopped at one cell where a child sat wrapped in a shawl that swamped her small body. She picked away at a pile of rags, her face hollow and hungry. I stopped to look at her, and her tear-swollen eyes met mine. I tried to smile at her in reassurance, but she scowled and wiped her eyes with a grubby arm, then went back to pulling at the rags.

"How old is she?" I asked in horror.

"Yes, she's a young'un. Mary Kirkley. Eleven years old. Stealing scrap iron. Two weeks hard labour and a good thing, too, for it's her first offence. Next time she won't be tempted to take what's not hers."

We passed on to the other cells.

"Perhaps I could talk to one of the women," I said. "They might welcome a friendly face."

She looked around, scanning the row of doors. "Not today, ma'am. Mrs Buckley gave strict instructions just to show you around. Mebbe you'd best wait here for her. I must push on and do my rounds."

Just then a stout, rosy-faced woman with peppery-grey hair swept in through a nearby door. I recognised her as one of the matrons who'd been walking with Mrs Cotton.

"Miss Dunn," Mrs Callahan barked. "Do you have a moment to take this lady visitor around the other part of the ladies' section?"

"Begging your pardon, Mrs Callahan, I was about to have a bite to eat."

"It can wait," said Mrs Callahan, striding off in the other direction.

"I'm sorry to have interrupted your routine," I said, standing to greet her. "I'm Clara Blackstone."

"No matter, ma'am. Miss Dunn, assistant wardress, but you may call me Bertha," said the woman, taking my hand and shaking it with a firm grasp. "We're often asked to miss our meals. But it's worse when we have to give up a Saturday night out or a Sunday holiday." Her eyes were soft and brown, a fine network of wrinkles etched around them by the wide smile on her face. I felt a rush of courage, a sense that this was my best opportunity to get to the poisoner.

"Are you wardress to Mrs Cotton?" I asked with some hesitation.

"Aye, one of them. I often accompany her to the exercise yard."

My heart thundered in my ears. I summoned up every ounce of confidence I could muster. "Might I visit her?" I asked.

Frowning, she looked me up and down as if trying to gauge my intent. "Well, the governor tells us not to encourage nosey folk. He says we're not a travelling show here, but a sober place of correction and punishment."

She began to walk away, but I was determined to see Mrs Cotton. I had come this far and could not turn back.

I held up my Bible. "I am a devout follower of Reverend Buckley. Only yesterday I listened to his sermon about reaching out a healing hand to our fallen sisters who crave forgiveness of their sins. I have some words of faith I'd like to share with her."

Bertha stopped and turned to look at me.

"I seek only to guide her towards the path of redemption. Surely you cannot deny her that."

She narrowed her eyes and thought for a long moment, stroking her fleshy chin.

"Well, she's allowed her share of visitors, so I don't suppose it would do any harm as long as she agrees to see you." She glanced around to see if anyone was listening. "Just follow me."

# Folkestone

## Spring 1873

I FEEL A sense of hope now that I can see the English Channel from the train window. The sight of the wide-open sea always thrills me with the promise of faraway lands that lie beyond the horizon, just waiting to be explored. And I've felt so light and comfortable since I rid myself of my widow's clothes in London and changed into a rose-coloured travelling dress. I handed the stiff black gown to a beggar woman on the steps of Charing Cross station. She scuttled away clutching the rustling silk to her heart. I hope she will eat well for a few months on the proceeds.

The train eases into Folkestone Harbour station and we alight under leaden rain clouds. Moored by the pier, the Folkestone-to-Boulogne ferry rocks in a choppy sea the colour of wet leaves, its three chimneys sending snail trails of steam into the air. Sensations overwhelm me—the slap of waves on the ship's hull, the flapping of flags, the air redolent with briny decay. The distant bellow of foghorns from hazy ships that move like slow animals across the horizon.

A nearby coal ship with dirty smokestacks belches foul smoke into the air, reminding me of the north and all my despair.

Fear kept me prisoner for so long. When the boat casts off, I will leave it behind.

In Bethlem, a rich woman told me she'd never felt more free than at the asylum. *Free from the daily constraints of womanhood,* she said. The voices forever whispering—place your teacup just so, fold your hands demurely on your lap, cast your eyes modestly downwards, sip your cordial like a bird at a feeder, do not squint or speak in a vulgar, strident voice. Sit and nod, nod and smile. In the asylum she could screech like a parrot and polka barefoot around the hallways all day long, twirling a ragged shawl around her head and the attendants would smirk and say, "It's just Martha dancing at her imaginary ball."

I found nothing but confinement there.

And my marriage was a prison.

If freedom means rebelling against all constraints, I felt the first stirrings of it when I met Mary Ann Cotton.

I was a naïve, vulnerable woman then. I approached her cell with all the zeal and idealism of a missionary, blind to reality and unmindful that when I stepped over the threshold into her cell, I'd crossed the line all good and virtuous women must never cross.

That first time, I saw a haunted forty-year-old woman beset by troubles, her eyes as dangerous as these dark, fathomless waters.

Her story was a siren call, tempting me—enticing me into forbidden places.

For we humans cannot resist the lure of the abyss.

# 11

I FOLLOWED BERTHA along a maze of musty corridors, until we emerged into a narrow stone-walled passage. At the end, a studded iron door led into a cramped room where two wardresses sat at a wooden table set with a brown teapot, stained mugs, and the remains of a sponge cake.

"What mischief are yer up to now, Bertha?" said the heavier one.

"I've brought a lady that wants to meet Mary Ann," she said, winking.

The younger one, with laughing eyes and a flat, fleshy nose, hauled herself from her chair. "Well, you wouldn't be the first."

The older one laughed a hearty belly laugh. "Why, everyone wants to meet Mary Ann. To see the women that packed off all her husbands—isn't that so, Miss Mullin? She's become quite a curiosity for a great number of well-meaning folk. The women in particler—seems some of 'em want to get a few tips on how to rid themselves of the old man."

"You've got a loose tongue, Thompson," said Bertha. "Mrs Blackstone's a respectable prison visitor."

I held my breath as they bustled about, opening another heavy door that would let *her* out. The murderous wife and mother. The cold-blooded killer of husbands and children.

I heard a light drag of footsteps across the floor and then a soft, flat voice, unlike the animated tones of Bertha and the other women.

"Has Mr Stott come for me?" asked the voice. "For I'm innocent of the crimes."

"No, Mary Ann," said Miss Thompson. "Your stepfather is a working man with a family to provide for."

"I must tell him that there are five or six bad'uns that would see me all done for and they cannot bring a witness to testify against me."

"It's a lady visitor to see you. She's kindly taken time out of her busy day to come and talk to you," said Miss Thompson.

I heard the dry scraping of chair legs on stone. Unable to resist, I peeped round the doorpost. A small figure in a chequered shawl hobbled across the room, clutching her distended belly.

She stood listening, her face obscured in the shadows, and for a moment she appeared unreal—a shifting image from my nightmares, a pen-and-ink caricature from the front page of the newspaper. And yet I drew back when the flames cast a fiery glow across the room and she stood silhouetted against the crimson firelight, the dark, brooding figure from my dream. The whole world went silent as we stood still, studying each other, the cell so quiet, I could hear the sound of flames licking across the wood. Then my eyes adjusted to the darkness and the illusion materialised into flesh. The long, pale face with the cap of black hair parted in the middle and smoothed across her ears. The black brows above deep-set eyes that had watched babies writhe in agony. I shivered, feeling a powerful need to step away from her slack, sullen gaze. But the shadows enveloped her again and I could only see the glint of her dark eyes, hard and cold as slate. They fixed on me as if she would pin me like a butterfly to a spreading board. The silence seemed to buzz in my ears. I was trapped with her in that moment, in that dark, musty space. In that tiny box of a room with its cold stone walls.

"Is it the woman that waved at me?" she said, seeming to sniff at the air like a blind creature. "The kind lady with the sad eyes?"

I held my breath, afraid to make a noise.

"I was expecting you," she whispered intimately. I remembered that in my dream she called me *sister*, and my breath came short and shallow as the voice in my head said, *She has summoned you here.*

Bertha was chatting with the other women, oblivious to our conversation.

"Don't be afeared, pet. I only want company," Mary Ann said in a high, wheedling voice. "Come closer so I can see you."

I approached and stood in the doorway, only a few feet away from her.

"I saw you somewhere before," she said, her flinty eyes weighing me up from head to toe.

"I don't think so," I whispered, holding my breath.

"Fine coat and bonnet. A real lady," she said, moving towards me, so close that she could touch the edge of my coat.

So close that I smelled the musky odour of sweat from her clothes.

"Back off and keep your hands away from the lady visitor, Mary Ann," said Bertha, holding the door open. Mary Ann shuffled back a few steps into the darkness, mumbling under her breath.

"Will you be all right now?" said Bertha, placing a stool by the door. I nodded and she went back to the other women.

"Impudent bugger," said Mary Ann, once Bertha's face had disappeared from sight. "Treats me like I'm vermin."

I perched on the edge of the stool, my insides charged with a feeling that was neither fear nor excitement, but something in between—as if I held the cover over a basket of snakes and felt compelled to glance inside.

"Tell me, what brings a fine lady like you to the prison?" she asked, jolting me back to reality.

"Spiritual guidance," I muttered, though the words seemed hollow in that dank place. "Charitable work. Mrs Buckley, the chaplain's wife, arranged it."

She straightened her shoulders, her mouth set in a tight line. "You think me a charity case? I'm no poorhouse skivvy and I don't need charity, Mrs . . ."

"Blackstone."

"I'm not in need of charity, Mrs Blackstone. I need a good lawyer to plead my case."

"You have no lawyer? How can that be?"

"Aye, they don't put that in the papers. They don't tell all their good Christian readers that I must beg for someone to speak for me and nobody will take me on. That my first lawyer, Mr Smith, was a scoundrel if ever there was one. That all the world has deserted me and my innocent child."

My eyes flickered to her belly.

To the baby growing there, oblivious to its circumstances.

"You have bairns, Mrs Blackstone?" she said, suddenly snapping back to the present. I shook my head, conscious of the intense heat radiating from the fire. My neck was slick with sweat.

"And you're married for how many years?"

"Five."

"Ah, that's a whole story, I suppose."

"I-I prefer not to speak of my personal life," I stuttered, my tongue so dry, I couldn't get the words out.

"I suppose they tell you not to get in too deep with the prisoners," she said, leaning forwards and rocking a little so that I caught the faint yeasty smell of her skin. "Are you new at this visiting business, then?"

"Today is my first visit."

"Well, if those common thieves and sluts can have a lady visitor, why can't I have company to help me through the long hours? After all, I'm an innocent woman. No court has proved me guilty yet." She inclined her head as if daring me to say otherwise. "And the newspapers are packed full of lies. They have nowt better to talk about. Have you read the stories about me, then?"

I could not lie. I knew my eyes would betray me. "Some of them."

She craned her head forwards, cupping a hand to her ear. "Speak up, miss, so's I can hear you."

My throat was dry as sand. "I said I've read some of them."

"Then I shall keep you all to myself from now on," she said, her pale hand reaching out from the shadows as if she would rest it on mine. I flinched and she stopped halfway, her eyes darting to the peephole. "Best not, I suppose."

She placed her hands together again, retreating back into the darkness so her face was veiled in shadow.

The air in the room grew close and cloying. I remembered my purpose—the reason I had come there. "I-I am here to talk to you and share your troubles, ease your burden and offer you guidance."

I thought I saw a flash of teeth, like a ferret baring its fangs. But she was smiling. "Nonsense. I'd wager you're after a bit of excitement. Looking for some juicy gossip to share with the other ladies at your genteel tea parties."

A sudden rush of heat flushed my cheeks and my scalp prickled. She had ripped away my pious pretence. Laid bare my delusions. My mind reeled with doubts. Was it nothing but ghoulish curiosity that had brought me here? A thirst for the morbid details of her shocking story? I'd combed the newspapers for stories about her, driven by utter disbelief that one woman could be capable of such evil. Perhaps I longed to hear her own account of the lurid tales that filled the newspapers.

*Stifle your emotions,* said the small voice in my head. *Do not show your true self if you know what's good for you.*

I pulled my shoulders back. "Why, I-I came here in good faith. I am concerned for your soul and for the welfare of your child, being born in this prison."

Now she brought her chin up in a posture of defiance. "Then you're just another one of them nosey rich folk seeking to steal my baby."

I shrank back, away from her. "No—I only wish to help you pass the time whilst you wait for your hearing."

I jumped when a piece of coal flared into flame, throwing a bloodred light across her face. She was smiling.

"I like you, Mrs Blackstone. You seem an honest type of woman. Not like those other do-gooders with their hoity-toity airs and a hanky stuffed in front of their noses. Cheeky beggars, they are. But I think we might become friends. And once I tell you my story, you'll know the truth about my life. You'll tell all those doubting folk out there that I'm innocent. Will you come back to visit me?" she asked, her dark eyes daring me to say no.

For a moment I faltered, then the voice inside my head muttered, *Say you will,* and before I could change my mind, I nodded, my heart rising to my throat.

"I thank you. It'll give me and the bairn something to look forward to." I stared in fascination as she patted her belly. "Now I must lie down. The baby tires me so."

She shuffled back towards the plain wooden trestle bed. "And don't forget your promise, Mrs Blackstone," she said, disappearing into the darkness.

That night I felt driven to write, though Henry had strictly forbidden any brainwork, as he called it. But I hadn't felt so alive in months and I burned to record my thoughts about the prison and my meeting with Mrs Cotton.

I had just settled at my writing desk when the door creaked open and Henry swept in without knocking. I shoved the papers underneath my shawl.

"Secret musings?" he asked, his lips curling in a wry grin. "You know I forbade any intellectual exertion, Clara."

I shook my head. "Just some harmless sketches. Dr Shepton recommended drawing as a calming activity."

"Typical of that quack. Dr Barnsley should have exposed him as a charlatan," he grunted, pursing his lips tightly.

*Ignorant fool,* said my secret voice. *He was the only man with courage amongst a pack of bullies and tyrants.*

I took out the paper and began to sketch a flower, watching from the corner of my eye as Henry jammed his hands on his hips and started to pace back and forth. "Nature can be very soothing," I said sweetly.

He stopped and glared at me. "Then you will enjoy Emma's embroidery circle. She has invited you to attend tomorrow."

*I would rather pierce my eyes with needles than sit for hours picking at a blank square of linen.* But the quiet voice took on a sudden urgency. *Do not openly defy him.*

"Perhaps I'll call in there for an hour or two and visit the prison afterwards. There's a wretched child of only eleven who desperately needs guidance."

"And you will provide it?" he asked, his brow wrinkling in a frown.

I quashed the surge of vexation—the response. "Make yourself cooperative, ladylike, not oversensitive or emotional. Just the kind of woman one likes to meet with," Mrs Parsons had urged.

I arranged my face in an amiable expression. "It will be so rewarding to try."

My answer seemed to satisfy him and he left me in peace. Eager to write before the sleeping draught took hold, I returned to my journal and my hand flew across the paper as thoughts and impressions poured onto the page:

*Her eyes disturb me the most. They are so deep and black, the pupil and iris merge together into one. Their expression is not cold or sly or cruel, as in the newspaper portrait. I can only describe them as dead eyes, lacking any shred of human emotion. She can bring tears to them, affect a smile, but it is only her lips that form themselves into something approaching laughter. Her eyes have no fear. They are steeped in death. And when she fixes her gaze on you, those eyes bore deep into your soul and know you for all your fears and weaknesses and hidden intentions.*

# 12

ALICE STOOD OVER me at the breakfast table, holding out the day's newspaper with its garish front-page headline: **THE EXTRAORDINARY POISONING CASE AT WEST AUCKLAND.**

"Thought yer might like the paper, Mrs Blackstone," she said, smirking before retreating to the kitchen. The banging and scraping of pots soon followed.

The article detailed the evidence given during the hearing before Mrs Cotton's committal to the prison. They had described her as *a woman of medium height, with a self-possessed air about her* and said that *during the examination, the prisoner held a white handkerchief to her face whilst the following evidence was presented.*

*During the week previous to the death of Charles Edward Cotton, Dr Kilburn saw him three times. The child had been vomiting and was somewhat purged and complained of pains in the region of the stomach on all three occasions. The third time he saw the child, he was considerably weaker. He then changed the medicine and saw no more of the boy till the next morning, when he was dead.*

My stomach turned over as I scanned the terrible details of the postmortem—external appearances were emaciation and distention across the bowels—membranes of the brain slightly congested and the brain was softer than natural. Stomach a dark brownish red and covered with a thick mucus scum—two or three particles of white powder detected in the stomach.

Dr Scattergood of Leeds had received the samples from Kilburn. He had found arsenic in the *contents and substance of the stomach and the bowels, in the liver, lungs, heart, and kidneys,* confirming the suspicions of the police officer and the parish overseer, Riley, who had first alerted the authorities of his concern. The boy had been poisoned by arsenic in large enough quantities to kill a grown man, let alone a child.

*Mrs Cotton was heard to say, "People are saying I poisoned him, but I am innocent. I made application to the relieving officer to get him into the workhouse, but they wouldn't take him. I also wrote to an uncle of the child, up south, to take the boy, but he refused. I am only the stepmother. I had no right to keep him. He has prevented me from earning many a pound. I have had a great deal of trouble with the Cotton family, with so many of them dying in such a short time."*

*When asked if the prisoner had anything to say in response to the evidence, she replied no in a low but decided tone of voice. The magistrate, Mr Hicks, then said, "Prisoner, you stand committed to take trial at the next Durham assizes for the murder of Charles Edward Cotton."*

I put the newspaper down. Why did she still protest her innocence even after the autopsy revealed poison in such large quantities? Perhaps she was mad or deluded. Or were the doctors mistaken and there was some miniscule shred of a chance that she was innocent, as she claimed? My mind drifted to the image of the white handkerchief held to the side of Mrs Cotton's face. It contradicted the idea of her having a proud, self-possessed air. Or perhaps she'd been so overcome by the details of the child's postmortem and the gruesome consequences of her actions, she'd tried to hide her emotions from the curious onlookers crowding the courtroom.

*Stomach a dark brownish red and covered with a thick mucus scum.*

I shuddered and glanced over at the breakfast dish—at the spongy pink lumps of meat lying on the plate. Grilled kidneys. I could not even touch them. Cold tea was all I needed to settle my stomach and take a quick walk to Emma's in the welcome fresh air. Then I'd excuse myself after an hour.

The clock at the prison showed three minutes past ten when I finally arrived. I had suffered more than an hour of Emma's excruciating chatter about how to handle the servants and how best to baste a goose to ensure the most succulent flesh. With the promise that I would actually attempt some embroidery the following week, I managed to extricate myself from the circle of simpering ladies with the excuse of an oncoming headache. That justified the calling of a carriage and I was soon on my way to the prison without any further protests.

Mr Boxted looked on as I signed the book, the lines of his face blurred by the steam rising from his mug of tea.

"Nippy out there," he said, turning the book around to check my signature. "Mrs Clara Blackstone. I remember you. On yer own today, then?"

"Mrs Buckley was busy on a social visit, and I didn't want to miss another day. Is Mrs Callahan about?"

He searched through my bag then unlocked the studded metal door. "First office on the left, soon as you turn the corner," he said, tipping his hat.

Mrs Callahan sat in a tiny cubbyhole of an office, sorting through a pile of papers. She glared at me over the top of her glasses. "So you're back for more? We didn't scare you off, then?"

"I thought I could read to one or two of the women," I said, indicating my bag.

"As you wish. I'm busy trying to sort out the shifts, so I'll send one of the junior wardresses to accompany you today. Just stay away from the chronics."

I nodded and thanked her.

"And remember, Mrs Blackstone, whenever you wish to visit, just ask Mr Boxted for the wardress doing the rounds. I'll let them know you'll be a regular."

I breathed a sigh of relief. Working with the other women would give me easier access to the prison, and once I was inside, I'd find Bertha to take me to Mrs Cotton.

The junior matron introduced herself as Miss Honeywell. She looked to be barely eighteen, with wisps of yellow hair peeping out from her white bonnet, scrubbed pink cheeks, and limpid blue eyes. As she passed the cells, the women called out to her.

"Miss Honeywell. Pretty lady. Let me tell your fortune. A young man with dark eyes waits for you. I dreamt of him last night."

"Silence, Packer!" she shouted, rapping the bars with a stick.

Another woman reached her hand through the bars. "I made you a rag doll, Miss Honeywell. Now can you get me a biscuit or a scrap of tallow?"

"Pay no heed to them. They try every way to gain favour with us."

She showed me to the cell of a thin, mousy-haired young woman bent over her rag mat. "You can start with Edith Parker," she said, unlocking the door. "She likes a bit of company. Just rap on the door and call for me when you wish to leave."

Though I felt a little shaky when the door shut behind me, I stood close to Edith and introduced myself. I offered to read to her, but I soon learned that all she wanted was a sympathetic ear to listen to her story.

"I was a servant with a wealthy coal merchant," she said, turning watery blue eyes on me. "They didn't treat me well, so I ran away and fell in with a bad crowd that led me wrong. A false friend was the culprit. I shall never trust another soul again as long as I live. She took me to the concert room and then the pubs. Every night we went out until the drink turned my head and I was forced onto the streets."

After listening to her story for a good ten minutes, I read a few Psalms to her, then excused myself and moved on to visit her neighbour, a vivid dark-eyed woman named Viola. Her white hands looked as if she'd never seen a day's work. She declared that the other prisoners were *rude and vulgar and not fit to wipe the muck from her shoes.* But her face lit up and her eyes took on a faraway look when she claimed she had an inheritance. "A little property is coming to me soon, with the blessing of God. Quite a snug little cottage overlooking the river, with its own kitchen garden. I shall grow beets and cabbages—oh, and flowers to dress my dinner table. I shall be set for life," she said, clasping her hands to her heart.

"Why is she here?" I asked Miss Honeywell when I left the cell.

"Common thievery. She stole a pair of ladies' evening gloves from a dressmaker's shop."

"And the inheritance?"

"Not a likely prospect," she said, shaking her head. "Viola's mother was the housekeeper in a great house. Her father was the master. When Viola was old enough, her mother tried to hang on to the master's favour by presenting her daughter as a gift to use as he wanted."

My hand flew to my mouth.

"Aye, it's a sad story. She still believes he might choose to redress the wrongs done to her, though I highly doubt it."

I wandered after the wardress, feeling a weight of sadness on me. Viola had been so wronged. And her inheritance was probably just an idle dream, conjured up to kill the terrible monotony of the prison.

When I was in Hoxton, I would often think of Izzie's lovely country home in Oxfordshire. The place where I'd spent my childhood. I'd lie in the narrow bed and try to imagine myself walking amongst the flowers that bordered the front lawn: fragrant roses, hydrangeas, tall lupines, and hollyhocks shading blue forget-me-nots, sweet peas, and a profusion of velvety pansies. I'd stand amongst all that beauty, marvelling at the tangle of ivy climbing the walls, the graceful arched windows, and the upper balconies with their wrought-iron railings.

*One day you will inherit all this,* Izzie had told me.

A rush of panic almost knocked me sideways. Now that she was away, who was looking after the place?

The doctor had ordered her to India in the seventh month of my pregnancy. He feared her lungs would give out in the smoggy London air. She begged me to write every day and I'd done so until the week before the stillbirth. But my life had been in such turmoil, I'd only written a few times from Hoxton. And Henry hadn't mentioned a letter from her since I'd been back.

"Mrs Blackstone, Mrs Blackstone." Someone tapped my shoulder and a familiar voice shook me back to the present. I turned to see Bertha peering at me, her brow knit. Miss Honeywell stood behind her, puzzled.

"I swear you were off somewhere far away," she said.

"Just thinking of my grandmother," I said, blinking my eyes into focus.

"You look a bit peaky. Are you sure you want to see Mary Ann today?"

I nodded. "I'm only a little tired, but I don't like to go back on a promise."

I thanked Miss Honeywell and followed Bertha along the corridor.

"Mary Ann's been asking after you. You must have made quite an impression on her. She thought you'd be stopping in earlier."

"I was busy," I said as we approached Mrs Cotton's cell. My head felt so foggy, I could barely think. The aftereffects of the sleeping draught still lingered, making my legs feel thick and stiff.

# 13

THE DOOR CLANKED open and Bertha announced, "A visitor for Mary Ann," as she ushered me into the anteroom next to her cell to receive instructions from Miss Thompson, the wardress on duty.

"Bertha says you'll be coming here on a regular basis, so we'd be obliged if yer don't engage the prisoner in any talk about the case. Also, yer'd be advised not to become overfamiliar with her or share any personal matters. The women here are troubled, desperate souls. Liable to grasp at straws and use that knowledge to cause all manner of trouble for you. Best to just listen and offer sound Christian guidance."

I held my Bible up for her to see, but my insides lifted and turned over as she led me to the cell. Though a good fire burned there, a cold sweat beaded my temples. "Miss Thompson, could you bring us some tea?" I croaked, my throat suddenly dry again.

A flat, unaffected voice interrupted the silence. "Aye, Miss Thompson, and might you spare a better candle? For how shall we read the good book in this darkness? And I *should* like to see Mrs Blackstone better."

My hands trembled as Miss Thompson handed me a flickering candle. I gasped when the light danced on the walls, throwing Mrs Cotton into sharp relief.

She sat on the edge of her plank bed, watching me, her hands crossed in her lap and the same chequered shawl across her shoulders.

"Put the candle down on the side table, dear, afore you burn the place down. Your hand is shaking."

I did as she told me, forcing myself to breathe steadily. To still my fidgety hands.

I studied her face. The strong chin and deep eye sockets appeared slightly masculine. Her mouth and eyes were unsmiling as they looked up at me, seeming to assess my clothes and gloved hands.

"I thank you for coming back to visit me," she said in a low and lifeless voice. "For I'm in sore need of a friendly face."

I settled myself on the stool by the door, clutching the Bible to renew my resolve. "Well, that is why I'm here. Shall we read a few verses together?" I said, hoping my voice had not faltered too much.

She waved the book aside with a flick of her hand.

"Bugger that nonsense," she said, glancing downwards. She had no intention of receiving my spiritual guidance. Instead her eyes devoured my buttoned black boots. The tip of her tongue slid across her lower lip. "Beautiful quality leather. Must have cost a good bit of money."

I placed the open Bible on my lap. "My grandmother brought them from Paris."

"Of course they're French. Fine workmanship. Nowt like that in these parts," she said, drawing herself up straighter and narrowing her eyes. "And I know nice things when I see them.

I'm no gutter rat. I taught Sunday school and when I was fifteen, I went to work for Mr Edward Potter, the manager at South Hetton Colliery. He lived in a grand house with silver candlesticks and lace tablecloths and china teacups. He still speaks highly of me. He'll vouch for my character in court. I'm a respectable woman. Always have been. I know what it's like to have money. I hired cleaning women to scour the floors in my own house and I had my share of good clothes and food."

I remembered the insurance money she'd received on the death of her children, then pushed the thought away under her penetrating gaze.

"Might I call you Mary Ann?"

She nodded. "And what shall I call you, then, dear?"

"Mrs Blackstone."

She leaned closer so the candlelight fell on the curve of her brow. "That doesn't seem right. If you can call me Mary Ann, then surely I can use your Christian name. I'm a respectable Methodist woman and not yet convicted of any crime."

I glanced behind me to see if Miss Thompson was listening. She'd warned me not to get too personal, yet here I was about to reveal my first name, which seemed an intimacy I shouldn't entertain. And yet when I turned around again, Mary Ann's eyes glittered with such menace—like a coiled snake ready to pounce—I felt compelled to tell her.

"Clara."

She sighed, unwinding herself with a breathy whisper. "A real lady's name. Now I wish I had a nice piece of cake to serve you. I always had good china for special occasions. Never served the funeral cake on cheap pottery. Used the best tea leaves, too. I have a taste for good tea. Not like the horse piss they serve here." Her hand flew to her mouth, which twisted in a strange, simpering smile. "Oh, you must pardon me. I quite forgot myself. Didn't mean to offend you on your first proper visit, Clara."

I shook my head. If only she knew what I'd seen and heard at the Bethlem Hospital. "I've heard worse. Perhaps I'll bring some tea next time and maybe a few biscuits."

She smiled again, though her eyes remained cold. "Oh, you're so kind. I do enjoy biscuits with my tea. I'm partial to shortbread. Made with butter, of course. Not lard."

"Then butter shortbread it will be," I said.

*"Clara, Clara are you always so willing?"* she chanted, as if reciting a children's rhyme.

"What do you mean?" I shrank back. She was mocking me.

"Just a little song I recalled from my childhood days," she said, grinning and revealing a row of uneven grey teeth. "Now look, your hands are still trembling. Hold them still, Clara. Never show your fear, for you know in all the fairy tales the fierce wolves always sniff out the gentle ladies."

I clasped my hands together to stop the shaking. "Tell me about your childhood," I said, eager to change the direction of our conversation.

She gazed at the wall beyond me. "Oh, them were the happy days when I was a Sunday school teacher and strong in my faith. Though my youngest sister, Margaret, died young and I missed my dear father, who met a terrible end. When I was only ten, he fell headfirst down a pit shaft trying to mend a pulley wheel. The heartless bastards brought his body back to the house in a wheelbarrow. Mam tried to keep us away, but I saw his dead body wrapped in a filthy sack labelled *Property of the South Hetton Coal Company.* He were a slave to those bastard pit owners. That lovely man, in the prime of his life, reduced to nowt but a heap of flesh and bone. His dear body crushed as if they'd dragged it through a mangle."

Her voice faltered and stopped. Only the crackle and spit of the fire filled the silence as she gazed at the glowing coals.

"You must miss him?" I said.

"Aye, he brought me up to fear the Lord, and made sure I attended the Wesleyan Sunday school in Murton. But after he passed, death came into my life and has never left me alone since." She shook her head and rocked back and forth. "They say the devil seeks only the souls of the pure and innocent, and I believe it. I was but a child then and he came to me, forked and hoofed, and has shadowed me ever since."

I had described her eyes as dead eyes, lacking any shred of human emotion. Now I realised they were haunted. Possessed.

Feeling a sudden chill in the air, I drew my shawl around me.

"I was only nine when my parents passed, so I also know something of tragedy," I said, noticing how her eyebrows twitched as soon as I mentioned my family. How she moved closer as if to suck the story from me.

"Your people died young, then?"

"Father died of influenza. Mother never left his side and wouldn't let anyone else tend to him."

"I supposed she pined away for love of him," she said, tilting her head and scrutinising my face.

"She took to her bed and would not eat."

"And left you all alone?"

I nodded.

"You were an only child, then?"

The close, stale air of the room wrapped around me, and with it came a creeping sense of terror that turned my insides over at the memory.

"I was," I whispered.

"Poor bairn. It must've frightened you so."

I nodded. "A waking nightmare. Mother screamed and cried for him from morning till night. 'He is hiding somewhere,' she'd wail. 'He is only waiting to be found.' I remember rushing about the house, searching every cupboard and corner and closet in case she was right."

"She was a hysteric, then?"

I looked away. "I cannot say."

"I was a nurse, dear. I've seen all manner of conditions."

Her voice was soothing, her wide eyes intense and piercing, as if she could read my thoughts. I was powerless to stop myself. "She refused to eat even though the doctor said she must. They ladled broth into her mouth, but she spat it out, all the whilst screaming, '*I see him, I see him!*' Then she died three months after Father."

"So she left you a poor orphan. All alone in the world."

"Alone and afraid," I said, glancing over as she folded her arms and nodded.

"Love drives some poor folk into a frenzy. I've seen men and women killed over it, though I can surely say I've never met a man that I'd be willing to die over."

A brief image flashed into my head. Clad in funeral black, Mary Ann hovered over the bed of a man with a sickly grey complexion, her hand propping up his head as she eased a cup into his mouth. I blinked and the picture went away.

"Are you feeling canny, Clara?" she asked in a soft voice that brought me back to the present.

"Just a little sad."

"Only, you came on a bit strange just then," she said, trying to pull herself up. "Let me take a closer look at you."

She sat back down in a rush as Miss Thompson came in carrying two mugs of tea. "I hope our Mary Ann's cooperating," she said, setting the cups down on the bare wooden table beside us.

"We've just been through the first three Psalms," Mary Ann said before I could utter a word. "Isn't that so, Mrs Blackstone?"

I nodded, reaching for the tea.

Mary Ann studied the rough white cup. "Is this how you serve tea to two fine ladies, Miss Thompson? In a common pitman's mug?"

"By you're a cheeky one, Mary Ann. Mebbe I'll get the good china out next time. Would that suit you better?"

"Aye, it would. Mrs Blackstone isn't accustomed to drinking from colliery pots."

Miss Thompson swept out, laughing as Mary Ann took a long drink of tea.

"Perhaps now is a good time to read some verses together," I said, patting the Bible that still lay open on my lap.

Her brows knit as she slammed her cup down on the table, making my heart leap. "Like hell we will, Clara. I told you I taught Sunday school. You think you can teach me my Psalms? I know them all by bloody heart."

I almost choked as the tea caught in my throat.

"Save the lies for Miss Thompson, Clara. You're here to find out the truth about me, aren't you?"

The blood roared in my ears and I nodded.

"So now you've told me about your life, I suppose I shall have to tell you how I came to walk through the valley of the shadow of death. How William Mowbray, my first husband, led me into the depths of Hell."

She spoke with a low, soothing voice.

"I was a clever dressmaker when I was a young lass. I could run up a dress from an old set of curtains and I would have made a fine minister's wife. But William Mowbray come along with his silver tongue and soft hands and led me to a life of shame. I fell pregnant and married him, though I was not yet twenty," she said, rubbing at the swollen hump of her belly. "He convinced me, against my better judgement, to go south to Cornwall, for he'd found work on the railways. That place were worse than Hell itself. Ten of us crammed into a miserable shack and you couldn't set foot outside. The pathways were thick wi' clarts and ashes, and armies of rats ran through filthy streams of water. T'were like the devil's den. Navvies and thieves prowling like demons in the back alleys, drinking and fighting. Ready to throw a poor lass on her back and give her a fright. 'Tis there I had four bairns and all but one sickened and died. Poor things caught the typhus fever from the privies leakin' shit into the wells.

"But I never harmed them bairns. I had four babies down there and brought only one back from Cornwall. My poor dear Margaret Jane was the only one left. I told Mowbray, 'I cannot suffer another child of mine to die that way, so we must leave and go home to my mother and stepfather at their pub in Hetton.' Now I curse those devils who write lies about me in the newspapers. They claim I killed every child I bore. Even the poor babies that died in Cornwall. But I grieved for those bairns then and I still do now."

I thought of the longing I felt for a baby I could barely remember. How it gnawed at my heart. So I couldn't imagine watching three beautiful children die, one after another. To hold them in my arms and watch them breathe their last breath, helpless to do a thing about it. I wondered then if something in her heart had died in Cornwall and could never be resurrected. If it had hardened her to the reality of death.

She placed her head in her hands and looked up at me with damp eyes. "God wouldn't have granted me another child if I was a murdering monster. Would he?"

I couldn't answer her.

"Clara," she said, her voice sharp as a razor. "I canna spend more time with you if you've already set in your head that I'm nothing but a common murderer. Tell me you have an open mind."

I searched for the right words. Miss Thompson had warned me not to discuss the case and yet here I was, breaking every rule in the book. I looked up at Mary Ann. "You must have faith in the courts. If you are innocent, you will be spared."

She sighed and wrung her hands, the sharpness in her voice softening to a childish whine. "But can you help me? Can you help me get a proper lawyer? My last lawyer, Smith, is nowt but a rascal. He's pawned everything I own and now has his thieving hand out for more."

"I'm not sure what I can do . . ." I said, my throat suddenly dry. "But I'm here to listen to you. Ease your burden."

She chewed her lip and looked at me with narrowed eyes. "I don't want talk. I need practical help. A petition. Money for them bloodsucking lawyers."

"I have no money of my own, but I can help you write a letter or compose a petition."

She slumped back in her chair and rubbed a hand over her belly. "Aye. I suppose that'll do. And bring me something more than kindness next time you come."

"I promise to bring the shortbread, and some tea, perhaps?"

She nodded and I turned to leave, but her hand clamped on to my wrist with such force, I sat back on the chair, my pulse racing.

"Wait and listen," she hissed. "Fair's fair. I mean to be your friend and friends help each other out. You understand?"

I glanced at the small window in the door to make sure nobody was listening.

"I was a nurse in Sunderland Infirmary for years. I just want to have a look at your eyes, pet. You can tell a good deal from a person's eyes. Come here, closer to me."

I leaned in far enough to see the fine dark hairs on her upper lip, to smell the stale odour of unwashed skin. Those dark, glittering eyes fixed so intently on mine, she seemed to burrow her way into my head.

"I knew it. Laudanum. You can tell from the size of the pupils. Like pinheads."

Needles of fear pricked my skin. Already she knew too much about me and in such a short time. "You must be mistaken."

"Mind you, it's none of my business, but if I were you, I wouldn't touch it. Makes a person fidgety one minute and then melancholy the next. Then the more you have, the more you crave."

"Could it be in a sleeping draught?"

She threw her head back and laughed. "I'd say there's a good bit of it in every sleeping remedy and blood tonic and pain cure."

"But my husband tells me it is for my own good."

"Do you know what it's made of?"

I shook my head, mortified at my ignorance.

"Why, it's tincture of opium mixed with alcohol—pure evil and leads to a lifetime of suffering. I've seen it ruin a few good people in my time. Grown men reduced to walking skeletons and mothers so drugged, they forget to feed their own bairns."

"I'm taking it under doctor's orders," I said, glancing at the door again.

She squeezed my wrist. "Tell me, Clara. Why does your husband dose you with that poison?"

My head spun. How cleverly she'd worked her way into the secret parts of my life, like a spider easing through a crack in the plaster. "I have insomnia."

"Does he force it on you?"

I looked away and shook my head weakly.

"Mebbe I'll put it in a different way, then. Would you rather not take it?"

I turned back to her unflinching eyes. "It makes me drowsy—I cannot think clearly."

"Of course it does." She released me with a wink and settled back onto the bed, her eyelids flickering. "Now, listen to me. I'm just giving you some friendly advice, you understand? I've had my fill of well-meaning doctors and scheming husbands, and if I wanted to keep my head clear of laudanum, I'd take a good look through the house—all the cupboards and shelves and hidden corners—even your husband's coat pockets. And if I found a small brown bottle with a cork stopper, I'd pour it out and fill it back up with a bit of water and brown sugar. Mebbe some sweet sherry or vanilla. Then nobody's any the wiser. Not even your own husband. You catch my drift?"

I nodded, stunned at how quickly she'd rooted out my secret. Then I stood up to go, but she touched my hand again.

"Take care, Clara, and watch out for those wolves. For when they get their teeth into your flesh, they'll tear you to pieces."

# 14

I HURRIED THROUGH the crowded marketplace, the cries of the merchants ringing in my ears—*"Winter turnips, penny a pound." "Best russet apples, no worms or rot."* I shouldered my way through them all, shuddering as I passed the butcher's shop, where spongy sheets of tripe hung in frilled pink curtains beside garlands of plump sausages.

*The child's organs were completely saturated with arsenic.*

I turned my head away. Mary Ann had seemed so distressed when talking about her first three children, yet the newspapers made no mention of that chapter in her life, nor suggested her first children had died of natural causes.

And now this accused murderer was offering me advice. Sound advice.

I had permitted Henry to dose me with laudanum—to soften my brain and keep me in a drowsy state, as if I'd never left the asylum.

*It's tincture of opium mixed with alcohol.*

My mind swelled with visions of squalid, smoky rooms. Only three years ago, Mr Dickens had laid bare the horrors of the opium dens guarded by the wrinkled crone sucking at her ink-bottle pipe. She'd lead you in and pull aside the ragged curtains to reveal rows of wretched cots that housed comatose husks of humanity—the hollow-cheeked cleric sinking into the bliss of oblivion, the starving artist's model dying for love.

At home, a brooding silence blanketed the house. I waited a moment until the steady *tick* of the grandfather clock calmed my breathing, but the brisk walk had left me ravenous. I bit ragged chunks from a heel of bread as I threw open cupboards and drawers, searching every corner for the sleeping draught. My mouth watered at the sight of the sliced roast lamb in the pantry, but I pushed it aside and searched behind the flour bag and bowl of eggs until finally I found the small brown corked bottle tucked behind the tea caddy.

I pulled out the stopper and sniffed the sweet, flowery odour. My head suddenly felt light. I could drift into a dream-filled sleep if I just tipped some onto my tongue. Then I'd float through the house like a sleepwalker, all the terrible memories blown away like wisps of smoke.

Was that the kind of wife Henry wanted? A meek, brainless dolt who muddled through the day in a somnolent state, tied to her master because her body craved more with each dose?

*Pure evil, and leads to a lifetime of suffering.*

It was all I could do not to smash that hateful bottle to pieces, but I took a deep breath and waited for the quiet voice to calm me.

*Take control, Clara. You will have the advantage of a clear head, and he will never know it.*

So instead, I turned the bottle upside down and dashed the contents down the sink, sluicing the inside with fresh water. Then, as Mary Ann had instructed, I refilled the laudanum bottle with water, brown sugar, and a few drops of vanilla. After shaking it thoroughly, I replaced it in the exact spot I'd found it.

After supper, Henry sat by the kitchen fire, hands resting on his stomach, his waistcoat buttons strained almost to bursting. Alice's roast leg of lamb and buttered parsnips had lulled him into a rare state of contentment.

Since he was gazing into the depths of the fire with a satisfied smile on his face, I decided it might be a good time to ask him about Izzie, but my hands would not stay still. I perched on the edge of my chair, fidgeting with the lace ruffle on my dress, and was just about to speak when his eyelids began to droop.

"Henry," I ventured. His eyes snapped open and he blinked as if disoriented.

"What is it, Clara? Do you need your medicine?"

I took a deep breath. "I have a question."

"Well, out with it, Clara. Don't hover."

I steadied my voice and sweetened its tone. "I was wondering if Izzie had tried to write to me when I was in the asylum?"

He pressed his fingers into his eyes and sighed. "I am tired. Must we talk about this now?"

"But it's been well over a year since I heard from her."

He sat up straight and began jabbing at the fire with the poker, throwing a shower of sparks up into the air. "Do you think you've been in the right frame of mind to worry about Izzie's health when you have been so unwell?"

"I am better now, Henry. Dr Shepton said I had made a good recovery."

"Damn that man," he snapped, slamming the poker down and pulling himself out of the chair. "His head is softer than his heart."

Though I felt the sting of his sarcasm, I persisted, determined not to become agitated. "But I should like to know if she's all right."

He shrugged on his jacket. "Why would you ruin a perfectly tranquil evening, Clara? I had hoped to take a nap by the fire, with you sitting peacefully at my side. But you're bound and determined to pester me tonight."

I followed him through the doorway, my body trembling with suppressed fury. "I'm worried, Henry. Izzie is the only family I have."

He stopped and shook his head. "And you are *my* wife, Clara. I'm the only family you have here. You might show some more appreciation of that."

*Cease with your questions,* said the voice. *Begging will get you nothing. Artfulness is the only way.*

I dropped my head. "Forgive me for disturbing your nap, Henry. We'll talk about it another time, when you're rested."

He brushed past me into the hallway. Pale yellow light spilled from the streetlamp through the glass pane on the front door, but did nothing to soften the rigid lines of Henry's face.

I lay in bed, studying the ceiling and wondering why Henry had been so agitated about Izzie's letters. Did he wish to spare me bad news? I cast my mind back to his visits. Had he even mentioned Izzie in all the time I was away?

He hadn't set foot in Bethlem until the day he took me out of there, and had only visited Hoxton two or three times.

The bitter taste of resentment rose in my throat when I remembered his first visit. I was sitting in the morning room, only a month after I'd arrived. I'd barely opened my mouth to speak, since I was in a constant state of nausea. Constance, a distinguished-looking dowager with a halo of frizzy white hair and a pronounced squint, was perched on a chair beside me, her face twisted with concern.

"It's the antimony, my dear, that makes you sick. They give it to curb the violent streak. You must have lashed out at someone. Did you, dear?"

I shook my head and tried to wipe my mouth.

"Well, they wouldn't have bound your hands if you weren't a feisty one. I know because I broke the attendant's nose when they brought me in. I told them I shouldn't be here. I told them my shopping trip was rudely interrupted. I thought I was going out to purchase new boots when the two crafty devils, my son and nephew, spirited me away and landed me here. In an asylum . . ."

Then, I remember, Henry appeared. Tall and handsome in an immaculate black coat.

"Is this the blackguard who decoyed you away?" said Constance, looking him up and down. "Quite the dandy, I see."

Henry turned to a nearby attendant and muttered in her ear. Immediately the woman bundled Constance back to her room.

Henry smirked as she twisted and struggled to pull herself from the attendant's grasp.

"He's out there living the high life, my dear," she shrieked, "whilst you waste away here until you're nothing but a ghost!"

I remembered looking at Henry then and marvelling at how his white shirt seemed starched to perfection. How his coat was stylishly cut and his shoes polished and shining. How his gaze seemed to linger on his reflection in the morning-room window. This was not the earnest young man in the threadbare jacket I'd met at Izzie's recital.

Now my bedroom door swung open and Henry stood holding a flickering candle.

"Are you feeling better?" he asked, his features seeming to shift and rearrange themselves in the dancing light.

I sat up, nodding. He perched on the edge of my bed, placed the candle on my table, and bowed his head. "I was hoping not to burden you with this news until you were ready to hear it."

My blood chilled in anticipation of what he was about to tell me.

He looked at me with mournful eyes. "I'm afraid your grandmother's health is failing."

"You mean her pneumonia has returned?"

He nodded. Time seemed to bend and warp until I barely felt the bed beneath me. "How can that be? Someone would have written to tell me."

He glanced away, his mouth twitching in the candlelight. "I wrote to her after the . . . the stillbirth, but you were in no condition to worry about her health. You were struggling with your own troubles and you know how badly your mother took the news of your father's illness. I couldn't risk the same thing happening to you."

I fell back against the pillows. *My mother again. Will he ever cease to remind me of her breakdown?*

"I cannot believe it, Henry. I wrote to Izzie from Hoxton. So many times. Surely someone would have responded."

"As did I, Clara. But I didn't hear anything until her doctor wrote to inform us she was growing weaker each day."

"When? How long ago?"

"A week before you came here."

"I say it can't be true." I turned away, my lower lip trembling. Now the cracks on the ceiling seemed to writhe as if the gnarled tree branches were pushing their way through the crevices. He kept talking, but his voice was distant. As if it were coming from the bottom of a deep well.

"I was going to tell you when you were stronger and more able to bear the bad news."

"I cannot believe it," I said, my hands pressed to my eyes.

Then he came close and pulled my hands away until I could see the tangled hair of his whiskers, the sharp glint of his eyes. "Poor Clara. You will always be my little orphan. But I promise I'll never leave you. How could I ever desert my long-suffering wife?"

I lay rigid and took the false sleeping draught without protest, but even still he gripped my head, his thumb pressing against the softness of my throat whilst I swallowed it. Then he sat by my bed until I pretended to fall into a deep sleep, the taste of sweet vanilla fresh on my lips. I sensed him hovering above me, the rasp of his breath magnified in the silence. He watched me for a good few minutes until he was sure I was in a deep sleep. When he strode out of the room, I lay still, stomach churning until his bedroom door slammed shut.

I'd last heard from Izzie just two weeks before the night of the stillbirth. Now I ached for my grandmother, with her lullabies and kisses and warm lavender hugs. When I was a child, I'd curl up on her lap like a kitten, her papery hand stroking my hair as she sang to me.

*When little Birdie bye-bye goes,*
*quiet as mice in churches,*
*he puts his head where no one knows,*
*and on one leg he perches.*

*When little baby bye-bye goes,*
*on Mama's arm reposing,*
*soon he lies beneath the clothes,*
*safe in the cradle dozing.*

My eyes smarted with tears and when I finally drifted off to sleep, I dreamt I had entered a long black tunnel illuminated at the end by the reddish glow of flames. Weightless, I floated towards a blazing fire where a dark-haired child stood sobbing, her face buried in her hands, her body shaking.

At her feet, a shapeless lump wrapped in sacking lay on the stone floor. Soon the shape began to twist and turn, doubling up on itself then straightening out again until a blackened hand appeared at the opening. The child grew still and turned her face to me, her eyes black and glittering as freshly hewn coal. "My father must fight the devil for his life," she whispered as the filthy hand pulled down the sacking and I saw my mother's head burst out from the top, the pallid skin stretched like wax over the bones of her face. Thin tufts of hair sprouted from her scalp and her eyes were sunken hollows.

"I will not eat. You cannot force it down," she hissed as her head jerked and twitched from side to side until the entire bundle rolled onto the fire, exploding into flames then sputtering and burning like a bale of dry hay.

# 15

AT BETHLEM, ANNIE had always said, "Never trust a man—most particularly your own husband."

I told myself to keep those words close to my heart as I sat by the parlour window the next morning to compose a letter.

*Be wary of Henry's every word and action,* said the quiet voice as I put pen to paper and scratched out the words *Dearest Izzie . . .*

A knock at the door interrupted me mid-sentence. Alice scurried in, her face flushed and shiny. "If you please, mum, Mr Blackstone says the Buckleys will be calling here tonight."

I put down the pen to rest my forehead on my hand.

*Be wary of his every word and action.*

"What time?" I said, glancing up at the way she wrung her hands.

"He said four o'clock sharp."

*Dammit,* said the voice. *Why has Henry not mentioned this arrangement before?* My mind was so taken up with worry about Izzie, I was in no mood for small talk—especially not with the Buckleys.

"Shall I fetch some Eccles cakes from the baker's?"

I searched my mind for memories of Izzie's great tea parties. The tables laid with lavish canapés, dainty finger sandwiches, and towers of fluffy meringues.

"No, Alice. We'll make finger sandwiches and I'll get some cakes from the baker's on the way back from the prison."

Alice's eyes widened. "I never made dainty sandwiches, mum, only me dad's bacon baps."

"Don't worry. I'll teach you."

It took a whilst to allay Alice's fears and compose a list of provisions for her to buy, but soon the back door slammed and I watched from the parlour window as she plodded along the lane, swinging a basket on her arm.

In the kitchen, the fire was low, the air chilly. A dull pounding throbbed behind my eyes. Was I missing the laudanum already? Without it, my sleep had been fitful and now my head was thick and muddled. I struggled to the table, where I drank a cup of cold tea and tried to piece my scattered thoughts together so I could finish the letter to Izzie. My message was brief. I wanted only to let her know I was well and in Durham, and urged her to get in touch. I did not worry her with talk of the asylum.

Once I'd sealed the envelope, I glanced across the hallway to Henry's study. How strategically it was situated at the foot of the stairs. Like a sentry in a prison, he could monitor every movement from behind the fortress of his desk. And last night I had shown my weakness—my concern for Izzie's life. Mary Ann's words echoed in my head.

*Never show your fear, for you know in all the fairy tales the fierce wolves always sniff out the gentle ladies.*

Now the study door was shut, but I needed to get inside. To find more news of Izzie.

I tried my front door key in his lock, but it would not budge.

I searched the hooks next to the back door. All the keys were gone. On the nearby wall, another row held scarves and aprons. I shook them all until I spied the sack of clothes pegs hanging low on the scullery wall. A spare bunch of house keys glinted inside.

I tried three keys before finding the right one.

Henry's study door opened with a crisp click. I drew a deep breath.

This was forbidden territory. Henry's hallowed sanctuary.

When I stepped inside, the faint scent of his lemon shaving soap gave me a start. It seemed as if he'd stepped out of the room just seconds ago to find a pen or pamphlet and would swoop back in at any moment. I waited and listened but could hear only the rushing of wind down the parlour chimney and the ticking of the grandfather clock in the hallway. Tiny hairs prickled on the back of my neck and I dared to glance behind me, imagining I heard the scuffing of feet across the tiles. But not a soul stood there. Only a rainbow of light played on the walls: a reflection of the sun through the stained-glass window on the front door.

I sorted through the papers and envelopes stacked on Henry's desk until I spied Buckley's name on a note attached to a playbill for a London theatre which read:

*Such a wonderful evening. Emma and I look forward to many more such outings.*

Strange. I hadn't realised Henry and Buckley had spent time together in London. Yet it seemed reasonable that Henry could have learned about his new position if Buckley had been down south, visiting Henry's college.

I replaced the playbill and note and shuffled through the papers.

Nothing but formulae scrawled across the pages of notebooks.

A bookshelf crammed with academic texts revealed dry mathematical treatises and textbooks. The drawers of a battered mahogany bureau were filled with pencils, letter openers, and bottles of ink, but a lever behind the rolltop cover revealed a sheaf of envelopes addressed to Izzie in my own handwriting.

The letters I had written from Hoxton, all cleanly sliced open with a letter opener. Intercepted by Mrs Parsons and scrutinised, no doubt, by Henry. I sorted through them, realising not one of my letters had reached Izzie.

Henry had held back my letters and was lying to me about sending them.

Just then the grandfather clock struck the half hour. I had to leave now if I was to get to the prison as I'd promised. I stuffed the letters back into the small compartment and pulled down the rolltop cover. After making sure everything was in its place, I locked the door and placed the keys back in the peg bag. But all the whilst my mind turned over and over, wondering if Izzie was worse or if—Heaven forbid—she had died and Henry was keeping it from me.

I posted my letter to Izzie, saying a silent prayer that she had somehow made a miraculous recovery and was sitting in her garden enjoying the sunshine. Feeling somewhat calmer, I made my way to the prison, thankful for the distraction of a morning spent there, but I was forced to sit and wait at Mr Boxted's desk for half an hour before they'd let me in further.

Mrs Callahan swept by me without speaking, her face white as a sheet.

"Is something amiss?" I asked Mr Boxted.

"One of the women has gone over the edge. Raging and taking headers against her cell wall and smashing the furniture up. We have to make sure she doesn't tear the gas pipes down or we'll all be in trouble."

When they finally let me through, I passed Mrs Callahan and two other male warders standing outside Viola's cell, the prisoner I'd only recently visited. One of the warders held a rough grey canvas garment with straps and buckles on the sleeves. *A strong dress.* A tide of panic froze me to the core, for I, too, had felt its roughness chafe my skin, had suffocated as they bound me tight and left me in solitary confinement.

Viola was propped up against the cell wall, her ragged head lolling like a puppet's. In an instant, Mrs Callahan and the two men sprang inside, rolled her onto her back, then slipped on the straitjacket. And whilst she sobbed and howled, the pounding on the other cell doors grew louder as wild cheers from the prisoners echoed to the ceiling. The warders set the mattress straight and placed her onto it as Mrs Callahan swooped out of the cell, raced along the rows, and smashed her stout club on the doors.

"Show's over. Back to work or no supper tonight!" she shouted, and the banging ceased.

Miss Honeywell passed by, a broom and bucket in her hand. "Move along, Mrs Blackstone. We have a cleanup to do and you don't want to get under Mrs Callahan's feet after this ruckus."

"What happened to Viola?" I called after her.

She stopped and turned to me. "It's the cottage. Her old master gave it to his maiden aunt."

My ears rang from all the chaos, but I hurried on, anxious to push aside the tragedy of Viola's absolute destruction and get to Mary Ann's cell.

Bertha stopped me in the corridor, her mouth set in a tight line.

"Mary Ann was fretting something terrible when you didn't arrive at nine o'clock this morning."

"It couldn't be avoided. I was late leaving the house and had to post a letter."

"Only, and you'll excuse me saying this, Mrs Blackstone, I'd urge you not to get too close to her or make any promises you can't keep. That woman's in a desperate state. Like a drowning woman swept away by a tidal wave, she's liable to grasp at any poor soul that comes along, to stop herself from going under. She'll drag you down with her, if you know what I mean."

"I promise to be mindful," I said, feeling a nagging sense of unease, for when I last spoke to Mary Ann, I'd felt as if I stood on the precipice of some great unseen danger. "How is she today?"

Bertha shook her head. "Very unhappy. You should know they've exhumed the body of Joseph Nattrass, another of her supposed victims."

"Was Nattrass her husband?"

"As good as," Bertha muttered. "Some say she took up with him after William Mowbray, her first husband, died. Then she moved him into her house after Fred Cotton, her fourth husband, passed. She claimed she nursed Nattrass until his last breath."

# 16

MARY ANN STOOD by the window, silhouetted against a dull sky the colour of wet clay. The soft swell of her belly appeared jarringly at odds with the cold stone walls and rigid iron bars.

"They tell me the authorities have dug up Nattrass," she said with a long, shuddering sigh. "So now they canna leave the dead to sleep in peace."

She turned towards me, the grey light throwing her face into sharp relief—the hollow, burning eyes, the deep ridges etched from her nose to her mouth.

"You're two hours late," she said, her voice razor-sharp.

A rush of panic caught in my throat. "I was delayed in the other wing. One of the women ransacked her cell in a rage and the warders wouldn't let me through."

She shuffled towards her bed, shaking her head. "Brainless sluts with no sense of dignity. Many a night I've imagined myself dashing my brains out against that wall when the darkness closes in like death and the madness comes like an itch you canna scratch. But I'll never give them the satisfaction to see me grovel like a beggar. I'd tell that girl to keep her eyes wide-open and stare down the darkness as if she were its equal."

I followed her to my usual place on the wooden stool. "She must be in a desperate way to harm herself like that."

"Dinna waste your breath on riffraff, Clara. They're undeserving of your time. The minute them frowsy baggages leave the prison gates, they'll be back in the shops with their thieving fingers on some worthless bauble. You must come straight to see me. I'm an innocent woman. I never took anything that wasn't rightly mine."

She settled herself on the bed, fidgeting with her shawl until her eyes snapped upwards, locking me into her gaze. "If you'd got here a few minutes later, they would have sent me out for my exercise. Then you would have missed me."

"My life is somewhat complicated at present," I mumbled.

"You took care of your laudanum troubles, then?"

"I did."

"I thought so. You seem more sharp today, though I sense something's weighing heavy on you. Tell Mary Ann about it, pet. Mebbe I can help."

I swallowed and glanced behind me. The door was shut, the wardresses drinking tea in the next room. "They canna hear you. You might just as well be reading from the Holy Bible for all they care. Speak up."

I took a deep breath. "My grandmother is sick. I'm worried for her."

"Then mebbe you should be tending to her instead of sitting here with me."

"She's far away—in India," I said, shaking my head.

She placed her hands over her belly. "Well, all you can do is say your prayers, pet. The Lord might answer. Though I canna fathom why such bad luck always comes my way when I pray every night for the souls of my dear departed children *and* my first husband, Fred." She patted the hump of her belly again. "I'm certain God will not send an innocent woman and mother to the gallows. Though only the Lord knows what he has in store for me."

My eyes were drawn to her belly and the way she caressed it so protectively. *The child is her insurance*, I realised. *Her protection*. Whilst it lived inside her, she was a mother, not a murderer.

She leaned close to me, cupped a hand to the side of her mouth, and whispered, "You know, the religious men come every day and try to make me confess—breathe their fusty breath all over me and beg me to lie. But I send them all away. A pack of fools, the lot of them. I'll tell you summat, in my time working at the Sunderland Infirmary, I've seen some odd men of the cloth. I remember one old vicar with a bad case of pneumonia. Seems he'd decided he had a calling as a priest *and* a mermaid. He'd made a wig out of seaweed, stripped himself naked save for an oilskin round his legs, rowed out from the beach at South Shields, and sat out on the big rock near Marsden Grotto, singing his heart out until he fell in the water and caught his death of cold."

I couldn't hold back a smile. "That can't be true."

"Not a word of a lie. I heard he spent the rest of his days wandering around the rectory in his dressing gown until the pleurisy took him. Now, have yer brought me something other than kind words and confidences?"

The sudden sharpness of her question brought me back to the dank light of the cell and its cold, confining walls. How easily her mood changed. I quickly rummaged through my bag and produced a packet of barley sugars, some shortbread biscuits, and a packet of tea leaves.

She gathered them onto her lap. "Well, that won't fetch me a fancy lawyer, but I'll enjoy them all the same. We'll have the biscuits with a cup of tea. Of course, I would've preferred a bit of fruitcake. I got in a good piece for the neighbours when young Frederick Cotton's laying out was done. I liked everything to be nice. Had clean linens and white stockings ready for Nattrass when he passed. Every bairn got a new nightdress when it drew its last breath. Like little angels, they were—all laid out in snowy white. Treat the dead with respect, I say. What else can you do for them?"

"The doctors showed no respect for my child. I never held my baby. Never knew if it was a boy or a girl. They threw its little body away whilst I was unconscious under the ether." I covered my eyes for a few moments whilst Mary Ann chewed at the shortbread. She waited for me to collect myself, regarding me with an impassive expression. But no matter how deeply I looked into her eyes, I could see nothing. Only emptiness.

"Well, that's a heartless and cruel way to treat a stillborn baby," she said, wiping a hand over her mouth. "Mebbe it were ill-formed in some way."

I remembered Henry's eyes, like dark tunnels in the livid white of his face.

"Mind you, Clara, a bairn canna help the way it comes into the world and even if it's a cretin, it still deserves some kindness. Is that why your husband gave you the laudanum?"

"It's more complicated than that," I said, dropping my gaze to the grimy cracks etched into the stone floor.

"Well, you'll tell me sooner or later. When the secret is too heavy to hold on to. But I'll tell you again, Clara—he had no business giving it to you, though I'm not surprised. Most men have no sense. They're like arses, best out of sight."

I tried to smile at her bluntness.

We sat in silence whilst she finished another biscuit and brushed the crumbs from her lap. Finally she folded her arms and rested them on her belly. "Well, as they say, it's all in God's hands. Even the wealthy are not spared when it comes to losing bairns. But the poor. Their lives are built on suffering. I've had twelve of my own bairns and only two survived, and they live with Robinson, their scoundrel father. Truth is, the poor have no time to grieve. Their babies die of disease and starvation every day. When Mowbray and me came back from Cornwall, I couldn't escape the greedy clutches of death. My poor, dear Margaret Jane sickened and died. The doctors said it was gastric fever. But I say different. That bairn was forever running about with no shoes on. I say she caught a cold and ate too many eggs. We buried her at South Hetton church and only Isabella was left."

"How could you endure so much sorrow? After losing all those children?"

"Why, Clara, I just had more. I had no choice. A year after that, I had another girl. I named her Margaret Jane in memory of the first and then I had my boy, John Robert. We moved to Sunderland. That's when William went to sea with my uncle John, a master on a steamer. But within the year my dear little John died. I buried him in the Holy Trinity churchyard. I remember that day so clearly. We stood by the graveside wi' the rain hoying down in buckets. The two little girls clung to my legs whilst I shook from head to toe with sorrow. I cried so hard, I couldn't tell the tears from the rain."

She began to rock, her arms wrapped tightly around her chest. "Twelve years. That's the time me and William Mowbray had together, and death took him next. At first it were only a bad foot, but he were worse than a lame horse—couldn't do a stitch of work. Then he caught the typhus. The doctor told me he'd die within the week. He was not a strong man but a gentle one, and he suffered. High fever, confusion, delirious most of the time. He were a brave lad, and struggled on, but he was no match for death. The papers say I murdered him, too, but

I have the death certificate, signed by the doctor. Typhus took him. Not me. You see, Clara, how they twist the truth?"

I thought of how the newspaper had laid the blame for up to twenty deaths at her hands, and how easy it would be to fall back on rumours and stories that might be nothing more than idle gossip. And yet so many people had died under her care. How could I believe this woman whose mood changed as quickly as the wind, pulling me back and forth until I lost all sense of reality?

"See, now you start to question all those scandalous stories. Written by folk who know nowt—only what gossip they can gather from nosey old mares that never had a good word for me. They didn't see how I was at the end of my tether. Dr Gammage, who attended William, said himself he'd rarely seen such distress in a widow. I could not eat nor drink for days. The angel of death had its wings spread over me like a black and terrible cloud, taking Margaret Jane next with the gastric fever."

"How could you keep going?"

"I did what I had to. I took the insurance money, left Isabella at my mam's, and went to work at Sunderland Infirmary. How else was I to live? A woman has no choice but to struggle on. If there's no man to help her, she must do it alone."

"Weren't you ever afraid?"

"I had no time for fear. I just carried on alone until I met George Ward, a patient at the infirmary. He seemed a respectable, healthy man. Turns out I was wrong. He fell sick and I nursed him for weeks. He was unconscious for five days before he died and were only thirty-three when he passed away in his sleep. Skin and bone he was, and so thin that I could carry him from his bed in my own arms. Dr Evans certified the death and said it was cholera and typhus that struck him down. And now the papers say I killed him, too. They have no idea of the pestilence that creeps through Sunderland like a plague. But Clara. You've got money. A nice house, most likely. Have another bairn and forget the heartache. That's what sensible people of means do."

I was just set to answer when the door creaked open and Miss Thompson came in. "It's time for your exercise, Mary Ann."

"All right. If I must." She sighed. "Mrs Blackstone and me were just having a good natter."

"Say your goodbyes and I'll be waiting outside," the wardress said, turning to leave.

Mary Ann's hand darted out and clasped mine, giving me a terrible start. In the half-light, her fingers appeared maggoty-white. I held my breath.

A faint smirk flickered across her lips. "It's no wonder that man of yours has the upper hand. You're like a timid mouse jumping at the slightest noise," she said.

I pulled my hand away, my heart racing.

"Losing a bairn is common as losing a tooth, Clara. Don't take on so. Just carry on and have another one and you'll soon forget about the one you lost. And I'll make sure to pray for your grandma, but don't be late next time."

"I won't. What shall I bring you?"

"A black-hearted bugger like your husband probably holds the purse strings tight, so I suppose you're poor as a tinker. Bring some writing paper and a pen, for the women that look after me here are daft as floor mops. They canna write a decent sentence. I'm in need of a lawyer and the only way I'll get one is to advertise for one in the newspaper."

# 17

"I FEAR WE are entering a time of escalating decadence, Henry," said Buckley, biting into the crust of an almond tart. He chewed for a minute, searching the ceiling for further inspiration. "An unprecedented rise in the numbers of undeserving poor has resulted in a plague of crime and degeneracy. The ruffian's boot is marching even here into our fair city of Durham, though it is far worse in the slums of Gateshead and Sunderland. Why, there they are drinking, copulating, and reproducing in overcrowded tenements a dog would refuse to lie in."

He paused to bite off another mouthful of pastry. We were sitting in the parlour, the blazing fire reflected in the silver surface of the teapot. Outside, a mist had fallen, scattering the light from the streetlamp into a dim halo. I thought of Mary Ann sitting by her bed, praying for Izzie, and as I watched Buckley's plump, flapping lips, I was reminded of a great codfish swimming around that mermaid priest with the seaweed hair and oilcloth tail. I put my napkin to my mouth and feigned a cough to stop myself from laughing aloud as he continued.

"One has only to look at the burgeoning numbers of public houses and gin palaces on every street corner. I read that there are almost five hundred public houses in Sunderland and no fewer than one hundred of them in the area that spans from the foot of High Street to Sans Street. The authorities were forced to issue orders for police officers not to drink in a pub whilst in uniform. The result of all this intemperance? Immorality and decadence. Soon we who have ascended into a higher order of humanity will be overwhelmed by ever-increasing masses of drunken degenerates and criminals."

"But what is the remedy?" asked Henry, perching on the edge of his chair, eagerly digesting the impromptu sermon. Now his eyes shone with relish at every nugget of wisdom Buckley spat his way.

*Henry is weak,* said the small voice in my head. *Like a lamb being led towards the butcher's knife. And I had once thought him earnest and ambitious—driven by a desire to excel. Now I see a gullible, malleable man. A minion, fawning to his betters.*

My mind snapped back to Buckley's voice, droning on in the background. "Why, if the underclasses encroach any further on us, no respectable woman will dare to venture out alone."

"Well, I for one am quite happy to stay at home, Donald," chirped Emma, reaching for a chocolate éclair.

Buckley chewed at his tart whilst regarding his wife. They had wolfish appetites, the two of them—masticating their food with well-honed jaws, whilst their eyelids drooped with the pleasure of the whipped cream and chocolate.

"Not surprising," said Buckley, finally mopping his lips with a napkin. "As Darwin says, women are fashioned by evolution for maternity and the home."

Henry glanced over at me, his eyes twitching. "But Clara has been going out alone almost every day since she arrived here. Perhaps that is not advisable."

I swallowed some tea. "Only to do good work, Henry. To share words of faith with the unfortunates at the jail. I told you—some are barely more than children."

Henry appeared not to have heard me as he regarded the remains of his finger sandwich. "And yet these ox tongue sandwiches are very tasty, Clara."

"Though I do hear," said Buckley, brushing aside Henry's words, "that these days even the butcher must be watched for dishonesty. Apparently they've stooped to adding large wedges of fat underneath the meat to raise the weight and cheat the customer of their hard-earned money."

And so the dull voices buzzed around me until they became one monotonous droning sound.

I smiled sweetly to the company and poured more tea.

Later, when Henry took Buckley into his study, Emma tried to make conversation.

"In light of what Donald was saying, you might try gentler pursuits like sewing or knitting, Clara. Perfect for calming the most troubled souls."

I balled my fists until the nails dug into my palms whilst Emma continued, oblivious. "I was so clever with embroidery when I was a girl." She sighed. "Now I can barely tell one end of the needle from the other, and my fingers have become so stiff."

"I prefer to paint," I replied.

Emma continued to chat endlessly about the weather, her garden, her servants, and her daughter, Amy, who was soon to return from Europe. All the whilst my mind kept drifting back to the prison and the mind-numbing monotony of the oakum-picking and rag-tearing, mechanical tasks meant to quell the passions of the female prisoners. To occupy their days and wear them down into blind subservience. Only then would the authorities let them out in the hope that they'd fit back into their place like cogs in a machine. Now Henry was trying to dull my senses into obedience until I fit in neatly with all the other wives.

Emma took a pamphlet from her reticule and waved it at me. My mind snapped away from thoughts of the prison.

"I know you are struggling to find your place here and be a good wife to Henry, so Donald felt you might benefit from reading this particular article," she said, putting on gold-rimmed spectacles. "It is written by the excellent Mrs Linton. I will read you an excerpt." She took a deep breath and held up the booklet. "'The ideal on which marriage is founded is love, and no true-hearted woman that ever lived, who loves her husband, desires anything but submission. If she loves, she desires her husband to be greater than herself, and she believes him to be so.'"

Glowing with triumph, she put down the paper. "If you can only take those words to heart, Clara, your home will be a place of harmony and peace."

I swallowed my distaste. Buckley had trained her well. "Most illuminating, Emma. I thank you for your kindness."

"Keep it, dear, and think on it," she said, handing me the hateful pamphlet. Unable to bear her toadying voice, I excused myself to the kitchen, but hesitated near Henry's study by the half-open door when I heard the guarded tone of Buckley's voice.

"I should say that the majority of respectable women, happily for them, are not very much troubled with sexual feelings of any kind, Henry. In fact, the best mothers, wives, and managers of households know little or nothing of sexual indulgence. Love of home, children, and domestic duties are the only passions they feel."

A pregnant silence followed as Henry cleared his throat. "But what of men and their desires—that is, if—if they encounter, er, certain difficulties," Henry stammered.

"One incident of failure might be enough to annihilate a man's sexual feelings, but you must know, as a general rule, that a modest woman seldom desires any sexual gratification for herself. She submits to her husband to please him and gives up her own wishes and feelings—save her maternal yearnings—for his sake. Have confidence, Henry. Clara should willingly perform her wifely duties if you take charge. And the sooner, the better."

A creak of Henry's chair sent me scuttling towards the kitchen, where the heat from the fire crept like a hot glove around my throat. I struggled to unfasten the top button of my dress, unsettled by the distant memory of Henry's naked chest with its dusting of red hair, the shadowy indentations of his ribs, and the sharp but stale tang of sweat as his thin arms folded around me, pressing me down onto the mattress.

That night, the rain lashed against the windows. I lay in bed watching ribbons of water stream down the panes until I heard the floorboards creak behind the door.

I heard soft breathing and my body went cold.

The handle turned, the door swung open, and Henry stood like a ghost in his long white nightshirt. "Are you awake, Clara?"

My tongue was paralyzed.

*Just lie still,* said the quiet voice that had spoken to me in the marble bathroom at Hoxton. *Lie still and it will soon be over. Cast your mind to some other place.*

By now he was at the bedside removing his slippers. The candle sputtered, throwing twisted shapes on the walls as he grasped the corner of the blankets, pulled them back, and climbed in beside me.

"You must be lonely here in your bed," he whispered. His dry lips grazed my cheek, whilst his fingers groped under the sheets for the hem of my nightdress. I felt a sudden draught as he hitched the petticoat up to my waist, his cold fingers paddling at the insides of my thighs.

Now another voice screamed in my head—the wild voice that had urged me to kick and bite and strike out with a scalpel.

*He locked you away for the better part of a year; he let them torture you with primitive cures. He withheld your letters from the only person who loves you.*

"I will be gentle, Clara," he mumbled as he climbed on top of my rigid body and flapped up his nightshirt. A waft of dried sweat and lemons made me turn my head away to look out at the tree scratching against the window. I clenched every muscle in my limbs as he shifted and pressed on my belly, his bony knees bruising my hips as he spread my legs wide then jostled for position. Jerking my arms upwards, he pinned them down and seemed to rear above me, his face twisted, his mouth hanging open as he grunted and thrust until he fell like a dead weight, crushing the breath from me. I prayed that I would leave my body so I could feel nothing, but just as my mind began to float on a featureless plain, he cursed and rolled himself off.

"Dammit—it's no good," he said, sliding off the bed and pulling himself upright. "Your indifference prevents me."

I clutched the sheets to my chin, the nausea rising in my throat as he bent over me.

"Have you nothing to say, Clara?"

I bit my lip. "Perhaps in time."

His face creased with anger. "How much time? The degeneracy is in your blood, Clara. You couldn't even bear a healthy, well-formed child. I should have known you were tainted from the start."

The candle sputtered and died as he swept out from the room, leaving me in complete darkness, a faint spiral of smoke still hanging in the air.

# BOULOGNE-SUR-MER

## SPRING 1873

BOULOGNE-VILLE IS A pretty, grey-roofed station built of cream and yellow brick, its windows trimmed with fresh white shutters. We stream down the gangplank of the ferry, a festive parade of travellers dressed in straw hats and bright cotton dresses and carrying light parasols. Gusts of warm sea air send my bonnet ribbons fluttering as I cross by clusters of white-hooded local women holding baskets of fish, through to the bustling terminal and the platform where the Marseille train waits.

My good humour is marred only by the knowledge that I must don widow's black again.

On the crossing over from Folkestone, a tiresome little man latched on to me. Bluff and hearty with a puff of pomaded brown hair, thick muttonchop whiskers, and a laugh as tuneless as a donkey's bray, he persisted in shadowing me on my walks around the deck to *protect me from the uninvited attentions of dishonourable fellows* and to shield me from the sight of those stricken with seasickness as they hung over the ship's railings and vomited into the wind, or lay writhing on the deck moaning that they were at death's door.

Halfway through our crossing, a broad-shouldered matron in tartan wool mantle and tam o' shanter bustled over and took my arm, ushering me towards the tearoom, where her dalmatian lay sleeping, tethered to the leg of a heavy leather sofa.

"You are fair game for all such scurrilous characters, my dear. They believe you to be one of the fishing fleet. Young single women sent out to India with the sole purpose of making a good match."

So I am forced to purchase another mourning dress, from an intimate little shop near the station. But its playful French stylishness delights me—the pretty ruched mantilla hat with a veil that drapes the chin and fastens with a flower-trimmed bow, the tailored black grenadine dress with its lace-edged bustle and organza neck ruffle. Faced with unwanted male solicitations, I will simply unpin a cunning little rose clip and *pull down the curtains* so that I may concentrate on my readings.

I settle myself into my carriage and take out the books I picked up in London. On this journey I mean to educate myself. Talking to Mary Ann opened my eyes to the harsh realities of a woman's life, and now I will read the scholars: Harriet Martineau, Mary Wollstonecraft, and John Stuart Mill. I have Mill's book, *The Subjection of Women.* I hear he died only a few weeks ago, so in a sense I am in mourning for this good and wise man. I have already marked many pages of his treatise as having particular significance. His words sing to me with such clarity and logic.

> *The wife is the actual bondservant of her husband: no less so, as far as legal obligation goes, than slaves commonly so called. She vows a livelong obedience to him at the altar,*

> *and is held to it all through her life by law. . . . She can do no act whatever but by his permission, at least tacit. She can acquire no property but for him; the instant it becomes hers, even if by inheritance, it becomes ipso facto his. In this respect the wife's position under the common law of England is worse than that of slaves in the laws of many countries.*

I find myself scrutinising the faces of the young women who wander by my window to board the train. How many of them are out here fishing for a husband? Passed over by eligible bachelors at home, they undertake such a gruelling journey with the sole purpose of securing a good marriage. I should warn them of its perils and pitfalls. Show them Mr Mill's pamphlet. But the young and headstrong will never listen. Izzie certainly tried her best with me.

The night Henry tried to force himself on me, I swear I heard her voice in the stillness.

*I raised you to have your own mind, Clara. Why have you fallen so quickly under the spell of the first young man to pay you some attention? And there is a hunger burning in Henry's soul. A hunger for material possessions.*

Blinded by his attentiveness, I dismissed her wise words.

Now, closing my eyes, I will myself back to her house. To the Blue Room, with its aqua-coloured walls, grey silk curtains, and the crystal chandelier that sparkled like frozen teardrops.

That room was always alive with music and conversation. Filled with young singers, musicians, and dancers dressed in bright silks and prints like the colours in a summer garden. The night I met Henry, I wore an ocean-blue dress. I stood by the piano to recite a poem, but the intense young man in the threadbare black jacket distracted me. Perhaps it was the way he laced his fingers together, tapping their tips on his knuckles as if impatient to burst out of his genteel surroundings. Perhaps it was the way he stared at me with unflinching adoration.

I stumbled over my lines—felt a slow heat warming my face.

Afterwards I drifted around the company, listening to idle scraps of gossip.

*I hear he's far from well-off, but quite a brilliant mathematician and a junior professor at King's College.*

*Obviously used to keeping humbler company.*

*A kind man. He brought his cousin Ava, a budding cellist. I hear she's consumptive.*

Later he approached me. "A sincere and heartfelt recitation," he said. Ava was transported to the caves of ice with Kubla Khan.

He began to call on me daily. We read the newspapers together. He'd scan the financial section and the vast charts and columns of antlike figures littered across the pages. "Though stocks and bonds can be unpredictable," he said, "there is something comforting in the strict rules that govern numbers, and those who have a true understanding of these laws hold power that others can only dream of." At those times, his eyes gleamed with the fever of grand future dreams.

"Henry finds beauty in the most unexpected places," I told Izzie. "He says nature is governed by mathematical laws."

"Just remember, Clara, never surrender your own free will and bend to someone else's," she replied.

Henry proposed to me in the morning room. He grasped his gloves and leaned towards me, the tips of his ears glowing scarlet. "My dearest Clara, though I cannot offer you the finery and wealth you are accustomed to, I offer you the treasures of my intellect, my love, my guidance, and my protection."

Then he handed me a basket of rose petals with a silver locket buried amongst them. Inside the locket were our hand-painted portraits. “A token of my undying love,” he said.

When I told Izzie, I thought she’d embrace me with joy. Instead tears glistened in her eyes.

“Take your time and do not be impulsive,” she whispered. “You will inherit a significant fortune one day and money can make an opportunist out of the most steadfast person, especially one driven by ambitions of wealth.”

I refused to listen.

We were married at the small country church near Izzie’s home, its pathway bordered with early summer roses. Storm clouds billowed across the sky, but the rain held off until we were inside.

Henry’s shy cousin and soberly dressed parents were the only guests from his family, whilst the pews on the other side of the church were filled with Izzie’s wealthy friends and a restless crowd of bohemian artists. Later my new mother- and father-in-law gawked at the lavish wedding breakfast, at the trays of chilled lobster and French duck pâté that Mrs Adeline Blackstone passed over with a wrinkled nose as if sniffing piles of cow dung.

“Fancy food does not sit well with us,” she barked. “Hubert and I are people of simple tastes and prefer the modest ploughman’s fare.”

I overheard Henry’s father’s caustic comments to his son. *A scandalous crowd of pretentious sluts, fops, and nancy-boy artists.*

But it was too late to turn back.

Now, watching the sunshine play over the weathered timbers of a sleeping French village, I think of Mr Mill’s assertion that oppression of women is one of the few remaining relics from ancient times and we, as humans, will never progress until we erase it.

Mary Ann had never read his works, but she had the measure of his meaning when she talked about marriage, and in her own strange and twisted way she brought me to an understanding of my own wretched situation. To the sad realisation that my marriage was nothing more than a business arrangement, one that my husband hoped would eventually reap handsome financial profits.

# 18

THE NIGHT AFTER Henry came to my room, I hurried to the prison, realising I had nowhere else to go. No person to listen to my troubles except an accused murderer, but I'd just spent eight months in a madhouse, so it wasn't surprising that I was drawn to society's misfits. I laughed aloud at the thought, attracting stern glares from two elderly ladies pushing an ancient man in a wicker wheelchair. They stopped to watch me as I hurried along the street, paying no mind to their disapproval.

A different wardress was on duty at Mary Ann's cell. A younger, plump woman with bright auburn hair who introduced herself as Mrs Falks.

Her face was slick with sweat as she wiped her forehead with a handkerchief.

"She's in quite a state this morning. She's expecting a visit from her old lodger, Lowry. Seems Smith, her lawyer, forced him to hand over every scrap of her furniture and clothing—even the sheets from the bed—and now he's run off with every penny he could raise from pawning her few bits and pieces. Now he refuses to help her anymore."

I clasped my Bible to my breast. "I'm a regular visitor here. I come to offer her guidance and support, which will benefit her unborn baby."

She placed both hands on her ample hips. "Then you wouldn't be the first to show concern for the innocent mite. The prison authorities are up to their ears in letters from do-gooders keen to step in should the hangman orphan the poor bairn. One o' them's even a Bishop Auckland judge. You should see the parcels of baby clothes they've sent. You could clothe a whole street of bairns with them. And the religious folk flock here like a plague of locusts. Why, there's enough prayer books here to stock a chapel." She threw her head back and laughed so hard, her eyes watered. "They all beg her to confess her sins to God, but she sends them packing. Oh, aye, we've got the Queen of Sheba in there. Pure as the driven snow and full of her own importance."

When she opened the cell door, I heard a low moaning sound.

"The baby is a big'un and makes her poorly. It's due in a few weeks," Mrs Falks explained.

The air was murky with dried sweat and musty clothing. Mary Ann lay on the bed, her face to the wall.

Mrs Falks tapped her on the shoulder and she stirred. "Yer have a visitor, Mary Ann."

"Is it that thief, Smith?" said the weak, reedy voice. "Or is it Chapman? I must tell him off and send him packing with his tail between his legs."

"Why no, lass—it's a kind lady visitor just come to pass some time with you."

"Is it Mrs Blackstone? Clara?"

She sat up, rubbing her swollen belly, then bowed her head and began to rock and moan in a plaintive, childish voice, stopping only to turn her eyes towards me as if to gauge the extent of my pity for her. My breath caught in my throat at the sour expression on her face. "If you have a spark of kindness in your body, you'll know that I'm as innocent as this unborn child. I never poisoned that boy."

"You know you're not to speak of that, Mary Ann," said Mrs Falks. "Especially in front of strangers."

"Clara is no stranger," said Mary Ann, fixing her dark eyes on me. "Are yer, pet?"

My skin prickled at the chill in her voice that contradicted the intimacy of her words. "No, I'm not," I whispered.

Mrs Falks wasn't to be put off. "All the same, you know the rules. You'll get your say in court."

"Aye, but I'll still need someone to speak for me and now that Smith's buggered off with everything but the bloody poss stick, I'll be lucky to find a decent lawyer."

"Watch your mouth, Mary Ann. Don't swear in front of a lady," said Mrs Falks, wagging a finger.

I raised my hand to appease her. "I've heard worse. You may leave us now. I'll talk with her."

She left and pulled the door shut, glancing in through the little opening before locking it.

"So what shall we talk about, Mary Ann?" I said, taking the Bible from my bag.

"Yer can put that bloody thing away for a start. I've had my fill of the good word today and it's done nowt to get me out of here. Let's talk about what's eatin' at you, Clara. I see you're troubled. Your eyes are wild and your mouth is sulky."

A memory flashed across my mind—Henry's body crushing mine, his hot breath dampening my skin, his blunt fingers creeping up my leg. I bit down hard and fast on my lip. "I cannot talk about it."

"Then shall we talk about the weather?" she said in a haughty tone, arranging the shawl on her shoulders as if it were a velvet evening cape.

I shifted myself on the stool, every nerve in my body on edge. "You wish to make polite chitchat?"

She glanced up at me. "Why no! I expect you'll get plenty of that empty blather at your fancy ladies' tea parties."

I grimaced. "Polite conversation is so dull, it makes my teeth ache."

She chuckled and winked at me. "Then I have a mind to talk about men."

I thought of Henry's dry lips brushing my neck, his lies and false accusations. "Must we?"

"Summat's bothering you today, Clara. You can tell Mary Ann about it," she crooned.

"Answer me this first—did you love your husbands?"

She shifted her feet and arranged her grey skirts around her legs. "Love, that's for the young and soft-headed. And marriage, it's worse than a jail sentence. It's hard labour. Slavery. Penal servitude. But you do it because you must. How else can a woman survive?"

I gazed at the fire, my heart close to bursting with regret. "Before we were married, my husband gave me a locket with our portraits inside. He said I was a precious flower and he'd love me forever. Like a romantic fool, I believed him."

"And now?" she asked, chewing at her fingernail.

"Now he deceives me and lies to me," I said, my voice faltering, but I could not cry in front of her.

She shook her head and wagged a finger in the air. "Clara, Clara. When will you learn? All that fancy love talk is nowt but a story men make up to get summat from you. Tek it from me. I'm an expert when it comes to men, and I'll tell you for certain—there's only one thing drives a man and yer'll find it right between his legs. They've got their brains in their galluses. Right from the lowly pit labourers to the posh gents who come slumming around the colliery villages lusting for young lasses and running after poor girls of no more than fourteen. And I've seen those same wealthy gents marry a woman that's plain as a pikestaff to get their hands on her money."

*I should have run away at the wedding and gone to India with Izzie,* I thought, digging my nails into the soft flesh of my palms.

Marriage had been the only option for Mary Ann. Her survival depended on it. But I'd blithely cast away my freedom and married Henry without a thought for the consequences. How could I have been such a fool?

She tapped my hand. "Don't tek on so, Clara. Women are different. They still believe in love. When I was a young lass full of fancies, I thought I loved Joe Nattrass. I remember the first time I saw him on the beach at Seaham—a fine, handsome fellow with such a swagger in his walk. He had an eye for the ladies, but he always came back to me, for back then I was still young and comely. He said my eyes were dark as the coal glittering under the pitman's lamp. Said he could lose himself in them. That man had a lovely way wi' words. And what a lover he was. A real stallion."

A giggle tickled my throat and I covered my mouth to stifle it.

"I believe I've scandalised you, Clara."

"I'm a married woman, Mary Ann."

"Ha! Doesn't mean you know anything about real passion. Most proper ladies spread their legs, fix their eyes on the ceiling, and do their wifely duty whilst the old man grunts like a winded hog on top of them." She grinned and leaned so close,

I saw the coarse grey strands that silvered her dark hair. "But a woman has needs, too, Clara. Even though most of 'em won't admit it. Proper ladies keep their feelings all bottled up until it chokes them. Well, I never settled for that. I made sure I got my needs met in the doings that went on under the sheets. Even when my husband Mowbray were away, I had Nattrass at the back of the coal shed. Fucked him good and hard and took pleasure in it."

She pulled away, her dark eyes gleaming. "I've run my hands over many a fine man's naked body and felt my insides shiver at the joy of it. There's nowt like it. And no man was ever my master. They gave in to my needs and were bound to me forever. Until death took them away from me."

Her eyes blazed with a terrible power as she sat back in her chair and licked her lips. I imagined her head thrown back in the throes of passion. Two bodies in a cluttered attic bedroom, rearing and bucking like rutting animals.

"It's warm in here," I whispered. A sick, dizzy feeling swept over me as I thought of the candlelight flickering in Henry's eyes.

"Yer going to faint, are yer? That's what all the fine ladies do when their passions get the best of them. But I'll give you some advice, Clara. If your husband's good for nothing, move on and find another. That man of yours. Mebbe he's the one that canna father healthy bairns. Find yersel' a real man. There's plenty of them in the mining villages if yer don't mind slumming it a bit. They'd be happy to oblige a comely looking woman like you."

The door creaked open and Mrs Falks strode back into the cell. She took one look at me and planted her hands on her hips.

"Eeh, what've you been up to, Mary Ann? Mrs Blackstone looks like she could crawl under the table with embarrassment."

"Why, nothing, Mrs Falks. Clara were just saying how the weather's turned cold."

"A likely story," said the wardress, shaking her head. "First time I saw a fine lady discomfited by the good book."

Mary Ann gave her a sideways glance. "Don't you know your Bible, Mrs Falks? Why, there's parts of the Old Testament would make your hair curl."

Mrs Falks snorted and swept out. I turned back to Mary Ann, but the moment of intimacy had passed. She gazed into the fire, a faraway look in her eyes.

"Joe Nattrass fancied me the moment he saw me. And I felt the same. Mebbe things would've been different if we'd stayed together, but it turned out he was just like all the other brainless arseholes. Found himself a young girl never been bedded. Bloody hypocrite thought I was all used up. And that's another thing, Clara. Better watch out or your man will be seeking a younger girl. Someone new and fresher than his poor, suffering wife."

She shook her head slowly, rocking back and forth until her eyelids drooped. Soon I heard the faint rasp of her snoring and rose to take my leave. My skirt swished against hers and as I turned to go, she called out to me, her eyes half-closed.

"I told you, Clara. Look your enemies square in the eye. Face them without fear and never show your weakness or it'll be the end of you, pet. They'll squash you like a common housefly. Promise me you'll take heed."

"I promise."

"And one more thing," she hissed, her eyes snapping open so wide, I stumbled back against the stool. "I don't need empty pity, hinny. I need money to get a proper lawyer. Do you know my old lawyer, Smith, refuses to represent me now he knows of the extra charges? And that's after he pawned Nattrass's silver watch and took the money as well as the bed, the carpets, and even the knives and forks. Pawned it all for thirteen pounds. They're heartless scoundrels. Think they're too good to stand up for me in front of the judge. Can you help me, Clara?"

"I have no money to give you, Mary Ann."

"Not even a scrap of jewellery that might fetch a few pound?" she said, staring at my locket. I grasped it as if the chain were searing my neck.

"You can have it. I don't want it anymore." I unfastened it and held it out to her, feeling a wry sense of satisfaction that I was about to give Henry's treasured gift to an accused murderer.

She grinned and tucked it into her lap, her eyes devouring it. "That's a fine piece, Clara. Are you sure your husband won't be angry?"

I shook my head. "It's of no use to me anymore."

She held it up so that it glittered in the firelight. "I'll be hard-pressed to part with it, Clara."

"It's yours. Do what you want with it," I said as the door swung open and Mrs Falks bustled in. Mary Ann stuffed the necklace into her pocket.

"It's like a railway station here," she said, turning to two dark-jacketed men waiting in the room beyond. "Your visitors have arrived, Mary Ann."

Mary Ann craned her neck to see behind the wardress's plump body. "Move yer rump then, so I can see who's here."

"Cheeky beggar," said Mrs Falks, stepping aside.

"It'll be Lowry and his marra Joe Thornley. Better watch yersel', Clara. Our Joe is quite a looker."

"Take no notice of her cheek," said Mrs Falks. "I'll show you out."

I passed the two men in their rough work jackets and chequered mufflers. The stocky older man with thinning grey hair, a wispy moustache, and hooded eyes I guessed was Lowry. But the other man's tall frame filled the doorway and he looked to be in his early thirties, with broad shoulders and black wavy hair. Clean-shaven, his face glowed ruddy from the cold, and with his strong, aquiline nose, clear grey eyes, and finely shaped lips, he resembled a Roman warrior, though the effect was marred by a network of scars running across his left cheek.

"Mrs Blackstone," said the wardress. "Are you ready?"

I blinked, conscious I'd been staring too long at the younger man, and my cheeks flushed with heat. Both men clutched flat caps in their hands and nodded briefly in greeting as I hastened out, only stopping to look back at Mary Ann, who dangled the locket in the air, her eyes glittering greedily. I felt no regret at losing it—only a hollow emptiness when I realised I had no love left for Henry.

I burst out from the side door into a small stone courtyard. All around me, the cold brick prison walls towered upwards, leaning inwards as if they would squash me. A flock of birds flew in arrow formation across the bright blue rectangle of sky. Flying onwards to warmer climates, to lush gardens and tropical groves.

I pressed my back against the wall and caught my breath as Joe Thornley's face flashed across my mind, and I remembered Mary Ann's words.

*Find yersel' a real man. There's plenty of them in the mining villages if yer don't mind slumming it a bit. They'd be happy to oblige a comely looking woman like you.*

# 19

HENRY BARGED INTO my bedroom next morning without knocking. He stopped inside the doorway and scanned the room with mistrustful eyes, clearing his throat with some discomfort.

"The winter ball is tonight. Donald reminded me only yesterday and insisted I bring you," he mumbled, his eyes downcast.

I moved away to the window. The bare branches of the elm tree shook in the wind. Winter was upon us and a feeling of darkness and dying swept over me like a wave, sucking away my hope. I was in no mood for dancing, especially with Henry. "Perhaps you'd prefer to go alone," I said, hardly able to feel myself breathing.

He scowled and tapped his foot on the floor. "I cannot do that. The entire faculty will attend and I need you to be there by my side like all the other wives."

I bit my lip and kept my silence.

"Dammit, Clara. I'm giving you a chance to meet new people—to prove that you can still act like any sane, normal wife. You will go. Be ready for five this evening."

After he left, Alice rushed in. "Sorry, mum, only the master said I must help you go through your dresses."

I waved her towards the wardrobe, scarcely able to rouse myself from my chair. "Look in there and pick one. I don't care which."

She opened the door and began rummaging through the gowns, finally pulling out an evening dress Izzie had given me. "You should wear this lovely white one with the pale green trim." She stroked its foamy lace skirts, her eyes wide with wonder, and her innocence touched something in me.

*Never show your weakness or it'll be the end of you, pet.*

I sprang to my feet. *Enough of this moping,* I told myself. Wallowing in a state of hopeless desolation would get me nowhere. I let Alice help me into the dress, then I stood in front of the mirror. The bodice gaped and loose folds of fabric drooped around the waist—not surprising after a year of asylum slop. I had her pin it up, then sent her off to wait for it at the dressmaker's. Keeping her occupied for a few hours would give me ample time to search Henry's rooms again for more letters from Izzie.

I quickly took the spare set of keys from the peg bag and let myself into Henry's bedroom. The air still reeked with the waxy smoke of a snuffed-out candle. Alice must have been at work already because the bed was made, covered with a bottle-green bedspread embroidered with thick gold stitching. The room had an air of lavish grandeur—dark maroon walls, moss-green velvet curtains, a polished walnut dressing table set with an embossed silver brush-and-comb set, a weighty crystal flagon of eau de cologne next to a bottle of Macassar oil. Two tall lamps stood atop a marble mantelpiece, on either side of a grand onyx mantel clock, their figured tortoiseshell bases and crimson silk shades reminiscent of a private gentlemen's club.

It seemed like another world, completely at odds with the shabby simplicity of the other rooms in the house.

I rifled through the writing desk drawers, finding only pencils and pamphlets and a few calling cards. But in the bottom drawer, under a sheaf of playbills, I pulled out a photograph of a beautiful dark-eyed woman with bold pencilled eyebrows, painted lips, and tumbling black curls. Across the bottom was scrawled: *To my dearest Henry from your own Piccadilly songbird, Minnie.*

More evidence of the *suffering* Henry had endured whilst I was away in Hoxton.

Under that was a bundle of notices that appeared to be demands for payment from a variety of men's clothiers and florists. I sat down on the bed and sorted through six bills from an exclusive men's tailor on Regent Street for morning coats, a Norfolk jacket, a dress coat and trousers, a selection of linen and cambric shirts, waistcoats, ties, cravats, and an expensive Ulster overcoat. Three final demand notices—one from a milliner's in Piccadilly listed the purchase of a top hat, a straw boater, and a bowler; the second from a shoemaker's on Bond Street where he'd bought handmade shoes, boots, and slippers; and the third from a wine merchant's on the Strand where he'd purchased several crates of burgundy and champagne. At the bottom of the final demand notices a small stamp indicated they had been paid, but on closer scrutiny the scrawled handwritten note said *outstanding balance forwarded by Donald J. Buckley.*

Feeling a sudden chill, I shivered and pulled my shawl around me. He'd been living the high life on borrowed money whilst I was shut away.

I was about to stuff the bills back into the drawer when I spied the corner of a sheet of lavender-sprigged paper peeping out from under a packet of mints.

Izzie's stationery.

I pressed the paper to my face. The letter had come only a few weeks ago, and the faint scent of lavender still lingered on it.

*My dearest, darling Clara,*

*I write this whilst sitting on a shady verandah surrounded by lilies and purple hibiscus. I wish you, too, could see the beauty of the gardens and hear the hiss of the fountains. My cough has quite disappeared in this balmy climate. My doctor informs me, however, that I must stay another year, so sadly I will not be returning to England in the spring.*

*I know that you must be settled in Durham, and therefore I do not wish to alarm you, but I feel I must make you aware that I have sent many letters to you over this past year, but since I have not received any reply, I suspect you did not receive them. I know that you lost your precious baby. My heart weeps for you and my dear departed great-grandchild. I say a prayer for its innocent soul.*

*Please write to me immediately and tell me you are well and happy.*

*Your loving Izzie*

I clasped the letter to my heart. This was absolute proof of my husband's lies.

Then I went over to his wardrobe and flung the doors open. A collection of fine suits, jackets, shirts, and coats hung above a row of highly polished boots and shoes.

All the trappings of Henry's secret extravagances.

Another life I knew nothing about.

# 20

LATER THAT EVENING I watched from my bedroom window as the Buckleys' carriage pulled up at the front door. But only Reverend Buckley stepped out onto the street into the pool of yellow light. Immaculate in a black evening suit and silk-lined cloak, he clasped a gleaming top hat in his hand. Seconds later I heard the sharp rap on the door knocker, followed by Alice scurrying across the hall, then the creak of the front door as he entered. The deep murmuring of voices from below told me Buckley was in Henry's study.

I dreaded the evening ahead. How could I look Henry in the face now that I knew of his deception? But the quiet voice spoke to me again using Mary Ann's words.

*Never show your weakness or it'll be the end of you, pet.*

I checked my reflection in the mirror. The cream lace dress fit like a glove, accentuating my slender waist. Sapphire earrings glittered like blue ice in my ears. Alice had braided my hair and wound it into a crown studded with Izzie's diamond butterfly pins. My cheeks were flushed with apprehension, but the eyes that gazed back at me were wounded and furtive, the smile strained.

*Look your enemies square in the eye,* Mary Ann had told me. *Face them without fear.*

I pulled my shoulders back and regarded myself with a steady, confident expression.

I would carry myself with poise tonight. I would not bow my shoulders or cast down my eyes like some beaten dog.

I stood at the top of the stairs, listening to the low murmur of male voices coming from the open study door, then tiptoed a little way down and leaned in closer. Henry's voice seemed flat and listless.

"She's become a pallid, feeble creature. Not the vigorous-looking girl I first met."

Buckley's deep baritone voice boomed out into the silence. "The doctors say when the bosom shrinks to the size of an average chicken's breast, nature wisely prohibits such a woman from increasing her breed."

I stuffed my fist into my mouth for fear of crying out, and held my breath, afraid of making the slightest sound. He spoke of women as if they were nothing more than livestock to be weighed, measured, then disposed of.

Henry continued: "Mother always said girls of good country stock are far hardier and have bodies better suited to childbearing, but I still find myself drawn to the more delicate highborn types."

"Sadly, I fear that sometimes a higher pedigree correlates with a more highly strung disposition," said Buckley.

"But I must admit she was a tantalising prospect—vivacious with prosperous connections and the promise of a substantial future inheritance. A good family apart from her unstable mother."

"All the latest scientific evidence suggests a greater tendency of mothers to transmit insanity to their female children," said Buckley. "And the degenerated reproductive capacity results in a calamitous chain of events—atrophy of the breasts, total loss of pelvic power, and ultimately sexless sterility."

"My God," said Henry. "No wonder she needed the dressmaker's aid to disguise her wasted body."

I fell back against the wall, the darkness seeming to roar around me.

"It's a sad truth, Henry, that the power of feminine vanity is so strong, a woman will use all her wiles to conceal physical defects from her husband's watchful eye."

A long pause followed before Henry replied. I leaned forwards as far as I dared, my breath wild in my ears. "But there's the problem of Shepton's report. The man's a bloody thorn in my side. Says there's nothing wrong with her."

Buckley lowered his voice. "Leave it to me, Henry. The present system allows for a person to be incarcerated in an asylum at the will of another private individual by means of documents procurable by anyone who can pay for them. The signatures of only two medical men are needed, and I think you'll find many practitioners in these parts are of a more conservative inclination when it comes to women's troubles. I myself have pecuniary interests in several such *therapeutic* homes. Perhaps we could come to a mutually beneficial arrangement considering the little matter of your outstanding debt."

"In good time, Donald. We must be patient or we will lose the old lady's trust and jeopardise the inheritance."

"You said she was on her last legs," said Donald, an edge of urgency creeping into his voice.

Henry sighed. "She has rallied, but her condition is chronic. The doctor has given her less than six months, though he hasn't told her."

The whole world went silent as my legs weakened and faltered. Horrified, I stumbled forwards, making the floorboards creak. Henry appeared at the study door, a black figure silhouetted against the light. He glanced up at me and my insides dissolved. "Why are you creeping around the place like a house cat, Clara?" he said, his eyes barely meeting mine.

"I didn't want to disturb you," I said, trying to regain my earlier resolve.

He waved me down, then surveyed me from head to toe. "The dress is quite charming, Clara, but put a smile on that glum face of yours. Don't you know that a frown puts years on a woman's appearance? Get your cloak on and we'll join you shortly in the parlour."

He swooped back into the study, slamming the door behind him.

I gritted my teeth and forced myself to be calm. *Don't falter now. He's nothing more than a vain, superficial fool.*

But a dangerous one who sought to rob me of everything and then cast me away forever.

I placed my hand against the wall to steady myself as Alice emerged from the kitchen.

"You look beautiful, Mrs Blackstone. Shall I get your wrap for you?"

I nodded and pulled my shoulders straight to let her fold the fine velvet shawl around me, shivering as its cool satin lining slid over my shoulders.

In the carriage, Reverend Buckley sat opposite Henry whilst I gazed out the window, trying to compose my face into a placid expression. A blur of streetlamps skimmed by as we passed taverns brimming with patrons who had spilled out onto the street holding flagons of beer. Further along, a ragged cluster of children warmed themselves at a chestnut roaster's brazier.

"Henry, have you read anything further about the Auckland Poisoner?" said Buckley, rousing me from my thoughts.

Henry sprang to attention. "Why yes. Only last week I read an article about poisoning. The author claims it is akin to assassination and the product of a polished and voluptuous age."

Buckley scowled and stroked the ends of his moustache. "One could hardly call Mrs Cotton a person who has revelled in any kind of luxury; rather, she seems to have used poison in order to achieve only petty financial gains."

"Well, surely it is all relative," said Henry. "To a person steeped in poverty since birth, a few pounds might appear to be the passport to a life of comparative comfort."

I glanced at Henry's hawkish expression. I was his passport to a life of luxury and comfort, to that prosperous future he'd dreamt about as a young boy, when he watched his father stride by the pigpens and vowed he'd never muddy the soles of his own boots.

Buckley continued: "And yet other studies claim that the secret nature of poisoning makes it a crime favoured by women. Once the poisoner makes one kill, a sort of mania possesses her and she continues for no other reason than to satisfy a morbid fascination with her secret power."

"That makes a great deal of sense," said Henry, smoothing out a fold in his evening cloak. "There is something so sly and devious about the crime that fits with women's naturally cunning nature."

*Only a shameless hypocrite could be blind to his own deviousness,* I thought, glancing at Henry's smug face. My insides burned with the knowledge of his deception.

Buckley leaned towards Henry and lowered his voice. "Not to mention she comes from degenerate stock—descended from the pauper and mendicant classes. Why, Dr Maudsley states quite clearly that lunatics and criminals are as much manufactured articles as are steam engines and calico-printing presses. Imagine that."

"Then it is no wonder she drifted from one husband to another—merely to sate her naturally licentious appetites," said Henry.

A silent rage simmered deep in my gut, growing more intense at the sound of their self-righteous hogwash. Buckley's puffed-up lips and reddish face put me in mind of an overgrown goldfish in Izzie's ornamental pond that swam around gobbling up all the tiny water creatures into its cavernous mouth. And Henry was the skinny whiskered catfish, slyly skulking along the murky bottom of the pond, slurping up the putrid scraps of Buckley's drivel.

I turned to them, unable to keep my silence a moment longer. "Are you gentlemen aware it is quite common for widows to remarry? And as for equating Mrs Cotton with mendicants and beggars, I do believe her father was an industrious working man and she herself a well-respected nurse at Sunderland Infirmary."

Both men turned to glare at me, their mouths gaping in outrage, just as the coach lurched to a screeching halt when a dray horse and cart thundered across the road in front of us. I felt a sudden lightness in my head.

Henry set his hat straight. "Donald speaks from a scientific viewpoint based on hard facts and research, not naïve, irrational emotions."

Buckley dismissed Henry with a wave of his hand. "Clara, you are not exposed to the wickedness I encounter amongst the female prisoners. A plague of evil is sweeping the women of our nation and Mrs Cotton is the embodiment of it."

*But not so evil as the two of you scoundrels with your cunning schemes,* said the wild voice, now demanding to be heard. I was done with blind compliance now.

"Pardon me, Reverend Buckley, but perhaps it is a plague of poverty and ignorance that forces those women to commit desperate actions, most often for the sake of their children."

Henry's eyes grew wide with horror as Reverend Buckley threw his head back and laughed. "This is not mere desperation, Clara. These impoverished colliery villages you speak of are rife with alcoholism and coarse desires. They are the breeding grounds of the criminal underclasses. Social underworlds associated with filth, contagion, and animal instincts. Those monsters fight like mongrels, murder, lie, and steal just to satisfy their base desires."

I straightened my shoulders and felt the blood rush to my head. "Are you saying, Reverend Buckley, that a respectable middle-class man is incapable of using cunning, lying, and deceit to get what he wants?"

Henry's eyes burned. If he'd held a knife in his hand, he would have stabbed me in the heart.

Buckley's voice rose. "My dear Clara, you only need to read all the latest scientific texts to know that through natural selection, we men of the higher classes have ascended our lower nature and, with our superior capacity for reason, developed a well-fashioned will characterised by self-restraint and self-control."

"On the contrary, Reverend Buckley, that has not been my experience. I would say that men's inherently competitive nature causes them to use every trick in the book to satisfy their ruthless ambitions and get exactly what they want, regardless of their social class and irrespective of the consequences to those they step over then cast aside."

The silence was immediate. Henry's face transformed to a ghastly white, Buckley's went beet red, but it was too late, the blood was coursing through my veins like quicksilver.

"Enough," hissed Henry. "You're talking utter nonsense."

Buckley sat back, glowering at me, whilst Henry sank against his seat, his face livid. "I must apologise for Clara's outburst. She has been acting irrationally for some time now and is liable to blurt out stupid, ill-considered opinions."

"I say you should keep your wife in check, Henry, or you'll come to regret it," Buckley grunted.

The rest of the ride passed in silence. I bit the inside of my cheek to quell the exhilaration that swelled up inside me. I'd finally spoken out, but I feared the consequences. Feared that I'd pushed Henry too far.

When the coach pulled to a halt, I barely noticed the lights and the finely dressed guests streaming into the hall. Buckley marched on ahead whilst Henry held me back, pushing me under a grand archway. He gripped my arm and shoved his face so close to mine, I could see the oily sheen of Macassar oil on his moustache.

"Now I know you're truly mad," he hissed. "What in God's name possessed you to insult Reverend Buckley in that way?"

Other guests streamed in behind us, but Henry held me fast, his face pinched like a snarling fox, his fingers digging into the soft flesh of my upper arm. "Well, answer me."

I turned away from the sour reek of alcohol on his breath. "Let me go, Henry. You're making a spectacle of yourself."

He shook me again, his grip tightening like a vice. "Don't toy with me, Clara."

I looked down at my reddening arm. "You want me to walk in with bruised arms, Henry? What will your colleagues think?"

"Brainless fool," he whispered, releasing his grip, his face flushed and red. "You'll regret this."

He stamped on ahead of me towards the gaily lit ballroom, where Buckley, his face creased with vexation, thrust his hat and cloak at one of the footmen. I looked round in wonder at the grand ballroom and its elegant Grecian pillars. Twinkling chandeliers cast a lacework of light onto the dance floor. Couples twirled and spun by in a blur of silk and muslin, ruffles and flowers. Sprays of green foliage in crystal vases decorated the tables, and an orchestra played from a gilded stage. The air was thick with laughter, conversation, and the fluttering of fans held in white-gloved hands. I hadn't seen anything so beautiful since I'd lived with Izzie, but a cold fist pressed against my heart. I was an interloper here. An outsider. Deceived and utterly alone.

The bitterness swelled in my throat as surely as if I'd swallowed acid.

"I have sent someone to find Emma," said Buckley peremptorily, glowering as he scanned the crowds. "You would do well to stay by her side tonight, Clara. Henry and I have important people to meet."

Henry stood meekly at his side, adjusting his white evening tie and smoothing down his ivory silk waistcoat. I appraised his fine suit with its velvet lapels and sleek tails, and imagined him in a London tailor's shop—perhaps one of those intimate establishments nestled under the arches of the Burlington Arcade—turning to admire himself in a gold-framed pier glass. Perhaps he'd worn it the night he went to the theatre with the Buckleys, or when he'd gone backstage to present Minnie, the *Piccadilly songbird*, with a bouquet of roses, whilst I languished, half-conscious, on a frigid bathroom floor.

His eyes lit onto me. "Why do you stare at me like that?" he whispered, leaning close enough so Buckley couldn't hear.

"You are my husband. May I not look at you?"

His eyes darted round the room. "Keep your voice down. You glare at me as if your eyes are daggers."

"Now *you* are imagining things, Henry," I said, smiling at a woman I remembered from Emma's dinner party.

"I see you are in the grip of some kind of perversity—some fit of foolish recklessness. I should take you home if your nerves are too ragged."

"What is all this talk of going home?" said Emma, sweeping towards us, regal in a deep maroon gown, a posy of greenery clutched in her gloved hand. "Clara shall be *my* companion tonight."

Henry sighed and thrust me forwards. "I trust you'll keep a close eye on her, Emma," he said just as Buckley stepped forwards to greet a tall, imposing man with glossy black mutton-chop whiskers, a drooping moustache, and dark, unflinching eyes.

"Henry, you must meet my good friend, Superintendent John Henderson, who has the distinction of being the arresting officer of our infamous poisoner, Mrs Cotton."

"I am not sure if that will be a blessing or a curse on my career," he said, his eyes alighting on Henry. "Though I have been in constant communication with the Home Secretary since the arrest, which has brought considerable recognition to our fair cathedral city."

"And that can only serve to advance your career," said Buckley, nudging Henry towards him. "My colleague Henry Blackstone, professor of mathematics."

"Never had much of a head for the higher forms of mathematics. Too abstract for me," said Henderson, stroking the end of his moustache. "I'm more of a practical man. Always had an eye for detail. Those little trifles the average person might miss."

Buckley leaned in close. "And that, of course, is how you caught a vile murderer."

"I do not give up until I have rooted out the evil truth," he said, his gaze flickering across my face. One corner of his thin lips twitched upwards. "And these charming ladies?"

Buckley took Emma's arm. "My wife, Emma, and Mrs Clara Blackstone."

He dipped a shallow bow. "Delighted."

Buckley narrowed his eyes. "Unfortunately, Mrs Blackstone is under the impression that you may have arrested an innocent woman."

All eyes turned to me. My insides squirmed as Henderson straightened his shoulders like a soldier. "Do not fall victim to charitable delusions, Mrs Blackstone. The wholesale murderer is clever—an expert liar and manipulator. We have uncovered corpses saturated with arsenic, and still the do-gooders send her misguided letters of support and fuel her ridiculous claims of innocence. We will convict her. We must. I will see to it. A woman cannot be permitted to get away with murdering her children and her husbands. Think what kind of example would be set by leniency."

Buckley clapped him on the shoulder and directed a broad smirk my way. Henry's face had drained of colour. "Quite so, Superintendent Henderson. I will make sure to correct my wife's foolish misapprehensions."

Henderson directed a quizzical look at me. "I urge you to do that, Henry. Far too often foolish thoughts become dangerous ones. Give them an inch and the next thing you know, our women will be attempting to overthrow us."

"A ridiculous idea," said Buckley, guiding Henry and the superintendent towards a clutch of colleagues gathered by the stage.

"What is going on, Clara?" said Emma, her gaze following the retreating men. "Is everything well with you?"

"Just a misunderstanding," I said, trying to silence the rushing in my ears.

"Good, because tonight I am overjoyed that my darling daughter, Amy, has returned from her travels. You must meet her," she said, steering me towards the refreshments table.

Tiny frosted glasses encircled a swan carved entirely from sugar. But beside it, Amy, a slender raven-haired girl with alabaster skin and startling blue eyes, was the most glorious swan of all. She towered above the lesser mortals, her bare shoulders gleaming like polished marble. The women chirped around her like brightly coloured hummingbirds, pecking daintily at the canapés and drinking in the nectar of her every word.

When Emma introduced us, Amy inclined her head and graced me with a faint smile. She offered a silken white hand to shake, then turned immediately back to her audience, who begged for more stories of the Venetian gondoliers and the charming Florentine piazzas. I had no appetite for food or idle chitchat and backed away from the spectacle just as Buckley led Henry towards Amy, who shone like a beacon of youthful perfection amongst the older folk.

I watched the scene unfold. Henry stared unblinkingly at Amy as she tossed her raven curls so they glinted in the candlelight. Buckley wrapped an arm around her slender waist and introduced Henry, who took her outstretched hand as if he were handling a sliver of ivory, bowing over it like a supplicant to his queen. Then he snapped to attention and directed a rakish smile in her direction. She, in turn, held her fan to her face, her glinting indigo eyes sparkling out at him.

*They were flirting. Right before my eyes.*

I hadn't seen Henry so spirited since our wedding day. He chatted animatedly with Reverend Buckley, whilst his gaze kept straying in blind adoration to Amy, the goddess incarnate.

Mary Ann had warned me of this.

Turning away from the sight, I hurried in the other direction, towards the dance floor, where a small grey-haired man snatched at my dance card and scribbled on it with a gold pen.

"Such a pity you are alone. I'd be honoured, madam," he said, sweeping me in amongst the dancers. Speechless, I surrendered myself to the music and the banks of flowers that swirled by in a rainbow blur.

The strains of the waltz became a dissonant cacophony, and as we turned to weave amongst the other bodies, I was reminded of the weekly ball at the asylum. Like some weird nightmare masquerade, the Lunatic Ball, as it was known, was the only time the women were permitted to mix with the men. It was a bizarre affair where murderers, pickpockets, and prostitutes danced with hysterics, melancholics, and syphilitics. Garish paper flowers adorned the grey prison dresses and many inmates danced alone, each one keeping his or her own time as a fantastical private orchestra played in their head. Then, at nine o'clock sharp, a shrill whistle sounded and the keepers chivvied us away, back to the monotony of our rooms.

My mind was so scattered, I stumbled over my partner's foot.

"Perhaps you need a breath of fresh air?" he asked.

"Please excuse me," I said, pulling away from him and making my way to an open door that led onto a balcony. Shadowy shrubs lined the terrace and the frost-rimmed leaves crunched under my feet. I pulled my shawl around my shoulders and carried on along a pathway to the side of the building. The moon shone between the trees, its reflection scattered like broken eggshells on the river down below. I stayed there in the quiet and imagined how I would paint it.

Later, Henry staggered out drunkenly from the ballroom, his hat askew, and draped a heavy arm across my shoulders. "Buckley mustn't see me like this," he hiccupped, his voice hoarse from too many cigars. "He claims to abhor intemperance and yet he holds a skinful of whisky as if he's spent the entire evening sipping at lime cordial."

Together we stumbled towards the carriage. He clambered up the steps after lurching backwards twice, then sat hunched in the seat opposite, glowering at me from beneath drooping lids. As the carriage pulled away, I wished I'd made my own way home earlier. His face twisted into a drunken smirk.

"My life here is close to perfection," he slurred. "I have fine colleagues, my position at the university is secure, I have the respect I've always dreamt of, but you, my dear wife, seem bound and determined to destroy all that with your flapping mouth and your damned frigid ways."

A deathly chill crept across my skull, and a tightness constricted my chest.

The carriage bumped over the cobbles, dislodging his hat from his head, and still he sat there scowling and belching out a foul odour of stale spirits. "Some men would horsewhip their wives for speaking out and making a fool of them. And for failing to fulfil their wifely duties."

He lunged across the space, slumping down beside me on the seat. "Or perhaps you have found other habits, Clara, that prevent you from being a proper wife."

He pulled me towards him, so close that I could smell the brandy on his breath. I recoiled, but he tugged at my hair until my head lay on his shoulder. "Show me a little attention, Clara, or must I force the affection from you?"

I ground my teeth, my eyes scanning the coach for some means to escape, but his arm snaked around my shoulders then tightened suddenly across my throat like a noose. I fought to draw breath, my arms beating against my sides like a panicked bird. Mary Ann's words flew into my head.

*Watch out for those wolves. For when they get their teeth into your flesh, they'll tear you to pieces.*

I gathered all my strength and flung out my right foot, kicking him sharp against his shins. He yelped out in pain and dropped his arm enough that I could roll away from him and dive across to the other bench. The carriage picked up speed as I pounded on the roof of the cab, but Henry was on his feet and back over to me before I could make enough noise to alert the driver.

He grasped my hair and yanked my head upwards. A sour wave of fear rose in my gut as an image flickered in my head: A strong hand pulling me by the hair from a bright sewing room where machines buzzed like a thousand angry insects. Someone had pulled me to the ground and dragged me away by the ankles so that my head bumped across the flagstones. Was it Bethlem or Hoxton? I couldn't remember, and now Henry pushed his face so close, I saw the tiny red veins in his feverish eyes.

"Buckley claims that nymphomania is rife amongst female lunatics. Or perhaps you sated those fantasies by abusing yourself with masturbation. Is that why you run to the prison, Clara? To seek dissipated women with lewd appetites like yours? Buckley has told me about those women and their *pets.* Their lustful cries and endearments when the lights go out."

"You are revolting," I hissed as he leaned forwards and crushed his wet mouth onto mine. I squirmed and clawed at his arms as he clutched at my breasts. Panicked, I twisted my body from side to side.

"No appetite for me now, Clara? Then see what you are missing."

He grasped the back of my neck with one hand and shoved my head towards his groin.

"You want to talk like a brainless slut, then act like one," he snapped as he forced my cheek against his member. Screaming, I tore myself away, choking with rage.

"Well, I have no appetite for a filthy lunatic," he said, laughing aloud and falling back against the seat, where he held himself fast and with ever-quickening strokes until he shuddered in climax. Shrinking into the far corner of the carriage, I watched the lights fly by in an orange blur and waited until he'd fumbled with the buttons on his trousers. Afterwards his eyelids drooped and he dozed off, snoring like a bear.

When we reached the house, the coachman helped me drag him inside and to his bed. He lay there, inert, his mouth gaping open with deep, rasping snores.

I stood over him, my heart thudding as if it would leap from my chest. Imaginary scenarios raced through my mind. I saw myself pushing him from the moving carriage with such force, his head cracked against the cobblestones, or pulling a knife from my reticule and sticking it in the soft flesh under his ribs until the blood rose to his throat and drowned him. Or greeting him for breakfast with a smile and a pot of tea laced with arsenic.

I grasped a pillow in my hands. How easily I could crush the life from him. I'd say he died from choking on his own vomit. But would the police believe me? *Would Superintendent Henderson root out the evil truth?*

The door creaked open behind me.

"Does the master need some water, Mrs Blackstone?"

I turned and saw Alice's face, a white blur in the shadows, her eyes heavy with sleep. I dropped the pillow onto the bed.

"You can leave some on his bedside table," I whispered, sweeping by her and into my room. "And when he wakes tomorrow, tell him I'm indisposed."

# 21

I WAS IN a wild state when I reached the prison the next day. Last night I had wished Henry dead. I had seen his face crushed in the dirt, watched his blood stain the winter slush.

Terror gripped me. My body felt slight and insubstantial—a flimsy husk that could blow away with the slightest puff of wind.

Bertha was on duty, boiling a kettle for the morning tea, when I swept into the anteroom, my head reeling, my movements skittish.

"Are you feeling canny, Mrs Blackstone?" she asked, her brow furrowed with concern. "Only yer flew in here like a hare chased by the hounds. Sit quiet here for a minute before you go in."

I perched on the stool, pulled off my hat, and rested my forehead on my hand, massaging my temples to stem the panic that coursed through my blood.

"Tek a minute and settle yourself, dear. I'll have some tea ready soon."

"It's just the wind—it's fierce today," I said, my eyes drifting to the locked cell door. "How is Mary Ann?"

She measured the tea leaves into the pot. "There's been good and bad days. Mr Backhouse, the Quaker, an old employer of hers, was just here for a visit and promised to vouch for her good character should it be needed. But then when she learned they'd exhumed the bodies of her own little baby Robert and Cotton's son, Fred, that set her back a bit. You'll see when you go in."

Mary Ann was sitting on her bed, propped up against the wall, her face pale and drawn. She clutched at her belly. "Oh, 'tis a terrible thing when your bairn canna rest peaceful in his grave. And now them scavenging old doctors will pick over his little body and make up more lies about me."

My head was so filled with my own troubles, I sat on the stool and chewed at my thumbnail. Now where were my high and mighty ideas about spiritual guidance? I was like a blind person stumbling through the wilderness.

"Yer've got some fight in your eyes, pet," she said, frowning and pulling herself upright. "Summat's eating the life out of you."

I couldn't speak. Izzie was dying. Henry had lied to me, forced himself upon me, and now he was scheming to lock me away again.

"Poor Clara. Fine house. Beautiful clothes. Educated professor for a husband and no bairns. What's the trouble? Is your husband still tormenting you? Are you still sleeping alone like a nun?"

I turned away from her searching eyes, the hopelessness welling up inside me like a great tide that would sweep me away.

"Not talking today, Clara? Or mebbe yer think I'm as common as muck, Clara. With a sluttish mouth. Don't you?"

I shook my head. "I think you've had a hard life."

She grinned and wagged a finger at me. "No, no, hinny. Not as hard as yours. You've never felt the joy of suckling a babe or watching its little fingers curl round yours. You've never had a man lust for you so much he can't keep his hands off you."

A tear trickled down my cheek.

She touched my hand and I shivered as if a spider had crawled across my skin. "Tell me everything, Clara, for summat's eating at your soul."

She waited, lips slightly parted, a keenness in her eyes that glinted like cold steel, daring me to tell that dark and forbidden secret she'd been longing to hear.

I took a deep, shallow breath and let those fathomless eyes draw me in. "You think I've never known hardship. I come here to offer you kindness because I know what it's like to be locked away in a cell. To stare at four stone walls and feel as if you could rip the nails from your fingers trying to claw your way out."

Her mouth hung open, spittle beading her lower lip. "You were in prison?"

"An asylum," I said, studying the floor.

I heard her quick intake of breath. "The madhouse?"

"My husband put me into an insane asylum."

"Tell Mary Ann about it, pet. Now's the time to cast that heavy burden off yer chest."

Her voice was low and coaxing—an incantation that mingled with the crackling of the fire.

My secret was a live thing growing inside me, pushing at my heart—pressing the breath from me.

*Tell her,* said the voice. *If you hold this burden too close, it will break you.*

Soon the words spilled out like poison from a festering sore.

"When I lost my baby, I also lost my mind. The doctor took my baby's body and threw it in a bucket. I screamed and begged him to bring it back."

She leaned closer to me. "And then—then what did you do?"

I closed my eyes, trying to block the memories of that night, but I could see it—smell it as if it were happening right there in that cell. I remembered the hospital. Its sickly yellow walls, the mingled smells of ammonia and fresh blood in the air. "I was dizzy from the ether—the pain was like fire searing my gut. I bit at the doctor's ear and struck out at the nurses. Then I seized a scalpel from the tray and when they tried to pacify me, I stabbed a nurse in her eye with that scalpel. They thought she would die from the blood loss. They saved her, but I had blinded her in one eye."

Mary Ann's eyes were saucer-wide as she sat back, appraising me. "Well. You're a real wildcat. Who would have thought it? I suppose they didn't set the police onto a high-class lady like you."

"They took me to Bethlem and locked me in a cell, even though my body burned with fever. I lay there for days, delirious."

Her voice was a soft whisper. "And how did they treat you in that place?"

I felt my gorge rise at the memories I'd held back for so long—the choking feeling of rubber tubes snaking down my throat, the slime of raw egg on the doctor's fingers. "When I wouldn't eat, they forced the food down my throat. When I gouged at my eyes with my own fingers to stop seeing the eyes of my stillborn baby, they wrapped me in a strong dress and strapped my wrists to the sides of the bed. I cursed and spat at them until they dosed me with chloral, then I slept for days. When I awoke and my body was healed, they set me amongst the chronic lunatics. My husband kept me there for two long months, then sent me to a private asylum in Hoxton."

"And how was it there, pet?" she said in her wheedling voice.

The shame and guilt were so great, I could barely meet her eyes. I focused instead on the dusty hem of her dress.

"Unimaginable horror—hours of confinement to a bed, daily freezing showers, my body spread out like a carcass on a cold slab whilst they gave me the icy douche . . ."

I heard her tongue *tut-tutting* against her teeth. "Eeh, that's terrible. I would've got rid of that bugger long ago," she said in a blunt, matter-of-fact tone.

"You mean Henry?"

"Aye. The scoundrel that put you away like that. One thing they'll never say about me, pet, is that I'm mad. I have a sharp head on my shoulders and I know what's what. I'd fettle any man that tried to lock me away in a madhouse, especially when he had no reason to."

"But I was deranged—a wild beast."

She shook her head. "You've nowt to be ashamed of, Clara. Remember, I was a nurse at the Sunderland Infirmary and I've helped to deliver many babies. I've seen childbed turn the heads of all kinds of women. Women who took one look at their newborn baby and tried to push it from the bed. Who pinched its tiny arms or tried to stick pins in the poor bairn's soft skin. Some of them were respectable women who cursed and swore like tinkers and clawed at us like cats, or spoke in gibberish and soiled their own clothes. We even had one woman—just had her tenth baby in ten years—she tried to jump from the hospital window."

"What happened to them all?"

"One or two died of the fever, but most got better after a few weeks and went home. The doctors said it was often due to a difficult labour. Or maybe a bad infection because the midwife was careless or the doctor had a heavy hand using the forceps and tore the woman's body. Maybe there was too much blood lost. Having a bairn is no easy task and some women have bad luck when it comes to babies. Rich or poor. Makes no difference."

Her eyes narrowed and her lips set themselves into a straight line. "I'm poor, not stupid, Clara. Your man is a scoundrel. He should never have locked you away. And once you get into the hands of those mind doctors, they think they know it all. But they know nowt about women's lives. They canna imagine the pain of giving birth year after year, the drudgery of keeping the place clean with a houseful of bairns running round your feet, and the hopelessness when you have barely a penny to your name and the pantry's bare. When you can't even set foot outside the door for the little ones clinging to your legs with their crying and their sickness and their whining."

It was the first time I'd seen her pale cheeks flushed with anything close to passion. "Then who am I to complain about my life when so many women live in misery?"

She sat back and nodded. "Now you know, Clara. Those wretched women have no hope. Their life is finished. But you have the means, though you canna seem to see it. Keep a sharp head on your shoulders and listen carefully to me now. Get yourself some money. Set aside a bit of the housekeeping. A little bit each week. Then pack yer bags and go somewhere else. Damn your respectable name. It won't do you any good when you're stepping over puddles of piss and jabbering lunatics. That scallywag's going to lock you up again if you're not careful."

"I know he will."

"You're not mad, Clara, and he has no right to put you away."

"He's a liar and a cheat. He'll do anything to destroy me."

She looked at me then with an expression of complete understanding—the first time I'd seen any shred of humanity in her eyes. "I'll tell you, Clara, it's a wicked thing when your husband turns against you."

The walls of the cell seemed to blur and fade away until only Mary Ann and I existed. Two women deceived by their husbands. "Do you think that all the men in your life were evil?" I whispered, afraid to break the connection between us.

"Most of them. They all wanted to beat me back when I got ahead. Like Robinson, who said I stole from him, and Riley, who couldn't abide to see me happily married to a respectable customs man, and had me arrested."

"Surely there are some good men."

"Even the good'uns are afraid of a woman who just wants to get a piece of things for herself. Who wants to have summat nice without having to beg a man for it."

I remembered something I'd read in the newspaper. "Is that why you took money from your third husband, James Robinson?"

She sat back, her face fallen in on itself as if I'd slapped it. "More wicked lies. As it happens, I did set aside a bit of money from Robinson's building society accounts. I had to. He was a stingy bastard with the housekeeping money."

"But the papers say you took more than fifty pounds and pawned your husband's linens and furniture."

"I know the gossips say I spent it at the races, or gave it to Nattrass. It's all false. I did keep a bit aside for mesel'. I mean—I like a few nice clothes. What woman doesn't? And I deserved it for all the sacrifices I made for him. When I met that man, he were a widower left with five children, his wife having recently died. I moved in to look after him, and in a week, the ten-month-old baby died. Poor mite couldn't survive without his mother. But Robinson didn't waste any time. He got me into bed and pregnant a few months later. Then I was called to look after my own mother at Seaham."

"How did your mother pass away?" I asked, careful not to betray any trace of suspicion.

She narrowed her eyes like a prowling cat. "Been doing some reading, have you, Clara?"

She continued to weigh me up, her eyes drilling into mine, then she seemed to collect herself and the hard set of her mouth and jaw suddenly softened as she looked away to deliver her story.

"Well, the neighbours said it was a surprise that my poor mother died, but as soon as I set eyes on her, I feared she was not long for this world, she were that sickly. And just because I took a few bits of linen and some clothing, my own stepfather told me never to set foot in his house again."

"Did you go back to Robinson then?"

"Aye—and it were a bad year. I had to take my own little Isabella Mowbray back there into a house filled with sickness. And no wonder—the place was filthy as a midden. First little James Robinson was taken, then his sister, Elizabeth. I had Dr Shaw in to see them twice a day sometimes. And worse still, my own Isabella—my last child from dear Fred Mowbray—she went down with it, too. Vomited in my face, she did. I canna get the memories out of my mind. All of them rolling around in the bed and foaming at the mouth until their little bodies gave up. I was so sick myself, I took to my bed and couldn't crawl out from under the sheets.

"John was good to me then, and wanted to call for the doctor to look at me, but I wouldn't let him. And the two of us were that broken by grief, we had to ask a friend to report the bairns' deaths. I cried every day after the funerals. Three children gone in two months. It was too much to bear. But James still saved me from gossip. I was pregnant through all that sickness and he still married me just afterwards. We had two bairns together. George and little Mary Isabella. Poor lamb. Only lasted three months and then God took her."

I couldn't tell if the tiny drop glistening on her cheek was a tear or just a pinpoint of light from the fire.

"But afterwards Robinson wouldn't listen to me. And those conniving sisters of his were forever nattering in his ear. Turned him against me. Told him, *It's thy Mary Ann that has poisoned your bairns.* Bloody mares—forever tattling. So one day I went out with baby George and when I came back, the door was locked. I had to wander the streets like a beggar, a helpless baby in my arms, with no home and no place to lay my head."

"How did you survive?"

"I was desperate. And when you're driven that low, you throw yourself on the mercy of your friends. I had to leave the baby with a neighbour so I could get a job and buy a crust of bread. I'd sold everything of my own to care for Robinson and he listened to lies and gossip. Left me with nothing. What was I to do?"

I bowed my head. "I should not have bothered you with my worries when you are fighting for your life."

"I don't need pity, Clara," she snapped. Her body stiffened and her chin rose. "You see, there's barely any difference between us, Clara. Your man is out to destroy you, too. He'll put you to rot in the madhouse and that'll be the end of you. At least—if the worst happens—the hangman'll release me from my misery." Then she sighed a deep, shuddering sigh and lay back on her pillow. "I should've run away when I had the chance. But like a fool I stayed in West Auckland. And that were enough time for Henderson, Riley, and Kilburn to get their heads together and make summat out of nowt."

"You're tired," I said, standing up. "I should let you rest."

She closed her eyes, her face twisted in a grimace as she clutched her belly.

"Is it the baby?" I said, leaning over her.

"Mebbe, but don't worry about me, Clara. I'm an old hand at this. You look after yer own troubles."

She was moaning slightly by the time Bertha opened the cell door.

"Are yer feeling canny, Mary Ann?"

She drew her knees upwards under her skirt. "I think the pains are coming."

"Best be on your way, Mrs Blackstone. I might have to call for the midwife. And give her a couple of days afore coming back here so she's out of the hospital wing."

As I passed through the narrow hallways, my mind twisted and turned. The baby was on its way. My belly ached with the faint memory of my own pains, and I felt a stab of envy. She'd birthed so many children in her forty years. What was one more? And yet, it was maybe her last.

Maybe her salvation.

I ran more swiftly then, as if pursued by devils, until I reached the door and burst out into the open air, where I steadied myself against the prison walls.

*How was it that a murderer understood me better than anyone else in the world?*

She knew that my own husband was conspiring to lock me away and let me rot in an asylum. Was it possible the same was true for her? That Riley and all the others had conspired to send her to the hangman?

But maybe after bearing so many children, and watching them die, something broke inside her heart and deprived her of reason.

I clutched at my forehead. *Innocent or guilty? Murderer or victim?* The thoughts buzzed through my head like a cloud of angry wasps until I could not sort one out from the other, but my mind snapped back to harsh reality when Reverend Buckley burst out from another door only yards away from me. I ducked behind a nearby shrub to watch him as he stopped at the foot of the steps to pull on his gloves and survey his surroundings. He sniffed at the air like a feral creature—a hungry wolf scenting blood. Then he spat onto the ground and wiped a sleeve across his mouth as he strode off towards the gatehouse. Once he had disappeared from view, I crept out from my hiding place and hurried to the gates.

On the way home, Mary Ann's words swirled around in my head.

*Your man is out to destroy you, too. He'll put you to rot in the madhouse and that'll be the end of you.*

I stopped on impulse outside an unassuming office, housed in a narrow slice of a low white terrace. I had passed it many times on my way to the prison. The brass nameplate on the blue door read Hepplewhite and Clarke: Solicitors and Notaries. Now I stood a good few minutes, wondering if I should step inside to find out if there were any legal means to leave Henry and escape to India. Could I pursue a divorce or separation on my own? Could I even utter those dreaded words to another man who might be part of the staunch, unyielding brotherhood that included Buckley and Superintendent Henderson? How long before word would get back to Henry that I was sullying his good name and reputation with my unthinkable demands?

And yet I had read of recent cases where women had been granted a divorce. I could not sit back and let Henry jeopardise my freedom and lock me away—maybe forever this time.

I looked round to check that no one was about and, heart pounding against my ribs, I pushed open the door and entered a cavernous room made warm by a blazing fire.

The solicitor was a dour man with a sullen mouth and bald pate that glimmered through scant strands of hair. I sat opposite him at a desk cluttered with papers, balls of string, and leather binders. To his left, a globe of the ancient world sat on a brass stand. I studied it, trying to spot the Indian peninsula.

He inhaled deeply, pressing his lips together in a tight line. My mouth was dry like sandpaper as I waited for his response.

"If you're seeking a divorce, you must have a strong case against your husband. For as the law stands, a man can divorce his wife for one instance of adultery, but a woman can only obtain a divorce if her husband is physically cruel, incestuous, or—" He coughed and reached for the cup of tea beside him, sipping at it before murmuring, "Pardon me, or . . . has engaged in bestiality—in addition to being adulterous."

I met his milky brown eyes. "It seems then, Mr . . . Mr . . ."

"Hepplewhite."

"It seems, Mr Hepplewhite, that the law is heavily stacked in the husband's favour."

He blinked as a cascade of sparks burst onto the mat from the fireplace behind him. "There are many people campaigning to change that reality, but as it stands, the present laws do undoubtedly give the husband an easier way out of a marriage."

"Then is it true I have no rights—only those my husband chooses to bestow on me?" I said, slumping to the back of the chair.

He shook his head. "No—not entirely true. As a free human being, you do have rights. I must tell you, things have improved since 1857, when the Court of Divorce and Matrimonial Causes was established. But I don't wish to waste your time on a long history lesson—only to say that many wives have enjoyed a higher rate of success with their divorce and separation actions since the system was modernised."

I felt a slight inkling of hope that was soon extinguished when I noticed his brows furrowed by a frown.

"But you must be cautious with your expectations, Mrs Trevelyan."

Since Durham was a relatively small community, I had used a false name as a precautionary measure.

"The divorce process is long and tortuous. The court sits in London, though they will accept evidence from petitioners in local courts. It will take considerable time before your case is even heard, especially if your husband contests it. And even when you get to court, your husband could easily convince a divorce court that he is a respectable and entirely reasonable man and you are the one at fault."

"But how can that be?" I said, my heart sinking with the solemn realisation that he was making perfect sense. That would be Henry's first line of defence.

Mr Hepplewhite held up his hand. "Truth be told, the court is most interested in keeping husbands and wives together and they still favour the word of a husband, especially if he is a respectable man. Is your husband a gambler?"

I shook my head.

"A drunkard?"

"No."

"A philanderer who runs away to pursue a dissolute life?"

"None of those things."

"Then why would you choose to divorce him?"

"It is a matter of deceit and cruelty."

"I see," he said, twirling his pen between ink-tipped fingers. "Then you could pursue the avenue of a judicial separation. A husband's cruelty is the most common basis for a separation, but claims of cruelty are heavily scrutinised and the most successful motions involve extreme violence, with proof of injury to be demonstrated to the court. If you were granted a judicial separation, you would be treated as a *feme sole*—a single woman, with all the rights that entails, but you would not be free to remarry."

"How long would that take?"

He sighed. "Six months to a year to go through the entire process."

*Far too long.*

I looked towards the window at the pale winter sun, now sinking below the horizon, bleeding its primrose light onto the trees outside. "I thank you for the advice, Mr Hepplewhite," I said, placing my hands on the desk and rising. "I'll consider my options carefully."

His expression suddenly softened as he rose to show me out. "Though I might appear stern and aged, I maintain strict neutrality in these delicate situations, Mrs Trevelyan. I would be pleased to be your advocate should you choose to pursue this course of action."

I nodded, thanked him, and stepped out into the street, my heart cold and heavy as the damp mist that crept up from the river.

Though Mr Hepplewhite had restored my belief that there were still some decent men about, his advice had shown me I had no other option but to escape—run away.

Abandon Henry before he disposed of me.

# Marseille

## Spring 1873

THE PORT OF Marseille is lined with grand five-storey buildings of soft ivory stone. A mild Mediterranean breeze blows across the harbour and I feel a quickening in my heart at the promise of warm nights under the stars, sailing an ocean haunted by the ghosts of ancient Phoenician, Greek, and Egyptian mariners.

The sight of the tiresome little man from the Boulogne ferry suddenly jars me—sets my teeth on edge. He has attached himself to a bevy of pale young women in grey gowns and modest bonnets, shepherding them along the quayside towards the ship. He shows off his French with a flourish and plenty of guttural *rrr*'s as he orders the porters to take care with their mountain of luggage.

Thankfully, I have only one trunk. Once I had gathered up all of Henry's belongings and sold his lavish clothing and personal effects, I had enough to pay off Buckley, buy my passage to India, and have a little left to tide me over until I reach Izzie.

My matron friend stands at the foot of the ship's stairs, transformed by a light summer ensemble in cream linen. She looks at my black dress and her wispy grey brows knit together in a frown.

"I am recently widowed," I explain.

She throws her head back and laughs heartily, displaying a solid set of yellow teeth. "That may keep the suitors at bay on the journey, my dear girl, but in India the demand for wives is so great, even widows have been propositioned on the way out of the funeral service for their departed husbands. Why, some women are so desperate to maintain their security, they entertain prospective suitors whilst caring for their failing spouse."

I feel a sudden stirring of panic. That these women would travel so far to submit themselves so willingly to a life akin to slavery. With barely any legal recourse to remove themselves from it. But I remind myself I have left that stifling existence behind me and must banish such negativity from my journey, so I smile and quickly make my way up the gangplank. I will not need a husband in India. Izzie will be my security, I remind myself, as the obnoxious man corrals his little harem into a corner of the promenade deck to watch the ship cast off.

The blue, red, and yellow triangles of the P&O flags flap like carnival streamers under a brilliant blue sky. Everything here is vivid and sun-washed—to be painted in a palette of bold primary colours touched with light. Like the golden statue of the Madonna and child perched on the towering belfry of Notre-Dame de la Garde—a monument to motherhood.

I sketched Mary Ann and her child in those weeks before the trial. I can see the picture clearly.

It is a prison cell. A fire burns, casting the subject in crimson, a mother cradling her baby to her breast, its shock of black hair glinting in the light. But the mother doesn't look at her baby. Her coal-black eyes, set deep into shadowy sockets, stare out at me, blank and impassive and utterly unreadable no matter how carefully I study them. Her mouth hangs slack, with the slight suggestion of derision in her expression.

But maybe it is mockery, or contempt for the artist who, like an insect caught in a jar, flutters vainly back and forth in her feeble attempts to escape her situation until she falls spent, beaten, and broken to the bottom.

# 22

I WAS NOT prepared for the transformation when I first visited Mary Ann and her baby. She sat in a comfortable armchair, glowing with pride and cradling the child. The round head with its downy black hair nestled against her shabby grey dress and she'd wrapped the chequered shawl around its tiny body.

She looked up at me, her eyes more gentle than I'd ever seen them. The blank, impassive expression was gone. The baby had lit them with new life.

"See how I am still blessed, even in this miserable place, Clara? She's a beauty. See her pretty fingers and the nails like little seashells." When she beamed at me with the pride of a new mother, my body went cold. Was it envy of her blissful motherhood or shame that I'd given birth to an ill-formed child? Guilt that my body had somehow blighted the budding life as it formed, killing it as surely as if I'd poisoned it? Or was it the thought of those other pale corpses lined up like lifeless dolls in their new white nightgowns, whilst their mother calmly served fruitcake to the neighbours?

"This is my little Margaret. Margaret Edith Quick-Manning Cotton," she crowed as the tiny, trusting fingers curled around hers. "Only two days old and already she smiles at me. Come here and see."

She beckoned me closer and I sat down on the stool, my eyes devouring that beautiful baby.

She stroked the silky head. "This bairn will have a better life than I had, for her father is Mr Quick-Manning, a respectable customs man. I know he will come for her and for me when he finds out all the accusations are lies. And I have vowed with every ounce of my strength to do better for this one. She is my last hope."

When she reached out and grasped my wrist, her eyes glittered with tears. "I'm a good mother, Clara. You must believe me. I never killed my baby, Robert. Dr Kilburn said himself he'd seen babies die of the teething pains, and that bairn was having terrible fits. I swear I never gave him anything but the breast. And I didn't abandon my little Georgie. I left him at the neighbour's house. I knew she'd take him back to his father. It was the only way he'd be safe, for them streets were no place for a woman with a baby in her arms. The sailors down at the docks would make you put your baby away in a drawer whilst they had their way with you."

She set the child against her shoulder and patted its back, her rough hands cradling the fragile bobbing head. I realised then, this cell had been a dark place where the hangman's shadow lurked in every corner. But now that a new life had entered here, the fire blazed cheerily in the hearth and the sun shone brightly through the barred windows, bringing with it a new sense of hope.

"A good lawyer will take all that into account and make a case for you. Have you found one?"

"Not yet. And I'm to appear at the Bishop Auckland hearing soon. There'll not be a witness to speak up for me."

"You must put a notice in the paper. Shall I write one for you?"

She sat forwards in a rush, oblivious to the child clinging to her shoulder like a newborn kitten. "Aye, we must or I have no chance in the courts."

I went to the door and asked Bertha for the paper and pen I'd left on my last visit. They'd kept it in a cupboard in the anteroom, since pens or similar implements were not allowed in the room without supervision. I settled on the stool and wrote:

*Those lawyers committed to a fair and balanced judicial process, who have an interest in representing Mrs Mary Ann Cotton at her hearing in Bishop Auckland and her subsequent trial at the Durham assizes, are invited to submit their names promptly to the accused, care of the governor of Durham Prison.*

I handed the finished product to her. "Brief and to the point."

She scanned the page, her tongue slowly tracing her upper lip as she concentrated. "Very fair handwriting. At Sunday school they always said I had a good hand, but my spelling were poor."

"Good, then you must instruct your matrons to show it to the governor, then place it in the newspaper tomorrow," I said, trying hard to smile.

"Summat's eating at you, Clara. You know you can tell me about it."

I shook my head. "You're happy today. I don't want to spoil that."

"You're afraid, Clara. Scared of being a pitiful creature with nowt to your name except the clothes you stand up in. That's why you stay with that man of yours. Am I right, Clara?"

I nodded, my stomach heavy as a lump of raw dough. "If I leave, he will come after me."

"So you come to an accused murderer for advice? You think I can help you do away with your man?"

I shook my head. "No—you misunderstand. I'm afraid of what lies out there for a woman with no family."

"You could find another man to help you, Clara. Though that never did me much good. For I always tried to put the needs of others first—like the Bible tells you to. I was still married to Robinson, but when he abandoned me, I went straight into poor Fred Cotton's house because Margaret, his sister, begged me. I helped him grieve after his wife and their newborn baby died of typhus. I comforted that man every way I could and in return I supped nowt but sorrow. The world can be a cruel place, but let me tell you, Clara, the Lord won't condemn you for trying to survive on your own. Keep your freedom, Clara. Don't look to a man to aid you. They're all bloody cowards who'll suck the very soul from you, then leave you wi' nothing."

"But where can I go? I have no money. No friends."

"A woman like you won't last five minutes on the streets. Go back to your home and look for money. If you canna find any, take something to pawn. Silver, jewellery, clothes—anything. Then use it to find another, safer place to lay your head."

I felt a glimmer of hope. Mary Ann was right. I'd pawn some of the treasures Izzie had given me. What use were they now?

Just then the baby began to fuss, its tiny mouth rooting at her bosom until she unbuttoned her bodice and put it to her breast. I watched her mouth turn up at the corners in an unfamiliar smile, her eyes half-open in a state of blissful contentment. She began to sing in her low, flat voice to the suckling baby.

*Dance to thi daddy, sing to thi mammy,*
*Dance to thi daddy, to your mammy sing.*
*You shall have a fishy on a little dishy,*
*You shall have a fishy when the boat comes in.*

Instinctively, my hand began to fly across the blank sheet of paper in my lap as I sketched mother and daughter—the severe white parting in her hair, the thin arched eyebrows, the grey hollows that framed the heavy eyelids, the shadow of fine hairs above her lip, and the fragile velvety globe of the baby's head, its weight cradled in the chequered shawl.

"Show me," she said, finally glancing upwards.

I handed the sketch to her. Her eyes darted across the paper with a hungry look.

"It's a canny portrait, Clara. Yer never told me you were an artist."

"I haven't painted for a long whilst."

She pulled the child away, its eyelids fluttering in sleep. "Yer wasted on that man. No doubt he's jealous of your talents."

"He used to say I shouldn't cheapen my art with commerce."

"Yer mean he'd begrudge you making a few pound from your handiwork?"

"It made him uncomfortable," I said, remembering Henry's impatience when visitors lingered too long on the series of fairy paintings I'd made for the nursery. "He said when I painted I became too excitable and my wild imagination would lead me down the same path as my mother."

She lowered the baby gently into the cradle and pulled the knitted blanket over the tiny body. "Eeh, I never cease to wonder—the excuses men make when a woman wants to do summat for hersel'. Bloody men like to run the show. Try to knock them off their little thrones and they'll give you what for. They twist everything around until your head spins so fast, yer canna tell the truth from the lies. That's why I'm here, Clara—because I took charge. I wouldn't let any man get the better of me. I always made my own way in the world and they don't like that in a woman."

I had so many questions to ask—to have her reassure me that I could really leave Henry—to spur me into some sort of action, but the door creaked open and Bertha stood, tucking a stray curl into her cap. "Bairn's asleep?"

"Aye, but see, Bertha. Look what Clara's done." Mary Ann beckoned her over. They stood, admiring my sketch. I'd forgotten how much I loved to draw—how I longed for the feel of a paintbrush in my hand, how I craved the oily scent of paint. The dream of supporting myself with my painting emerged like a distant mirage. Shimmering, beautiful, but presently unreachable. Unless I freed myself from Henry's clutches.

"Eeh—it's beautiful," said Bertha, looking at me as if for the first time. "Yer never said you were an artist, Clara. It's a fair likeness."

"Keep it as a present for little Margaret Edith."

Mary Ann held it up to the light again, then glanced at me, an injured look twisting her face. "This is a true portrait of me—not the murdering monster's face they plaster across the front page of the newspaper."

Neither Bertha nor I spoke. Was it doubt, suspicion, or pity that quivered in the air? The baby sighed and Mary Ann's eager voice broke the heavy silence.

"Well, don't stand there like a soft-brained bairn, Clara. Come here and put yer name on it like all the artists do. Don't they, Bertha?"

Bertha nodded and suddenly Mary Ann was animated again. The severe lines of her face softened with pure joy as I signed my name on the portrait.

“Lowry’s come to visit. Brought two friends with him,” said Bertha, tapping my shoulder. “Best be on your way, Clara, or we’ll have a crowd in here.”

“You’ll come to Bishop Auckland? To the hearing?” said Mary Ann as I put on my gloves. She held on to my wrist, her eyes entreating me. For weeks all I had seen there was emptiness—a blank void—but now life had returned to her with the arrival of the baby. I nodded that I would try to be there, and left her fussing with the baby’s blankets.

Outside, three men waited, cloth caps in their hands. Lowry, who I’d met last time; another tall, square-shouldered man I judged to be in his mid-fifties, with a wide, ruddy face, thick greying hair, and the flat, crooked nose of a prizefighter; and Joe Thornley, who carried a small basket covered with a white cloth. His grey eyes followed me as I straightened my hat, and he flashed such a smile, I felt the heat rise under my collar.

“Mrs Blackstone,” he said, dipping his head in greeting. “This is me dad, Clem Thornley.”

The older man nodded, directing a gap-toothed smile at me.

“Best bare-knuckle boxer this side of the River Tyne,” said Joe.

“Aye, until the law caught up with him and the judge bound him over to quit the fighting,” said Lowry. “Now he don’t talk much, but he’s got a heart of gold. He’ll do anything for a friend.”

The older man nodded, his eyes straying to the door behind me and Bertha, who had followed me out.

"Eeh, I didn't mean to leave you alone wi' these ruffians, Mrs Blackstone."

"I think me da's sweet on Miss Dunn," said Joe. "Canna keep him away from her bonny eyes."

"Go on with you," said Bertha, her face lit with scarlet patches at Clem's broad grin. "Mrs Falks will be back any moment and she'll report me to Mrs Callahan for unladylike behaviour."

"Canna have that," said Joe, winking at me. "Can we, Mrs Blackstone?"

"I would never want to jeopardise her position here," I said, the words spilling out stiff and formal amongst this casual company. How I envied their humour and ease.

"All right, then," said Bertha. "I'd better check this basket in case yer brought forbidden goods here, though I'm sure Mr Boxted did his job at the front door."

As Joe pulled the cloth back, I took in the glossy arch of his brows and the thin moustache—lightly waxed at the ends so it curled up above the full curve of his upper lip. His skin glowed with a pale olive sheen, broken only by the crooked scars.

"It's just a stotty loaf and a bit of spice cake to wish the baby luck," said Lowry.

"It's what we do to welcome a new baby into the world, Mrs Blackstone," said Joe. "We bring cake and a silver coin for good fortune."

"It's a beautiful gesture," I said, my heart weighed down with thoughts of returning home.

"Well, it is a kind gesture," said Bertha as Mrs Falks rushed in, her head darting around like a chicken's at the sight of the assembled company.

"Are we having a shindig here, then?" she said. "In a prison, of all places."

"I was just showing Mrs Blackstone out, Mrs Falks. You'll look after the visitors, won't you?"

I wished the men goodbye, only turning to see the three men troop into Mary Ann's room under the watchful eye of Mrs Falks.

*A silver coin for good fortune.* I realised then that with each new baby came a brightness—its shining, innocent face a miracle that might signal a turn in family fortunes. But the hope was temporary. Soon the grinding monotony of filth and poverty would dim their joy and the baby would become just one more screaming mouth to feed along with all the other hungry children.

Bertha unlocked the outer door, the jangle of her keys jogging me from my thoughts.

"She seems so happy," I said as Bertha fell into step beside me. "It's hard to believe she . . . she's . . ."

"An accused murderer?"

I nodded, glancing over at Bertha's stern face.

"We wardresses can never forget it, Clara. She canna be left alone with that baby. Not for one minute. Them's our orders and we must follow them to the letter. For the evidence is piling up against her. The doctors found that little baby Robert Robson's body was full of arsenic, as well as young Fred's. And that's a hard thing to overlook when she's the only one that tended to them when they were sick."

"But she holds the baby so tenderly."

"Aye, meks a person wonder, doesn't it?"

"When will you take her to Bishop Auckland?"

"Tomorrow. You can go too, if you wish. We'll be on the half-past-eight train."

# 23

A HEAVY FOG had covered the sun by the time I left the prison, muting the street sounds to a distant echo and passersby into dim, moving shadows. My feet disappeared into the mist and I felt light and disembodied, as if I were walking through a hazy dreamworld. Wrapping my scarf over my mouth, I staggered onwards, my head muddled with thoughts of Mary Ann's trial, the baby, of Henry and his cold creeping fingers on my throat. Izzie was my only hope. The last person on earth that cared for me and yet I could not reach her. All at once, my longing for the safety of her fragile arms and the papery softness of her wrinkled cheek so overwhelmed me that I had to stop and steady myself against the dripping wall of a baker's shop.

Nearby I could make out the glow of the main post office windows. I stumbled forwards and pushed the damp wooden door open, letting myself into the bright warmth of a cavernous room lined with polished wooden counters, the air redolent with the mingled scents of paper and ink.

I approached a young clerk with an acne-scarred face and the faint beginnings of a moustache. With quiet patience, he deciphered my desperate pleas and explained that I could send a telegram to Izzie and receive a reply by the next day at a personal box that only I could access. I could even receive a money order or tickets for a passage on a ship bound for India.

I imagined Izzie standing on some sunlit pier, her yellow silk shawl fluttering as she waved her hand to welcome me after my long voyage.

The young clerk tapped his pen on the counter. "Will you send the telegram, then?"

I remembered Mary Ann's words: *Well, don't stand there like a soft-brained bairn, Clara. . . . The Lord won't condemn you for trying to survive on your own.*

Why would I waver? Unlike Mary Ann, I had the chance to free myself. And even she had said Henry would think nothing of putting me away and leaving me to rot.

My heart raced. Tears of joy and hope caught in my throat. "I will," I said, glancing away so he could not see the moistness of my eyes. Soon I was scribbling a short message on the form he'd handed to me.

> *Must come to India at soonest possible date. Please send money or tickets for passage.*
>
> *No cause for worry. All is well. Your own dear Clara.*

I assured myself that she'd have people working for her who would know exactly what to do when they received it.

"Call in late tomorrow," said the young man. "We may have heard something by then."

I arrived home having formulated a loose plan for my escape. I would secretly pack a bag in readiness and leave as soon as I'd heard from Izzie. Though the voyage was long, I would take only the barest essentials—enough to last me for several months.

The house was quiet, Alice still out at the market. I stood in the hallway, looking around at the familiar sights—the grandfather clockface painted with gold scrollwork and bunches of primroses, the wrought-iron umbrella stand, the sunlit parlour beyond the doorway. I felt a creeping sadness—I could have been happy here. I had grown fond of the city, with its ancient churches and quaint cobbled streets. But leaving meant I'd never have to lay eyes on Henry, and that was worth the sacrifice.

His study door was shut, but since I was alone, I felt a sudden urge to uncover more secrets. I hurried into the kitchen and took the keys from the peg bag. Within minutes, I stood over his desk, imagining how I might scramble and muddle all his carefully stacked lecture notes or pour cold tea over them just to spite him.

Instead I rifled through the drawers until I came upon an envelope from India, but it was empty, the letter gone. Underneath it was a letter written in Adeline's looped handwriting. Cautious not to disturb any other documents, I slid the letter from its hiding place and read.

*Dearest Henry,*

*I am hoping this letter finds you well and more settled in your new home, though I fear that is not the case since your wife returned.*

*You said in your last letter that she is withdrawn and still shows signs of belligerence and unpredictability. Might I remind you, I had reservations about that woman from the start. I told you she was a flighty one with a mind like an unhinged door. Not surprising, considering her people were loose bohemian types. You should have held out for a girl with class and a good family. Worse than that, she has failed to produce a healthy child, which has caused your poor father no end of sleepless nights. Only yesterday, I found him tearing at his straw hat and lamenting the possible death of the Blackstone name.*

*You must face the truth now, Henry. You have a barren and unstable wife. How must this appear to your colleagues and especially to your esteemed mentor, Reverend Buckley? Why, I'm sure it is food for gossip of the most unsavoury kind. For that reason, you must keep your wife's activities firmly in hand. Keep her away from your colleagues. You cannot risk any further smears on your reputation.*

*Despite all this gloom and doom, I was overjoyed to learn that you received a notice from India, regarding the eccentric grandmother's failing health. You must write and tell me the details.*

*I always said you would raise yourself up in the world and you would never be like your father, with the stink of the pigsty on your hands. That life is not for you, my dear son. You are bound for better things, and I do not want to see that girl lead you to an empty, fruitless life. You deserve the best, so keep your chin up. In a few months, you will grasp the golden fleece and finally discover the true value of the old biddy's worth. You will then be wealthy enough to make some hard choices about this so-called marriage of yours.*

*Ever your loving mother,*
*Adeline.*

I threw the letter back onto the desk.

*What a disgusting, odious serpent was Adeline Blackstone with her venomous words! How fiercely she had tried to engineer Henry's future.*

I remembered the first time I met her—a stout, forthright woman with eyes so sharp, even a spider could not escape her scrutiny. She was in the habit of wearing plain dresses of severe black or navy with starched white collars, whilst Henry's father was an unwieldy, rumpled sort of man covered permanently with a fine dusting of wheat chaff. He sported a battered straw hat, which he left on each time he blustered into the kitchen. His wife's eyes flashed and her eyebrows rose to alarming heights. "Remove that donkey's breakfast from your head in company," she screeched.

Later I caught Mr Blackstone conversing openly with his late mother's portrait in the parlour. I drew back too late. Glancing over at me, he mumbled, "No matter," and made a great show of stoking the fire. Afterwards, he stormed into the dining room and chided Henry—in the midst of studying a weighty mathematical treatise—for *burying his nose in a book like a pinch-nosed priest.* This insult had precipitated the swift intervention of Mrs Blackstone.

"Hold your tongue, you old *nincompoop.* My boy will never slaughter a pig or muddy his feet with cow clarts," she blazed, though her head barely reached her husband's shoulder. "He's bound for the better things in life."

Mr Blackstone struggled to articulate a response until he thought the best of it and slunk off to a wicker chair on the front porch to smoke his pipe. Henry sat, head buried in the book, seemingly oblivious to the pantomime going on around him. Or he just chose to ignore her, like his father. Both men, utterly beaten into submission, had surrendered every aspect of their lives to the machinations of the formidable Adeline Blackstone.

And I knew she had always considered me an absolute failure as the wife and future mother of her beloved Henry's children.

"Motherhood is the holiest function bestowed on women, Clara," she'd announced after my first miscarriage. "So we must hope there is no physical incapacitation preventing you from undertaking this most hallowed duty."

But now that I'd failed to give birth to a healthy child, she looked for Henry to replace me with another wife who could produce a brood of healthy babies to bear the Blackstone name and inherit the legacy that was rightfully mine. I would never allow it. When Izzie heard of Henry's wicked scheming, she would do all in her power to stop even a penny from reaching his greedy hands.

I replaced everything as I'd found it in the drawer and hastened upstairs to begin packing my belongings. Until the tickets arrived, I would tread softly in the house and wear a face of utter obedience, leaving no room for Henry to suspect I was up to anything. Only two, maybe three more days, and I'd be free.

After almost a year in the asylum, I was an expert at fading into the shadows.

At becoming a ghost of a woman.

# 24

I WOKE UP with a start the next day. Henry hadn't returned home until after midnight, and I'd spent a restless night waiting for the morning light to break through the darkness. For then I could get out of the house, make my way to the train station in time for the half-past-eight train to Bishop Auckland, attend the hearing, then hurry back to the Durham post office to see if word had come from Izzie. But Alice bustled into my room with a breakfast tray and reminded me that we were to accompany the Buckleys to the seaside in an hour.

I flopped down onto the bed, fighting the urge to beat my fists against the bedposts and cursing myself that I'd forgotten Emma's whispered invitation as we'd left the ball a few days ago.

"Tell Mr Blackstone I'm feeling unwell," I told Alice as she scurried off, shaking her head and muttering. Now every moment spent near Henry had my stomach in turmoil. My insides knotted and twisted at the sound of his footsteps on the stairs and I was forever checking the door in case he burst in. But soon the clatter of hooves sounded outside, signalling the Buckleys' arrival. I ran to the door and listened to the commotion of footsteps and voices, praying they'd leave without me so I could go about my business. But it was not to be. Heavy footsteps echoed on the stairs followed by a loud rapping on my door.

"Clara, are you there?" said Emma.

My heart fell. Why couldn't they leave me alone?

"Let me in, Clara."

I got up and opened the door. Emma swooped inside in a flurry of veils and stiff woollen skirts. "My goodness, dear. You're pale as a ghost. You must come to Seaham and get some fresh air. Bring the colour back to your cheeks."

"I-I have a headache," I mumbled, sinking back onto the bed.

"Come, come," she said, throwing my wardrobe doors open. She took out a warm jacket and bonnet. "We'll wrap you up so snugly, you won't feel a draught, and the sea air will clear your sinuses. You'll see. You'll get such an appetite after a brisk walk. We'll eat fried fish afterwards. You've never tasted anything as good as freshly caught cod."

She led me downstairs, supporting my arm as if I were an invalid. Henry stood at the bottom, glowering. Buckley stood behind him. I met their eyes with a stony glare and Henry averted his gaze, busying himself with the arrangement of his muffler.

"Good news, she is coming," said Emma.

"Very well," said Buckley, sighing with impatience. "Our Amy is waiting in the carriage."

Reverend Buckley took it upon himself to act as our tour guide, insisting that I, as the newcomer, should sit near the window. I was glad to distract myself with the passing view rather than force myself to talk to any of them, especially Henry, who seemed oblivious to everyone else but Amy, sitting opposite, a picture in deep green velvet. Each time she smoothed out her gloves or fidgeted with her reticule or tapped her mother's shoulder to whisper in her ear, Henry's eyes flew to her, devouring every dainty action. I turned away to watch the stubble-filled fields and frosted hedgerows as they passed by in a blur.

Soon the autumn fields gave way to a vast sweep of cliff top. Beyond the rocky outcrops, the sparkling sea spread out towards the horizon where water met sky, merging into a blue-grey wash of colour. A lighthouse stood at the farthest point of a long pier, and a vast sandy beach stretched in both directions as far as the eye could see.

Mary Ann had met Joe Nattrass here at Seaham, and I imagined her as a young woman, walking along that windy beach, her black hair streaming behind her. Could that vital young girl have ever imagined the twisted course her life would take? Or could he have known the terrible way he would die, his body riddled with arsenic?

We assembled on the cliff top, ready to begin our descent down the steep iron stairway to the sand. Reverend Buckley paused at the top of the stairs.

"I must warn you," he said, wrapping his scarf under his jowly jawline. "Take care not to invite the attention of beggars, vagabonds, or undesirables on the beach. The children are particularly persistent when begging for pennies or sweets or . . ." But then the wind whipped around our heads and stole the rest of his words, whisking his red hair upwards like a stiff rooster's comb.

We seemed such an intrusive presence as we made our way down to the quiet sands, Buckley's loud observations disturbing the soothing rhythm of the waves washing onto the shore. Despite the winter chill, he persistently wiped his forehead with a large handkerchief and his face glowed as red as a boiled lobster, but the fresh sea air stung my face with such a frosty bite, I wished I could take off and run away from them all. Seek refuge in one of the stone cottages nestled along the cliff top, their chimneys smoking and windows bravely facing the brisk sea winds.

Today the sea was a steely grey ribbon, rippling and foaming as the tide came in. Ragged clusters of people waded through the icy water. A mother and three barefoot children pulled a cart along the sand, stopping now and then to gather rocks at the shoreline, their tattered jackets soaked with water.

"These humble people are gathering sea coal," Buckley explained. "It will last them through the winter if they can find enough."

"Such a futile struggle for survival," said Henry, watching the solemn group as they stared openmouthed at us before continuing with their gathering.

I was relieved when he hastened on ahead to catch up with Buckley, who had gone to watch some curlew hunters grouped around the higher rocks. I turned to follow Emma and Amy in the direction of the lighthouse.

Just then the wind picked up, whisking my bonnet ribbons across my face and sending the waves crashing onto the shore. The family of coal gatherers had moved further along the beach and left their youngest child squatting in the shallows, where he poked amongst the rock pools with a piece of driftwood.

The tide was so strong that the waves swept in, flooding the rockeries with foamy brown water. The mother, heedless of her youngest child, plodded away in the distance, her other children hanging on to the cart. I cursed her carelessness and moved closer to the little boy, in case a wave should rush in and swallow him up. He was no more than three and his feet and legs were blue with the cold. He crouched down low and though he shivered, his mouth hung open in fascination at the crab that scuttled away from his stick. Sandy curls of hair covered his head and his eyelashes fluttered like two rows of feathers. He licked at the sticky column of mucus that oozed from his nose. I moved so close, I could see the rime of dirt on his neck and the scabs and bruises on his little legs. I longed to pick him up, wipe him clean, then feed him warm soup until he fell asleep in my arms, safe from neglect and harm.

Suddenly a huge wave washed into shore, knocking him backwards onto his bottom. He floundered about in the wet sand awhilst until he pulled himself up and began to wail, wiping a tattered sleeve across his sticky nose. In an instant I picked him up and gathered him into my shawl.

"There, there," I said, drying him off. "This will make it better." But he took one look at me with his wide blue eyes and began howling even louder.

"No—no, don't cry," I pleaded, hugging him harder though his sharp little feet kicked at my ribs. "I'll look after you." I staggered along the beach towards the shelter of the steep cliffs.

From the corner of my eye, I spied his mother running towards us, yelling, her voice whipped away in the gusts of wind. The child's cheeks were raw and red from bawling and his tiny body shuddered with sobs as he strained to escape my grasp. And though the bitter stink of urine wafted from his clothes, I held him tighter, afraid to put him down for fear he would run back towards the incoming tide. But the more I held him, the more he shrieked.

The mother, a rag-haired slip of a girl, bore down on me, screeching, "Baby-stealer, she's trying to kidnap me bairn!" Scarlet-faced from the wind, she bared a row of broken teeth, snarling like a wildcat as she snatched the infant from my hands and gave me a good hard shove that sent me stumbling backwards until I landed with a thump on the sand. A sharp pain shot up my back.

"I ought ter call a policeman. Kidnapping an innocent bairn—she should be locked up."

I slipped and slid in the wet sand as I tried to struggle to my feet.

"What the devil is all this fuss about?" boomed Buckley as he and Henry and then Emma ran up to me, their chests heaving.

"I-I was just trying to help," I stuttered.

"More like trying to make off with my little Luke!" she screeched.

"No—that's not what happened. I picked the boy up when a wave knocked him over. The child was in danger."

At this the mother became agitated. "Well, that's just like you posh buggers—telling barefaced lies. I wonder what the judge'd have ter say about it."

"That won't be necessary," said Buckley, producing a few coins from his pocket. "This should clear things up."

"No, Donald—I won't let you," Henry said, darting poisonous looks my way, but the woman's hand shot out too quickly and grabbed the money.

"But I did nothing wrong," I insisted, watching the woman yank the sobbing child away and march off towards the rest of her brood, still mumbling curses.

"Let Donald handle this, Clara," said Emma, bustling up behind me. "We should go to the teahouse until all the fuss dies down."

I hesitated, but Henry flashed such a black and terrible look at me, my heart rushed to my throat. Suddenly clouds blocked the sun and the sky seemed leaden. I turned away from him and trudged across the sand, my skirt hem soaked with seawater. Emma and Amy walked ahead, turning to stare at me as if I were a mad, hopeless creature.

When I heard Amy ask, "Is she drunk, Mama?" I turned in my tracks and ran in the other direction, towards the staircase and the cliff. Some wild voice in my head told me that if I could just get to the top, I'd knock on a cottage door and beg for sanctuary—away from all these people who sought to destroy me.

I ran, oblivious to their calls, which were carried away by the fierce gusts of wind. Henry tore after me, his hat swinging in one hand, the other frantically beckoning me back. But that small voice told me to keep running.

*Faster, faster.*

*Get away from him whilst you can.*

A stiff burst of wind swept my bonnet up and off my head, sending it skittering across the sand. But I flew across the beach until I reached the stairs and began to climb, my lungs bursting with the effort. Holding on with both hands, I pulled myself upwards, determined to reach the top. The rusty rail grazed my palms, but I staggered on until I spied the scrub grass and jagged rocks at the summit.

Mounting the last step, I took off into the open field. The sea spread out on three sides like a heaving black cloth. To my left, a group of men unloaded fishing rods from their carriage. Their heads turned as I ran by, but my mind was focused on the tiny pinpoints of light that danced in front of my eyes. I staggered forwards a few hundred yards only to find myself staring over the edge of a sheer cliff, at the dark sea that frothed and boiled around the rocks.

A wave of nausea washed over me.

*It's not so far down, then you'll be rid of him forever.*

Now the wind moaned and shrieked around the rocky inlets, wetting my face with an icy spray. Wet snakes of hair coiled around my neck.

I could taste the salt on my lips.

*It's not so far down.*

I heard the thundering of footsteps behind me and glanced around to see Henry, gulping for air, his face purple from running. He stopped a few feet away and bent over, hands on his knees. After a few moments he spoke in a strange, quiet voice.

"You want to jump, Clara? It could be so easy. You'd fly like a bird over the edge and then you'd feel no more pain. Your wretched life would be over and no one would miss you."

My body shook with sobs. He was right. Who would miss me? An accused murderer? Izzie, who was dying and out of reach? I was utterly alone.

He continued in a slow, hypnotic voice. "You know there's no one left to cry for you. Not your mad, deluded mother, and that miserly old scarecrow you call your grandmother will be food for worms soon."

I covered my ears with my hands and shook my head. Rage welled up like acid in my throat until I screamed out the words I'd held inside. "She tried to warn me about you and I refused to listen. You are a vile, disgusting liar—a pathetic excuse for a man—not worthy to even utter her name. I would rather dash my brains out on those rocks than spend another moment with you."

My heart raced. Bright rays of sunlight seemed to warp and buzz around my head. I turned and stepped forwards until my toes were a few inches from the cliff edge, until the sky and sea spread out before me like a blue-grey sheet. So welcoming, I could have launched myself out towards the horizon.

"Jump, Clara. You know you must."

A gull dove down into the foam, then swooped back upwards, leaving shimmering beads of water in its wake. I turned to look at Henry, his eyes reddened by the gusty wind, his face paper-white and pinched, his heart barren and empty. My foot slid forwards, sending a barrage of pebbles skittering down the cliffside. I swung back round. The ledge was crumbling beneath my left foot. I heard Henry's sharp intake of breath, then I sensed Izzie's voice above the rushing of the wind.

*Never surrender your own free will and bend to someone else's, Clara.*

I took a step back, away from the ledge.

*I would not die to benefit him.*

Just then a gull shrieked overhead and someone yelled, "Stop her, man! She'll fall!" I twisted round. One of the fishermen had broken from the group and was racing towards us.

Henry's eyes widened with fear and confusion. Before I could draw another breath, he lunged forwards and sent me crashing sideways to the ground. I slammed down on the grass with the full force of his body on mine. A thousand white sparks exploded across my eyes. The sky seemed to spin in circles above me as I clawed and wriggled to pull myself out from under him, but he held my arms fast, pinning me facedown on the grass.

I threshed and twisted to free myself. "Filthy, lying beast!" I screamed, my cheek grinding into the rough ground until I tasted soil and bitter grass. "Murderer. You would kill me to get what you want."

"Shut your mouth, you fool," he hissed, pressing the flat of his hand across my mouth. "You've gone too far this time."

The man came thundering towards us, his face streaked with sweat. "Sir, you are a hero. She was about to jump."

Henry scrambled to his feet then held out an arm to pull me up, his eyes blazing as if daring me to utter one word. "First I had to convince her that her life was worth living," he said, brushing the soil from his jacket then shaking the man's outstretched hand.

"We have hot tea and blankets," the man said. "You must bring her over and warm her up."

Henry's arm snaked around my waist and he pulled me tightly to him as we followed the man to his carriage. I stumbled over the rough tussocks of grass and rocky outcrops as he put his mouth close to my ear.

"Breathe one word of this to anyone and I'll have you locked up in the madhouse before you can blink."

That night a storm blew in. Cold draughts wheezed in under the doors and the whole house seemed to bend and creak in the wind. I drifted in and out of dreams, waking to jagged white flashes of lightning across the window. Then came a deafening thunder crack that stirred the very bones of the house. I sat bolt upright to see Henry sitting on the chair by my bed. Lightning bleached his face to a livid white. My blood froze. I pulled the sheets up to my neck, squeezed my eyes shut, and prayed I was only dreaming.

But when the lightning subsided and I could hear only the patter of rain, I opened my eyes again. He was still there, a dark figure cast in shadow.

He placed his fingers together as if in prayer. "Don't be afraid, Clara. I'm your husband. May I not come to your room?"

"How long have you been watching me?"

"Long enough to witness your troubled sleep."

"The storm disturbs me."

He shook his head. "No, no, Clara. Perhaps it is your guilty conscience that troubles you."

"Or yours," I whispered.

"Why should I be guilty?"

I remembered standing over the sheer cliff face and the water foaming around the jagged rocks below and the low, hypnotic drone of his voice above the rushing wind. "You want me dead. You said so on the cliff top."

His eyes were sunk in dark pools of shadow, but they shifted sideways in a lie. "Paranoid ravings of an unstable woman. Not a soul would believe you."

"I know what I heard."

"But Clara, who would trust the words of a miserable liar that sneaks around behind her husband's back and befriends a notorious murderer? Did you think Reverend Buckley wouldn't hear about your little *visits* and tell me that you have been seeking out the company of a wholesale poisoner? Not a soul would believe your ravings. Your mind is broken." He rose to his feet and began to pace across the carpet, stroking his chin and glancing at me every now and then. "Reverend Buckley assures me I have a good chance of promotion, and I mean to surpass his expectations. I have always dreamt of being a senior professor at such a prestigious university."

His face softened a little and he gazed towards the window as if regarding something perfect and beautiful—a ripe fruit hanging just beyond his reach. I sat up in bed, my heart racing.

"Then let me go, Henry. I will leave quietly, go to India, and you'll never have to worry about me being an embarrassment to you again."

He stopped in his tracks and shook his head, his voice low and threatening as he reached into his pocket and pulled out a slip of paper. "Never, ever speak of leaving me. And you can forget any ideas about going to India. Just this evening I received a telegram from Izzie's doctor. It seems you sent a rather puzzling message to your ailing grandmother. Of course, considering your volatile state, Dr Price has strict instructions to inform me of any correspondence bearing your name. You can assume then that there will be no *rescue* or tickets to India,

Clara. Instead you will stay here like a dutiful wife and never mention going away again."

"You want to keep me from seeing Izzie?"

"Your duty is here with me, your husband."

I imagined launching myself at him—tearing his smug face to shreds with my bare hands, but I tamped down the fury and let it simmer deep inside. Nothing would be gained by arguing with him. Slyness and secrecy were my best weapons.

He stood by the bed, leaned towards me, and spoke in a strange but quiet voice. "It's in your hands now, Clara. If you make any mention of today's events or even try to leave me, I will find you and I will commit you. Buckley assures me I need signatures from only two medical men, together with my own, to have you put away with no hope of ever getting out again. All I ask is that you act as an obedient wife. You can have your prison and your morbid association with a murderer and I will live my own life, free to pursue my own interests. Agreed?"

*Until you get your hands on the inheritance and put me into an asylum again.*

The darkness seemed cloying. Suffocating. My entire life dominated by this cold and calculating man.

He straightened up and rummaged in his pocket. "I'll take your silence as agreement. Now, you'll need an extra dose of sleeping draught to ensure you get a good long rest. Sleep is the best remedy for all you've been through today."

I clutched at the sheets as he opened a new bottle of laudanum, clasped my chin, and tipped a quantity into my mouth. I fell back on the bed as the hateful drug trickled down my throat.

When I finally drifted into sleep, I dreamt I stood outside Mary Ann's house on Front Street. It was a clear starlit night and the full moon cast a silvery sheen onto the road. She stood on her doorstep still as a stone statue. When she saw me, she held out her arms and beckoned me into a dark kitchen occupied by a long wooden table covered with knotted lumps of rags. "Come and see my dear husbands, Clara. See how they tried to abandon me," she said, covering her eyes. Her whole body shook with convulsions.

"Don't cry," I said, grasping at her hands until I pulled them away from her face.

She was not crying, but laughing so hard that tears streamed from her eyes.

"I held them down until the last breath shuddered through their miserable bodies," she whispered in a strange, hoarse voice.

And then I looked closer at the lumpy mounds and saw they were not rags, but naked corpses, stiff and grey and piled on top of one another like carcasses at a butcher's shop. I strained to look closer at the whiskered face of the body on top and it was Henry, lying cold and dead, but his face moved and shifted in the shadows. "He still lives," I said, peering closer, but drew back in horror as maggots squirmed from his hollow eye sockets, wriggled into his open mouth, and writhed all over his body. Then thick white grubs split and transformed into fat winged insects until clouds of buzzing flies filled the air, swirling and boiling like great thunderclouds.

# 25

WHEN THE FRONT door slammed shut the next morning, I peered through a gap in the curtains and watched Henry stride out onto the street. A fine drizzle speckled the black silk of his umbrella whilst the blustery wind pushed and pulled at its ribs until it appeared like a large hovering crow. I could not tear my eyes away until he'd turned the corner at the end of the street and disappeared from my sight. Only then could I take a deep breath, knowing the house was rid of his vile presence for the rest of the day. He had cut off my best means of escape. Now Izzie had no idea I was in trouble.

I paced back and forth across the room, thoughts veering across my mind. *My husband wants me locked up or dead; then his way to Izzie's money is clear.* Even if he decided to keep me trapped here alive until Izzie passed away, he was bound to rid himself of me afterwards. I steadied myself against the bedpost to stem the waves of panic.

*Death was better than a lifetime in the madhouse.*

*But I wanted to live.*

*What to do? What to do?* But the ideas fled from me like wisps of fog until I could not grasp on to anything substantial except the knowledge that I was trapped in a loveless marriage at the mercy of a man who regarded me only as an obstacle standing in the way of his blind ambition.

*A man without conscience or any shred of human feeling.*

I ran to the window and heaved it upwards, forcing myself to gulp in mouthfuls of cold air until my mind began to slow down and I could think more clearly. Alice was still clinking pots in the kitchen below and I remembered Mary Ann's advice. I busied myself scouring my room for things to pawn. Her voice urged me on.

*Look for money. If you canna find any, take something to pawn. Silver, jewellery, clothes—anything. Then use it to find another, safer place to lay your head.*

I set my carpetbag open on the bed and began to fill it with my silver vanity set as well as Izzie's crystal perfume bottle, several pairs of earrings, a sapphire necklace, and a china sweet dish. What good were trifles like these when my freedom was at stake? The only item I kept was my mother's jade-and-walnut jewellery box.

Five minutes later, I slipped out of the pawnshop with a small leather pouch of money that I fastened to my petticoat strap after the pawnbroker alerted me to the dangers of walking the streets with a large amount of ready cash. But it was still not enough to get me to India. I would have to find more valuables to pawn and that meant returning to the house. But that thought was so abhorrent, I drifted instead towards the prison. In my desperation I thought Mary Ann might have some other suggestion—some way to rid myself of the man who would condemn me to a madhouse where I'd moulder away until my mind degenerated into complete submission to a grizzled tyrant of a doctor, or I was knocked silly with a kneeling board by some scoundrel of an attendant.

Bertha was folding baby clothes into a pile when I arrived. I felt her eyes on me as I took off my gloves.

"I couldn't sleep," I said, my hand flying to my hair to check for stray strands. "But how is Mary Ann?"

She shook her head as she held up a tiny lace-trimmed nightgown. "Not so good. When you didn't come to the hearing, she was worried you'd abandoned her like all the other fair-weather friends. And after the new charges, she took a turn for the worse. She is to be tried first for the murder of Charles Edward Cotton, then afterwards for the murders of Nattrass, young Frederick Cotton, and the baby Robert Robson Cotton—bless their poor little souls."

I cast my eyes to the floor. "I wish I could have been there."

Bertha planted a thick red hand on her hip. "I never thought I'd utter these words, but that trial were a mockery of justice. Mary Ann had no one to speak for her. No witnesses, and sixteen pressmen were there looking out for every little twitch of her face. But thankfully, she's found a lawyer and that has helped a bit. Mr Thomas Campbell Foster has been appointed to represent her and has already attended to her here, but should he return, I must ask you to step outside."

"Will she talk to me?" I asked, glancing towards the cell.

"You can try," she said, leading me to the door, "but she's not in a hopeful frame of mind. Though a visit from a friend might buck her up."

Mary Ann was sitting on her chair, watching the baby sleep in the cradle. When she turned to look at me, I stopped short, stunned by her stringy, unwashed hair, combed severely back so it hung in tangled rattails around her shoulders. Her thin pale face was smudged with dark hollows under her eyes, her dry lips chewed to scabs.

She twisted a washcloth in her hands. "I have a proper lawyer now. A fine, respectable man. Mr Thomas Campbell Foster, Q.C. He tells me we can make a case of accidental death."

"How would you claim that?" I said, settling myself on the stool.

She leaned closer and spoke in a low, confidential voice. "It's all scientific, you see. The arsenic come from the green wallpaper on the bairns' walls. It says here it's full of arsenic. Learned men have done all these studies," she said, taking up a handful of papers from the pile stacked on the stool next to her. "Foster told me the damp and heat makes the paper flake off and the children breathe it in whilst they're sleeping."

"And what about adults?"

"Them too. The poison's lurking everywhere. In curtains, cushions, medicines. I told him I saw clouds of it come off the bedposts and mattresses after I'd cleaned them."

"But why did it not affect you?"

"Some folk have a weak disposition, Clara, but I'm made of stronger stuff." She glanced over as the baby stirred in her sleep, her eyelashes fluttering against her cheeks. "Aye—she's a little beauty, and sweet-natured, too. I wish . . ."

She stopped mid-sentence and we listened for a moment to the baby's soft, even breathing. I thought then about the terrible reality that her mother might be strung up on a gallows in a few weeks. The idea hung unspoken in the silence between us, tainting the air with gloom. Mary Ann's fear of the death sentence would be the creeping, clutching thing that stopped her from combing her hair or tidying her clothes or wiping her face with a washcloth. What purpose did those trivial routines serve when your neck might soon be broken by order of the crown?

"You didn't hear what they said about me in Bishop Auckland," she said, breaking the silence.

"I am sorry I couldn't be there."

"No matter. It was all just gossiping neighbours lying through their teeth to get a bit of attention. I never gave them bairns arsenic. Even though the police searched every inch of my house, they never found any, and all the teapots were clean. That bastard Riley stirred up all the gossip against me. Got everyone nattering about how I laid my own dead baby out in the same room as Nattrass when he was sick. What was I to do? I hadn't the heart to leave the bairn alone and I had to tend to Nattrass and his fits. They'd have people think I buried the two of them together to save time. That's not true: the bairn was buried on the Sunday. Nattrass died the next day and we buried him on Wednesday."

"Your lawyer will clear all that up now."

She shook her head and rocked back and forth. "I was in a bad way then. A terrible way. I knew my baby was going to die and so I asked my neighbour to make a nightdress. I wanted him to be laid out nice and pure like a little angel."

"But can you see how bad that might look?"

"I cared for all of them. On my own. I did what had to be done." She looked up at me with a wan smile. "And let me tell you something they didn't put in those newspaper stories or talk about in court. Joe Nattrass had a filthy habit—he was an arsenic eater. He had that poison all over the house and now they blame me for it. It's no wonder his whole body was steeped in arsenic."

"But why would someone knowingly take poison like that?"

She chewed at a strand of hair, her wild eyes darting from me to the sleeping baby. "It's like this, Clara—some men tek arsenic so they can feel like more of a man—if yer catch my drift. And when it come to these types of *habits,* the more yer tek, the more yer need, until yer gambling with yer own life. And when yer sick—as Nattrass was with his kidneys—yer'll do anything to forget the pain. So it's not surprising that the poison found its way into the bellies of them innocent bairns. He were none too careful at that time, for he were suffering terrible from kidney disease and we all knew it."

"Why couldn't you tell that to the court?" I said, incredulous that such important evidence had been completely ignored.

"Smith didn't do his job and it was too late to call witnesses for the defence."

"Then you must tell Mr Campbell Foster."

She caught my wrist and thrust her face towards me, her eyes so wide, the whites showed around them. "There's more, Clara. I swear Kilburn, the chemist, and his addle-headed assistant, Chalmers, are both liars. They're afeared folk will find out they made a mistake. See, the poison was in the medicine Chalmers made up for Kilburn. Those two don't know if they're coming or going with all those bottles on the shelves. The arsenic is out there in the open for all to see. Chalmers was so busy, he didn't check the labels. I know it."

"Do you have proof?"

She shook her head. "When the police searched my house, Dr Kilburn took away the empty medicine bottles. Probably knew what Chalmers had done. Even Sergeant Hutchinson said he saw him make away wi' them, though Kilburn denies it."

"You must tell your lawyer everything. He'll decide how that information can be used."

"I have. But Clara, I'm poor. A nobody. Kilburn and Chalmers and Riley have got the better of me. But you—you've got money, and you know what I told you about that. Make plans to move on, for there's always someone standing in the way of a person's happiness, trying to stick a knife in their back and twist it until they drop. Get out of there and leave your rascal husband behind."

"I wish I could rid myself of him forever." Once spoken, the words seemed to hang in the dank, musty air. My hand flew to my mouth. "I shouldn't have said that."

A long silence followed. She placed her palms flat on the edge of the cradle and tilted her head, smiling a strange, crooked smile at me. "Why, Clara. Everyone considers murder at some point in their lives. Even proper ladies like you."

"I couldn't contemplate such a thing," I said, breathless.

Wiry strands of hair fell across her temple as she leaned closer and hissed, "But you just did, Clara, and I was your witness."

"Forget I said it," I whispered, my heart thundering so loud, I swore she could hear.

She wiped a hand across her mouth. "Well, mebbe I will, pet. Yer secret's safe wi' me, as long as you believe that all I did was buy arsenic and soft soap to get the fleas out of the bed frames and mattresses."

I took a deep breath. "Where did you buy that arsenic?"

Her eyes flickered towards me. "You want some for yourself, Clara? Mebbe put a bit in the old man's tea?"

"No—no," I stuttered, shaking my head. "I was only curious."

She smiled a sly, knowing smile. "Of course you were, pet. You wouldn't 'White-powder' your own husband."

"White-powder him?"

"That's just what folk call arsenic poisoning. But I never bought poison. I only bought arsenic and soft soap-mixture. Summat everybody uses to rid themselves of the ticks that carry disease. You can buy it at the chemist's shop. And now look at me. Forsaken by the world, and all those bastards won't rest until I'm strung up on a rope. You'll see, Clara. I shall be swinging at the end of a noose before you get up the courage to do summat about your scallywag of a husband."

"I have no stomach for it."

"If there was no other way, you could do it."

I glanced at the door to see if Bertha was watching us. "How?" I whispered.

"First look me in the eye, Clara, and I'll tell you once again I'm an innocent woman, wrongly accused."

I reached out and took her rough, scaly hand. It was cool and dry and flinched slightly at my touch.

"I believe the courts and the newspapers have wronged you. I believe they will be hard-pressed to give you a fair trial."

"Then come closer, dear, and I'll tell you all I know."

I leaned inwards until my hair mingled with hers.

Until my cheek brushed against her lips.

I remember thinking, *The lips of a monster are grazing my ear,* as she whispered, "Some folk dilute the arsenic and soft soap with water until the powder sinks to the bottom of the bottle and then—not too much at once . . . only a little at a time . . ."

When I pulled away, the last words I heard were *two penn'orth of arsenic dissolves nicely in a hot cup of tea.*

"Make your move, pet. I would if I were in your shoes. I mean, if I were the type of person to commit such a crime."

She held one finger to her lips and I stared at her for a long moment, and between us there passed a look of such understanding, I was shaken to the core.

"Will you come to my trial, then?" she said. Her eyes searched mine, moist and shining but devoid of tears.

"I will. If you look up to the gallery, I'll be there."

"That will be a comfort, I suppose," she said, bowing her head again. Then little Margaret Edith began to cry and the other matron, Mrs Sewell, pushed the door open, a pile of baby clothes in her arms.

"I have fresh laundry for the bairn. Clean nightdresses and bonnets. We'll change the little flower so she's comfortable," she said. As she placed the linens on the bed, her eyes fell on the few gifts I'd brought—a knitted shawl and some baby soap I'd bought on the way to the prison.

"What's this, then?" she demanded.

"Just a few little things I bought for the child."

"She can keep the shawl, but I'll be taking the soap," she snapped. "Best leave Mary Ann to rest now and come along with me."

"Aye—go on with you, Clara, but don't listen to any of her bloody lies," hissed Mary Ann. "I'll be telling the governor I want a change of wardress. This one canna keep her gob shut."

Confused and vexed at the interruption, I followed Mrs Sewell as she bustled out, her head down and the soap clutched in her hand. She locked the cell door shut and turned to me, her face set in a frown.

"I know you are a regular visitor here, but I believe you were warned to exercise caution around the prisoners, and now you bring presents to Mrs Cotton without having us check them. That cannot be allowed. We have to keep a sharp eye on her at all times. Only the other day one of the other matrons caught her stealing slivers of soap and hiding them in her pockets."

"But what's the harm in that?"

"The soap's not to wash the bairn, pet. But to feed her little pieces and make her sickly so Mary Ann will get more attention and the hearings will be postponed until the bairn's well again."

My throat tightened. "I had no idea. I would never knowingly harm the baby."

"I know. You're most likely a well-meaning woman who only wants to see the best in people, but I'll tell you again: you cannot trust her, no matter what she says." She patted my shoulder and spoke in a softer voice. "I didn't mean to scare you, pet. I only thought to warn you that now the trial's fast approaching, we must be more vigilant, for she's bound to grow more desperate, then who knows what she's capable of?"

I mumbled my apologies and left before she could say another word. My head felt so light. *I am like a gullible child where Mary Ann is concerned.* She had spun her web and caught me in her silken lies. And now I'd jeopardised the safety of her innocent child. I fled the prison, thoughts of arsenic and teapots whirling around in my head.

# 26

I SPENT THE next morning packing my carpetbag with a few articles of clothing and more belongings to pawn. My plan, hastily put together during a restless night, was to visit the pawnshop again and scrape together enough money for passage to India, then catch a train to Folkestone and wait until the steamer sailed.

I'd barely slept, afraid that Henry might burst in through the door and find I was fully dressed and had stowed a bag filled with valuables at the back of the wardrobe. But when the sun rose in a great blaze of red, I sat up, rubbing my swollen eyes, and realised it was time to leave now for good.

Steadying myself against the door, I waited and listened. Henry had already left for the university. Alice was in the kitchen, washing dishes and singing as if it were just another ordinary day, so I would slip out the front door before she spotted me. I tiptoed down the stairs, holding my dress up so it wouldn't make a rustling sound, but as I turned the front door handle, a looming figure darkened the stained-glass panel.

I tried to push the door shut, but Reverend Buckley peered around the door, blocking the opening with his foot.

"I-I was just going out," I stuttered, my heart lurching.

"I came here to wait for Henry," he said, stepping forwards so the door swung shut behind him. He stood silhouetted against the light from the doorway, blocking my path, his feet planted firmly apart, his shoulders squared and his face set in a hard, unyielding expression.

I backed away. "I'm afraid he is out."

"You were going somewhere, Clara?"

"I have an important appointment," I said, trying to push past him.

He shifted sideways, cutting off my escape. Beads of sweat dampened my forehead. I was only steps away from freedom and yet I could not get past him to the door. A scream rose in my throat, but I stifled it, afraid he'd never leave if I broke down in front of him. On impulse I threw the carpetbag under the hallway table as he unbuttoned his coat. "Of course—your work at the prison. I'm sure that can wait."

"Reverend Buckley, my husband isn't here," I said, edging towards the door. "I must leave now. You may come back when he returns."

He drew himself to his full height and glared at me, his eyes bloodshot and watery from the wind.

"*You* ask *me* to leave. I think not." He moved so close, I could smell the acrid scent of dried sweat from his clothes and feel his damp breath on my face. "Your husband tells me you have been causing him great concern lately. Since he trusts me implicitly and respects my considerable expertise in the medical field, he has asked for my assistance in helping to ascertain your mental state."

Alice rushed out, her eyes wide as dinner plates. "I'm sorry I didn't get the door, Mrs Blackstone."

"Take my coat, girl," said Buckley. "Then put the kettle on. Mr Blackstone will be here shortly with an important visitor."

I fled into the parlour, thinking I might be able to leave through the scullery, but Buckley followed close behind.

"We aren't expecting anyone," I said, my eyes darting to the kitchen and the back door.

"Henry is on the way with a very well-respected doctor. He has travelled here specifically to see you, so you would do well to settle yourself and await his arrival."

"But I feel perfectly well. I'm not in need of medical attention," I said, trying to still the tremor in my voice.

"Let me explain, Clara," he said so intimately, my flesh prickled. "Just sit down and hear me out."

I backed far away from him and perched on the edge of the sofa, clinging to the velvet cushions for comfort. Buckley flipped up the ends of his jacket and eased himself onto the straight-backed chair opposite. He crossed one leg over the other, and knit his fingers together. Then he let out a deep sigh and watched me from beneath glowering brows.

"It is well-known in medical circles, Clara, that the female mind is more excitable than the male's. Generally, religion and moral guidance provide the strength needed to curb a woman's naturally volatile temperament, but when these are weakened by reproductive troubles such as yours, the subterranean fires become active and the crater gives forth 'smoke.'"

"Smoke—what do you mean by smoke?" I said, wondering what on earth he was babbling about.

"Figuratively—I'm speaking figuratively, of course. I mean mischief, Clara. Mischief. Woman is by nature a salacious creature. Whilst the modest, well-trained wife and mother keeps her baser instincts under control in her daily life, you, on the other hand, have demonstrated a propensity for wild, impulsive behaviour that threatens the very foundation of your family."

I swallowed back the rancour that burned at my throat. "Is my family now *your* business, Reverend Buckley?"

"When a trusted colleague comes begging for my help, it is my business," he hissed with such venom that beads of spit foamed at the corners of his lips.

I wedged myself against the cushions just as the front door flew open and Henry stepped inside, followed by a tall wraith of a man dressed in a black frock coat. Buckley sprang from his chair and went to greet them.

"Have you told her, Donald?" Henry said, glancing sheepishly in my direction.

"I have, Henry. She is waiting for us."

The tall man shook Buckley's hand, then followed Buckley into the parlour. Strangely, Henry lingered in the doorway, avoiding my eyes.

"This is my learned friend, Dr Beardsley," said Buckley, his hand grazing the doctor's shoulder. "Dr Beardsley, this is Henry's wife, Clara Blackstone."

Beardsley was a middle-aged man in his forties with a lanky, skeletal figure and the pallid face and lofty, domed forehead of a monk. His arrowlike nose had flared nostrils above bushy whiskers that straggled down to his collar. But his eyes were so piercing, I felt an unsteadiness in my legs as I stood up to greet him.

"Sit, sit," he muttered, motioning with his hand.

"I have no need of a doctor. I am quite well," I protested, wishing above all else that I could fly out of the door and leave them all behind. I remembered the day at the beach when I'd watched the curlew hunters as they closed in on a frightened bird, determined to ensnare it. Now I felt that creature's terror as these three men hovered around me, measuring my reactions with their hawkish eyes.

"She hasn't been herself since she came to Durham," said Henry, stepping into the room. "Even though I've tried every way I can to make her feel safe and welcome here."

"Yes, yes, Henry," said Buckley, waving Henry aside and turning back to me. "Dr Beardsley will simply ask Clara a few questions and make some learned observations about her general demeanour and health."

They had me sit in the front parlour by the writing desk. Dr Beardsley sat opposite, perusing handwritten notes from which he read excerpts.

"'Admitted to Bethlem Hospital in an agitated state after a vicious assault of an attending nurse. The patient required restraints, due to violent outbursts of obscene language and cursing—'"

"I watched them dispose of my dead child. I saw its face. They would not let me touch or hold my baby," I cried, glancing up at Henry, who hovered in the doorway, eyes cast to the hallway floor.

"Please do not break my concentration, Mrs Blackstone," said Beardsley, sniffing and pinching at his nose. He continued reading: "'Periods of agitation and distress followed by long periods when the patient will not eat unless forced to. Will not dress or undress herself. Tears at her clothes and speaks in gibberish. Attempts to involve her in rehabilitative activities result in stubborn refusal and defiance. Patient must be physically removed from the workroom.'" He looked up at me with weary eyes. "Mrs Blackstone, do you believe you deserved to be committed?"

"Dr Shepton said extreme behaviour can often follow a difficult birth and that rest and gentle care would have been preferable—"

"I am not here to dispute another learned colleague, but to form my own opinion. Mrs Blackstone, do you believe your husband confined you unjustly?"

My throat was parched. "I do. If they had let me hold my baby, I would have grieved and made peace with its death."

"And do you continue to shun your husband's affections because you harbour a grudge against him?"

*I would rather hold a venomous snake to my breast than let that selfish cheat and liar even touch me.*

"It is called grief," I said, clenching my hands in vexation.

He tapped a finger on the table and sighed. "Grief is one thing, but to be morbidly obsessed, to wallow in self-pity, is another. Many women lose several children then go on to have large families."

*Not with impotent weaklings and fortune hunters.*

I stared at my feet, trying to pull my thoughts together.

When I dared to glance up again, he was scribbling notes across the page, his tongue moistening his drooping tobacco-stained whiskers.

"Now, regarding your activities since your arrival here in Durham. How have you spent your time?"

"I write in my journal. Do charitable work."

"Do you involve yourself in social events with the other university wives?"

"We attended a ball."

"Once. At your husband's insistence?"

"I have visited Reverend Buckley's home."

"On two occasions, and once you excused yourself because you felt unwell."

He glanced at Henry, then back at me. "On a seaside outing with the Buckleys, you tried to kidnap a pauper child and caused a scene that resulted in Reverend Buckley paying off the child's mother."

"It was a misunderstanding. I saved a young child from the oncoming tide. His mother had abandoned him. Should I have left him there to drown?"

"Enough," Beardsley snapped, eyes blazing. "Directly afterwards you ran away to the cliff top and threatened to jump to your death. It was only your husband's brave and speedy actions that saved you."

I stared in disbelief at Henry and opened my mouth to speak. "He—he—"

"I have witnesses to the event, doctor. You may read their statements," Henry said in a low, trembling voice, his eyes carefully avoiding mine.

"Thank you, Henry. I will look them over." He straightened his shoulders as if he were a lawyer prosecuting me in a court of law. An image of Mary Ann facing a row of solemn magistrates flashed before my eyes. I grasped the arms of the chair and focused instead on the slight twitching at the corner of Beardsley's lips.

"Now, how else do you occupy your time?"

"I do charitable work."

"In several settings?"

I shook my head. "At the prison."

"And how many prisoners do you visit?"

"Two or three," I said, conscious of the rush of blood to my face.

"But chiefly only one?"

I glanced at Henry, who seemed to hold his breath, awaiting my answer. I nodded and his shoulders drooped.

"A wholesale poisoner?"

"A woman awaiting trial."

"For murder. Do you believe you have formed a special sort of bond with this person accused of murdering her own children and her husbands?"

I looked over at Henry's burning eyes and my hands shook. I hid them on my lap under the table. "I speak to her. Share words of faith."

"And do you believe this prisoner is innocent of her crimes?"

"It is not my place to determine that."

"But you are deluded enough to argue with your betters that she may be innocent?"

"Of course I do not believe she is innocent," I said, struggling to quell the tremor in my voice. "I merely said she deserves fair legal representation."

"And yet your fascination with this woman causes you to seize every opportunity to run to the prison to visit her even though your husband would prefer that you form more suitable friendships with the other wives in your social circle?"

"I offer her guidance so she may face her trial with courage."

"And this accused murderer is pregnant?"

Fingers of heat crept up my neck. "She has already given birth."

"Have you formed ideas about taking this person's baby should she hang?" A half-smile played across his lips, revealing dull yellowish teeth.

I swallowed. "No. I have not."

Beardsley's steely eyes seemed to drill into mine. He waited for what seemed like an eternity. I bit the inside of my cheek. I would say no more to these monsters.

He sighed and began gathering up his notes. "Gentlemen, I believe I've seen enough."

"For what?" I said, rising from my seat.

Dr Beardsley stood up and regarded me sternly. "You would be advised to curb your agitation, Mrs Blackstone. It will not help your cause."

He straightened his papers, tapped them into perfect order on the tabletop, and manoeuvred them back into his case.

Henry and Buckley watched in openmouthed awe, jumping to attention as he snapped the case shut and turned to address them.

"Gentlemen, it is well-known that a woman is a prisoner of her reproductive system, and if she experiences severe problems, neurasthenia can result. The *wandering womb* has been talked about since the days of the great Hippocrates, father of medicine."

Eager, Buckley leaned towards him, moistening his lips. "And how does that manifest itself, Dr Beardsley?"

"Why, if the womb is underused, as in Mrs Blackstone's case, it becomes akin to a wild beast wandering around the body and causing all manner of disorders, including anxiety, tremors, convulsions, nervous hysteria, and many other afflictions. Mrs Blackstone desires a child and will do anything to get one. Even take the child of a serial poisoner."

"I knew it," said Buckley, slapping his knee.

"Never," gasped Henry.

I rose from my chair again. "But I just told you that is not my intention."

"She is lying," said Dr Beardsley, waving me aside. "I will contact another of my colleagues to give her a thorough examination. He is an expert in gynaecological matters."

"Can he cure her?" asked Henry.

"Curing the body will cure the mind; therefore, correction or removal of the uterus, ovaries, or both could possibly restore sanity. There are other options, but these are too delicate to discuss here."

I had heard enough. I sprang from my chair as if to leave, but Henry caught me by the shoulders and pushed me back into the parlour. "Do not make this worse, Clara. We are only looking to save you from yourself."

"You may expect my report early next week," said Dr Beardsley, raising his bushy eyebrows. "In the meantime, I recommend you administer this sedative three times daily to calm your wife's nervous agitation." He rummaged in his bag and produced a small blue bottle. "Chloral hydrate is an effective sedative. But use it sparingly, for too large a dose can cause confusion, seizures, irregular heartbeat, and, in extreme cases, such a marked drop in blood pressure that the heart will stop."

He measured some out onto a large spoon and nodded at Henry, who threw an arm across my chest, pinning my back against his body. Panic swelled in my throat as I sucked for air. I whipped my head to the side, hot tears streaming down my cheeks. Dr Beardsley cupped my chin with a cool, clammy hand and tipped the medicine into my mouth. I choked, then swallowed, conscious of the sticky liquid dripping down my chin. Henry held me tight, crushing the breath from me until the outline of the back door shifted, shimmered, and dissolved into a blur.

The pawnshop, the money, the tickets—escape. *Even the good'uns are afraid of a woman who just wants to get a piece of things for herself.*

A tear squeezed out from the corner of my eye and a slow, creeping heaviness finally took my legs out from under me as I heard the doctor's bag snap shut.

# ALEXANDRIA

## SPRING 1873

WE APPROACH ALEXANDRIA under a bronze sunset sky. The air shimmers with heat like the inside of a kiln. I imagine how I would paint the fiery heavens with streaks of burnt umber, ochre, and cadmium orange, streaked with rose red. Grand white buildings bathed in a magical wash of gold line the harbour. It is no wonder Alexander the Great called this city the beloved of history.

The fishing fleet girls gather by the ship's rail, heads bowed in rapt attention as the tallest of them reads aloud from a small handbook. They giggle and chatter like eager children, oblivious to the glorious Egyptian city unfolding on the horizon, with its tall spires and minarets and the tangle of masts and sails in the harbour.

"Mrs Davidson recommends a door wedge for safety and convenience as well as a compass for the solo lady traveller. And here is a most cunning device—an eyestone for picking off dust motes in one's eye," chirps the red-haired reader.

"I read that in India, fashion does not move at such a rapid pace," says a short, stocky girl with brown curls and a generous mouth. "So last year's bonnet or hat will not appear démodé. And I gather the locals are passable dressmakers, though without the finesse of European seamstresses."

The girl with honey-coloured ringlets draws back, her mouth twisted in distaste. "Well, my aunt told me that in India, the sewing and even the laundry is done by men, not women. She says they have rough hands and reduce one's fine lace trimmings to a ruined mess in no time."

I move away, unsettled by their idle chatter. To be engrossed in such daily trivia is an idle pastime of the affluent.

On the quayside at Alexandria, I watch in horror as a beggar with a withered stump of a leg and a filthy cloth tied over one eye approaches us holding out a battered tin pail. A stout man in official uniform seizes the poor wretch's ragged overshirt and throws him to the ground. The hollow thud of heavy boots on the beggar's scrawny ribs echoes louder than the slamming of trunks onto the stone slabs of the pier. I catch sight of the beggar's wild face. Moaning like a wounded beast, his good eye blazes with such hatred, he could tear that policeman apart limb from limb.

I, too, have felt hatred so intense, it clouded my mind. Trapped me in a state of confusion and bewilderment.

Donkey-driven carts ferry us to the rail terminal. This is a place of contrasts. Square sun-bleached buildings stretching far as the eye can see, oases of glossy palm trees clustered around glittering mosques, a bandstand with white colonnades on a street of elegant Westernised buildings. Then we veer off into a narrow warren of alleys that teem with white robed men and veiled women swathed in black. Beggars squat everywhere, their bony arms outstretched—sitting by wretched butchers' shops, where greying haunches of meat hang like decaying corpses abuzz with flies. My mind suddenly fills with a terrifying clarity.

I read somewhere that man is the only animal that devours his own kind.

I believe it to be true. We humans are possessed of savage instincts—to protect, to survive, to avenge, but the evil ones amongst us are ferocious predators, deriving pleasure and power not only from preying on the weak, but from destroying them slowly, deliberately, and cruelly.

# 27

ADELINE BLACKSTONE ARRIVED at our house just before midnight. A fitting hour for such an evil creature.

I shrank to the side of the window when she emerged from the carriage, her stiff black cape flapping around her like the wings of a bat. The wind blew her bonnet back, and she glanced upwards at the creaking elm tree as if she sensed me standing beyond it, watching her.

Henry strode out into the blustery night, his fists clenched. She swooped over and cupped his chin, but he pushed her gloved hand away. And when the coachman unloaded three large travelling trunks, he seemed to argue with her, gesturing angrily until she waved him out of her way and bustled towards the front door. I imagined old Mr Blackstone, back at the farm, jamming on his straw hat and dancing a jig around the empty kitchen as his wife's coach disappeared over the far horizon.

A cold draught swept through the house as the door slammed shut and Alice's frantic footsteps pattered across the front hallway. I could hear her high-pitched chatter, promptly quelled by Adeline's sharp orders, whilst Henry's low-toned placations ebbed and flowed in the background. Anxious to avoid contact with Adeline, I crept over to my bed and slipped under the sheets. I woke less than an hour later to a light shining under my doorway and the sound of Henry and Adeline squabbling outside. The doorknob turned and I shrank beneath the sheets, peeping out to see them standing in the open doorway, their shadows elongated like quivering giants in the candlelight.

"Well, do not make such a pretence of sleeping, Clara," snapped Adeline. "Will you not have the decency to greet your mother-in-law?"

I sat up in bed, blinking to accustom my eyes to the darkness. I stayed silent, having retreated to the muteness I'd maintained at the asylum. It was safer to let her words wash over me so I was impervious to their sting.

Henry leaned against the doorpost, holding a candle. "Mother, I have faithfully and anxiously watched, cared for her, and guarded her from her own excitable temperament and still she does not appreciate my devotion."

Adeline shuffled into the room, candlelight playing on the fleshy folds of her cheeks until her face resembled a carnival mask. "You hear my son? He has gone to considerable expense to give you the best private care and you make him suffer for it. Now he employs expert doctors to discover the source of your chronic maladies, yet you persist in acting like a woodenheaded fool? Have you no consideration?"

She waited, her eyes flashing. I imagined launching myself at her, knocking that stout body to the floor, where she'd lie, limbs waving like an upturned beetle. I'd seen the attendants topple over plenty of women at the asylum by grasping their ankles and taking their legs out from under them. They'd fallen to the floor with a crash like skittles in a child's game.

"Well, speak up, girl."

"I only wish for my basic right to freedom."

Henry's hands clutched into fists. "You have no rights. I am your only protector and I will decide what's best for you."

"And let me remind you, Clara," added Adeline, placing a hand on Henry's shoulder. "You'd better open your foolish ears to your husband like a dutiful wife should."

I threw the sheets off and swung my feet onto the floor. Adeline edged away from me. "So your son is to have complete dominion over me and allow them to cut up my body without my permission?"

Adeline's mouth drooped as she looked from me to her son. "What on earth is she talking about?"

"Tell her, Henry. Tell her what your expert doctor plans to do," I said, trying hard to quell my anger.

"Let her be, mother," said Henry, taking her by the shoulder and trying to chivvy her out. "She is a hopeless case. It's the mania that makes her conjure up these ridiculous delusions."

I stood, shaking from head to toe, holding down a scream that would have taken the roof off the house. Instead I clenched my hands and kept silent.

Adeline's eyes blazed open. She steadied herself against the doorpost. "See the poisonous look in her eyes, Henry? And she has been counselled by a murderer. Can you not find something to settle her or will she come to our rooms and murder us in our sleep?"

"I have everything in hand, Mother. Don't be overdramatic," he said, handing her the bottle of chloral and a spoon.

He lunged towards me and threw his arm around the back of my shoulder then across my throat. "You'd be advised to keep your mouth shut with all your far-fetched stories," he whispered, his lips brushing the edge of my ear. "Mother, measure out a spoonful."

She poured out the mixture and handed the spoon to her son, a smirk twisting her mouth. Henry pressed against my windpipe until I gasped for air, then he emptied the draught down my throat.

"See how sweetly that went down," he whispered, kissing my temple and lowering me onto the pillows. "Pleasant dreams, my dear."

"Well, I will be here from now on to see that you stay put," said Adeline before turning to leave. "We'll put an end to your clandestine escapades and all the other nonsense you've been up to."

My stomach churned as I descended the stairs the next day for breakfast. The chloral had muted my senses. I felt as if I were walking in a fog, and when I reached for the dining room door, my arm seemed separated from my body by a shimmering curtain of light. I grasped both hands together to seize the knob and turn it, terrified that the whole world was spinning out of control around my head.

"Don't loiter in the hallway, Clara." Adeline's sharp voice gave me such a start, I pushed the door open. "The porridge will go to waste."

Smoothing down my hair, I staggered into the dining room, waves of nausea forcing me to tread carefully.

Adeline had grown more stout and moonfaced since I'd last seen her. A result of her partiality for apple pie and clotted cream. But she wasted no time in looking me up and down, her eyes as narrow as cracks in a dinner plate.

"A trifle thin, I'd say. And an unpleasant pallor in the cheeks. But that's what comes from having a nervous disposition."

I stood there tongue-tied, my eyes drawn to the lacy ruffle that cradled her wobbling chin.

"Well, don't stand there gawking, girl. My son cannot afford to waste good food. Tell her, Henry?"

All this time Henry had buried his face in a newspaper, a tactic used by his own father. He looked up at me with simmering eyes.

"Do as she tells you, Clara, for Heaven's sake. Sit down and eat something."

All through breakfast Adeline nattered about the best recipes for semolina pudding and how eager she was to meet Donald and Emma Buckley and their remarkable daughter, Amy. Then she sucked at her teeth after clearing off a heaping bowl of porridge and brown sugar. "And of course, it is quite fortunate that my visit coincides with the trial. The newspapers have been filled with a litany of the infamous Mrs Cotton's crimes."

"Mother, why are you interested in such a sordid case?" said Henry, sniffing at the kippers laid out in front of him.

"In my lifetime I have had the misfortune of encountering two such villainous women," Adeline said, pulling the plate of kippers towards her. "Thirty-five years ago, I witnessed the hanging of Anne Fair, who murdered three husbands, two children, her brother, and two other persons—all by poison. I had hoped never to come across such evil again, but this Cotton case is far worse. I cannot fathom such wickedness."

"I, too, have been wondering how it is possible for a woman to commit such atrocities without a shred of regret," said Henry, tugging the kipper plate back towards him.

"Apparently, she offers no explanation and insists on her innocence. Unless she has confided in you, Clara," said Adeline, scowling at me.

I lowered my eyes and moved a piece of egg around my plate.

Henry glared. "Don't encourage her, mother. She will not be visiting that place again and besides, the woman is sure to be hanged."

"How can the punishment be otherwise?" said Adeline, reaching for a slice of toast.

I tried to ignore the incessant chatter, wincing at the way it grated on my nerves like fingernails scraping across a rusty tin plate, but I watched Henry from the corner of my eye. How imperiously he sat at the head of the table, like a puffed-up emperor in his petty little kingdom.

Adeline stuffed a napkin against her mouth and belched. "Perhaps Clara could accompany me to the trial. The experience might make her realise her folly when she sees her precious *friend* reduced to nothing but a common criminal at the hands of those fine lawyers."

Henry stroked his chin. "I will think on it. Would you like to go, Clara?"

But all I could hear was Mary Ann's voice, urging me to make a move.

*There's always someone standing in the way of a person's happiness, trying to stick a knife in their back and twist it until they drop. Get out of there and leave your rascal husband behind.*

"See how she sits there smirking and dreaming, Henry," squawked Adeline. "It's no wonder you're at your wits' end."

Henry wiped crumbs from his lips. "Don't worry, Mother. It's the chloral that makes her drowsy. Beardsley will deliver a thorough report."

Adeline glared at me. "Well, you have only yourself to blame, girl. With all your ridiculous fits and turns, not to mention the rank disobedience you've displayed towards your husband. You know that Henry must make a good impression with his colleagues and you seem bent on destroying his good name."

The toast was like sawdust in my throat, so I pushed my plate away and stood up to leave.

"Now she sulks, Henry. A guilty soul cannot face the harsh truth." She nudged her son, who'd retreated back behind his newspaper. "You must use a strong hand to deal with her, Henry. Impress upon her the importance of obedience."

Frowning, Henry put down the paper. "Go to your room, Clara."

Adeline slammed down her cup. "Speak up as if you mean it."

Red blotches spread across Henry's face and neck. "I said go to your room!" he roared.

Adeline was still nattering at Henry when I slipped out into the hallway, overjoyed to be away from them.

"A louder, more commanding voice is bound to instil fear in her."

The nagging went on for a whilst until I heard the slam of a fist on the table and raised voices. I stopped on the stairs and listened to Henry raging at his mother. Within a few seconds, she appeared in the kitchen doorway, mopping at her eyes. When she looked up and saw me standing there, she sniffed and thrust the handkerchief into her sleeve.

"Well, what are you gawking at, you silly fool? Get up to your room and out of my sight."

# 28

ALL AFTERNOON I fretted, wondering how I could escape Adeline's eagle eyes. Henry had gone to a university meeting and would not be home until evening, and Adeline had been in fine fettle, sailing around the kitchen, dining room, and parlour like a great battleship, with Alice puttering along in her wake. On arrival she had promptly wrested the house keys from Alice's hands and attached them to her dress with a large safety pin so that they clinked against her ample hips.

The two of them had gone through every room in the house, dusting, scrubbing, and polishing until Alice could barely drag herself upstairs to bed. I watched her cling to the bannister, damp strands of hair hanging from under her cap, her dress patched with sweat. Soon her door shut and the slight thump of her body falling onto the bed was followed by absolute silence.

I went back to my desk by the window and looked over the letter I had hastily scribbled to Dr Shepton, begging him to verify my sanity by sending me a copy of his final report. Now it seemed desperate—ill-conceived that I would ask him to answer in secret. Henry was bound to intercept the letter; or Shepton, kind though he had been, might choose to correspond first with Henry, since he had been the person to sign for my release from Hoxton. I ripped the letter to shreds and stuffed them into the corner of a hatbox.

The walls were closing in. All legal avenues of escape now blocked.

Desperate to flee the suffocating confines of my room, I poked my head out into the hallway and heard a low, droning sound coming from the kitchen. I tiptoed downstairs to find Adeline sleeping by the fire, the bottle of chloral sitting between her hand and a plate of cleaned chicken bones. Her mouth hung open, a silvery ribbon of saliva dribbling down her chin. How helpless she looked and how simple it would be to take the pillow from the footstool and press it to her fleshy face, watch her limbs thrash about like a drowning woman's until they hung limp and still. But she shuddered and snorted a little, and instead my hand shot out and snatched the bottle, burying it in my pocket. But just as I went to find my carpetbag, she stirred.

"What are you doing up, Clara, sneaking around the place like a thief?"

Feeling a steady pressure rising in my head, I turned and forced a smile. "Why, I'm making some tea. Would you like a cup?"

She yawned so wide, I could see the glint of gold in her teeth. "I suppose I could manage one with a piece of that rhubarb pie Alice baked."

Luckily, she still seemed a little sleepy and the kettle was still on the hob, so I filled the teapot and brought her food before she noticed the absence of the chloral. Whilst she made short work of the big wedge of pie, I tipped a dose of chloral into her cup and then poured the tea. "One spoon of sugar or two?"

"You know I'm partial to sweets," she mumbled, her mouth full. "Three will do."

I sat by the fire sipping my tea and watching her drink. "You know, Clara," she said, sighing deeply, "if only you could always be so sweet and genial towards Henry, he might give you another chance."

"I promise I will try," I said as her eyelids began to droop.

She held on to the chair arms and tried to pull herself up. "I think—I think I must go to bed."

But her arms gave way and she fell back onto the chair.

"Stay here in the warmth for a whilst. I'll take you upstairs later."

She struggled to keep her eyes open. "Yes—yes, I'll just close my eyes for a . . ."

In seconds she was fast asleep, snoring through her slack mouth. I stood above her, realising now was my only chance to leave, so I unfastened the safety pin from her waist and attached the keys to my own dress.

The carpetbag of valuables I'd stowed under the hallway table was still there—not surprising, since I'd heard Adeline barking orders to Alice all throughout the morning, complaining about the shabby state of the kitchen, the meagre supply of food in the larder, and the tarnished silverware in the dining room. They had barely ventured into the hallway.

Finally I put on my warm coat and stood at the foot of the stairs, watching the milky winter light filter through the glass door panel. But first I let myself into Henry's study, thinking he might have left money somewhere.

I rifled through the drawers, finding only pamphlets as well as a few calling cards. But I found some letters in the bottom drawer—Adeline's letter to Henry, a telegram from Izzie's doctor, and one from Buckley. I seized the telegram first, burning to find out how Izzie was.

*Good news. The patient is weak, but her condition has improved. She may last at least six months with the new treatment.*

If only I could get there—to be with her for her last few months. Tears pressed at my eyes, but I could not waste time. Buckley's envelope had a short handwritten note folded inside a longer letter:

*Dear Henry,*
*You'll be pleased to read this letter from Dr MacReary of the Sedgewell Asylum.*
*Donald*

The other letter was from Dr MacReary:

*Dear Reverend Buckley,*
*Can you please inform Mr Blackstone that when he is ready—within the next six months—I am prepared to receive Mrs Blackstone upon the certificate of Dr Beardsley that she is* hopelessly insane. *In this way we can get her entered without any sort of trial or hearing and avoid any undue embarrassment to her husband. You must be prepared to "spirit" her here on some other harmless premise so there is no fuss on her arrival.*

*You may assure him we have the finest institution here, a veritable boon to suffering humanity. It is only twenty years old and houses seven hundred lunatics. We maintain a strict daily routine, and males and females are housed in separate wings, supervised on a continuous basis by trained attendants to prevent unruly or immoral behaviours. We also boast marvellous conveniences, including padded cells for the protection of the self-harmers, and our own farm, water supply, fire service, and unique breed of hog. I feel confident Mr Blackstone will be more than happy with our amenities.*

*Yours Respectfully,*
*Dr Cameron MacReary*

I stuffed the letters into my bag, my heart raging at the icy dispassion of Dr MacReary's tone. All the faces of those wronged women flashed before me—Ivy with her scarecrow's hair, clinging to me in a drug-addled haze; Annie, discarded like a piece of used clothing; and Constance—duped by her own family into taking a journey that ended inside the asylum gates. There was no way on God's earth that I'd ever let Henry dispose of me in that place.

Just then the hall clock struck four.

I prayed the pawnbroker's shop would still be open, for once I had pooled all the money, I planned to take a room at an inn near the prison to consider my next move.

I crossed the silent hallway, unlocked the front door, and stood on the step for a moment to take in the blazing sunset. A woman in a purple coat and black hat hurried down the street, holding the hand of her eager little boy. She nodded at me and continued on her way as a carriage drawn by two chestnut horses clattered by. Then I stepped out into the coming night, welcoming the cold bite of winter air on my cheeks.

When I left the pawnshop, the sky was already darkening. I had a pouch of money—almost forty pounds all told—and the clothes I stood up in. I'd purchased some servant's clothes for a few pennies and now unrolled the rough cloak and wrapped it around me, then took off my good bonnet and swapped it for the servant's plain felt hat with its limp cotton frill. The wind blew steadily, but I stooped to shield my face from the cold and hurried on, clutching my carpetbag.

Once I approached the marketplace, I kept my head down, careful to avoid the eyes of the passing groups of merrymakers who poured out from the pubs, linking their arms like drunken comrades. I passed the grand façade of the Royal County Hotel and walked on until I came to a modest but respectable boardinghouse situated in a long white stone terrace just opposite the prison gates. Gathering up my courage, I pushed the black-painted door open and walked inside.

Fifteen minutes later, I looked through rose-sprigged curtains at the high prison walls on the opposite side of the street. This was a perfect spot. A place to hide until I made arrangements to sail for India. I threw my bag onto the quilted bedcover and studied the room, which was plain and simple with a wardrobe, a dressing table, and a brass bedstead.

I stood for a few long moments, relishing the privacy and the silence of the place. I'd promised Mary Ann I'd attend the trial, but I had no doubt that Henry would be scouring the city for me as soon as he realised I was missing, and yet I could not go back on my word to Mary Ann. I would take a chance and go to the trial tomorrow. The servant's clothes would be a sufficient disguise.

# 29

NEXT MORNING, I woke with a start at the rumbling sounds outside my window. Pulling the curtains aside, I saw crowds of people swarming towards the assizes court. Carriages were caught in the crush of bodies, their horses unable to advance any further. Smartly dressed people simply left their carriages and walked the remaining distance to the courthouse.

I wrapped the servant's shawl around me and hastened downstairs. The landlady was up and about and busy in the breakfast room with the other guests, so I seized an apple from an earthenware bowl and left before she caught sight of me.

My gaze cast downwards, I stepped outside into the teeming mass of bodies. The mob was a living creature that flexed its muscles and pulled you close, then cast you away by taking your legs from under you, but I planted my feet hard on the ground, stuck out my elbows, and shoved my way forwards until I broke through the front line of the crowd and arrived at the grand courthouse doors.

An army of sympathisers to Mary Ann's cause were stationed outside, holding painted placards calling for mercy.

Bertha had told me that many of them were well-connected and ready to campaign for clemency should she be condemned to death. But a huge rabble of outraged souls gathered opposite, screaming, “String up the monster,” “Kill the evil bitch,” and “Send her to Hell!”

The crowd carried me through the doors and into the vast hall with its polished marble flooring and imposing arches that spanned the entire perimeter. A grand staircase stretched upwards towards tall wooden doors on an upper floor where barristers in their flowing robes and white wigs walked back and forth or huddled in close groups. Extra clerks were on hand, directing spectators to a further flight of stairs and through a doorway into the public gallery, where rows of benches were arranged before a wrought-iron railing. Below was the courtroom—a dark space lined with polished wooden panels, relieved only by bright jewels of sunlight that spilled through coloured glass panels in the ceiling.

I sat at the back with the rest of the humble folk, well hidden behind a row of soberly dressed ladies and close enough to the door so I could slip out quickly should someone see me, though I’d pulled my bonnet down low enough to shade my eyes.

“So the monster will finally get her due,” said the woman in front of me, straining forwards to see the reporters filling up the rows down below.

“This is but the first trial,” said her neighbour. “A greater judgement awaits her on the other side.”

“Quite, quite true. No doubt she is bound for the fiery furnace and all the wrath of Hell,” said the first woman.

Silence finally descended on the crowd as Mary Ann entered the courtroom looking frail and aged as she leaned on a stick to help her in. Strange, I thought, I’d never seen her limp or falter. Was this some kind of attempt to earn sympathy from the crowd? A difficult task, considering how the spectators gawked at her as if she were a mere curiosity. Her hair was not combed back tidily as before, but brought forwards, almost over her eyebrows, giving her a weird brooding appearance. Her matrons accompanied her to the dock and she hobbled into her place, leaning heavily on the stick. She winced as she sat on the hard wooden bench, then shrank back into the seat, her eyes darting around at the sea of staring faces like a cornered rat.

"All in all, a pathetic, bedraggled-looking creature," whispered the first woman. "Not quite the evil fiend I was expecting."

"And the child is absent," said her friend.

"What a pity. I'd hoped to take a look at it," the other replied. "To see how much of a resemblance it bears to its mother."

So the baby, Margaret Edith, had become an object of curiosity, and now the whole proceedings had taken on the tone of a circus with ogling onlookers ready to pay good money for a front seat to the proceedings.

I felt a faint stab of guilt. Surely, that same ghoulish curiosity had driven me to visit Mary Ann in the first place. I pushed that thought aside and turned my attention to the entrance of Mr Justice Archibald, a commanding figure in his long grey wig and dark robes. His eyes were heavily hooded, though not unkindly, and he was clean-shaven, his mouth a thin slash above a dimpled chin. His face wore a grave but weary expression as he looked down on Mary Ann. I imagined the wrenching in her gut. I'd cowered like a trembling creature under the scrutiny of Beardsley, Buckley, and Henry, my insides writhing in fear. Now Mary Ann was entirely alone, contemplating these formidable men whose sole purpose was to squash her with the heavy hand of the law.

Her eyes darted to the twelve sombre men of the jury, who sat black-clad and stone-faced like a group of undertakers, then she glanced at the rows of male reporters, whose eager hands held pencils ready to record every detail of the proceedings. When her lawyer took his seat, she stared straight ahead at the judge, her gaze unwavering, her face white as damp paper.

Mr Charles Russell, Q.C., a heavy-browed man with piercing dark eyes and aristocratic bearing, led the prosecution, and Mr Campbell Foster, the defence, appointed only three days prior. When Mary Ann was asked how she pleaded to the charge of wilful murder of her stepson Charles Edward Cotton, she replied in a firm voice, "Not guilty." Her words set off a ripple of chatter amongst the spectators. Mr Justice Archibald slammed his gavel down and the silence was immediate.

Mr Russell opened the case by going over all the particulars of Mary Ann's background, though no doubt the crowd was already aware of every sordid detail, from the many newspaper accounts that had appeared since her arrest.

Mr Russell continued with the charge: "The presence of poison in all the child's organs indicates it could not have been given accidentally, but was administered over the course of two or three days to work its deadly mischief. By whose mind and hand?"

He turned and looked over at Mary Ann, then spoke in a commanding tone, emphasising each word with care. "This crime was planned, deliberately, secretly, in security, in darkness." He paused. There was not a sound in the courtroom. Not even a breath was drawn.

"No arsenic was found in the prisoner's house when it was searched, but six weeks before the boy's death, he was sent by Mrs Cotton to a chemist's shop to purchase two or three pennyworth of soft soap and arsenic, apparently for the purpose of applying to some iron bedsteads for the destruction of bedbugs." Mr Russell then turned to the jury. "The chemist refused to give the mixture to the child and, at the request of the prisoner, her neighbour Mrs Dodds, a charwoman, went and bought it instead. She applied some to the bedstead, and the rest she gave back to the prisoner. The quantity of arsenic contained in the soft soap was about half an ounce—three grains of which was sufficient to kill an adult. It is a simple thing to dissolve the mixture in water and let the arsenic fall to the bottom."

I shuddered at the memory of Mary Ann's whispered last words to me about the mixture of arsenic and soft soap, but I forced myself to focus again on Mr Russell's commanding voice.

"Now we must consider the motive. To a mind depraved or morally weak, to one with a fancied sense of security, who could say what motive might be adequate? There was some small pecuniary motive. There was the irksome tie of a child not of her flesh and blood. There was the feeling of poverty. The prisoner had motive—had the opportunity. No one else had either."

There followed a succession of witnesses who testified about the boy's condition and Mary Ann's relationship with the child. Only one neighbour said the boy was kept comfortably during his illness and Mary Ann's new companion, Mr Quick-Manning, liked him so well he "adored the ground he walked on." The rest told a completely different story. First, Mary Tate took the stand, watched closely by Mary Ann.

"I was often in Mary Ann's house, washing and cleaning. I saw her ill-use the boy many times and I told her to go canny on him, but she just said, 'The boy is mine and I'll do what I want to him.' On Easter Sunday, Mrs Smith gave the boy an orange and a paste egg. Mary Ann put them in her pocket and when he was crying for the orange, she threw it into the fire and said it would make him bad. The boy went on crying and she took a leather strap and thrashed him. That poor lad didn't get enough to eat and I told her that. All she said was that the Cottons were weak-stomached children and couldn't bear too much food."

Another neighbour, Mary Priestley, said, "I saw Mrs Cotton call for the little lad. He ran to her, and as soon as he reached the doorway, she struck him with her hand, dashing his head against the wall. Then she followed him across the floor, and smacked him with one hand, then the other, then kicked him with her foot. Afterwards she took him up and put him in a chair, wiped his face, then sent him out on an errand. I saw her beat that poor boy many times. She was very vicious with him and wouldn't let him play like other children."

My gut twisted as they described how that child suffered in the final weeks of his life. According to witnesses, he had not only endured beating, kicking, and starving, but Mary Ann had locked him outside alone during a thunderstorm whilst she went out for the whole day. Whilst other women in the spectators' gallery held handkerchiefs to their eyes, Mary Ann sat blankly staring ahead.

Sunbeams gleamed through the windows, splintering into a thousand tiny shards of light. My temples throbbed as I struggled to focus on the judge and lawyers, who seemed to shimmer like mirages at the edges of my vision. I had spent so many hours in that dark cell, listening to Mary Ann tell her story. She had tried to paint herself as a victim—had traded her advice for my belief in her innocence, but here was the real truth from the people who had been inside her house and witnessed her cruelty day after day. I grasped the wooden seat to anchor myself as Dr Kilburn gave his evidence.

"I attended the child as requested by Mrs Cotton. There was no one else in the house but the child and the prisoner, who was looking after him. The boy's body was wasted, his belly distended as if starved, and though I gave him medicine, the prisoner said the child was unable to keep it down, and he subsequently died."

Despite Mr Campbell Foster's objections, Russell was allowed to introduce evidence relating to the poisoning of Nattrass, Frederick Cotton, and the baby, Robert Robson Cotton, his reasoning being that it demonstrated a damning pattern of behaviour. Mary Ann's face drained of colour when the judge allowed the witnesses to talk about the other cases.

I listened to the parade of misery as one witness after the other described the horrific events.

"When Nattrass was sick, she never left his bedside and wouldn't let anybody else help him. I said many times he should have some food, but Mary Ann said he couldn't have anything. Towards the end, he had fits. Mary Ann would hold him down; otherwise, he would have thrown himsel' right out of the bed. He gnashed his teeth and his eyes turned up in his head."

One tearful woman described the last days of ten-year-old Frederick Cotton. "I saw Mary Ann trying to stop the bleeding from a leech wound on the right side of little Freddie's body, above his bowels. That child was thin as a stick and complained terribly of thirst. And when Mary Ann gave him drinks out of the same teapot, the bairn vomited so often, he couldn't get his head to the basin. The night before he died, the poor bairn was weak as a newborn lamb, but he still begged me to fetch someone to pray with him and so I went for Elijah Atkinson. The bairn died shortly after."

Sarah Smith fidgeted with her shawl as she gave her testimony about baby Robert's death. "Robbie was prattling away on his mother's knee in the morning and by the afternoon his tiny body was racked with the most terrible convulsions. Mary

Ann said, 'The teething has made him poorly,' but after an hour or two he seemed to be improving. At dinnertime, he even took his scrap of bread, dipped it in the syrup, and put it to his mouth. I said to Mary Ann, 'Look, little Robbie is all right now,' and she said, 'He is.' Well, when I came back that night, she was kneeling by the cradle upstairs, her eyes wild and staring out with fright. Nattrass was ill in the bed, and the baby gave such a heavy fetch and took such a long time to start breathing again, and his eyes were fixed as if he were clinging to his life. I said to Mary Ann, 'Robbie's dying. Who shall I get?' And she looked right at me with a straight face and said, 'Nobody.' Well, I begged her to let me get Dr Kilburn, and when I got back, Mary Tate was there and she says, 'Have you ever seen such a change as this?' I says I never had, and I looked straight into Mary Ann's eyes and says, 'What on earth have you been giving him?' 'Well,' she says in a huff, 'nothing but a teaspoonful of syrup.' Then the doctor came and when he was examining the bairn, Mary Ann went into a fit at the sight of the bairn's convulsions, but she soon came out of it.

"When the doctor left, she says, 'Tek the bairn from the cradle, Sarah. I'm afeared to touch him.' I took the poor mite out and had him on my knee for about an hour. He kept fetching up until he could bring up no more, and when I put him back in the cradle, he never fetched again. His little body was stiff and cold. I told her then, 'Robbie's dead.'"

Another neighbour held a handkerchief to her eyes as she explained, "The day before little Robbie died, Mary Ann begged me to make the poor thing a nightdress. I thought it were strange, but I did so. I made a beautiful white cotton dress. Well, the next day I had to help her lay that little angel out in it."

Dr Scattergood confirmed he found arsenic in the stomach, bowels, and liver of both children.

I curled my hands into fists and cursed myself for my stupidity. I had been a fool to think I could give her spiritual guidance. She was far too clever for me. She had rooted out my vulnerabilities, entrenched herself in my head, and manipulated me as if she were a puppet master holding the strings that would make me dance.

There followed a long period of questioning of Kilburn by Campbell Foster regarding the location of arsenic bottles in the surgery, with the implication that he had made a fatal error with the medicine.

The prosecutor sprang to his feet and objected to the suggestion. The judge allowed the objection and Foster paused, momentarily confused. Then he sorted through his notes, and turned back towards the doctor. He continued with a line of questioning about the arsenical properties of dyed wallpapers, but the doctor dismissed any validity to that theory.

At that point, the judge intervened, addressing Campbell Foster sternly. "Your question is very speculative and can hardly be asked. This entire cross-examination is of a speculative character."

Mary Ann leaned forwards, her hands pressed flat on the arms of her chair, the knuckles white from pressure. Her lawyer was ill-prepared and she knew it.

The lady next to me turned to her friend and whispered, "They are grasping at straws. As if a learned man like that would make such a mistake. And as for the wallpaper theory—I should have been dead ten times over if that were true."

That night, a heavy rainstorm swept in. I lay on the bed in my room by the prison, listening to the raindrops pounding on the roof, slashing against the windows and shaking the panes. For the first time in days, I felt the faint stirring of fear that I would never escape Henry unless I left tomorrow.

Finally, my skin icy with fear, I drifted into restless dreams.

I was standing in a cobbled courtyard surrounded by high brick walls. A simple wooden gallows stood against a sultry sky the colour of mercury. At the end of the freshly hewn wooden beam, a noose stirred slightly in the wind. The hangman stood beside the lever, a black mask covering his face.

I stood at the base of the gallows and watched as dark-clothed figures dragged Mary Ann out from the tunnel, but when they saw me, they threw her aside and seized me, grasping my arms and pushing me up the steps to the scaffold, whilst around me a crowd of onlookers jeered and raged with deafening cries. The hangman slipped the noose around my throat and I felt its rough fibres chafe my skin as the wind picked up and shook the very boards I stood on.

*Let the bitch swing!* the hangman cried, and it was Henry's eyes that blazed through the holes in his mask as he moved to pull the lever that would launch me into the drop. I awoke at the snap of the rope. Clutching at my throat in terror, I opened my eyes to see ribbons of rain streaming down the windowpane. A low rumble of thunder filled the air.

# 30

I PACED BACK and forth in front of the window the next morning, watching the rain beat down on the rooftops and rush in small rivers down the street. But the inclement weather had done nothing to deter the crowds. A sea of umbrellas and sodden hats ebbed and flowed below me as the people filed into the court buildings for the final day of the trial.

I kept going to my bag to open and then close it again, convincing myself that I should leave the city. Now. Wait until everyone was safely inside the courthouse and then go. Today was my best chance. But then I would go back to the window and think of Mary Ann sitting in the court, awaiting the closing arguments and the inevitable verdict. I was caught between the two choices. Pulled this way and that until the pain of indecision froze me to the spot and the blood pounded in my ears.

I should not go to the court again.

Springing to my feet, I crammed my clothes into the carpetbag, secured the purse of money to my bodice, and slipped out of the room.

Driving rain bounced off the cobblestones as I hailed a coachman sheltering under a broad oak tree. I pulled the rough cloak around my shoulders and climbed into the cab after instructing the driver to take me to the station. The horse splashed through rain-soaked streets, slowed to a walk by the oncoming crowds who were making their way to the courthouse. Raindrops beaded the windows and I struggled to wipe the condensation from the glass, but hard as I wiped, a damp film spread across it again. Finally, after an eternity of sitting back, trying to still the doubt that raged in my head, we began the climb towards the station. Mercifully, the rain had stopped, leaving the streets slick and gleaming.

The window finally cleared and I glanced out as the cab approached the station entrance, but I fell back against the seat, my heart racing.

Henry was waiting by the gate.

I looked again. Two other coaches had pulled in ahead of us and two burly men, stationed beside him, had stepped forwards to scrutinise the passengers leaving the first carriage. Henry shook his head and retreated as a man, a woman, and two children passed him by. The second carriage was about to stop when I realised I had less than a minute to escape.

He was on the lookout—ready to head me off should I try to leave the city.

I clenched my fist and beat it on the ceiling of the cab, which lurched and shook as the driver climbed down. His face appeared, a white blur at the window. Easing the door open a crack, I whispered, "We must turn back. Now."

His brows knit, but I thrust a shilling at him and he touched his hat. "Back to the inn?"

I nodded. "Be quick about it."

Back at the inn, I asked the coach driver if he could take me to Darlington or Bishop Auckland, but he told me the roads would be thick with mud, making the journey far too treacherous to attempt. So, trapped in the city, I waited in my room until after the lunchtime adjournment, then put on my servant's clothing and slipped back into the courtroom for the final hours of the trial.

I hid in the crowded back row, straining to see Mary Ann gazing with hollow eyes at the judge, her lower lip trembling with fear. In all the times I'd visited her, I couldn't remember seeing such terror in her eyes. The frightening reality of her situation had suddenly dawned on her as all her hopes of petitions and reprieves were fading away to nothing.

The judge asked for the closing remarks, beginning with the prosecution. Russell puffed out his chest, turned to the jury, and readied himself for a grand performance.

"You are here to consider only the charge that the prisoner did deliberately murder her stepson Charles Edward Cotton. She was left alone in the house with a seven-year-old boy, a boy she did not want and had tried to have admitted to the workhouse. He was a tie upon her, a tie she had tried to get rid of but failed. But even the joyless character of his life that was never warmed with the sunshine of a mother's love could not stamp out the spontaneous joyousness that was planted in his breast."

By now Mary Ann had wiped a hand across her face, her lips twitching as if she were fighting back tears.

He continued: "On that very day when the prisoner was complaining that the boy could not be taken into the workhouse, and she was afraid that the Poor Law relief would be stopped, that healthy child took ill, and before seven days had passed, that child was dead. His young life was snapped as the blasted and withered blossom on the trees might be."

After spending some time refuting the defence's case that the poisoning was accidental, he finally turned to the jury and summed up his case.

"You are to enquire into the history of one of the most dangerous, one of the most appalling, and one of the most atrocious crimes that has ever disgraced this country. The death was by poison deliberately administered. If there is no witness to the actual administration of poison, then the search has to be for whoever had a motive. Surely, no one else but the prisoner had a motive." He pointed a finger at Mary Ann, who sobbed and bowed her head. "The household had been reduced to just the prisoner and the child. Could anyone else be guilty?" He concluded by cautioning them to consider very carefully if there was any reasonable doubt that the prisoner had poisoned the boy. "If so, it is your solemn duty to say so."

The men of the jury sat gravely, their eyes fixed on Russell. The room was eerily silent. Now it was up to Foster to try to turn the tide of opinion that seemed firmly set against Mary Ann, who sat transfixed. Her life hung in the balance and depended entirely on his words.

"Members of the jury, there is no direct evidence to show that the prisoner administered the poison, and it is doubtful she even purchased it, since she was living in a different town at the time the prosecution alleges she bought it. There was also no poison or trace of poison present in the house when she was arrested, and even the many learned doctors we have heard from have admitted it would be impossible to remove all traces of arsenic from a teapot by simply washing it. We do know there is everything to show it was not in the defendant's heart or mind to commit such a heinous act, so you must give her the benefit of the doubt. You must ignore the sensational claims printed in the newspapers and the gossip and rumours you may have heard. There are signed death certificates to prove the other victims died of natural causes. These alleged murders are a crutch to help the prosecution with a weak case. The prosecution has not shown any evidence of the prisoner being in possession of the poison. There was no motive. She lived by lodgers. Nattrass was her lodger. And more—they were engaged to marry.

"My learned friend has insinuated that she poisoned her own infant, fourteen-month-old Robert Robson Cotton. Unimaginable! A mother poisoning her own child! A mother nursing it, calling in the doctor, dancing it upon her knee, looking fondly at it, listening to its prattle, seeing its pretty smiles, whilst she knew she had given it arsenic, making its limbs writhe as it looked into her face, wanting support and protection!"

Mary Ann doubled over and began to shake. Her matron held her by the shoulders as the entire audience watched, mesmerised.

Foster moved on to characterise Mary Ann as kind and always ready to care for the sick. "Much of this so-called evidence rests upon the gossip of old women who were called one after the other and who tried to make three black crows out of one. You should come to the conclusion that the prisoner is not a cold-blooded fiend who would administer poison to her child, then watch the effects whilst she pretended to nurse it. You must try her without all these other suspicions. Do not balance the evidence by taking prejudice into consideration."

Mr Justice Archibald then addressed the jury, telling them to determine if the crime was committed with deliberate intent. And though he admitted there was a lack of direct evidence, he pointed out that many crimes are carried out in secrecy. All they had to do was arrive at a certainty because of circumstantial evidence, which excluded all reasonable doubt that Mary Ann committed the act.

No witness had spoken out in Mary Ann's defence.

But the jury still retired at ten minutes to four.

I turned my eyes up to the ceiling and studied its elaborate gilded scrollwork. Anything to numb my mind against the mindless chitchat around me that only subsided when the court came to order for a bigamy case. The crowd appeared restless, fidgeting in their seats every time a noise was heard from outside the courtroom, craning their necks to see if the jury would return.

I closed my eyes and waited, my hands clenched. Mary Ann had fought and scraped for her survival and left behind a trail of dead husbands and children, whether through sickness or by her own hand. It dawned on me then, the staggering extent of her determination and her cold, calculating callousness. She had lived through the most unimaginable horror and become immune to grief. But now she would pay the price. She was finally broken. The only thing left was to end her life in the most cruel and brutal way possible.

My mind snapped back to the courtroom and the frantic whispering that the jury was about to return. There was a rumbling below us, as if many chairs were shifting as their occupants stood for the arrival of Justice Archibald. The jury filed in. They had been out only forty-five minutes. The clerk stood before them and asked, "Have you agreed upon your verdict?"

The foreman of the jury stood up and said, "We have."

The clerk then asked, "Do you find the prisoner, Mary Ann Cotton, guilty or not guilty?"

The silence was almost deafening as every person in the room held their breath for fear of missing a word.

The foreman paused for a moment, then replied, "Guilty," at which there was a collective gasp from everyone. Mary Ann stared in disbelief at the twelve men, her face ghastly white.

The clerk continued: "You find her guilty of murder?"

The foreman clearly replied, "Yes."

Then the clerk asked again, "And so you all say?"

The foreman again answered, "Yes," then took his seat again.

With a strained expression in his eyes, Justice Archibald asked Mary Ann if she had anything to say as to why the sentence of death should not be passed upon her. She replied with a soft, wavering voice that she was not guilty. And then murmurings spread through the courtroom, until the clerk proclaimed that silence should be kept whilst the sentence was being passed. I held my breath as Justice Archibald spoke, the floor tilting beneath me when he assumed the black cap.

"Mary Ann Cotton, you have been convicted of this murder. You have been found guilty of poisoning your stepson, whom you ought to have taken care of. You seem to have been possessed by that delusion that sometimes takes hold of weak-minded people, wanting in proper moral and religious sense, that they can perpetrate these offences unknown to their fellows. The offence of poisoning is one of the most deadly and detestable crimes that can be perpetrated. The sentence I feel bound to pass upon you will ensure that others may be warned by your miserable fate, of the certainty of punishment."

As his low voice droned on, I remembered the murderous thoughts I'd had about Henry, and wings of panic beat in my ears.

*Everyone considers murder at some point in their lives. Even proper ladies like you.* Had she put the thought into my head or had I really considered it?

I blinked hard to focus my eyes on the deathly pallor of the judge's face under the black cap.

"It only remains for me to pass upon you the sentence of the law, which is that you will be taken from hence to the place from whence you came, and from thence to a place of execution, and there to be hanged by the neck until you are dead . . ."

Mary Ann gripped the rail and gave a strangled cry.

The judge continued: ". . . and your body to be afterwards buried within the precincts of the jail, and may the Lord have mercy on your soul."

She flopped back into the chair, her face ashen, her entire body convulsing with tremors. Bertha and the other matrons rushed to support her when she fell into a faint. A gasp came up from the crowd as the matrons picked up her limp body as easily as if she were a child, and the crowd surged forwards to see her carried into the waiting room.

I slipped out into the upper hallway only to find myself caught up in a swarm of people trying to push towards the staircase. Lack of food, together with the musty stink of damp wool and mothballs, turned my stomach and made my head so light that I went to grasp the bannister, but a stout woman stuck her elbow in my side and shoved me out of the way. Stumbling sideways, I felt my legs buckle underneath me until a strong hand clamped on to my arm and set me straight on my feet.

"Easy there, Mrs Blackstone," said a familiar voice. I turned to see Lowry, who pulled me away from the crush of frantic spectators. Joe and his father, Clem, stood by the courtroom door. Old Clem mopped at his eyes with a faded red handkerchief, whilst Joe's eyes burned from a face as pale as wax.

"Bastards," Joe hissed, crushing his cap in his clenched hands. "They didn't give her a chance. The newspapers had already published every damn piece of gossip they could muster up, so how could a jury have had any doubts? 'Tis the newsmen who declared her guilty."

"And not a shred of hard evidence to back up all those charges. Only the words of gossips and fibbers," said Lowry, beckoning me to follow him down the stairs. "Not even a single witness to speak on her behalf. The judge should have thrown the case out when he knew there was no proper defence."

"Perhaps you'll pay her a visit and offer some comfort, Mrs Blackstone," said Joe, "for she's bound to be in a desperate state now she has one foot in the grave."

The weight of their expectation was like a great stone crushing the breath from me. She had manipulated these men into believing her story, and now they attended to her like knights to their queen.

"I'll try to stop in there in the morning," I said, my voice swallowed in the hubbub as we surged down the final few stairs into the vestibule.

# 31

I WAITED AT my window until late the following afternoon, when I saw Mr Boxted leave the prison gates, followed by the other matron, Mrs Sewell, who hurried off in the direction of the marketplace. After another half hour, I spied Bertha walking up the street towards the prison. Throwing my shawl around me, I hurried out to intercept her before she disappeared through the main gate. I would have the last word with Mary Ann. A last attempt to hear the truth from her own lips. She owed me this at least.

The biting wind cut through to my bones. The shawl was so flimsy, it barely shielded me from the cold, but I wrapped it tightly around my shoulders and ran up to the wardress as she went to cross the broad lawn.

"Bertha," I said, tapping her on the shoulder. "Can you get me in to see Mary Ann?"

She started then turned to me, casting a puzzled look at the rough woollen shawl. "Oh, Mrs Blackstone. You gave me such a fright. I've been all jumpy since yesterday."

"How has she been?"

"She's in a bad way. I canna tell a lie. Thinks the whole world has turned its back on her."

I followed her as she picked up speed. "I must see her to say goodbye."

"You're going away somewhere?"

I nodded. "My grandmother is dying. She needs care in her last few months."

Her hand covered her mouth. "I'm sorry to hear that, and so you should go. Mary Ann's not long for this world. There's nothing you can do now."

"I could pray with her."

"Well, visitors are supposed to have a special note for admission now, but since you've been a regular here, I can slip you in for a few minutes. But you must be ready to leave if I tell you to. I suppose it canna do any harm to have a visitor at this point. Even God says mercy must be shown to the worst sinners." She knocked on the entrance door and once we were inside, we set off in an unfamiliar direction. "Mary Ann and her baby are staying in the women warders' retiring room. It's more comfortable for her last few days."

I was surprised at the comfort of Mary Ann's new quarters—well-lit and with a blazing fire. The cradle stood near an iron bedstead, a table covered with religious books, two chairs, and a stool. Two warders sat at opposite corners of the room. Bertha asked them to step outside the door whilst I visited.

The room was close, the air acrid with the scent of fear. Mary Ann perched on the edge of the bed, rocking the cradle, her head resting on the other hand. She beckoned me to sit by her.

"I thought you might have abandoned me too, Clara. Like all the others." Her eyes looked blankly at me. "Oh, I am done for. I am done. A miserable creature. Forlorn and abandoned."

She folded her arms and hugged them to herself, rocking back and forth. "A man wrote on my behalf to the Home Secretary, asking if they'd examine me to see if I'm mad. Can you fathom it? It's you who are the lunatic, Clara. Not me. I'm as innocent of the crime as that bairn in the cradle. That's what I told my auntie. She asked me why I did it and I told her the only crime I'm guilty of is bigamy. She told me there was no chance of a reprieve. That I must make my peace with God and prepare for the worst. But I ask you, Clara, would they truly murder an innocent woman?"

I searched for something to say, but words seemed as futile as her entreaties seemed hollow. "That is not for me to say, Mary Ann. But your letters might help in some way. There are still people speaking out and saying you weren't properly defended in the trial."

Her eyes brightened for a moment. "Aye, they tell me all manner of people have signed the petition—doctors, chemists, ministers, brewers, bank managers, innkeepers, and many others—all pleading for my life. But my husband, James Robinson, is a bastard and a coward. I wrote to him. I begged him to come here and bring the bairns to see me, and you know what the scoundrel did? He changed his mind at the prison gates and sent his brother-in-law, Burns, instead. That stupid bugger begged me to confess and make my peace, but I shut my mouth and wouldn't say a thing." She tore at her hair and moaned. "Oh, I fear death. I dread the noose."

"Mary Ann," I said as gently as I could. "Would you confess your guilt to me?"

When she looked up, her eyes were hard as flint. "I believe that is a matter between me and my maker."

I reached for her hand, noticing the thick blue veins on the back of it.

"I've told you my deepest secrets. I would swear to keep yours."

I watched her face, hearing only the rise and fall of her breathing above the crackling of the fire. She averted her eyes and gazed at the floor. "Sometimes things just happen. One thing leads to another."

It was the closest she'd come to a confession of sorts. I waited, barely breathing.

"You shut your heart away and then the world turns upside down. Wrong becomes right. Somebody makes an honest mistake and then those mistakes come easy as breathing." Her eyes snapped upwards, calculating my expression. "I told that porridge-faced minister the poison was in the arrowroot Riley gave me. All four of the Cottons took it and they all went the same way."

"You say Riley made the error. That he gave you arrowroot laced with arsenic?"

She clasped her forehead and gazed into the fire. "I canna say. I don't remember anymore."

"But you must. For the sake of your soul."

"I'll answer to God," she said, eyes burning with such a look of defiance, I pulled my hand away from hers. I'd had her, then lost her just as quickly.

I looked at the beautiful child, sleeping soundly in her cradle, oblivious to the horror surrounding her. "What will happen to Margaret Edith?" I whispered.

The corners of her mouth quivered. "You know, Clara, almost a hundred letters came to the jail asking to adopt her, but I've promised her to Mrs Edwards, a miner's wife. She lived five doors down from me in West Auckland. She keeps a clean, tidy house and has a good strip of garden in the front. Lowry wrote to me on her behalf. He says she's kindhearted but childless, and she longs to be a mother, so she'll cherish my baby as if it were her own. She says that she and Mr Edwards will bring her up in the fear of God." The tears brimmed over onto her cheeks. "I want her brought up by simple, common folk like her own mother, who live by the honest sweat of their brow. They will come for her today. "

She turned again to look at the child stirring in her sleep, her tiny thumb fastened in her mouth. I was speechless—no words could console her. They would soon rip her child from her arms so they could put its mother to death.

Mary Ann was silent for a good few moments. I was about to stand up when she seized my wrists, her eyes wild with terror.

"I've many sins to answer for but not this, Clara. You must believe me. I never murdered that boy. If they put the rope around my neck, it will not matter that I am innocent. I should've listened to my friends. Joe Thornley knows folk who'd do anything for a few pound. They'd have sprung me out of here if I'd given the word." Her eyes seemed wild and distant. "We could've run away together."

Her words chilled me. I had never considered the idea of even being near Mary Ann outside the confines of the prison walls. It was unthinkable—like opening the bolt on a lion's cage and beckoning it out to play.

"It's too late for me, Clara. But they'd get rid of your problem if I gave the word."

"I'm leaving him," I said, my voice quavering with fear. "There's no need."

"Aye, so you said. But you'll be forever looking backwards to see if he's coming after you."

I stayed silent as I held her gaze. "If he comes after me, I'll kill him."

She grasped my wrist tighter, her eyes gleaming. "Don't be a fool, Clara. You don't have the stomach for it. You're not like me."

Her words hung between us, like something I could pick out of the air and study—to examine later and wonder, *Was this her final confession?* But the moment passed, and the last rays of the sun filtered through the small barred window, lending a sickly sallow cast to her face. Her eyes suddenly hardened like glittering ice. She sniffed and her lip curled upwards. "Well, there's nowt else to be said, then. When they hang me, you must pray for my soul. Fair's fair, Clara. I've spent enough time listening to your troubles, so you must bear witness to my passing. Then I'll know I'm not alone when I leave this world."

"I will try," I said, terrified by her blazing eyes.

She let go of me just as the heavy wooden door creaked open and Bertha entered, her face set into a grave yet sad expression.

"Mary Ann, Mrs Edwards will be here soon. We must get the bairn ready."

Mary Ann bent her head and wiped a hand across her eyes. Then she took up the baby from the cradle. "I must give her the breast before she leaves, poor thing," she said, caressing the child's head. "She'll be hungry now."

"I'll give you a minute to say your goodbye, Mrs Blackstone," said Bertha. My feet were rooted to the spot as I watched the mother suckling her daughter for the last time, and the thought came again into my head: This was the end for her. In a few days, the men would come for her with only one purpose in mind—to put a rope around her neck and string her up like a trussed swine. The absolute brutality of that action knocked the breath from me. To use hammer and nails to build a gallows, to fashion a noose from rope, to measure a drop, to plan a solemn ceremony, and to assemble at a chosen hour to perform the savage ritual. But it seemed there was no other option. It had to be done.

I bent to touch her shoulder.

"I will pray for your soul. I promise."

She reached up and touched my hand.

"Hadaway, then," she said without looking at me, "and good luck to you."

I tore myself from her, turning at the door to watch her rock her child as if she could never be parted from her.

# 32

IT WAS DUSK when I left the prison, so I kept to the shadows, skirting the buildings, then cutting across the front lawn, now black in the moonlight. The bright windows of the inn were visible just across the street, so I ran through the damp grass towards the wrought-iron arch that curved above the far gate. A single lamp hung from it, casting a pool of light on the street. I paused there, shivering with fear and cold, my breath misting the air. No one was about, so it seemed safe to cross the open road. I ached for the safety of that room. To have some quiet to think of what to do about the hanging. Whether I should break the promise I'd made and leave tonight or take a risk and stay.

Just then a dark figure stepped out of the shadows from behind the manicured privet hedge. It was Reverend Buckley, striding purposefully towards me.

"How fortunate, Clara. Henry asked me to keep a lookout for you here. We knew you could not stay away from your friend, the murderer." His face was hazy in the moonlight. "We also posted men at the station. In case you took it into your head to leave the city."

I backed away, my heart thudding against my ribs, but he kept coming forwards, edging so close that I could see the frost-tipped ends of his whiskers.

"I told Henry you could never be tamed—that you continue to seek the company of society's outcasts."

"You're a monster and a fraud, unworthy to even mention God's name!" I screamed, backing away from him, but he grabbed at my arm with his thick fingers, the thumbs pinching my flesh. Just then I heard the hum of voices coming closer. Buckley pulled his hand away and turned to see who was approaching. I seized the opportunity and lunged forwards, running towards the knot of people walking along the path. It was Lowry, with a man and a woman who carried a basket between them. Mr and Mrs Edwards—coming for the baby. Buckley followed close behind as I approached Lowry.

"Mrs Blackstone," Lowry called, reaching out to catch me. "What on earth is—"

"I must hurry," I said, breathless, as I kept running, only turning to see him watch Buckley lumbering after me along the pathway.

Thinking only of survival, I ran faster, sucking in the freezing air until it burned my lungs. I turned to see Buckley had fallen behind, his face red from the exertion of running. I turned down an alleyway and ran until I reached the marketplace, deserted now but dangerous if I ran into the gangs of drunkards leaving the taverns.

I stopped for a moment and pressed my fingers against my temples. In a panic, I searched for a hiding place. Just a few yards ahead, the dark arches of the pant offered a quick refuge and I slipped inside its clammy exterior, where the only sound was the *drip-drip* of water deep in the well. My chest heaved as I tried to gulp air into my lungs.

Jagged shadow figures burst from a nearby alleyway and raced across a nearby street.

Once they'd disappeared from sight, I fell back against the mossy bricks and let the soft lapping of the water calm my ragged nerves. When everything was quiet, I crept out into the open and crossed the marketplace, tripping over empty crates and slipping on rotten cabbage leaves. I ran without heeding my direction, the cold air smacking at my face, my breath billowing out in a cloud. The unfamiliar pathway snaked like a crooked maze, leading me deeper into a place of shadowy passages, grimy pubs, and filthy lodging houses where hollow-eyed children played barefoot in stinking puddles and rag-haired women in tattered finery skulked in darkened stairwells.

I hurried past without meeting their sideways glances, intent on reaching the brightly lit streets ahead, where the narrow alleyway spilled out onto a wider thoroughfare with a blacksmith's, a milliner's, and a small chemist's shop, its frontage painted deep blue with a polished brass sign. The lantern in the window illuminated rows of neatly placed bottles and flasks and jars.

Somewhere amongst them was arsenic and soft soap.

I stood there, my chest heaving. I'd shaken off Buckley now, but how could I keep running? Henry would never let me get to Izzie.

*You'll be forever looking backwards to see if he's coming after you.*

# Port Said, Suez Canal

## Spring 1873

MY GUIDEBOOK TELLS me Port Said is not built on firm soil but stands on a bed of earth excavated from the Isthmus of Suez. It is a city claimed from the sea—a true symbol of the triumph of man over nature.

But as the train pulls into the city, I feel a sense of disappointment. It seems a temporary place, an arrangement of haphazard wooden structures reminiscent of illustrations I've seen of frontier towns in the Wild West of the New World. Even the Grand Hotel Continental on the quayside, with its timbered exterior and rough wooden colonnades, has the look of a cowboy saloon. This is a place of transitions, a strange mix of races and cultures passing through on their way to the riches and beauty of India.

Despite my dampened spirits, I feel a sense of excitement that I am closer to the end of my journey. That my life will truly start again with a second chance to enjoy the sweet taste of freedom. I will not squander it this time. I promise myself I will read, paint, and travel. I will devour new experiences and take in the world's beauty with sharp eyes and a clear head. Nothing can hold me back this time. No man will tell me how to behave or restrict my movements.

Because I almost lost everything. My mind, my freedom.

My life.

Mary Ann told me everyone contemplates murder at some time in their lives. I know that to be true. The instinct to survive can drive any person to violence, as can the hunger for revenge.

Vengeance that must be delivered—swiftly and secretly.

That was the way of justice in the asylum, where secret stabbings and unexplained beatings often went unpunished for lack of witnesses.

I took that lesson to heart when I had no other way to turn.

# 33

I GLANCED BEHIND me into the shifting darkness. Shadow figures materialised—eyes glinted, then faded into black. Without giving myself a chance to reconsider, I pushed open the door of the chemist's, startled by the loud *ting* of the doorbell. Behind the counter, an old man with a starched apron, wings of white hair, and bushy whiskers was busy pouring liquid through a funnel into a line of smaller bottles. He looked up and smiled. Before I could change my mind and beat a nervous retreat, I cleared my throat and asked the old man for a quarter pound of barley sugars and some soft soap and arsenic mixture.

"I disposed of my old mattress, but now I discovered lice on the bed frame," I said in a thin voice.

"Just a moment," he said, walking towards a locked corner cupboard. I turned myself away and pretended to inspect a row of ladies' face creams and skin tonics, whilst I reached into my bodice and struggled to take out some coins from the money pouch.

"This will do the trick," he said as I fastened the last button. He placed a small bottle on the counter. "Only, wear some gloves when you use it, and store it in a very safe place. Away from the young'uns."

I paid him for the mixture and was about to take it when he held his hand back and shook his head.

"Can't be too careful these days, miss. If you're buying this for your master or mistress, you must sign the poison register, ma'am. After all this to-do with Mrs Cotton, we must keep careful records."

He had taken me for a servant girl. A great relief to me. "Of course," I said, my ears echoing with the pounding of my heart.

He took out a small black book and thumbed through the pages, humming. When he laid the blank page in front of me, I paused for a few seconds, remembering Adeline's hateful letter and the crooked, spidery lines of her signature, then I wrote Adeline Blackstone.

"Can you direct me back to the marketplace?" I said without flinching as I stowed the bottle into the deepest corner of my reticule.

Moments later I sped past the statue of Lord Londonderry, pushing my aching legs to keep going. I was dizzy, my head churning with questions. How closely had the shopkeeper looked at me? Had he committed my face to memory? Could there be any chance of encountering him in some other setting where he might discover I'd given a counterfeit name? I had acted on instinct. Caught up in the terror of escaping Buckley. But now that I actually carried a bottle of poison in my bag, I feared I'd given in to base impulses that seemed inconceivable in the cold light of day. Had I actually contemplated murdering my husband?

Lost in thought, I stepped out onto the open street leading to the inn. Just then a carriage rattled down the road and stopped ahead, blocking my way. I shifted sideways to walk alongside it when the driver's helper sprang down from the carriage and lunged at me, seizing hold of my arm. I kicked and screamed and beat at him with my hands. Then the man threw the carriage door open and bundled me inside as the driver cracked the whip and we took off.

I landed inside the carriage on my knees, clawing at the seat with my fingernails to steady myself as the coach lurched and swayed across the cobbled street. The strange man seized me under my arms and hoisted me onto the seat, where I fell in a rumpled heap. Adeline sat opposite, grinning, her eyes shaded by the wide brim of a black silk bonnet.

I screamed and reached for the door, thinking I could wrench it open and escape before we picked up more speed, but the heavyset man sprang forwards and pushed me backwards. I flattened myself against the seat, my heart pounding.

"Behave yourself or Mr Murphy will be forced to use the restraints," snapped Adeline.

"Where is Henry?"

"Waiting for us to meet him. He will be overjoyed to see you."

I could have launched myself at her smug face and clawed at her eyes, but I bit back my anger. "Is he such a coward that he sends his mother to do his dirty work for him?"

"Hold your tongue," she said, her lip curling in disgust.

I turned away with a sinking heart as we left the confines of the city. Fields raced by and the trees appeared blurred and spectral through a steady sheet of rain.

Adeline began to doze, but the man called Murphy glowered at me, his pale eyes cold and implacable beneath the brim of a brown bowler hat. His long brown greatcoat, manicured whiskers, and impeccable gloves gave him the appearance of a military man. I closed my eyes, fighting ever-increasing waves of nausea and panic.

By now we were passing through a small village and out into open country again. The rain had stopped, but the moon was shrouded with mist, shedding cold grey light over a rambling stone building.

A wide driveway led to the barred windows, looming towers, and gloomy black doors of the front façade.

I knew exactly what place this was.

I turned away, sweat beading my temples and the back of my neck.

Adeline woke with a start, her eyes swollen with sleep. "We're here already?" she said, tapping the window. She straightened her bonnet as the driver came to a halt. "This is the Sedgewell Asylum. The residents you see here are quite harmless. The more wild and aggressive lunatics are locked up in cells."

I clutched the edge of the seat. "I don't belong here. You cannot force me in."

"That's what they all say," she said, smirking at Murphy.

She climbed out of the carriage first, then Murphy took my arm and dragged me down the steps. Gripping me tightly, he guided me to the front door, but I stopped at the threshold, certain that if I entered this place, I would never leave. I tried to wedge myself against the wooden doorpost, but he shoved me forwards into the gloomy interior with its wide brick arches and sweeping oak staircase. Stern-faced nurses in stiff white aprons and caps flitted back and forth, and a familiar moaning sound filled me with dread.

"Wait here with Murphy," said Adeline. "I'll go and find Henry and Donald, and don't make the mistake of trying to run. Murphy is ready and willing to defend himself against a vicious lunatic."

Murphy shoved me down onto a chair and I closed my eyes, wishing I could wake up from this nightmare. Suddenly a sharp tap on my shoulder made me jump. I turned to see an ancient lady clad in a ragged grey dress. A child's white frilled bonnet framed her wizened face. When she leaned towards me, her face split into a wide grin, exposing rotten black stumps of teeth. She cradled a rag doll in the crook of her arm and stroked its tattered hair with long bony fingers.

"I love me Ella Jane," she cackled. "For she's a canny bairn and not one for bubblin' all day."

"She's a very good baby," I mumbled.

She grasped my shoulder with a hand that was shrunken and freckled with liver spots. "You know I were a wild one once. I could ride bareback with the wind in me hair."

"You must have enjoyed that."

I caught the stench of rotten teeth as she spoke in a raspy whisper. "Father forbade it. And when he found me on my back in the hay wagon handling the serpent in the coal merchant's trousers, he put me on the asylum cart next time it come down the lane and here I am."

"How long have you been here?" I asked, sick at heart.

"Long enough for them to steal my baby away then open me up to tek out my women's parts!" she shrieked, jumping back from me. "And now the doctors say I'm a good girl that gives nobody any trouble." And with that she whirled away, spinning the rag doll then throwing it up in the air so that it landed beside me on the floor. I leaned to pick it up for her, but she bared her rotten fangs, leapt towards me, and clawed at my hand like a wildcat. I shrieked with the sudden, sharp pain just as Reverend Buckley strode in, with Adeline close behind. The woman grabbed her doll and scuttled away.

"Causing trouble already, Clara?" Buckley asked, his pale blue eyes drifting across my body. "Or perhaps old Verna's been pestering you."

"V-Verna?" I stuttered.

"The decrepit old hag. She's quite harmless, of course, unless one attempts to take away her doll. Then I gather she has a bite like a full-grown bulldog. But I see you got away with just a scratch," he said, glancing at the red welts on my hand.

I rubbed at the wound. "She believes it is her child and seeks to protect it."

"Precisely, her maternal instinct is as savage as a female bear's."

"If her own baby was taken away, then it is no wonder she became unhinged."

"She was deemed incapable to look after the child."

"But what was her crime?"

"Wildness—moral turpitude. The very underpinnings of insanity. Now, do you have any more questions, Clara?"

"Where is Henry?"

"Henry has arranged a very informative tour of this magnificent facility, but unfortunately he had to return to the university after sorting out some legal matters with Dr Beardsley, so we must hold you here until the doctor arrives."

I grasped the arms of the chair. "Why must he employ others to deal with his own wife?"

"Let us say, Henry is still learning how to assert his will. His mother and I both know how easily swayed he is," said Reverend Buckley.

Adeline stood behind Buckley, nodding as she muttered, "Alas, he is too soft-hearted."

"Besides, Clara, your paranoia betrays a most agitated state of mind. You'd be advised to behave more meekly or we may be forced to restrain you."

They took me and locked me inside a waiting room with dull mustard-coloured walls, empty except for a cane-backed chair and wooden table on bare floorboards. The tiny windows were too high for me to look through, but I could still hear sounds beyond the door—the endless clamour of shrieks and moans.

The sounds I'd come to dread from my nightmares.

The sounds of absolute and utter hopelessness.

# 34

A LOUD SCRAPING noise woke me. I opened my eyes to see Dr Beardsley in conversation with a short man in a grey jacket and loose tie, who was busy setting up a large photographic apparatus. I shrank away, my body stiff from sitting upright so long in the wooden chair.

"I must go home. I am here against my will," I said, but my throat was so dry, it came out as a whimper.

My head swam as the hazy figure of Dr Beardsley loomed above me. "We have neglected you, Mrs Blackstone. I'll send for fresh water. You must be thirsty."

Though my throat was parched, I pursed my lips. I would drink nothing they offered me. When an attendant arrived with a cup of water, I sniffed at it, wary it might be drugged. I touched one drop to my lips and my body cried out for water. I took but two sips and thrust it back.

"Still experiencing feelings of paranoia," said Dr Beardsley, fixing his cold eyes on me. "Now, make yourself comfortable so that Mr Tewson can take a likeness of you."

"For what reason?" I said, rising from my chair, but he caught me by the arm, his grip strong as a vice, and pushed me back onto the seat.

"Do not try to cross me. We have highly effective methods at our disposal to deal with women's disturbances."

He adjusted his tie, a faint flush painting his pallid cheeks. "Mr Tewson is an expert at reading a person's mental state from their photographic likeness. You would be surprised how one's face can betray symptoms of underlying mania, hysteria, and other violent disturbances. Now, turn to face him," he said, pushing my shoulders forwards, though I shrugged him away.

"I like to explain it thus," said Mr Tewson, emerging from the dark cloth behind the camera, his hair rumpled. "In the words of my esteemed mentor, Dr H. W. Diamond, 'The photographer catches in a moment the permanent cloud, or the passing storm or sunshine of the soul, and thus enables the metaphysician to trace out the visible and invisible in his researches into the philosophy of the human mind.'"

"Just another one of the many tools at our disposal," said Dr Beardsley, an edge of impatience in his voice.

"Dr Diamond was a man with a poet's soul." Mr Tewson sighed, gazing into the distance. But sensing the tension in the doctor's flinty eyes, he ducked beneath the cloth again. Soon a flash of white blinded my eyes, followed by the eggy stink of burning sulphur. Once my sight returned, I peered out into the hallway beyond, wondering how I might find a way to escape.

Dr Beardsley stood at the door, waiting for Mr Tewson to gather up his equipment. "Now we will join Reverend Buckley and your mother-in-law on a tour of this magnificent facility."

Adeline and Buckley were waiting outside the room with Murphy, who stayed close to me as we followed Dr Beardsley along a spotless corridor that smelled of vinegar and carbolic, an odour I'd come to dread from the showers at Hoxton.

We stopped at the open door of a room that resembled a large laboratory with a row of tall, upright wooden chairs across the back wall. Each chair had leather straps on its back and arms and strange metal boxes, from which sprouted rubber tentacles and wires, attached to platforms at the side. A middle-aged man with blank eyes and a twisted mouth was tied into one of the chairs. His bare feet sat in a basin of water whilst a doctor with a youth's dusting of hair on his chin attached a strange rubber cap and metal plugs to his head. Rubber tubing ran from the plugs into the basin of water.

"This is the electrical room, a marvel of modern science," said Dr Beardsley, beckoning us inside. I hesitated at the threshold, my stomach heaving from nausea, but Murphy pushed me in as Dr Beardsley continued: "Since insanity is primarily a physical disorder of the brain, it necessitates physical remedies, which can only be administered by the medically qualified. Here we are using the very latest scientific knowledge to harness the power of electricity in daily sessions of ten to twenty minutes to directly influence the brain. By placing the patient's hands and feet in water, we will send a current through both extremities at the same time, maximising its effects, but we must exercise caution. If too strong a current is used, epileptic convulsions will result."

He turned to the young doctor and held up a hand. "Dr Neasby. Let him be electrified!"

The young man turned a dial and a terrible buzzing filled the air. The man's eyes suddenly rolled upwards in his head, his teeth ground together, and his whole body twitched and jerked.

I covered my face, sickened as the stink of burning rubber flooded the room.

"It is not what it seems, Mrs Blackstone," said Dr Beardsley. "We have cured suicidal patients with this marvellous machine."

Adeline placed a handkerchief over her mouth and nose as a strangled, gurgling sound issued from the patient's mouth. After an agonising few minutes, we left the room. The poor man still twitched and jolted even as Beardsley shut the door.

"Very impressive," said Buckley. "Such a clever idea to harness the miracle of electricity."

"There is more," said Beardsley, ushering us along another long corridor and chattering to Buckley as he walked. "You could compare our treatment methods here to a game of chess. In other words, a complex sequence of offensive and defensive manoeuvres to bring about complete submission of the patient to the physician's total authority."

"Quite, quite," said Buckley. "The only reasonable solution to stem this plague of lunacy."

"And once we have established such a relationship, the patient will make a full confession of her moral wretchedness, then, isolated from family and other supports, we will unmask her deceitful stratagems."

Buckley stroked his chin. "After which, I suppose she may be returned to her menfolk's management and taught to make the will of her husband her own?"

"Precisely—in the more successful cases. But I fear many of the chronics will never recover sufficiently to find a way out of here. Or, in the case of certain delicate women's problems, we are forced to operate."

He opened the door to a room with glaring white walls and a cold marble floor. My legs went to jelly at the memory of the terrible showers at Hoxton.

He pointed to a scrubbed wooden table surrounded by gleaming trays of surgical instruments. "I apologise if I offend your delicate ears, Mrs Blackstone," he said, smiling at Adeline, "but our treatments here are grounded in science. If our insertions of ice water and ice into the female parts do not show results, we are fully equipped to operate by removing the ovaries or various other parts I cannot mention in female company."

Adeline mopped her face with the lace handkerchief. "I believe I have seen enough, Dr Beardsley. I have complete confidence in your expertise, but I must step out of the room for a moment."

She pushed past without glancing at me, her cheeks flushed livid red. I remained inside, unable to shake myself from Murphy's grasp.

Dr Beardsley leaned closer to Reverend Buckley. "That insanity arises from masturbation is beyond a doubt, Donald. In men and particularly in women, the chronic masturbator becomes self-mutilating and consumptive. We often see this afflict young girls as early as adolescence. For our male patients, we employ certain devices." He held up a large metal shield with a long hollow tube protruding from it. "But for some females, we must perform a clitoridectomy."

It seemed even Reverend Buckley swayed a little on his feet and coughed loudly, covering up his mouth. His florid face went pale as he turned to leave.

"I do not have the medical background to question a learned man like you, Dr Beardsley. But perhaps we might take a look at your dairy and hog barns. Henry's mother is something of a livestock expert and might consider making a donation to your farming operations. Besides, a little fresh air might be beneficial."

"Of course," he said, ushering us out into the hallway. "Perhaps your man will take Mrs Blackstone back to the waiting room whilst we venture outside."

I sat in the waiting room, staring at the blank walls and cursing my own stupidity.

Had I really thought Henry wouldn't use every method at his disposal to come after me? He would never allow Izzie's fortune to slip through his fingers without putting up a fight. Now I was hemmed in, all exits blocked, whilst Murphy smoked nonchalantly outside the room. All I could think of was how I wanted to barge through that door and run until I dropped.

Instead I forced myself to think of Annie.

*Never show them your true feelings, for then they'll have complete power over you.*

I made my mind go blank, let the calmness wash over me, but my body stiffened at the sound of rustling skirts outside. The door opened and Adeline hurried in. She stood over me as she pulled on her gloves.

"It's a shame you missed the hogs, Clara. Such modern, well-kept pens and very contented animals, but then I expect you consider such practical concerns beneath you."

I gazed ahead at the open door, the tip of Murphy's gleaming boots visible by the doorpost.

She placed a hand on her hip and took a deep breath, her face blooming with reddish patches. "So you're giving us the silent treatment? I see. Well, you should fall to your knees in gratitude to my son, who has generously made the decision to offer you a second chance to prove you can be a suitable wife to him."

I tried to temper my relief as I glanced at her smug face, her eyebrows raised in expectation of a suitably humble reply.

"I'm thankful," I mumbled, swallowing my revulsion.

"Let this be a warning to you, then. If you fail to improve yourself, you will end up here with no hope of release."

I got to my feet, my legs sluggish and cold. Murphy slithered into the room beside me, a cobra ready to strike in case I tried to dart away.

Following them both out, I realised I'd find myself here again if I didn't get away from Henry. Regardless of how dutifully I behaved.

This had been but a preview of my future home.

For once Izzie had passed, Henry would waste no time sending me back here for good.

# 35

"I AM LEARNING more about your condition, Clara," said Henry, leaning against the parlour mantelpiece. I sat mute, facing him in an upright chair, my insides seething. Behind me, Adeline barked at Alice in the scullery and the smell of roasting meat wafted in from the kitchen. "Buckley has opened my eyes with profound new works by Maudsley and Baker Brown. I see now that I am the true guardian of your interests, the custodian of your honour, and the one to protect you against your self-destructive urges. You must understand that we men are stronger; you, as a woman, are naturally weaker and therefore not in a position to dispute my wishes. In other words, you are here at my mercy."

There was a wildness to his eyes, a rapture—as if he contemplated the glory of his majesty and power. I studied the changes in his face. The bony swell of skull under the thinning hair at his temples. The aggressive jut of his jaw, and hooded eyes that seemed to dominate his shrunken cheeks.

I stayed silent. True madness was here. Right in front of me.

He shook a finger at me and smiled. "When you were a wild, untamed creature—filthy and unkempt, refusing your food, cursing and spitting, your wrists chained—how grateful you were when they removed your shackles. How your eyes shone in joyful gratitude when you looked at me. You will feel that again, Clara—the sweetness of submission. I will see to it."

He watched from the bottom of the stairs as I marched upwards, my stomach twined with loathing. It was a relief to get into my room and throw my reticule onto the bed, to go to the window and push it open to gulp in some fresh air. But it was shut fast. Nailed down.

I pressed my back flat against the window and tried to gather my thoughts.

It seemed the very house was shrinking—enclosing me within its walls. Now the silence pressed like a heavy stone. I ran to the bed and flung myself onto the covers, holding my hands over my face to shut out the feeling of being swallowed up and obliterated. Then I remembered the poison in my reticule. I tore through the contents of the bag until I found that small brown bottle, half-full with the mixture. I remembered Mary Ann's voice.

*Some folk dilute the arsenic and soft soap with water until the powder sinks to the bottom of the bottle and then—not too much at once . . . only a little at a time . . .*

Using a teaspoon from the cup of tea Alice had left, I ladled in some water from the jug by the washstand. One spoon at a time until the bottle was full. Then, in a fit of panic, I pried up a loose floorboard and hid the bottle in the space. It would stay there until I decided whether or not to use it. Once I'd put the mat back straight, I checked through my bag and took out the money pouch. The thick roll of notes and the weight of coins was a comfort to me. Money allowed the possibility of escape.

That night I ate supper in my room, then watched from the window as Adeline and Henry left for the Buckleys', Adeline's old-fashioned hooped skirt swaying under her wrap like a frilled lampshade. Once the carriage pulled away, I ran to my door and turned the knob this way and that. It was locked.

*Think,* I urged myself. *Be cunning like the women in the asylum. Act your way out of this.*

I remembered the shammers at Bethlem, fainting or throwing themselves on the floor and grinding their teeth in fits to catch the attention of the doctors when they came on their rounds. Most times the doctors were hardened to their games and would let them lie there until exhaustion wore them out. But occasionally a new attendant or a pink-cheeked young doctor would take pity and shower attention on them. Surely I could catch Alice out with some theatrics.

I placed my bag near the doorway and took a deep breath, then began to beat at the door with my fists, screaming Alice's name. In less than a minute her footsteps pounded along the corridor, then stopped outside.

"Mrs Blackstone, what has happened?" she said in a voice breathless with panic.

"I can't breathe." I gasped. "The sleeping draught . . . I can't . . ."

"But Mr Blackstone forbade me to open the door."

I whirled around, wheezing and puffing, then took the side chair and flung it to the ground with a clatter. A strangled scream came from outside and I heard the scrape of a key in the lock.

*Be ready,* the voice urged. *Now is your chance.*

I pressed my back against the wall so the door would conceal me, then waited as it creaked slowly open. A foot appeared first and then a hand. "Are you all right?" she whimpered, and I felt a stab of pity for the girl as she stepped in, peering around in the darkness to find me. Then, once she stood at the centre of the room, I took my bag, slipped into the hallway, and slammed the door shut, turning the key to lock her safely inside.

I could barely suck a breath into my lungs as I tore down the stairs, grabbed my warm coat from the stand, and pushed my way out through the open scullery door.

# 36

I LAY LOW at the inn for the next few days, not daring to show my face outside. Only venturing downstairs for meals, then returning to my sanctuary to consider how I could get away from the city without running into Henry or Murphy and his other cronies, who undoubtedly still lay in wait at the railway station or prowled the main roads that led out from the city.

Finally, the day before the hanging, I watched from my window until Lowry, Joe Thornley, and his father, Clem, trudged up the street towards the prison. Gathering my cloak around my shoulders, I hastened along the dank hallway and down the back stairs to the alleyway behind the inn. The cobbles were slick with morning frost, and the stink of last night's boiled cabbage wafted from the open bins nearby. Keeping close to the side wall, I crept to the front street, my insides churning. The three men approached, now barely three yards distant. I called Lowry's name and his head jerked to the side as he nudged his cronies, frowning. Cautiously, I stepped further out into the street until I caught Joe Thornley's eye.

"Mrs Blackstone!" he shouted, starting forwards.

I plastered a finger to my lips and pulled back into the alleyway. They glanced about them, bemused, then hurried towards me.

"I was sick with worry about you, Mrs Blackstone," said Lowry, touching my shoulder. "The other week it looked like the devil's horsemen were after you."

"We've not seen hide nor hair of you," said Joe Thornley, sharply appraising my rough cloak. "And now I have to wonder why a fine lady like you must cower like a frightened animal in a filthy alleyway?"

"I have a favour to ask," I whispered, knowing this was my last chance to get away from Durham. "But I beg you not to make me explain why."

"Anything for a friend of Mary Ann's," said Lowry. "What say you, Clem?"

The old man scratched the grey stubble on his chin. "I say we'll ask no questions to embarrass the fine lady and do owt she asks of us."

"Say the word, Mrs Blackstone," said Lowry.

"I need to get away from the city in secret. Can you help me?" My eyes strayed beyond them to the carriages that pulled up outside the inn.

"You mean smuggle you out in hiding?" said Joe, twisting his cap in his hands.

I nodded, watching a soberly dressed gaunt old man with a bushy white beard and a pallid face ascend from the carriage, accompanied by a younger man with the ruddy complexion of a farmer. Lowry glanced behind him, his expression grave as he turned back. " 'Tis Calcraft, the executioner. I saw his portrait in the paper."

We were silent for a moment, each considering the ghastly significance of his presence here, until Joe Thornley coughed and broke the silence.

"Me marrer Freddie Hawkeswell has a flat cart we can bring tomorrow. I'll warrant we can hide some cargo under the sacking."

"We'll be here for the hanging, Mrs Blackstone," said Lowry. "We promised to see her off."

"As did I," I said. "But afterwards I must leave the city. Could you meet me in the alley here behind the inn?"

The men exchanged glances. "Aye," said Joe. "There should be enough room to bring the cart around. Then we'll wait for you."

"Or do you need us to teach someone a sharp lesson?" said Clem, clenching his fists and ducking his head down. "I can still land a good right hook under the chin of any blackguard that dares to lay a hand on you. I'll mek him wish he'd never seen the light of day."

Joe steadied his father with a heavy hand on his shoulder. "We'll not be needing any beatings if we help the lady get away without being seen, Da. Settle yersel' down, now."

"Comes in useful sometimes, though," said Lowry, patting the older man's cheek. "Till tomorrow, then, Mrs B. We must mek haste now and say goodbye to our Mary Ann before the clerics get there."

"Mind you keep yourself safe till then," said Joe, winking and touching his hat.

I fell back against the wall, breathing a long sigh of relief as I watched them make their way towards the prison gate.

I woke at six the next morning to find my room bathed in a reddish glow. The crimson sky was streaked with jagged black clouds. As if the heavens were burning.

A fitting day for a hanging.

My stomach twisted and turned. So much was at stake today. Mary Ann's life and my freedom. I felt a sudden wrench in my heart that the moment she had dreaded was fast approaching. Now there was no escape from the hangman's noose. I would witness her execution, then slip away like a thief in the night, hidden in the back of a flat cart. Start my life over again—as long as everything went according to plan. I lay in bed, my whole body tingling as if tiny fish swam like quicksilver through my blood.

The plan was risky. But it was my only option.

I had sent the hotel's messenger boy with a note to give Bertha, begging her to lend me a wardress's uniform so I might sneak into the prison in disguise. She had sent him back with a bag of clothing and instructed me to meet her at the entrance to the prison at seven o'clock sharp.

Clad in the heavy woollen dress and with my hair scraped tightly under the starched cap, my stomach turned as I made my way downstairs, the smell of tea, toast, and greasy sausages wafting from the dining room. I couldn't touch a bite. Not today.

The sun shone through the gathering clouds, but a frigid breeze gusted around the crowds already assembled on the prison lawns. A small line of pressmen huddled at the prison gate. My heart beat fast as the line moved forwards, and each man's card was checked by a sober-faced guard. There were only two men in front of me at the gate when the reporter at the front of the line asked a question of the guard.

"Sir, could you tell us when the hangman arrived?"

The guard cleared his throat and straightened his shoulders as the reporters reached for their pencils and notebooks.

"Aye, since you're interested, I'll tell you. Calcraft, the hangman, was here yesterday. Like the angel of death he were in his black suit and white beard. His assistant, Evans, looked like a fresh-faced man. They say he's a farmer. And, rumour has it he keeps a hanging rope hung up in the sitting room at his farm in Wales. Takes a strange sort of man to be up to that sort of business."

"True," said another reporter. "We none of us take pleasure in executions."

The other men grunted and nodded. Encouraged, the guard continued: "He come to check the pit under the gallows. Told the governor it would have to be deepened and widened to take the chair. If the prisoner canna walk, she's tied into a chair and that's how she's hanged."

Just then Bertha appeared, cutting her way through the crowd as a scrawny man in a ragged jacket raised his fist and shouted, "String the bitch up and let her choke!" A loud cheer followed from the people around him.

"Nowt like a hanging to bring out the worst in people," she said, glaring at them before she caught sight of me. Hurrying over, she took my arm and steered me away from the line of pressmen.

"I must be soft in the head, but when she begged me to help you get to the hanging, I promised I'd try."

"I thank you for all you've done, Bertha."

"Then keep your mouth shut. Let me do the talking and I'll see if I can get you through," she said as we entered the side gate of the prison. The guard greeted us, his face drawn and serious.

"This is a bad business, Miss Dunn."

Bertha nodded. "Aye, this sad day's come far too quickly, Mr Boxted."

I breathed a sigh of relief that he didn't recognise me, just as Mrs Sewell hurried towards us in a dark dress and cape, her face deathly white, her eyes swollen and red. I turned away and fussed with my gloves.

"How was she this morning?" asked Bertha.

"They say she slept a little, then fell asleep reading the Bible. She woke this morning very pale and quiet, drank a cup of tea, and then asked us to join her in prayers. She prayed for the baby, Margaret Edith, then for little Robert Robson Cotton; for Robinson, her third husband; and for her stepfather, Mr Stott. We were all full of tears to see her going to her death without penitence."

"The ministers will be there now," said Bertha, "but I must help get her ready."

She sat me in a narrow corridor near the wardresses' resting room and bade me wait. The little wooden cradle sat there empty, a sad reminder of the baby that had brightened the place for a few days.

I must have drifted off, because I awoke to Bertha shaking me. "It's a quarter to eight," she whispered. "The hangman and his assistant are on their way to Mary Ann's cell to pinion her with the strap."

I staggered to my feet. "How was she?"

"She maintained her innocence to the end and all she said was 'I was the agent, the means, but not intentionally.' Make what you will of that, Clara."

"She still maintains Riley and Chalmers mistakenly put arsenic in the medicine," I said, remembering how she'd dwelled on it before the trial.

"Apparently, the reverend then asked how it could be but one accident, since it was many acts done over many months. And a whole string of husbands and children lay dead in the ground? But she wouldn't open her mouth more. I suppose she'd no more straws to grasp at. Now her two matrons will accompany her outside and then the male warders will take her up to the gallows to hold her in case she struggles."

"You won't go with them?"

"They said we could stand with some of the public witnesses, but I fear I don't have the stomach for watching such a scene."

"Can you get me out there amongst them?" I begged.

She gave me a questioning look. "You're a strange bird, Clara Blackstone, but I suppose I understand," she said, guiding me into a draughty white corridor.

Half an hour later I stood with the other public witnesses, shivering in the chill breeze. We were arranged into four rows in a nettled corner of the men's exercise yard. When the clock boomed eight times, a procession entered the area, led by a line of men in dark uniforms, bearing their wands of office. I felt a heaviness in my heart at the sight of them, heads held high as they marched towards the gallows, eyes fixed on the dark wooden structure, steel-faced like soldiers headed for battle. It seemed gruesome that such weighty company had gathered in all their pomp and splendour to witness the brutal destruction of a pauper woman.

"'Tis the undersheriff, the deputy governor, and the warden," whispered a nearby reporter as he scribbled in his notebook. "A mighty assembly for such an occasion."

The chaplain followed in flowing robes, black as the crows perched on the high prison walls, and Mary Ann came last, her matrons supporting each arm, her hands manacled and attached to a leather belt around her waist. The ground seemed to shift under my feet, but I regained my balance as she passed by. Bareheaded, her face was pinched and livid with fear, her mouth working as she looked up to the heavens, uttering prayers and wringing her hands as if she were sleepwalking, oblivious to the horror of what lay ahead. Her shrunken frame was wrapped in the old black-and-white chequered shawl. A gust of wind whipped her hair across her face, and her body shivered with the cold. My heart clenched as if a fist squeezed it.

The matrons accompanied her through the gate, then stopped and turned their faces away at the sight of the gallows, with its two eight-foot upright posts and transverse beam on the top. Below were the folded trapdoors, secured by a bar, which would be released by one push of the lever. On seeing the black-painted noose, Mary Ann stumbled and pulled back, sobbing and praying with even greater fervour, her eyes rolling upwards so only the whites showed, like a beast being brought to slaughter.

The two women steadied her, and she leaned towards them, appearing to whisper a few words as they cradled her arms. Then two male warders stepped forwards, grasped her by the elbows, and pulled her across the last fifty yards of gravel, where Mr Calcraft, the "finisher of the law" for Durham County, took her and placed her on the drop. Without a second of hesitation, he drew a white cotton cap over Mary Ann's face and placed the dangling noose around her neck, whilst his assistant pinioned her arms and legs. My heart thundered like a drumbeat in my ears, almost drowning out her last words. She cried, "Lord Jesus, receive my spirit. God have mercy on my soul!" as they strapped her feet together.

Calcraft gave the noose a last tug to see that it was properly adjusted, then, with a brisk movement, his assistant pulled the lever and Mary Ann fell heavily into the short drop, stopping with a loud thump as her body bounced slightly upwards. I thought then it was over, but she kept moving. Twisting and struggling as if she were fighting for life.

"She is not dead," whispered one of the reporters beside me. "Calcraft's bungled it again. The drop was too short."

To the horror of all assembled, Calcraft leaned forwards and held her by the shoulders for a few seconds, pushing her downwards.

Strangling her with his own bare hands.

The body reared up and down and he pushed harder in a final effort, glancing uneasily at the onlookers as he did so. Then he and his assistant stepped back as the body continued to writhe and twist, her chest heaving and her clasped hands jerking up and down, her white hood spattered with blood where her mouth and nose were. The reporters around me bowed their heads, coughing into handkerchiefs. One of the uniformed warders fainted, the matrons sobbed, but I forced myself to watch as her body writhed in agony, and her pinioned arms struggled to escape the leather belt.

I remained there for at least three minutes, watching until her body hung lifeless. I would not look away from the awful sight, unlike the men who had discovered they were not able to face the grim reality of her execution. I stood still as a statue and stayed with her until the end—saw her soul leave the earth, wherever it might be headed—to a forgiving God or to everlasting torment, and I prayed she might finally find some peace. Then I thought the terrible strength that drove her towards survival had stayed with her until those gruesome last seconds when she'd attempted to defy death and the hangman. This was the only way her life could end after everything she'd done, and yet it had seemed an obscene act of brutality.

At a few minutes before nine, the hangman cut down her body and lowered it onto wooden planks, ready for the waiting prison surgeon. The damp hood clung to the outlines of her face and her familiar chequered black-and-white shawl lay on the ground alongside the wooden planks of the gallows.

Next to her neatly placed shoes.

When I saw how they handled her body with a curious gentleness, the bile rose in my throat. They had brutalised her. Broken her. But their frenzy was gone now and the cold realisation of what they'd done was just dawning on them. At that moment, a black flag was hoisted above the prison to let the throngs of people outside the walls know that the sentence of death had been carried out. Their cheers rang out across the rooftops.

I followed the reporters out through the gate and hurried away from the prison, unable to dispel the image of her body, writhing in agony at the end of a rope. Cruel hands had dragged me by the hair across stone floors and cracked a gnarled club across my knuckles, had pinned me down and applied the icy douche until my teeth ground together as if they would break. Leather straps had pinioned me to my bed and fastened my hands across my chest in a strong dress.

I would never understand the terrible brutality that those in authority inflict on women.

I fled past the mob, now split into angry factions that called out at one another. The jeers of those who revelled in her death drowned out the petitioners praying for mercy for Mary Ann's soul. Outside the gates, a man was selling photographs of Mary Ann in her black bonnet and chequered shawl. I could not bring myself to buy one. Her face was etched in my memory. I would need no reminder of her now that she was dead and gone from my life forever.

I yearned to escape the place, and finally tore myself away from the prison, pushing through the crowds that cheered and shouted as they surged towards the taverns to celebrate. I shouldered my way to the front of the inn and slipped into the side alley that led to the back door, but turning the corner too fast, I almost collided with a man who stepped into my path, rolling an empty beer barrel. Beyond him, at the far end of the alleyway, I made out the dark shape of a flat cart rounding the other corner. I waved, but the horse screeched to a sudden standstill in front of a row of beer barrels.

My heart slammed in my ears, drowning the clamour of the jeering crowds out on the street. I ducked around the man who stood back to let me through, but as I turned my head to thank him, another, bulkier man grabbed me by the arm, pulled me to his chest, and held a cloth to my face. The sickly sweet stink of ether, the sound of Joe Thornley yelling my name, and the sight of Henry's face swimming in the shadows were the last things I remembered as the blackness swept over me.

# Aden

## Spring 1873

WE TRAVELLED ALONG the canal—a giant ghost ship floating through a vast, undulating desert. At times, I saw bands of camel riders stopped in awe, watching our ship slide through the narrow waterway, its black chimneys belching foul smoke into a velvet night sky pinpointed with silver clusters of stars. After entering the Red Sea at Suez, we sailed on to Aden to replenish our fuel supply.

Now I watch as dusk falls and the ship is lit with flares. Lines of sun-blackened porters stream onto the ship, bearing hulking sacks and baskets of coal on their backs, and intoning a low monotone chant, their sweat-soaked tunics clinging to their bodies. On the upper decks, the captain and his mate look on, roasting in their white uniform jackets. With the orange glow of the flares, the thick heat, and the livid red sky, I imagine I am sweltering in Hell.

Do I deserve to be in Hell?

I push the nagging reminder of guilt aside, clutch the ship's rail, and look out at the tiny peninsula. A bleak, arid-looking place, the city clings to the scorching red cliffs, baking under the blazing sunset. But my guidebook tells me Aden lies halfway between Suez and Bombay, so I am drawing closer to Izzie and my new life.

For a brief moment anxiety and uncertainty grip me like a false friend, whispering that no matter how far I run, I cannot escape my past. That I will never find happiness. That I do not deserve it after all that happened in Durham. Then I remember Izzie and the feel of her fragile arms wrapped around me, telling me that God forgives everyone—even the worst sinners. I know that the next stop—Bombay—will be the last one, so I banish those dark thoughts to a deep, hidden place and allow myself to revel in the prospect of absolute freedom.

Two of the fishing-fleet girls stand near me under a flapping awning. The blond-ringlet girl bows her head and her shoulders shake with sobs. I move closer as she gives her nose a loud blow. I hold my breath and listen.

"I have suffered this whole voyage with two awful old hags in my cabin," she sobs. "They natter at me from morning till night and tell me if I do not catch someone at the Bombay parties, I will be sent up-country to some remote plantation where the men are older and not so choosy."

The red-haired girl pats her shoulder. "You are too young and pretty to worry. Some handsome plantation owner or company official will scoop you up. It is Agnes, with her thick waist and short neck, who will be passed over. Why, she is twenty-four and well past the age of desirability. She will be lucky to be taken in by some toothless old widower with fingers like talons, sour breath, and unmentionable habits."

The ship's funnels blast twice, drowning out the rest of the conversation. I am thankful. I want no more of such talk. Mary

Ann was right. Marriage is a prison sentence. No more than unpaid servitude.

I will never marry again.

Izzie's money will ensure it.

# 37

I STOOD AT the foot of the scaffold, a simple structure—two upright posts with a beam attached to the top. A black-painted rope hung from the end, the empty noose swinging gently in the breeze. Below that, a wooden trapdoor was placed above a deep pit gouged into the earth. A deathly calm chilled the air.

*Where is she?* I called, but my voice was lost under a sudden beating of wings. A flock of crows scattered across the sky, circling like the eddying currents of a whirlpool. In my hands, I held a pair of tidy polished shoes with a buckle at each toe. A frayed piece of chequered shawl hung across my arm. I screamed again, *Where did you take her?* And then a line of black-masked men passed by the gallows, bearing a simple wooden coffin on their shoulders, led by a man with snow-white hair, bushy whiskers, and wiry white hairs sprouting from flared nostrils—Calcraft, the public executioner, his eyes shrouded by ragged brows. He held a Bible and recited the jumbled words of a Psalm as he walked. *In the valley of the shadow of death, you will walk with death in the shadows, let the devil take you. . .*

"She is still under the influence of the draught," said a sharp voice, stirring me into consciousness. I tried to push my eyelids open. So tired, eyelids fused shut, my body weightless—paralyzed, as if I floated on a cloud of ether.

"Can you not wake her?" said another, familiar voice.

My eyelids inched open to a dim, hazy world—like looking through a rain-blurred window. The shimmering shape of Henry's face hovered above me, flanked by two other faces that swam into my field of vision, their eyes magnified as if I were watching them through the curve of a goldfish bowl. One was Buckley, the other a stranger, and though I heard their words clearly, I could not move.

"We might classify her as a typical degenerate, cursed with progressive inherited degeneracy."

"Her mother was unstable. A victim of excessive passions."

"And she has exhibited mania, an obsession with the murderer."

"Only satiated by witnessing the brutal hanging."

"She refuses to fit in. Detests domestic tasks and avoids social gatherings."

"She is indolent. Keeps to her room and revels in an imaginary world. I cannot talk to her."

"She shuns her husband's affections and seeks an unnatural attachment to a female monster."

"She expresses contentious opinions and spurns the words of her betters."

"Gentleman, I will sign to her incurable insanity."

I opened my eyes to the darkness ringed with a flickering yellow light. Pain seared the backs of my eyes, and I shut them again to stop the heaving in my stomach.

"So they finally strung the poisoner up," said a voice to the side of me. My eyes snapped open and I saw Henry sitting by the fire, his chin resting on his thumb and fingers as he stared deep into the glowing coals.

"I hear reports that she died like a rabid dog, writhing in agony, no dignity even in her death. A fitting end for such a monster."

I pressed my eyes shut. I'd seen enough to know I was in my old bedroom. I could hear the elm tree outside, its branches scraping against the windowpanes.

"I suppose that will be the end of your morbid obsession with a murderer," he said, taking out his watch and winding it.

"How long have I been here?" I gasped, my tongue dry and thick.

He placed his watch back in his pocket. "Since yesterday. You've slept the sleep of the dead."

I tried to raise myself up on my elbows, but a swell of nausea forced me back against the pillow. "What do you want from me, Henry?"

He stood up. "What I have always wanted. A dutiful wife. But I see you are incapable of being that person."

I fell back onto the bed, the pain a tight band round my skull.

"You need to rest, Clara. Gather your strength for tomorrow. Then we will say goodbye. Forever."

"You'll let me go?"

He walked towards the door, shaking his head. "You know, Clara, it's quite fortuitous that your murderous friend died only yesterday. It provided me with the perfect excuse. Now I can tell everyone how you were plunged into despair at her brutal execution, and pushed to the limits of your sanity when she gave her wretched child to a pauper family instead of you. And I will be grief-stricken that my wife had to be committed to the madhouse on the recommendation of two learned doctors, when her devoted husband was trying so hard to save her from that fate."

"You're mad," I said, throwing the blankets away from me. "Izzie will never allow you to take me there."

"Izzie is thousands of miles away. She will never know." He turned, his hand clutching the doorknob. "So, my dear, the only other choice you have is death. They say the chloral mixed with wine is the speediest way to do it, though it might feel rather like drowning. In the meantime, stay here and think about it. If you are still here tomorrow, we leave for Sedgewell in the afternoon."

So I had not dreamt those faces and the doctor pronouncing his diagnosis. Now all channels of escape were closed to me.

I waited until Henry's footsteps had faded, then ran to the door. It was shut but not locked. I heard Mary Ann's voice beside me.

*You'll be forever looking backwards to see if he's coming after you.*

Could I run? Escape through the front door and find my way back to the inn? Wait there until I could board a train to London?

Holding the scream of panic down, I shut the door and ran to move the rug from the loose floorboards. Prying them up, I took the small bottle out from its hiding place. The soap bubbles had disappeared. The mixture had settled, and a layer of white powder lay at the bottom of the bottle. From there, just as Mary Ann had instructed, I poured off the water until only the powder remained. It would dry off by the fire. Tomorrow morning I would put some in Henry's tea. Just enough to make him sick.

But maybe enough to kill him.

Then I could escape.

I ran to the window. The moon was full, its dimpled face illuminating the street below. A shape moved in the shadows below the streetlamp. The tall figure of a man wearing a flat cap, his eyes turned upwards to my window. I blinked, thinking it an illusion caused by the chloral, and when I opened my eyes again, the figure was gone, vaporised into the night. I ran to my door and stood by it, hearing the slow swish of Adeline's skirts along the corridor, the thump of her heavy shoes on the floorboards. Her bedroom door creaked open, then slammed shut.

I pushed my door open a crack. The sound of clinking dishes echoed from the scullery. Alice was still about. Then I heard the low drone of Henry's voice and the neat click of his footsteps sounding across the downstairs hallway.

I let myself out and crept along the corridor to the top of the stairs. Hiding myself in the shadows, I watched Henry test the front door. My insides turned at the thought of him writhing in agony on the floor, his mouth foaming from the arsenic, his eyes turning up into his head whilst I looked on. Mary Ann was right. I did not have the stomach for murder. Instead I would wait until they were all in bed, then I'd get the keys from the scullery and escape into the night.

"Go to bed, Alice. I'll lock up," he called, taking the key from his pocket. His hand reached out to touch the bolt when the front door flew open, knocking him backwards. He stumbled, grasping at the umbrella stand, his mouth gaping open as he mouthed, *Oh, oh.*

Dark figures moved in on him, illuminated by the sputtering candle on the table. Henry's arms crossed like a shield in front of his chest. I caught a glint of grey eyes and a silvery strand of a scar on a cheek, then a short solid figure with a flat cap who snuffed the candle out. The figures merged together and the edge of a blade gleamed, then thrust down deep into

Henry's gut. I heard a dull grunt of pain as he slumped forwards onto the man who shoved him back. Then I watched my husband stagger backwards, towards the shorter man, his head thrown back, his face twisted in agony as he clutched his belly. The blade glinted again, arced in an upwards motion, and sliced across Henry's throat. My breath stopped as a fountain of blood shot into the air, followed by the heavy slump of a body—like a sack of potatoes falling onto the floor. The two figures slipped away into the night like jagged shadows, just as a blaze of light flooded in from the kitchen and Alice stood there screeching, her hands over her ears. Adeline's door burst open and she flew past me, her ghostly nightgown flapping about her legs. I pounded down the stairs after her. Alice was still screaming. "Murder—murder! Two men—in caps and mufflers—a knife!"

Adeline clattered down the last few stairs and stood shrieking at the sight of the sticky gouts of blood oozing like treacle from her son's throat. Then, staggering towards the wall, she slumped to her knees, falling to the floor into the bloody puddle beside him.

Alice stood like a stone statue, hands raking at her eyes. I caught her by the shoulders and shook her hard until she focused on me, her eyes staring out with fear. "Run to the station—fetch the police. Now."

It took a hard shove to rouse her, but she suddenly snapped into life and tore out through the open door, running and stumbling over the shrubs in her confusion. Henry was stirring, clutching at the mess of his throat. He gasped for breath, his mouth trying to work itself into soundless words, like a fish suffocating on a hook. And when his eyes finally fixed on mine, I smiled at the expression I saw there. Not hatred or anger.

But utter disbelief.

Adeline stirred and I covered my mouth to conceal the smirk as he breathed the final short, sharp rasps of breath from his ruined throat.

The constable, neat in his gold-buttoned uniform, stood over Henry's stiff body. Another officer combed over the scene for clues. Adeline lay in a stupor on the parlour couch. I had given her a large dose of chloral to stop her screaming. She'd kept the wailing up for a good ten minutes. The constable praised me. "A selfless act, thinking of others in the face of your own bereavement, Mrs Blackstone. He is her flesh and blood, after all."

"I will give her a regular course of it to spare her weak heart," I'd said, my face composed in a mask of sympathy and benevolence.

Alice shuddered and clung to me, whilst I rubbed my knuckles into my eyes to redden them.

"What did you see, Miss Kemp?"

"A man with a knife. Another with him."

"Young? Old?"

"I could not tell. It were dark."

I spoke up, my voice quavering.

"I heard my husband's cries. I saw from the top of the stairs."

"Did you see the men?"

I covered my mouth with a clenched fist and nodded.

"You saw them clearly?"

"Yes. One was tall, lanky, and powerful. I believe he was bald, with a bulbous nose. The other was an old man with thick grey whiskers and a stooped back. That is all I saw."

"Look here, Henderson," said the other officer, holding out a silver chain, a pendant swinging at the end of it. "The victim had this in his pocket."

"A botched robbery, most likely," said Henderson, clicking the locket open. He glanced at me, his eyes alight. "It has your likeness in it."

I remembered handing the locket to Mary Ann. Her clutching it and holding it up so it glinted in the light. *Joe Thornley knows folk who'd do anything for a few pound. . . . I just have to give the word.*

"Your husband must have loved you, Mrs Blackstone," said Henderson. "Because he gave his life to save this precious keepsake of yours."

As I took the necklace, prickles of heat tickled my cheek. The place that had brushed against Mary Ann's ear.

"I suppose he did," I said, watching it glint in the candlelight. "He wanted to make sure I would never forget him."

# Bombay

## June 1873

WE GLIDE INTO Bombay Harbour, past small islands glowing gold, turquoise, and amethyst in the hazy morning sunlight. Flocks of flying fish accompany us, leaping and skimming over the water.

Skinny brown boys in loincloths dive off the harbour wall, laughing and surfacing like glistening seals. A crowd gathers to greet us, and the faint sounds of a brass band become louder as we pull in. Everywhere, I see vibrant colours—saffron yellow, azure blue, deep crimson. The air is heavy with scents—the sweetness of jasmine, the briny saltiness of the sea, the peppery, musky perfume of spices and tobacco. My senses are alive with so much beauty. I cannot wait to get to Izzie.

On the quayside, a man in a faded linen suit approaches me with a sign bearing my name. Spider veins web his florid cheeks and his teeth are like yellowed piano keys. He smiles a sharklike smile and introduces himself as Dr Price, Izzie's doctor.

"My condolences on the untimely death of your husband," he says, glancing at my cream linen dress with one raised eyebrow. My heart shifts and suddenly the heat is a cloying, pressing fist that forces me to stumble against my trunks.

Dr Price snaps his fingers and two white-clad porters appear, swiftly transferring my luggage to a waiting open carriage.

I am conscious of a throbbing headache that worsens as we pass a river teeming with half-naked bathers and women scrubbing clothes on the banks. Then we plunge into a maze of narrow streets lined with many small shops and seething masses of people—turbaned men in long robes, beggars by the roadside, women in vivid saris, barefoot children selling trinkets, and stray dogs and cattle wandering into our path.

We finally pass into a wider street of towering palm trees and thick hedgerows studded with pink and yellow flowers. My heart lifts when I see the white roofs of elegant houses towering above the foliage. Finally I am home.

At Izzie's rambling bungalow, a warm wind rustles across the terrace and sets white silk curtains aflutter like butterfly wings. I step onto the front verandah and the air is scented with jasmine and honeysuckle. I follow Dr Price into the shady interior. Reminders of Izzie are everywhere. Dried flowers in bowls, her favourite books on the shelves, bright silk shawls draped across couches and dining chairs.

"I should warn you, your grandmother is in a weakened condition," says Dr Price, his voice taking on a sombre tone.

I step into an airy room where lavender barely masks the unmistakable odour of decay. A bed by the open window is piled with thick cushions and heavy quilts. A shrunken husk of a person—a wizened grey creature with wisps of cottony white hair sprouting from her pink scalp lies against the white pillow.

"Izzie," I whisper, drawing close to her so that I can clutch the bony, blue-veined claw that scratches at the bedspread. The crêpe-like eyelids flutter and the dank, toothless mouth opens and closes, gasping for air. Tears ooze onto my cheeks and I whirl round to look at Dr Price.

"I fear she is far, far gone and will not last the week," he says, bowing his head.

I spend the rest of the morning curled up beside her and drifting in and out of sleep. When I wake, she is still snoring faintly. I get up and make my way into the hallway, where Dr Price is waiting as if ready to pounce.

He clears his throat and his cheeks flush. "I have a delicate but pressing matter to discuss with you, Mrs Blackstone."

My mouth is parched and my stomach growls, but I follow him into the roomy parlour. The dryness seems to have taken my voice and my head is woolly with fatigue. I wish he would leave me alone to rest and sort out Izzie's business in my own time.

He clasps his hands behind his back and, in a manner eerily reminiscent of Buckley and Henry, leans against the fireplace with a proprietary air.

"It is a matter of money, Mrs Blackstone. Money owed and bills unpaid." He snaps himself upright in an indignant manner.

Every nerve end in my body tingles. "Money? My grandmother is a woman of great means, Dr Price."

He shakes his head and my legs feel weak, as if the bones have turned to chalk. "I fear she has been the victim of a scurrilous accountant who squandered her fortune in a series of failed business ventures and shady investments."

"But her house in Oxfordshire?"

"Mortgaged beyond its value and already gone to auction, as will this house very soon."

A low ringing sound echoes in my ears. The band of pain tightens across my forehead. "There is nothing left?"

"Nothing."

I slump back into a chair, my heart beating so violently, it might leap from my chest. He steps forwards, his face ashen white.

"Mrs Blackstone, do not take on so. I have a solution. Please hear me out."

Black demons of terror scamper across my mind. I don't want to hear the solution. I fear it.

"My wife and I have discussed this matter and are willing to purchase this house to cover the outstanding debts and prevent it going onto the auction block. You and your grandmother are welcome to stay here until she passes. Then—considering your situation—I am sure you will have no trouble finding an eligible bachelor or widower and making a suitable match here in Bombay to ensure your ongoing security."

I force a faint smile and try to silence the blood rushing in my ears. "Most kind of you, Dr Price. Could you leave me for a few moments to consider your offer?"

"As a matter of fact, I have rounds to do. I will be back this evening for your answer."

Once he is gone, I lie back on the velvet divan and close my eyes.

I have no choice but to accept Dr Price's offer. Izzie is dying, so she must be comfortable during the final week of her life. Then I will drink and dance and lure the richest, most powerful man to be my husband. After that . . .

I remember the small brown bottle tucked away in the corner of my trunk, wrapped in one of Henry's expensive silk cravats.

Oh, the irony of it all.

I rub my eyes and see a prison cell. A fire burns, casting the subject in crimson. Her coal-black eyes, set deep into shadowy sockets, stare out at me, blank and impassive, with the faint expression of derision. Or scorn.

She stands at the doorway, her outstretched hand holding a cup of tea. *Drink it, drink it,* she says, *for two penn'orth of arsenic dissolves nicely in a hot cup of tea.*

*Only a few grains. Slowly, slowly, so no one will notice.*

She taught me well.

She will never leave me now.

She made sure of it.

# Author's Note

*THE SAVAGE INSTINCT* is a work of fiction based on fact, which means I have taken certain liberties with characters. Some are based on real people, whilst others are entirely my creation, most notably Clara, Henry, the Buckleys, and the doctors. Also, for the purposes of this novel, I have compressed certain time frames and changed the dates of various events.

Mary Ann Cotton was regarded as one of England's most infamous and prolific serial murderers, arsenic being her poison of choice. I first became acquainted with her story when I discovered that she had been born just around the corner from the street my grandmother lived on, in a place called Low Moorsley, County Durham. I visited that street many times as a child.

I became fascinated by her story after reading an article in a UK newspaper that shed doubt on the scope of her crimes and suggested that if her trial had been held today, she would have escaped the noose and possibly gone free. No witnesses were called to speak in her defence, the evidence was entirely circumstantial, and she was without legal representation until a few days before the actual trial at Durham assizes. Of course, there are still many who believe she was guilty on all counts and received the appropriate punishment of death by hanging in the grounds of Durham Prison.

In my research, I read various accounts of her life, her actual letters from prison, and many of the articles that had filled the national newspapers. This case was notable for the media attention it received, and that inspired me to create a story, not necessarily about Mary Ann Cotton's crimes, but about the impact her arrest and trial had on Victorian society at the time, as well as what it revealed about that society's attitudes towards women who strayed from their natural "God-given" roles.

For those readers interested in learning more about Mary Ann Cotton, Victorian women, and "madness," and women's rights in Victorian England, you can check out the works listed below:

- The British Newspaper Archive at the British Library has many articles on the arrest and trial of Mary Ann Cotton.
- *Mary Ann Cotton, Dead But Not Forgotten* by Tony Whitehead (2000)
- *Mary Ann Cotton, Her Story and Trial* by Arthur Appleton (1973)
- *Mary Ann Cotton, Dark Angel* by Martin Connolly (2016)
- *Mary Ann Cotton, Britain's First Female Serial Killer* by David Wilson (2013)
- *Mad, Bad and Sad: A History of Women and the Mind Doctors, from 1800 to the Present* by Lisa Appignanesi (2014)
- *The Female Malady: Women, Madness and English Culture 1830–1980* by Elaine Showalter (1987)

- *The Diary of Alice James* by Alice James (1964)
- *The Subjection of Women* by John Stuart Mill and Harriet Taylor Mill (1869)

# ACKNOWLEDGEMENTS

MY SINCERE THANKS to everyone who read and commented on early drafts of *The Savage Instinct*, particularly my sister, Janet, for her interest and support; my friend Leslie for her insightful critique; my friend Kay; and writers Staton Rabin, Chris Huang, Jacqui Castle, and Lucy Hanson. Their honest and thorough feedback was invaluable to me.

Special thanks also goes to my cousins Alison, June, Erica, and Lauren in County Durham, who were great supporters of the book right from its inception and helped me with the complexities of "Durham miners' slang," as well as updates on the sale of Mary Ann Cotton's letters from prison.

I was fortunate to work with the amazing publishing team at Inkshares, most notably editor Adam Gomolin, whose brilliant insights, incredible story sense, and appreciation of language inspired me to keep going. Also thanks to Avalon Radys, whose intuitive notes and enthusiastic support of the novel came at a time when I needed it the most. To Kaitlin Severini, for her meticulous and incisive copyediting.

Thanks also to my brothers: Trevor, for his support and advice to keep going when I considered quitting, and Ken, whose honest but intuitive criticism has always been invaluable to me. To his wife, Linda, a keen reader who always cheered me on. To my son, Mike, and my daughter, Laura: your imagination and creativity never cease to amaze and inspire me. To my husband, Fausto: thanks for supporting my work and putting up with the hermit in the office!

Finally, this novel is also a tribute to the beautiful city of Durham. Though I haven't lived there since I was twelve, I'm frequently drawn back to visit, and many nights I walk its cobbled streets, old stone terraces, and leafy riverbanks in my dreams.

# INKSHARES

INKSHARES is a reader-driven publisher and producer based in Oakland, California. Our books are selected not by a group of editors, but by readers worldwide.

While we've published books by established writers like *Big Fish* author Daniel Wallace and *Star Wars: Rogue One* scribe Gary Whitta, our aim remains surfacing and developing the new author voices of tomorrow.

Previously unknown Inkshares authors have received starred reviews and been featured in the *New York Times*. Their books are on the front tables of Barnes & Noble and hundreds of independents nationwide, and many have been licensed by publishers in other major markets. They are also being adapted by Oscar-winning screenwriters at the biggest studios and networks.

Interested in making your own story a reality? Visit Inkshares.com to start your own project or find other great books.